WAKING CHAOS

PALDIMORI GODS RISING

T.L. CALLAHAN

DRAGON MOUNTAIN
PRESS

First published in United States of America by Dragon Mountain Press LLC 2017

2

Callahan, T.L. Waking Chaos, 2nd edition

Library of Congress Control Number: 2019904913

PB ISBN: 978-0-9991225-8-7 2nd edition

(ISBN 978-0-9991225-1-8 1st edition)

EB ISBN: 978-0-9991225-7-0 2nd edition

(ISBN 978-0-9991225-0-1 1st edition)

Edited by Book Nanny Writing and Editing Services

Cover design by: Covers by Juan

Artwork by: janko_m

Publisher: Dragon Mountain Press LLC, 1250 W. Ohio Pike # 199 Amelia, OH 4510

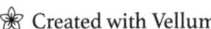 Created with Vellum

For my husband who believed in me and supported me in achieving this dream.

For my son who understands that Mommy visits dreamland when I'm at my computer.

PROLOGUE

Whoever said "third time's the charm" was a dumbass.

Here I was looking at number five and, apparently, he was as unlucky for me as the previous four had been.

Five boyfriends in three years. Five boyfriends and all of them cheaters.

It was enough to give a girl a complex—if I could still feel anything. But emotions were the luxury of others who hadn't had their lives torn apart. Who hadn't once abandoned the veneer of humanity to live on the streets where the bleakness of rage and despair were their only companions.

I shoved those thoughts back into their prison. A place deep inside me that I called my lonely highway. Once, it had run through lush pastures of hopes and dreams. Now, it cut through a barren wasteland with all the things that could destroy what was left of me painstakingly sealed away under its unforgiving asphalt. What did it say about who I had become that not one of those boyfriends had rated a mile marker on my lonely highway?

I stood in the doorway to my bedroom and felt absolutely nothing. Which only confirmed what I've known all along—I was meant to be alone. Reinforced by the fact that having to burn my new sheets bothered me more than stumbling upon my boyfriend and my assistant manager having sex in my bed. Natalie, my—until now—reliable and faithful employee, started moaning as if she were having the best sex of her life. I couldn't remember the last time I'd experienced an orgasm in that bed—or anywhere else for that matter. The vague sense of jealousy that my sheets were seeing more action than I did was another sad statement on my life over the past five years.

Like the proverbial train-wreck, I couldn't look away from the acrobatics taking place in my bedroom. How the hell did she manage to twist herself into that position? If this was what men wanted, I was doomed to a life of battery-operated relationships. Mentally I scored the performance as if they were contestants on a game show. Point deductions for this being *my* bed and *my* boyfriend, but definite high marks for creativity.

Daron picked up the pace and started groaning. A sound that usually signaled an unsatisfactory but thankfully quick end on the few occasions we'd had sex. I don't know why either of us had still been pretending there was a relationship—we had nothing in common and we barely saw each other. Massaging the temples of my pounding head, I backed out of the doorway. The grand finale could remain a mystery.

I trudged downstairs wishing I had stayed in bed today instead of forcing myself to go to work when I realized my sniffles had turned into something worse. I lived for the moments spent at my art gallery, Whimsy. It was the one bright spot that kept the memories from my past at bay, but it had been a bitch of a day. Starting with a shipping mix-up on a custom painting order. Then realizing through the fog of this cold and the drowsiness from the medication I'd taken that I'd forgotten my loan paperwork that was due today.

In the kitchen, I chugged a glass of water hoping it would ease the scratchy feeling in my throat. I toed off my shoes and snorted at the files lying on the granite countertop. Those files were the whole reason I was here in my condo witnessing acts that not even bleach would erase from my brain instead of being at work. That paperwork would have launched the expansion of my art gallery benefiting not only me but the network of local artists that I'd painstaking built since my business had opened three years ago. The papers had been due to the bank manager by noon today. When I realized I'd forgotten the files, Natalie had offered to pick them up and take them to the bank for me. She had been a trusted employee for a couple of years now so there had been no reason to doubt her. That's why I was shocked when the bank manager—Brice Kingston II, Port Lawson's very own small town royalty—called to say that the documents weren't received on time.

Brice's voice had dripped with smug satisfaction as he informed me that I would have to start the loan process all over again. Pleading with him to give me another hour had been pointless. He not only had snobbery down to a science but a chip on his shoulder to rival the Rockies where I was concerned since I'd snubbed his many sleazy attempts at dating. Unfortunately, he now took great pleasure in making my business dealings with the bank as difficult as possible.

After that disheartening conversation, I'd tried calling Natalie's cell since she hadn't returned to work. My calls kept going to voicemail, and I was worried that something had happened to her. Business had been slow at the gallery, so I'd left one of the other employees in charge while I made the fifteen-minute drive home. The rest, as they say, was history.

Please god, let us wrap up this confrontation quickly and quietly, I mentally pleaded as I washed down another dose of cold medicine, grimacing at the taste. Daron would get the boot. Natalie and I would discuss her poor life choices. We would all be civilized adults—ones that never mentioned this to anyone. Ever.

The gossips in this small seaside town on the Olympic coast of Washington were brutal. My best friend and I called them the GG's—the Gossiping Gaggle. A group of little old ladies that were sympathetic enough to make my teeth hurt whenever they heard of my all too frequent break-ups. I was pretty sure they mostly cared about juicy details as fodder for their gossip sessions but the last thing I wanted was to be the headliner for their next gathering. I liked my life predictable and low-key. Nothing to create a new mile marker on my lonely highway.

Weariness settled on my shoulders like a shroud. If only I could sleep for a while but there were the two surprise guests to deal with. I picked up the folder of paperwork, walked over to the large bay window at the back of the living room, and sank down onto the cushioned window seat to wait. My toes wiggled into the plush cream carpet. This was my favorite spot in the condo and the deciding factor in buying this place when I'd finally pulled myself out of the downward spiral after my parents died and came back to Washington.

Outside the window was the other reason. Windswept ocean waves crashed against the green shore not fifty yards beyond my deck. The afternoon storm rolled in almost like clockwork. Raindrops tinkled against the window. The low rumble of thunder sounded off in the distance. My eyes closed as I soaked in the moment of peace. Memories tried to edge in, the sound of the storm as it raged around us. My mother's screams. *No!* I pushed the memories down under the asphalt and opened the folder to read over the paperwork again.

The sound of giggling and footsteps on the stairs signaled the arrival of my guests. I hung my head for a moment contemplating the broken record that had become my life. Then taking a deep breath, I squared my shoulders and stood to do what had to be done.

There was nothing civil about the next hour. The conversation derailed so rapidly my head spun. The naive and sweet college girl I thought I'd known had been nowhere in sight. Her blue eyes had lit with a maniacal fire that had my skin pricking with unease as she gleefully told me how she had seduced her way through *all* of my boyfriends and my staff. The venomous words that Natalie lobbed at me left me feeling raw and exposed: "Oh princess, why so shocked? They all fall for your sweet and oblivious act at first, but they learn soon enough what a cold fish you really are." She'd pushed her tousled long blonde hair back from her beautiful face. Then ran her hands down her shapely body to suggestively toy with the hem of her short skirt. "Then I help them forget all about you."

After that I'd showed my ex-assistant and ex-boyfriend to the door, fervently hoping it hit them in the ass on the way out. There was only one thing I'd asked but the answer was as confusing as the rest of this debacle: "Why, Natalie?"

"Why? You stole from me first." Natalie snarled, but before I could ask what she meant she continued on. "I never forgive or forget."

She'd stomped out the door, Deron trailing along

behind her looking nervous. I gave myself a moment to rest my weary head against the door. The throbbing in my temples was so loud it could register as a second heartbeat. Then I gathered my strength and dragged myself up the stairs to my guest room.

My throat felt tight, and it took several tries to swallow— either from the cold that was coming on or the betrayal choking the air from my lungs—as I fought the tears that were threatening to fall. The acidic taste of betrayal was especially hard to swallow since trust didn't come easy for me. Natalie had proved herself a valuable employee, steadily weaving her way under my guard. As time went on, I'd treated her more and more like a partner in my gallery. She had access to everything. Not only about the business but a lot of details about my personal life as well. And she'd taken full advantage.

How gullible I must seem to them all.

I fell face-down on the bed. Tomorrow was soon enough to start cutting myself free from all of the people who had betrayed me.

1

Achoo!

Another tissue landed on the mountain that had collected in my trashcan. Another round of hand sanitizer and my skin felt like shriveled prunes. My cold had gotten worse adding to the struggle to make sense of the paperwork spread across my desk. The last two days had been spent firing my other employees and taking care of business. Sorting out all the details of my gallery that had included Natalie was harder than I had anticipated.

And, to make matters worse, my BFF, Dia King, had called to tell me that word had hit the town gossip circles within an hour of Daron dragging Natalie from my home.

My good-luck fairy must have been on vacation.

The leader of the GG's, Ms. Myrtle Jones, had shown up on my doorstep the next morning with a container of homemade banana pudding. She had taken one look at my scratchy red eyes and runny nose and called in the troops. The next thing I knew I was sitting in my ratty robe in a house full of elderly ladies telling me how men were only good for certain things. Like lifting heavy stuff and reaching the top shelf. Thankfully, Ms. Myrtle was one of the nicer members of the gossips and had run interference. Although the one time I'd tried to convince them that I was suffering from a cold rather than any heartbreak over Daron had garnered me enough "poor dears" to have me grinding my teeth to dust. They patted my arm and shoved more food at me until me and my fridge were filled to bursting.

Dia, of course, had enjoyed riling them up with well-placed comments that kept the man-bashing going for hours. By the time they left, I was too tired to move. And feeling sorry for the men in their lives.

The sound of the doorbell woke me early the following morning. My back protested every move as I shuffled to the door, stooped over from the awkward position I'd fallen asleep in on the couch. Pulling my old blue robe more securely around me, I attempted to smooth out my tangled bird's nest of hair. The fresh-faced young man on the doorstep—Ms. Myrtle's grandson—made me feel ancient. I scrubbed at my face in case there were lines left there from my decorative pillow and swiped at my chin, hoping I'd caught all the drool.

He presented me with a mixed bouquet of spring flowers and an invitation to lunch Sunday at his grandmother's house. He'd barely gotten the words out before a sniff of the flowers started me off on an instant coughing fit. I was a complete mess. Eyes watering. Nose dripping. Face hot as fire as I struggled to draw in each congested breath. The young man's look of horror said it all. He was kind enough to help me back to the couch—probably in fear of his grandmother finding out if he didn't. He agreed to send my regrets about lunch. Then he bolted so fast I'd barely been able to croak out a "thanks" before the door slammed.

To avoid well-meaning neighbors and matchmaking

grandmothers, my office was now doubling as my bedroom. Giving up on the paperwork, I wound my hair up, pinning it back with an antique silver clip from my desk, before heading to the gallery floor to stretch my legs and clear my head.

I weaved my way through the blown glass, pottery, jewelry, and various other art forms displayed on white pedestals of varying heights dotted about the gallery. Whimsy's art collection reflected its name in that the store contained an assortment of unusual items. The traditional offerings such as paintings were represented, of course, but my inner artist was always drawn to the unique.

Pride filled me as I scanned my shop. Whimsy was the only thing I had left in the world—besides Dia—that meant a thing to me. During the hours spent here I could lose myself in the artwork and let the echo of the past fade away. The quiet routine allowed me to relax my vigil over my lonely highway. Here I didn't have to fear what might trigger those memories to slip through the pavement and pull me back down a path of destruction. This was my sanctuary. My salvation when I didn't think there could be any.

It would have been so much more that that if I had gotten the loan from the bank. The term "starving artist" was all too real. I had been helping local artists reach larger crowds through my connections with other galleries, but it took time. The loan would have gone toward expanding my studio in the back, allowing those artists to teach classes to bring in extra income.

My fists clenched in frustration at what Natalie had ruined with her childish jealousy. And that's what it had been, I was sure. Our confrontation had played repeatedly through my mind as I struggled to understand. She had said that I had taken from her and referred to the men she had taken from me. There was only one man I had ever been involved with that she could possibly have thought I had taken from her. Douglas had been the first man to convince me to give dating a chance. Natalie had introduced us at an exhibition opening. He had been her professor, and they had both claimed they were only friends. Looking back now she had been very interested in the details of our relationship. Douglas had been a nice man but ultimately more interested in sleeping with his students. Namely, the Dean's daughter which had gotten him a black eye and a transfer to another university.

I sighed as I moved towards the large storefront window to watch the rainbows as light poured through the stained-glass edges and reflected onto the natural bamboo flooring. Stone pathways twisted and split from the bottom scene to wind through different landscapes on either side. The design had been my idea and the artist I had commissioned delivered with exceptional results. But it was very different from the glass sculptures I had dreamed of making when my career as an artist was still a possibility. What would my life look like now if I had taken a different path?

I shook my head and turned back towards the office, where I spent the day on the couch, the mountain of tissues growing even higher, trying to push through the ache in my head to get some actual work done and looking forward to my evening. Monday nights I eased into the workweek with pizza, pj's, and Netflix episodes featuring drool-worthy Agent Booth. Tonight, a pint of ice cream was joining me as my reward for finally ejecting Natalie from every aspect of my life. Maybe I would ask Dia to join me too.

Suddenly, the bell over the gallery door sounded. *Please don't let it be another of Ms. Myrtle's circle of friends stopping in to "pick up a little something" while trying to give me dating advice*. There was only an hour left before closing. I didn't want to be late for my date with Agent Booth.

I scanned the gallery, looking for my customer. The reflection of a familiar face in the oval antique mirror next to the counter almost made me want to sneak out the door. Brice Kingston II selected a necklace from the tray on the table and eyed it with distaste. He dropped it back to the table in a clumsy pile before picking up another. A shiver of disgust rolled down my spine as he held the necklace up in front of him and licked his lips, a heated look filling his eyes.

I eased back a step, fully intending to hide. Cowardly, I know, but I wasn't in good shape to fend off his advances. Unfortunately, my movement caught his attention and he turned toward me.

"There you are, Lia. Lucky for you I wasn't a homeless person wandering in off the street, or I could have run off with half the store by now." He smiled at me as if he hadn't made that snide remark about my business management skills. "I heard that you lost your staff. I'm sure it's a chore taking care of this little hobby of yours all by yourself."

I forced my lips to curl up into a semblance of a smile, but my expression may have been leaning more towards feral than friendly. He paused for a moment but decided to ignore his instincts and walked up to take my hand. Anyone else I would have cautioned to keep their distance so they wouldn't catch my cold. My first smile in days broke free when he stepped in to kiss my cheek.

Served him right if he got sick. I tugged my hand from his grasp on the pretense of tucking a loose strand of hair behind my ear.

"This is my business, not a hobby, Mr. Kingston," I reminded him for the millionth time. "Was there something I can help you with?"

His gaze dipped to my cleavage and got stuck there. "Huh-hum. Did you want to purchase that necklace, Mr. Kingston?"

His fingers tightened around the necklace in annoyance at my refusal to call him Brice. If I gave in an inch, he would turn our relationship into something it wasn't. He licked his lips again, sending a shudder down my spine. My leg twitched with the desire to knee him in the balls as he continued to ogle my breasts. However satisfying that would have been, I repressed my urge. That was how the old Lia would have handled him. Back when I was full of fire to take on the world.

Don't act recklessly. You aren't that young girl anymore. You're a respected business owner, and he holds the purse to your future. I took a slightly congested inhale and waited. He would get to the point of this unwanted visit—eventually.

"It's your birthday soon. May 22, correct?" he asked instead, his eyes finally traveling back up to my face.

"Yes, it is."

"There's a new five-star restaurant opening in Seattle. The chef is a friend of the family. I have a private dinner booked for us. Don't worry about not having anything to wear. I had my secretary pick out a dress for you. I know you prefer to dress . . . more casually, but this place requires more than jeans and T-shirts. You'll love it. I thought you would like to wear one of the trinkets from your store. This one should do fine." He dangled the necklace in front of my face, apparently expecting to be praised as though he were the most thoughtful man in the world.

What the hell? He couldn't be serious. I had turned him down flat when he had asked me out after he helped me get the initial business loan to open my gallery years ago and every time since. He had been a complete ass about it and had gone out of his way to make things difficult for me. Why was he acting as if it were a done deal that I would go out with him now?

"Y-You . . ." I stammered, completely at a loss for words.

Suddenly the door banged open so hard that the bell was knocked off. I winced as it hit the floor and continued to *clunk-clank-clatter* as it rolled toward a display of vases. Dia rushed headlong into the gallery, hunched over like she was ready to tackle someone. Apparently, I was her lucky opponent. I grunted as she grabbed me by the waist, almost knocking me into Brice.

Resting her head against my stomach, she struggled to catch her breath. "Th-thank god . . . I got here . . . just in time . . ."

"Dia, what's wrong? Are you hurt?" I tried to pry her arms away so I could check her over for injuries, but she wasn't budging.

"Hos . . . pital. Now." She groaned.

"Brice, you have to leave. I've got to get Dia to the hospital." I plucked the necklace from his hand and tossed it onto the nearest table. Then propelled him to the front door with my hand against his back as Dia trailed along, still clinging to me.

"This is absurd," he said, trying to force his way back through the door. "Just call an ambulance."

"Con . . . tagious." Dia moaned and grabbed his wrist. He squealed like a little girl and jerked out of her grip.

A tingling built in my nose right at that moment. *Achoo!*

His face turned white. "You stupid cow! Now you've infected us both!" He raced recklessly to his car at the curb and gunned the engine. With a squeal of tires, he shot out into traffic, barely avoiding collision with another car.

Dia's whole body was shaking against my waist now. Oh

no, she was convulsing. "Just hang on. I'll get you to the hospital."

I started toward my car, but Dia gripped me tighter, holding me in place. She shook even harder. "No. Not . . . sick."

"What?"

Dia stood up. Her face was red and tear-streaked. I reached for her again just as she burst out, "That. Was. *Awesome*."

I got it then. She wasn't in pain or sick. She was laughing so hard she was crying.

"Geez, Dia. You scared me to death. I thought you'd come down with the plague or something." My exasperation quickly melted. "Did you see his face?"

We slumped against each other laughing like lunatics on the sidewalk as people passed by giving us strange looks.

Finally regaining my composure, I said, "Thanks for saving me. How did you know what Brice had planned?"

"I'll tell you all about it over an early dinner at Mussels." She wiped the tears of laughter away. "Can you close up shop right now?"

"It's not Wednesday. Why are we going to dinner two days earlier than usual?"

Every trace of humor was erased as she said quietly, "I overheard some things at Myrtle's that I think you need to know about."

Dia was rarely this serious. Something was definitely wrong.

Dia and I walked along Harbor Street, saying hello to the locals we passed. Most of those greetings went unreturned which was unusual for our small town. I shrugged it off, maybe they hadn't heard me. We waited in silence at the corner for the light to turn. Normally, Dia would have been talking a mile a minute. Whatever was wrong must be pretty bad for it to have affected her this strongly.

"Dia, what—"

A crash sounded from behind us. We turned to the bakery shop where a tangle of arms and legs could be seen through the window. A dog was licking what appeared to be icing off of any limb it could reach. Two little boys were giggling as a young woman tried to untangle them from the mess while apologizing. Dia and I looked at each other.

"Donut Dash!" we chorused and immediately started laughing.

"Wow, it's been years since I've thought about freshman donut slavery. Man, were those seniors harsh if you didn't deliver the goods by six a.m. Remember that first time when we got attacked by the horde of senior zombies?" I asked.

"Yep, late-night study session hangover cure. Coffee and donuts." Dia frowned as she said, "I don't think I ever got the pink icing out of that shirt and it was cute. But I found my bestie so it was worth all the sprinkles I had to pick out of not so fun places when they knocked us to the ground, donuts and all."

"Absolutely," I agreed as we crossed the street. "Hey, do you remember Petty Betty? Did you hear she got arrested for drugs? They found a whole marijuana operation in her basement."

"Huh, maybe they helped improve her personality. Donut Dash day one she made me go back to the shop *three* times because her latte wasn't the right balance of foam. Good thing she never found out I used Piggy's blender to get it *just* right the rest of the year." Dia cackled.

"Wait, wasn't Piggy the one who hoarded food in her room?" We waved to our usual waiter and took our seats.

"Yep, that's the one. Remember how the dorms stunk like bleach for days after the seniors graduated? The admins finally had to come in and clean out the room. I don't know what all they found in there, but I never touched that blender without gloves." She shuddered.

"I remember. That's pretty gross, Dia. Betty could have gotten food poisoning."

"Like you can talk. At least I didn't make her break out in hives from rubbing a banana peel on her pillow. You totally knew she was allergic. Was that the time she broke your art pencils?"

"Yeah, I'd just bought those pencils too. I really shouldn't have done that." Remorse filled me as I thought back on the stupid things we'd done. "Her throat could have swelled up or something."

"She was a meanie. And it was our mission to defend the

oppressed, remember?" Dia put her hands on her hips in a classic superhero stance. "Lia and Dia, the Dynamic Misfits."

"Defenders of the underdog." I recited.

"Crusaders for freedom from mean girls everywhere," Dia added.

"And supports for chocolate as a food group," we chorused and laughed at our corny motto.

"All the pranks we pulled almost got us kicked out," I sighed. "But at least we got people to stop calling us by our horrible names. Jillian and Claudia should be reserved for little old ladies."

We shared a commiserating nod. We'd adopted our nicknames and refused to go back to the stuffy ones we'd been born with.

We relaxed back into our seats at our favorite table at Mussels—on the covered patio in front of the restaurant with a view of the marina. Our waiter came over, and we put in our usual orders, then clapped in appreciation as he showed off his moves for his next bodybuilder competition. I loved this restaurant. The wait staff bustled around the tables in their tight, cream-colored, muscle-hugging polo shirts and black slacks that showed off their corded thighs. The restaurant was known for its mussels, the seafood kind, and the hot-muscled wait staff kind. It was like a male revue, with more clothing and fantastic food.

The waiter left to get our drinks. Dia had gone quiet again as she stared at me across the stone tabletop as if trying to solve a complex puzzle. I didn't bother asking what had her so perplexed. She would tell me when she was ready. Dia didn't believe in holding back her thoughts. She was the sweetest, funniest person I had ever met. And a ball of energy that talked a mile a minute and sometimes bounced around like a caffeinated Chihuahua. She had tempered herself a bit in recent years, but she was still unpredictable even after all the years we had been friends. Whatever was on her mind right now would be presented in its own unique Dia way.

She tilted her head to the side, studying me from a different angle. Her hair spilled over her shoulder and brushed against her hips in a wavy blend of every shade of brown. Most people thought she had it professionally colored, but it was all natural. Like everything else about my bohemian friend. She believed that bras were torture devices and makeup was only meant for clowns. Today there were brightly colored feathers hanging from several braids in her hair. Her azure blue eyes looked startling against her bronze skin. As usual, they were alight with some new excitement. She was wearing a long turquoise skirt and a peach-colored peasant blouse with Daisy Duck on it that hung off one shoulder.

Everything about her was my polar opposite. She was the exotic free spirit who lived out loud. I was the boring buttoned-down businesswoman who liked it best when no one noticed me.

Ignoring Dia's staring, I leaned back in my seat and took in the beautiful spring day. Across the road, boats swayed in their slips at the Sea Salt Marina. Further out to sea, a large white sailboat powered through the water, kicking up waves. I watched in appreciation as the white sails rippled in the wind. Since I had grown up around boats, my dreams had always included owning one of my own someday. The sound of the water all around and the briny smell of the ocean on the breeze soothed me as nothing else could.

At least, it had before my world crashed down around me. Those dreams were long dead now. A sad longing filled me as I continued to watch the sailboat. And again, that same question nagged at me. What would my life have been like if that day had never happened?

My parents' deaths and that year when darkness had consumed me were mile markers on my lonely highway. Ones that I never talked about. Not even with Dia. The day my parents died in the boating accident my perfect world had shattered into a million shards that ripped me to pieces. The obituary saying "survived by their daughter" was a cruel joke; my heart had been laid to rest beside them in Lakeview Cemetery. It had always been the three of us, and their deaths had destroyed me so completely that I'd run to the other side of the world to escape the loss. Pain and rage had consumed me. A well of darkness had filled me and I'd sank into the depths of the underbelly of society. Eventually, I had pulled myself from the darkness and sought out the only person I had left in the world—Dia. She took me in without question and was by my side as I worked hard to find my place in this town. Gallery owner Lia had been born from those ashes, and I never wanted to go back.

I shook my head to clear away the memories. Dia gave me a sympathetic smile as if she knew where my thoughts had drifted. I pushed it all down and nodded, reassuring her that I was fine.

"Funny, you still look like the Lia I know," Dia said giving me a puzzled look. "But the Lia I know these days is obsessed with her business and way too serious for her own good. Huh. You never know about people."

"Dia, what're you talking about?"

"The GG's were at it again today when I stopped by to pick up some things for Mr. Skittles," she replied.

"Did he puke up a rainbow again?" I asked. "I know you love those candies, but I don't think they're good for cats.

And before you ask, the answer is still NO. Mr. Skittles is not getting an art show. Just because you hung up the stained comforter in your living room as evidence of his artwork doesn't mean people would pay to see a showroom full of cat puked-on items."

She was completely unfazed by my stern look. "Party pooper. I'll have you know that Mr. Skittles is a kitty Picasso. I'm thinking of starting a new T-shirt line. Didn't he do a great job on your birthday present?" she asked proudly.

Oh, holy hell, I was going to have to burn that T-shirt. "Uh, yeah. I loved it. Didn't know Mr. Skittles was the, uh, artist."

"Of course, it's a Mr. Skittles original. He wanted you to have one before he got famous. But that's not what I wanted to talk about. Have you been to Myrtle's lately?" When I shook my head, Dia continued. "I thought the GGs had started an X-rated book club or a PA group. I was ready to sign up even if they made me listen to them talk about how good girls wear bras. You would think they've never heard that good girls die young."

"Then I'm sure you'll live to be a hundred. Is a PA group like one of those parent-teacher groups?" My brow wrinkled in confusion trying to follow Dia's typical subject changes.

"Pornoholics Anonymous. I doubt the PTA is into dildos and bondage. Although the bondage would probably come in handy with a few of the parents who want to tell me how to do my job. Do you think the school board would approve ball gags for the more troublesome ones?"

The picture of Dia in leather as she cracked a whip at a bunch of first graders' parents wearing ball gags had me cracking up. "I doubt it. Why would you think the GGs were starting a 'PA' group?"

The GG's liked to gather at Myrtle's every Wednesday

night. No one knew exactly what those little old ladies did there, but if anything was going on in this town, they knew about it. They were the rumor mill, and when they had something juicy to grind their teeth on, the whole town would hear about it.

"Mrs. Kingston—the old hag—was talking a bunch of crap. She said she talked to Brice about you over lunch today. She wanted to make sure her son was not messing around with the kinky stuff that you're into." Dia snorted. "Brice apparently laughed like crazy, then ran off mumbling about making plans. Left her with the bill too."

Not having her only child cater to her every wish must have been a real shock to Mrs. Kingston. And if there was one person in the world Dia despised, it was Brice. I had the feeling that it wasn't only because of his treatment of me. Dia had grown up in this town and they were about the same age. I could only imagine that Brice had been even more obnoxious as a child.

"Mama Kingston was totally horrified by that. I'm sure Brice'll be getting an earful." Dia smiled gleefully. "I didn't like the sound of him having plans, especially when your name was mentioned. I dropped my groceries in her lap and ran to your gallery. You should have seen the look on her face! Anyway, it was a good thing I did. Imagine forcing a date on you. That's pathetic. I was glad to help foil his evil plans. But I want to know about the dildos and bondage. When did you turn into a sex-monkey?"

"Wait. What?" I asked in confusion. "What are you talking about?"

Dia scooted next to me and dropped her voice low. "Sweetheart, I hate to tell you this, but rumors are spreading fast around town about you being into all kinds of kinky stuff. They're saying that's why your boyfriends keep leaving you. And that your employees quit because they didn't want to be part of your real business. An underground porn network."

My mouth dropped open in horrified shock. "Oh my god. What? I wouldn't... I've never..."

Dia wrapped her arm around my shoulders and pulled me in for a hug. "I know, sweetie. I knew it had to be a mistake. People in this town respect you. I'm sure they'll all say it's ridiculous and the rumors will die down. It was probably Surfer Ken and Psycho Barbie. They're both a few french fries short of a Happy Meal. They were pretty frosted when you walked in on them, right?"

"I guess so. What am I going to say to people?" I wanted to crawl under the table. "Uh, I hate this!"

"I know you do. Just ignore it. The rumors will go away, I swear." Dia rubbed my arm in sympathy. "Remember when Dan and I first started dating?"

"Old Daniel Walters and the hot young substitute teacher." They had started dating right before we graduated college, but I hadn't met Dan until I moved here. Dia had told me all about being the star of the town gossip and labeled "the other woman" although her boyfriend had been divorced. "I'm still not sure what you see in a guy fifteen years older than you, but I guess everyone has their kinks."

"Haha. Funny." She elbowed me. "The rumors died off after a couple of weeks. I have it on good authority that we are now considered a 'cute couple' and the GGs are betting on when our wedding will be."

"You're probably right about it all blowing over soon. Damn Natalie and Daron! The GGs will have told everyone in town. I hate having everyone watching me and talking about me." I grimaced, then took a deep breath and let it out. "Ok, enough about me. How are things going with Operation White Dress?"

Dan, the stuck-up bastard—or Geritol, as I often called him—was never going to put a ring on her finger. Dia was the eternal optimist, though. She kept dropping hints that inevitably led to a blow-up from Dan about the pressure and what he called her "immature antics." My hope that she would see him for the condescending asshat that he was hadn't come true in the five years they had been dating. Dia suddenly became very interested in the bottom of her margarita glass, taking large gulps from the straw.

"Did you and Dan have a fight?"

"Dan is just acting weird," Dia mumbled dismissively. She finally glanced up at me and attempted a smile that fell flat. "Hey, I want you to know that I was ready to storm your condo the other night. But Dan convinced me that you needed a little time. I'm sorry, Lia. I should have been there for you after finding Natalie and Daron that way."

"Stop. There's nothing to apologize for. You couldn't have possibly done anything except catch my cold," I reassured her. "The Lia and Dia team will always be together no matter what. Dan is only jealous of my awesomeness." I winked, trying to cheer her up. "You *have* assured him that there was never an 'experimental phase' to our relationship, right?"

A bit of that vibrant spark returned to her eyes as she laughed. "No way. I told him your nickname in college was Lickalotapuss, and he could take pointers. It was totally worth the lecture to see the look on his face. He even got me a book on developing healthy friendships."

Imagining the look on Geritol's face sent me into another fit of laughter. "Glad you're helping Mr. Geriatric maintain a healthy heart with the occasional stress test. No wonder he always has you glued to his side whenever he sees me. He's afraid my sexual magnetism might be too much for you to resist."

"If I ever feel the urge in that direction, you'll be the first person I call." She giggled. "By the way, a friend told me about something I think you should check out. It could be just what you need right now."

"Uh, if this has anything do with servicing females, I'm not interested. I may have a bad track record with men and consider myself on hiatus, but I'm not into women." I eyed Dia sternly, hoping this wasn't another Save Lia campaign. Like the time in college when she thought I was eating too much junk food and slipped detox powders into my juice bottles. I'd lost ten pounds and a boyfriend in a week from those side effects.

"No, no, no. That's not what I meant. No sexual servitude required. Unless you want to, of course." She giggled at my expression. "This is a game hosted by some group of gazillionaires. Special invite-only. I don't have a lot of details, but I heard about it from a woman in my yoga class. She said she went last year, and it was the most amazing experience of her life. The contestants are taken to a remote location for a series of competitions, and they give big prizes to the winners. Like millions of dollars. She said it's all pretty swanky, and the people you meet are just there to have a good time. She gave me an invite. Hold on, let me find it."

Dia went digging through her large pink messenger bag that had pictures of dancing giraffes on the front of it, mumbling to herself about whatever treasures she was finding in there. It was like the clown car bag. You never knew what would come out of it or how it all fit into it.

"Ah-ha. I knew it was in here somewhere." Dia beamed at me and plopped what looked to be an index card on the table in front of me. I hesitantly picked it up, flipping it from one side to the other. The card was blank. Although, maybe my cold was still messing with me because when I looked again, there was writing on the card. I set it down on the table and frowned at Dia as she sipped her drink. She was now practically bouncing in her chair with her natural level of energy. Either the alcohol was starting to hit, or she had managed to dismiss whatever was going on with Dan that had been worrying her earlier.

"C'mon," I said, "do you really believe we would be invited to a millionaire's private 'game?' This is probably a kidnapping ring or maybe a cult of some kind. I'm open to trying new ways of meeting people, but I don't have the time for cult-level commitment."

"Lia, seriously, you can be so cynical sometimes." Dia twirled one of the feathers in her hair. "The woman from my yoga class is a divorce lawyer. No way she would have been part of something shady. Think about it. Pleeeease?"

"Even if it were legit, I'm not desperate enough to enter a contest with a bunch of juiced-up guys who are practically sporting an innie—and I'm not referring to their belly button. Not to mention the size-zero drama queens who think they gain weight from breathing air. Besides the need to do them bodily harm from sheer annoyance, have you seen the size of my butt lately?" I motioned to my plump body. "I'm lucky I don't have to have an airplane seat for each cheek. It's a near thing. Plus, you know about my luck with physical activity. Remember the barbell?"

Dia snorted. "Lia, you're gorgeous. You've got curves I would sell part of my intestines for. We don't really need all of our intestines, do we? There's like tons of feet of intestine, right? Better to make them a straight line; saves time. Anyway, that barbell incident wasn't your fault. So, you're a little accident-prone—everyone has their challenges. I really think you should check this out. It could be good for you."

The typical Dia stream-of-consciousness rambling had me shaking my head. Luckily for the kids in her class, she taught art and not biology. "I don't know, Dia. I need to hire new employees. All those rumors are flying around. I need to focus on my business right now."

"Lia, the gallery can't be your whole life. You used to love being an artist. When was the last time you created anything? I know you don't want to talk about what happened. I get it." Dia lay her hand on top of mine, a rare solemnity to her expression. "But sweetie, you've locked yourself down so tight that you barely even resemble the girl you used to be. I'm not saying that's all bad, but for a few minutes today, you let go and had fun. You let that bold and brave girl I met in college out of her cage. She's still there. Maybe this could be the adventure you need to bring her out again. I just want you to be happy. You deserve it. Will you at least keep the card and think about going? For me?"

Dia didn't get it because I had never told her, or anyone else for that matter. That girl I had been all those years ago had died alongside her parents.

"I have a business to run and bills to pay."

Dia gave me a pointed look.

"Fine, fine. I promise I'll keep the card and think about it," I replied. "I'm doing ok, though. Really. I'm not desperate enough to be part of some game."

3

ONE MONTH LATER

It's a good thing we hadn't made a bet on the rumors dying down. If anything, it was now worse. I was having a hard time finding new employees. The few people who had submitted their resumes wanted to know if I would be having sex with them to test their qualifications. On top of all that, my business was taking a hit. Everywhere I turned, people were talking about me—and not in a good way.

"That's her. That's the one I was telling you about," a woman down the frozen food aisle whispered loudly to her friends.

If there was a cycle of emotions for dealing with life crises similar to the stages of grief, I was going through it. Anger had given way to frustration. Then to sadness. Now I was just numb. Ignoring the women, I continued to look over the selection of frozen dinners. My bare fridge was the only reason I'd ventured into the store. Keeping Up with Myrtle Jones—better known locally as Myrtle's—wasn't usually that busy on a Tuesday night. Unfortunately, my being here could have had something to do with the increased traffic. My worst nightmare had come true.

The rumors had exploded all over town that I was the purveyor of a porn network, making it impossible to go anywhere without drawing attention. The nasty looks and whispers I could ignore. Being propositioned like a prostitute—which happened more than I would have believed—wasn't so easy. It was disgusting and demeaning. No amount of washing had been able to erase the offer some man had whispered to me yesterday. Avoiding everyone was my only solution. Even Dia.

She had called several times, but I'd let it go to voicemail. There wasn't anything either of us could do to calm the storm. Unplugging my work phone and letting my cell die was my solution to finally getting some relief from the revolting calls that had been coming in at all hours of the day. I couldn't handle anymore.

Exhaustion dogged my every step down the aisle. This whole ordeal had drained me mentally and physically. If I ate dinner tonight instead of falling asleep at the table—again—it would be a shock. Scanning the coolers, I looked over my choices. Chicken-like mystery meat. Beef-like mystery meat. More mystery meat. Oh, what did it matter? They were all the same. Grabbing some dinners, I threw them in the cart. A few more things, then back to hiding.

Hiding had become a skill these last few weeks. Sneaking into my gallery at dawn and back home after nightfall had helped me avoid most people. Even with my odd hours, though, it was impossible to dodge everyone. I had a business to run, after all. Every busybody in town had stopped in at some point to stare and listen in on every word. Eventually, I'd put up a sign that read: "*Anyone lingering within the gallery more than 20 minutes must make a purchase. Loitering will result in eviction.*" At least I made some money off the more persistent ones.

Unfortunately, my plan to wait until right before closing time tonight to do my grocery shopping had backfired. I'd been hiding out so much lately that I hadn't realized that it was the annual Founders Festival.

Port Lawson was founded by William Charles Lawson in the late 1800s. Lawson had been the youngest son of the Duke of Lewiston. He moved to America and became a merchant and, eventually, a well-known shipbuilder. He had established the Lawson Shipyard that was still owned and operated by the family today. Every year the city celebrated its roots and the still thriving shipping and marine industries with the Founders Festival.

Main Street had been teeming with people waving flags, wearing hats that looked like various sea creatures, and eating tons of seafood. Kids pedaled carts around that looked like tiny ships, and men bragged to their friends about how much "catch" they could haul at the game booths. Even sticking to the outer edges of the crowd didn't work when you were currently as infamous as I was. The whispering had started up before I made it down a block. You would think it was the 1900s by the way some of the women pulled their kids to the other side of the street to get away from me.

Thankfully, Myrtle's had been mostly empty when I got there. But by the time I'd grabbed the necessities, the crowd had doubled, and I doubted they were all there for the sale on canned tuna. *Were they following me?* At this stage, a lynch mob or stoning wouldn't have surprised me. Either way sounded like a horrible way to die. Time to go.

"I heard that she seduced poor Brice Kingston to get her business loan." It was the same woman from earlier. "Mrs. Kingston said *that one* told Brice they were going to get married as soon as her business started making money. He helped her get the loan, but then she started acting strange. Trying to get him to experiment sexually. When she invited her girlfriend to their bed, he broke up with her. Mrs. Kingston said *that one* tries to get him back all the time. Just last month she invited him to join her in a hotel in Seattle. Can you believe the nerve?"

That pathetic little weasel! How dare he imply that I would ever sleep with him. Ewww!

He was turning everything around to make me sound like the bad guy. I was the one who had turned him down after he tried to tell me that the time we spent together filling out my loan paperwork were dates. Then he started talking about picking out a house near his mother's after we were married. Now he was trying to pin that creepy invite to join him in Seattle on me. No doubt it was his way of getting back at Dia and me. I'd heard that he spent some time at the hospital having them run all kinds of tests on him after Dia's contagious illness stunt.

"Poor Brice," one of the other women replied. "He deserves to be with a good girl like my Maggie. Not some . . . Well, I won't say in polite company. You know my Maggie has always liked him. He never noticed her because he was stuck on *that one*. I guess he can move on now that everyone knows what she's *really* like. Brice is finally taking my Maggie out on a date, and she is over-the-moon excited about it."

Frustration at the lies and vicious rumors bubbled up to a boiling point. I couldn't even defend myself. Who would believe me against Brice, Natalie, and Daron? Tears stung my eyes as I quickly pushed my cart toward the checkout counter. My appetite was long gone.

How had my life come to this?

A loud popping noise startled me from my morbid

thoughts. A man was standing in the aisle holding a can of tomato sauce that appeared to have exploded all over him. Globs of red dripped down his shocked face. Guess my day could have been worse. Good thing I wasn't in the mood for Italian.

I quickly made my way to the front of the store. Ms. Myrtle and several of her friends were standing near the checkout. Their conversation cut off abruptly as I started unloading my cart. A shrill voice called out, "Ms. Jones, I thought this was a high-end establishment. I didn't know you were letting the common filth in off the streets."

Dread filled me. Of course, Mrs. Kingston would have to be here. The young cashier looked back and forth between us as if she wanted to crawl beneath the counter. My pleading look was useless, but I gave it a shot. Ms. Myrtle ran a tight ship; the girl looked to her for direction. My speedy getaway plans went up in smoke. Stiffening my spine, I turned to receive the verdict.

Five women stared back at me. Half of the GGs were accounted for and would apparently be serving on my jury. Mrs. Kingston's face was set in a fierce sneer of superiority that appeared only slightly more malicious than normal. A couple of the others were clearly on her side as they glared at me. The rest, including Ms. Myrtle, looked uncomfortable. My empty stomach dipped like I was on a roller coaster as I faced some of the most influential ladies of the town.

"Good evening, Ms. Myrtle. I'm sorry if my presence has caused you any trouble. I'm sure things will die down when I leave, if you'll give me a moment to finish checking out."

The silence stretched out for a moment. My heart pounded as I awaited my sentencing. *Would I be banned from shopping here?* That would mean driving to the next town for my groceries and general goods. On the bright side, that would at least get me away from all of this on weekends, even if it was inconvenient.

"Alice, finish ringing Ms. Davies up. I'm sure she wants to get home for dinner," Ms. Myrtle finally said.

Heaving a quiet sigh of relief, I gave her a tentative smile. "Thank you, Ms. Myrtle. I'll be done in a moment."

She nodded at me before turning to Mrs. Kingston whose face was scrunched up in anger. "Mrs. Kingston, were you calling my store common?"

"What? I was—" Mrs. Kingston said, startled.

"Did you insinuate my clients were filth?" Ms. Myrtle continued talking over her.

"No, it's . . . she—" Mrs. Kingston sputtered.

"My store is open to anyone who has the good taste to appreciate what I offer here and the money to pay for their purchases. I know you have at least *one* of those things, so I won't hold this against you." Ms. Myrtle said, pointedly glancing at Mrs. Kingston's lavish display of jewelry as evidence for the latter.

I pressed my lips together to keep from laughing. Paying for my groceries, I picked up my bags ready to go. "Good evening, Ms. Myrtle. Thank you again."

Mrs. Kingston's face was purple with rage as she huffed out of the store followed by the other two women who were her constant shadows.

Ms. Myrtle sighed. "I'm too old for this foolishness."

"My dear Ms. Jones, you don't look a day over twenty. What is this rubbish I hear about being 'too old'?" a teasing, British-accented voice asked.

A genuine smile tugged at my lips as Jack Lawson IV stepped into view from around a display of cat toys. His well-tailored navy suit emphasized his lanky frame. His pale gray eyes and heavily lined face would lead you to believe he was an old man waiting to punch his ticket, but he had too much fun making his family jump to his tune to give into a little thing like death. People often missed that sparkle in his eye and the quick smile that would have warned them that Mr. Lawson was a rascal. He loved to surprise people. At the age of 71, he could run circles around his adult children. His stories about the tricks he played on them kept me entertained for hours.

Ms. Myrtle blushed like a schoolgirl as he brought her weathered hand to his lips. "I for one find your store a tasteful delight and your clientele—most of them anyway—of good character. Now, my dear friend Ms. Davies looks to be a bit weary today. Do you think you could call up that nice grandson of yours to deliver those bags for her? I've just come back from my travels you see and would very much like to catch up with my friend." His subtle emphasis on "friend" did not pass Ms. Myrtle's attention.

"I'll give him a call right now. I'm sure you have much to talk about with your 'friend,'" she replied. Then she glanced at me with an assessing look before turning back to him. "Why don't you come for dinner at my house tomorrow night? I would also like to hear about your travels."

"Splendid!" He handed her a business card. "Ring me at this number with the details. I look forward to dinner tomorrow, Ms. Jones. Good day to you."

Mr. Lawson walked over to me, barely leaning on the cane in his right hand. He had once confessed that he had found the cane in his family estate and only used it because his daughter hated it. He held his elbow out for me. "Shall we, my dear?"

I left my groceries with the cashier and slipped my hand into the crook of his arm. The familiar scent of the ocean that he always seemed to carry with him filled my nose. "Mr. Lawson, it's a pleasure to see you."

"Ms. Davies, the pleasure is, as always, mine. Shall we adjourn to your gallery so that I can see what new works of art you have for me?"

I nodded, and we headed out. It took longer than expected to cover the few blocks to my gallery. Mr. Lawson was somewhat of a celebrity, and even with me by his side, everyone wanted to say hello. When we finally made it inside the gallery, I made us some tea at the machine near the sitting area, preparing his just the way he liked—heavy on the lemon. Then we settled into the plush gray chairs. My finger absently traced one of the vibrant purple swirls of the upholstery. A cheery fire leaped in the stone fireplace. Part of my attempt to pass the time during the slow business hours these days was tending to the fire.

"How are you, my dear?" he said in his soothing voice as he sipped his tea.

Reluctant to confess everything that had happened, I tried to divert the conversation. "I'm doing well. How was your trip to Tanzania?"

He smiled at me knowingly. "I will tell you all about my trip, my dear. But first I want to hear about how you are *truly* doing. I have heard some of what has happened here, so do not try to make this conversation all about me. You rarely speak of yourself, but this time I won't allow it. If you fear to tell me the truth, keep in mind that I have lived a very long time. There isn't much that would shock me. I do not judge how others wish to live their lives. All the same, I think the rumors are rubbish."

He flashed his perfect white teeth as he let out a raspy laugh at my expression. "Do not look so shocked, my dear. I may not know all there is about you, but I do know *you*. I also know who raised you. I told you that your father and I were business associates. Truthfully, we were also friends. I knew you would not remember me as you were in pigtails last I saw you, but I remember that little girl fondly. And, dare I say, we have become something of friends ourselves these last few years, yes?"

I nodded mutely at this new information.

"My dear, you keep me young." He chuckled again, slapping his knee. "I admit I started visiting your shop out of respect for a friend who passed away too young. That first day I saw you working side-by-side with the contractors to put this shop in order, you reminded me of your father. He was not afraid of hard work no matter how wealthy he became. He was a good man who loved his family deeply. I was very saddened by his loss."

We sat in silence for a moment lost in our memories. Mr. Lawson cleared his throat and continued, "I came to your gallery that first time for my own selfish reasons. I wanted to reconnect with a man I had lost touch with over the years through his daughter, but instead found a delightful young woman who has brought joy to my life."

I swallowed thickly as tears welled in my eyes. Mr. Lawson had shown up one day not long after my gallery opened to buy several paintings for a room he said he was having redecorated. Ever since he'd been a regular customer, buying up several items at each visit. When I finally got up the nerve to ask where he put it all, he had laughed. Then went on to tell me that he had several homes that could use some splashes of art, in addition to an ancestral estate in England that had enough space to display purchases of artwork from my gallery for generations to come.

"Thank you, Mr. Lawson. I may not remember you from

when I was younger, but you have been a great comfort to me these last few years."

"You are stronger than you give yourself credit for, my dear. I do not doubt that you will weather this storm." He settled back into his chair, crossing his legs. "Do you know who is behind the rumors?"

"I . . . no. It seems others are taking advantage of the initial rumors to add their own." I tried to hide the sickening feeling the situation brought on by taking a sip of my tea. "Natalie told everyone that I fired her because I was jealous of her. Brice has turned everything he's done around to make it sound as if I was to blame. But all of that happened after the rumors had already started. I have no idea who or why." I bit the inside of my cheek to stop my lips trembling.

Mr. Lawson patted my hand. "I thought not. I took the liberty of contacting a friend to look into it. He has some skill in this area." When I tried to protest, he patted my hand. "It was quite presumptuous of me, I know. But since your father has passed on, I feel he would want me to aid you where I can. Please don't be cross with me, my dear."

His unrepentant meddling had me smiling at him even though I hated the fact that I was in a position to need his help. "I see now why your son and daughter struggle to keep up with you. No wonder they call you Papa Pug—you really are the pugnacious patriarch."

"Humph. Papa Pug, indeed." He tutted. "Those children of mine have no respect. Their stunts of late have taken on a new level of stupidity. I tell you, they are trying to kill me so they can spend our family fortune on drugs and plastic surgery!" He rapped his cane on the floor. "What does a person need with a fake rear end, I ask you? It's bloody madness. My several times great-grandfather founded this town. As the youngest son of a duke, he was not expected to make much of himself. Yet he came to America and started his merchant business while his older brother sat on his pampered arse. He should have retired to the country when he made his fortune, as was expected, but he was a hard-working man. He taught his sons, just as they taught their sons. Generations of Lawsons have been shipbuilders."

I sipped at my tea again to hide my smile at this much-repeated rant.

His wrinkled lips puckered like he tasted something vile. "What do my children want to do? Get a tan and gamble. Bless my dearly departed wife, but she spoiled those two shamelessly. I blame myself. I worked day and night to build an empire. I should have worked on building my family—" He stopped abruptly and sighed. "Ah, love, I've gone off again. Forgive me. We were talking about you."

"I know you're worried about your kids and what will happen to the family business. It will work itself out, you won't allow anything else." I gave him a smile and set my tea on the coffee table. "You know, I never would have thought of having someone look into the rumors. I'm not used to leaning on anyone. Thank you."

"I'm sure we will soon get to the bottom of it. As for Natalie and Brice, shall I use my considerable influence to have them disappear to some third world country?" A mischievous glint entered his faded gray eyes. "I hear that the diamond mines are always in need of help. I'm sure backbreaking labor, and deplorable living conditions would cure most of their unfortunate dispositions."

The mental picture of them slaving away in a hole in the ground was the stuff of dreams. No doubt Natalie would sleep her way out of the situation and come back to wreak even more havoc on my life. "As much as I love the image, I think I'll have to pass. They're a couple of spoiled brats who used this opportunity to try to hurt me, though god only knows why."

"I grant you that Brice is not terribly bright and will soon trip over that ego of his. Your former assistant may be another story. She is young, but even the smallest viper is full of enough venom to do harm," Mr. Lawson cautioned. "I had the dubious pleasure of her acquaintance when you were away this last time for that art exhibit. I doubt sugar would melt on her honeyed tongue, but it's the eyes that are the windows to the soul, you know. You need only look closer to see she is full of rot and envy.

"Be careful, my dear, that you do not underestimate her or whomever has spread these rumors. It wasn't from Myrtle's that I heard the rumors directly myself, but from more than one of my colleagues while in Seattle last week." He rapped his cane on the floor once more, making me jump. "For the rumors to be making the rounds in my circles means that someone has some very influential connections."

A chill chased across my skin and my stomach dropped. Who would target me? I was nobody, and I'd made sure to keep it that way. Cracks split the pavement of my lonely highway, and a cacophony of screams rang out. Memories bombarded me. I saw my father swallowed by waves of water. Then I was shivering in a dark alley, my empty belly cramping with hunger and the stench of my unwashed body assailing my nose. Then I was in a squatter's camp in an abandoned building, the lifeless eyes of a man staring up in accusation at me from the trash-strewn floor.

I shuddered as my past tried to drag me down into the dark abyss buried beneath my lonely highway. The anger and fear these rumors had caused were far too familiar. What was I going to do?

4

The rest of the week dragged. I spent my time cataloging inventory and cleaning every inch of Whimsy. As Mr. Lawson had said, the rumors had spread well beyond our town and had taken on a new twist. A couple of the artists I worked with had called yelling that they weren't giving me money, and if I kept harassing them, they were calling the cops. I had no clue what they were talking about, but no one believed me. Unfortunately, Mr. Lawson's friend had not been able to find the source of the rumors. In the meantime, my business was still suffering and so was I.

I hadn't had any referrals in weeks from other galleries. When I called to talk to the gallery owners, they accused me of tacking on miscellaneous fees for purchases. Then there had been the disgusting pictures that had appeared on the gallery website and I'd finally had to take the whole site down. A police car parked in front of the gallery more than once, the officers watching but never approaching me. I'd had to cancel exhibitions and nearly every local artist had pulled their inventory from my store. I was stressed to the breaking point and my nerves were a mess. My world was spiraling out of control, again.

I'd done what I could to salvage the artists' careers, but there was no one to help me. I didn't want Dia tied to this in any way but the guilt of cutting her out of my life again was taking its toll as well. The asphalt on my highway was worn thin by the constant stress, anger, and helplessness. The doubts and fears of my past seeped through to taunt me. Every day I was closer to a precipice that would send me tumbling into the dark waters of my past to drown me.

I hated this. Hated it! There was no end and no solution in sight.

Desperation was creeping in. My sanity and my sanctuary were in jeopardy. The few sales from tourists and the morbidly curious weren't enough to keep paying the bills for the gallery. There was enough put aside to weather the storm for a bit longer, but that was money that should have gone toward art investments. I'd planned to make an offer on work from an artist a few towns over, but now that wasn't possible. My studio expansion was a long-lost dream. Every penny was going toward keeping the business afloat.

With nothing but time on my hands, endless questions for which I had no answers plagued me. Who was behind the rumors? What did they gain by ruining my reputation and damaging my business? How much longer could I go on like this? I had lost weight and it was getting harder to force myself to keep going through the motions every day.

The gallery was no longer my safety blanket blocking out the past. Yesterday I had tried to find some peace by creating my own artwork. It had been so long since I had tried that the tools felt foreign in my hands. My father's patient voice had filled my head. "*Steady. Steady. It's like building my ships. It takes a caring hand to bend it to your will with enough force but not too much to break it. That's it, little star.*"

The glass shattered. Rage had surged up and taken over, and the next thing I knew the punty rod I used for shaping was sticking out of the wall across the room. I hadn't lost time like that since the day I stood over that dead body in an abandoned building, its sightless eyes accusing me of something I couldn't remember. My lonely highway had been born in a moment of desperation soon after that when I sat at a fork in the road choosing between life or death. Every mile of asphalt I had laid had taken me farther from that place. Quiet and routine had become my tools to keep that highway maintained. My blackout that day in the studio had shaken me so bad that I hadn't set foot in there since.

The pavement was weakening, and I wasn't sure if I would survive its collapse.

The phone rang on the counter in front of me, startling me so much that I sent the jewelry I had been sorting scattering all over the floor. *Huh, why hadn't I thought of that?* It would take at least a half hour to clean that up. If I did it slowly. One piece at a time. Maybe I could "accidentally" drop a few more things.

"Whimsy Fine Arts, this is Lia. How may I help you?" I asked, trying to instill some cheer into my tone while mentally crossing my fingers that this was a client wanting to purchase something.

"Jillian, this is Brice. I'm glad I caught you. I wasn't sure if your little shop was still open," he said in that nasal little rat voice of his. Come to think of it, his resemblance to a rat was uncanny. That slicked back hair. Those beady little eyes. The big ears.

Dirty. Lying. Rat.

It took all of my effort not to slam the phone down.

Repeatedly. The silence stretched on for a couple of awkward moments while I struggled to say something that didn't start with an F and end with a you. All that came out was a garbled growl.

"Jillian? Hello? Are you there? You should have your phone checked. There's something wrong with the line."

Yeah, and my fist could set your nose back to pre-surgery ugly.

Ok, not helping. *You can't go around punching the man because he's an ass.* I could imagine it, though. Not quite as satisfying, but hitting people, even when they deserved it, wouldn't solve anything. Maybe picturing him as a rat would help. Wait, what was lower than a rat? A flea. He was the flea on the rat's ass. That's what I would picture when dealing with him from now on.

Deep breath. You can do this.

"Mr. Kingston. What can I do for you?"

"Well, I would normally do this kind of thing in person, but I have to pick Maggie up in a few minutes for our dinner in Seattle. I think you're familiar with the new restaurant that just opened? Maggie is so excited to meet the chef. We'll be attending the new art exhibition opening tonight as well." His voice turned even more nasal sounding as he gave me his fake version of empathy. "Oh, that's right, you know the artist. She was one of your clients, right?"

He knew that I knew her—he only wanted to twist the knife in my back.

Don't kill him. Remember that conversation you had with Dia about not wanting to service females. Prison isn't for you. "Yes, the exhibition was one I had planned to organize myself, but it didn't work out. Fortunately, the artist was able to find another gallery."

"Oh well, you won't have to worry about those kinds of

things when Whimsy closes. That's what I was calling about. The bank has reviewed your loan and decided to call it due in full. You'll be getting the letter in the mail with the payoff balance that will fall due in two months. It's a generous time frame; think of it as a gift between friends," he said cheerfully, as if he hadn't dropped a bomb on me. "I know you probably feel bad, but most businesses fail within the first few years. You'll have plenty of time now to get a real job."

"What? I-I-I . . . You can't—" Dots danced in front of my eyes as the oxygen was sucked out of the room. I felt numb with shock.

"Of course, you won't be able to pay off the loan," he went on, oblivious to the cliff he had pushed me off or that I was flailing to find a way to survive the fall. "I talked to the owner of the gallery we will be attending tonight, and they might be interested in purchasing your little shop. The name will have to change, of course. They can't be associated with all those nasty rumors. I can discuss their offer tonight. Don't worry, I think we can make enough to allow you time to look—"

"No!"

"I'm doing what's best for you." Brice lectured, as if he was talking to a small child.

"No, Brice, you're doing what's best for *you*. You're a self-centered asshole who has done nothing but make my life miserable. I'm not selling my gallery. One way or another I will find a way to pay that loan. Just remember this: karma is a bitch, and so am I," I growled at him. The beads on the floor rattled around my feet as if the ground were shaking. "One of these days I'm going to pay you back for being the creepy pervert that you are and spreading all of those lies. If you know what's good for you, you'll stay away from me and my business."

I slammed the phone down so hard I was surprised it stayed intact. Then, for good measure, I threw it at the wall. I stomped to the door and flipped the gallery sign to *Closed*, nearly ripping it from its hanger. It was the middle of the day, but so the fuck what? Customers weren't exactly knocking down the door to get in.

A seething rage fueled every furious step back to my office. The crunch of one of the pieces of jewelry under my foot spiked the fire higher. When I gripped the handle of the office door, the whole thing rattled on its hinges and then crashed to the floor.

Great, my gallery was falling apart too.

I walked across the fallen door, and threw myself into my chair. My fist banged against the desk, making everything on top of it jump an inch into the air. I had poured everything into this gallery. Everything. *Damn them all. All of those assholes and their . . . assholery! They aren't taking my gallery away. Not one single piece. This is mine.*

Damnit, there has to be something I can do.

My brain was spinning with the absolute knowledge that my gallery was going to be taken from me. The rumors, the lies, the blacklisting from the art community, the imposed isolation from Dia so I didn't bring her down with me. It all combined to obliterate my carefully crafted life. My breath panted out in short bursts as panic filled me. Thoughts rioted through my head chasing solutions that all ended with the same inevitable conclusion.

Prostitution. Robbery. The Lottery. None of those were going to solve my problem without creating more issues. I gripped my hair as if I could pull the answer out by the roots.

Darkness erupted from the brittle pavement of my highway threatening to consume me. My mother's scream filled my head as if I were back onboard that ship with my parents, unable to save them once more. Then that scream manifested as my own as I tipped my head back and let go.

The desk shook and my purse tipped over spilling its contents. The dam finally cracked, releasing a flood of tears. I was not one of those delicate criers. My eyes and nose felt hot and tingly already. I gulped down the sobs choking me, blindly reaching for the box of tissues on my desk. My fingers scraped across something sharp, and I jolted from the pain.

I wiped my eyes with the tissue and threw it in the trash-can. My chest felt hollowed out as I painstakingly repaired the highway and tucked everything away. Then I noticed the beads of blood along my pointer finger. I dabbed the blood away from the paper cut and, grabbing the offending card like it was Flea Boy's neck, I started to crush it in my fist.

Wait a minute. There was something familiar about this card.

A smeared drop of blood was the only thing on the white surface. Then, slowly, black writing started to reveal itself as if a fire was burning across the paper. I dropped the card to the desk, reluctant to touch the creepy thing.

Black symbols appeared—three on each side of the card. This was the invitation Dia had given me at lunch all those weeks ago. I'd put it in my purse that day as we left Mussels and hadn't thought of it since.

The center of the card read:

YOU ARE CHOSEN.
CHILD OF LIGHT.
WHAT YOU SEEK, YOU MAY FIND.
COURAGE. LOVE. PEACE.
ALL COULD BE YOURS IN THE PALDIMORI GAMES.

An e-mail address was listed at the bottom of the card, urging the invitee to join the Games. Curious, I logged into my laptop and entered the site address. There was a white background with the same symbols in a repeating pattern down either side of the page. The center consisted of a countdown box to the deadline for entrance and a short application. A list of very general requirements stated that the applicant had to be over twenty-one and available for the full four-week period in July. Dia had said something about this being an invite-only kind of thing so maybe the hard part was getting to this point.

The bottom of the screen had a long disclaimer that listed a bunch of legal stuff about nondisclosures and privacy agreements. However, it was the contest prize information that drew my attention. Contestants were able to win prizes in every competition of the Games. The grand prizewinner would take home three million dollars!

Is this for real? My god, that would pay for a hell of a lot more than my loan. I could make a fresh start if I wanted to.

The blinking cursor taunted me. Was I really going to do this? Me and physical activity were not a good combination mostly because I was accident-prone. It had been years, though since I'd had an incident—avoiding gyms had helped. Maybe things had changed? The stress of the last few months had whittled off a few pounds. Moving inventory around the gallery had built a bit of muscle. What did I have to lose?

I quickly completed the form and pressed Submit. A black circle with six flickering rays appeared. Stars twinkled into existence within the circle. Then tendrils of colors burst forward. The colors seemed to pulse in time with the flickering rays, like a heartbeat. When nothing new happened on the screen, I reached for the card again to study the symbols while I waited.

It had been a while since my art history class, but there was a certain style to the symbols that seemed familiar.

What the—?

The message that had been on the card before was gone. In its place were two lines:

LIGHT OF THE FAITH

ANERRHIPHTHO KYBOS

What on earth did that mean? The screen on my laptop suddenly went black, drawing my attention away from the mysterious card. A shiver raced down my spine as I read the bold white letters typing out across the screen.

Welcome to the Paldimori Games, Jillian Davies.

5

Sitting at my bay window in my condo the next day, I watched the waves lap on the shore beyond my backyard. It was mid-morning and I was still in my pj's. There wasn't any point in opening the gallery. I would drive myself crazy looking for things to do to kill the time. Besides, I needed a break from being stared at like I was a circus act.

Last night had been my first night of restful sleep in a while. Telling off Brice really was therapeutic. And maybe having a plan, even if was in the form of this mysterious game, made me feel more in control. Unfortunately, sitting around at home left too much time to think. Hugging my knees to my chest, I absently toyed with the hem of my pajama pants. Had I made the right decision to enter the game?

My internal debate was interrupted by a *thump* followed by a *sque-e-e-e-ak* sound from outside the front of my condo. Rushing to the front window, I stared in puzzlement at a large solid circle of pink surrounded by three rings of orange that someone had painted on it. The center circle had a happy face drawn on it in yellow, and what appeared to be glitter sparkled in the sunlight. Movement in the flowerbed caught my eye. Dia waved, then hefted my garden gnome onto her shoulder.

My head cocked to the side. *What is she doing?*

Dia squinted one eye while holding her thumb up in front of her face. She nodded to herself then spread her legs wide before she gripped the gnome with both hands. Her lips form the words "three." Then "two."

Oh shit!

I scrambled to the front door, my fingers clumsy in my haste to unlock it. "Dia, don't you dare!"

Finally managing to unlock the door, I tripped down the steps of the concrete landing, windmilling my arms as I tried to keep my balance while barreling forward. "What a Wonderful World" blasted from the pink phone lying next to Dia on the ground. Waving my arms like an air traffic controller, I tried to halt the unscheduled garden gnome flight she was lining up to pitch through my window. My neighbors were likely crafting new rumors to spread about my hostage negotiations with someone who looked like Rainbow Bright.

"Dia! Put the nice gnome down. He hasn't scheduled a flight plan. I don't need the FAA knocking on my door," I pleaded.

"The FAA only care about drones, not gnomes. I checked. Besides, I'm only a concerned citizen doing my duty to check up on a missing person. Did you know that the police don't consider someone who won't answer their phone as missing? Who isn't glued to their phone these days? I told them I also haven't seen this *supposed* friend of mine in about a month." She glared at me in accusation. "Although I've dropped in on her work and her home about a million times. It's almost as if my *friend* is avoiding me, but I know that can't be right."

Avoiding anyone? Who, me?

I would have some major making up to do. With Dia, that usually involved shopping. "I'm sorry. I know it wasn't right to disappear on you again. I just didn't want to bring you down with me."

"Sweetheart, you think you're keeping the bad things away from me, but you haven't figured out yet that bad things happen to everyone." Sympathy softened her glare. "I would rather experience everything life has to offer than live in a bubble. You keep trying to put me in that bubble by running as far away as possible like you're going to self-destruct and wipe me out if I'm anywhere near you. I don't need protecting."

How could I not try to protect her? She was all I had left. Dia was like a vibrant rose blossoming in a field of thistles. She was kind and so full of life. There was too much in this world that could snuff that out. I had seen it happen.

"What happened in your past was horrible. No one should ever have to go through that. You grew up with the perfect life, and then it all changed. Anyone would have been devastated. But when you disappeared, I spent every day wondering when I would get the call telling me you were dead too." A tear slipped down her cheek. "That was worse than anything that could have happened if you had stayed so we could work through it together. They may not have been my parents, but I felt their loss. Then I lost you too. What you're going through now sucks. I'm only asking that you try —for both of us—to let me be there for you. Ok?"

It finally dawned on me how upset she was, how scared. Her bottom lip trembled. Her fingers were white-knuckled where she gripped the gnome. There was a cautious hope in her teary eyes that I had never seen before. Guilt punched me right in the chest. This was all on me. I had taught the innocent girl she had been all those years ago to mistrust. I had caused her the very pain I was trying to protect her from. Swallowing down the splinters of guilt, I vowed that I would earn back that trust and erase the pain.

"Ok."

She smiled brightly. "You know what this means, right?"

"Let the torture begin." I rolled my eyes.

"Yay, shopping!" She squealed in delight as she rushed me. The gnome tumbled off her shoulder and made a sad crunch when it hit the ground. I winced. There went another phone. At least the music had stopped. Dia was too busy hugging me and rambling on about cute summer styles to notice. It was going to be a long day.

My arms ached from the mountain of jeans, tops, underwear, and whatever else Dia had managed to sneak into the pile. All clothing that I apparently could not live without. Sighing for the hundredth time since being dragged on this shopping trip, I tottered along precariously while she flitted from rack to rack like a manic butterfly. Why anyone needed anything other than well-worn jeans and comfy tees, I would never know.

Secretly, I enjoyed how excited Dia got when doing her fairy godmother routine. She would dress me up, and we would spend an evening out on the town. Generally, that meant driving to one of the larger cities since the nightlife in Port Lawson was pretty nonexistent. Then we would go back to my place for *my* version of fun, which involved comfy pj's, chocolate, and movie marathons. Dan-the-Downer usually called way too early the next morning whining about Dia coming home. The lectures would start before she even made it out the door about us being two grown women who shouldn't still be having sleepovers. That man seriously needed a stick-ectomy.

Today Dia had dragged me to a trendy shop in the downtown district of the large city just down the coast from us. The store, Starlets on Main, was classier than the regular ones she picked. The theme was red-carpet inspired. Mannequins dressed in chic summer dresses, halter-tops, and swimsuits posed amongst the clothes racks. The air smelled like lemon drops, and pop music was playing over the speakers. It made me want to run right back out the door.

"I'm so proud of you for doing this, Lia." Dia bounced around me.

I grumbled under my breath, shifting my bundle to navigate around a mannequin that looked like Marilyn Monroe.

"Oh, look at this swimsuit! This would look awesome with your skin tone." Dia squealed as she tossed scraps of fabric on top of the giant pile in my arms.

I nudged the swimsuit aside with my chin and worked my tongue to remove the stray thread that had managed to make it into my mouth. "Dia, I don't need a new swimsuit. I don't need twenty pair of lacy underwear. I definitely don't need the push-up bra that's going make me the first female to ever suffocate in her own cleavage. And I'm pretty sure the saleslady will be calling the news stations claiming she had a sighting of a walking mountain of clothes. Or, with the way she's been eyeballing me, it'll be the cops. Can we *please* go home?"

Dia finally noticed my struggle and sighed. "Fine, fine.

Spoil my fun." Then she tugged a few items from the pile—like that would reduce my burden. "Will you at least try on that burgundy romper? Please. For me?"

I huffed. "Ok, geez. I'll try it on, if only to set this stuff down and get the blood flowing back into my arms."

We made our way to the fitting rooms. Half of the room was a sitting area with a cluster of fainting couches in red brocade. The other side consisted of dressing rooms. I dumped the load of clothes onto one of the couches and started massaging the prickling sensation out of my arms. A streak of burgundy suddenly smacked me upside the head. I glared at Dia, grabbing the garment before it hit the floor.

"I thought you were in a hurry to get home, Lia." She smiled innocently. "What's taking so long?"

Dia's laughter followed me as I grumbled my way over to a dressing room. My friend may have been a hippie-wannabe about most things, but she was a tyrant when it came to her makeover missions. That pile of clothes was going to grow while I was in here trying on this torture device disguised as fashion. At least she wasn't making me try on everything.

The dressing room was larger than expected with a padded red bench and three mirrored sides. Setting the romper on the bench, I quickly stripped down to my plain beige underwear. Then I pulled the silky material up my body. It felt super soft against my skin. Huh, not as clingy as expected.

Cautiously, I peeked at the mirror directly in front of me. Deep brown eyes looked back at me in widened surprise. The high cheekbones of my round face were flushed a light pink from my war with the clothes pile and were even more pronounced from the severe bun I had piled my hair into. The deep V-cut of the garment showed off my plain bra and a shocking amount of my generous cleavage. My eyes wandered down to the flare at the waist that thankfully concealed my stomach. The loose shorts bottom looked more like a skirt and showed off smooth alabaster legs to mid-thigh.

"I know you're so quiet in there because you're in awe, right?" Dia asked from the other side of the door.

I would never admit it, but at that moment, I really was.

"What can I say, it's a superpower. I think I might need a cape. Do you think Shopping Genius or Fashion Defender would be a better name?"

Wow, I look pretty good.

Dia knocked on the door. "Lia, are you ok in there?"

I snapped guiltily to attention like I hadn't been staring at my ass in the mirror, and started removing the romper. "Ok, so maybe you do know a little about dressing me. But if you get a super-heroine name like Fashion Defender, then I get to call myself Obi-Wan Lia-nobi."

I smiled as she muttered something about my stupid movie fetish. My efforts to convert her into a fan hadn't worked in all these years, so I was probably safe from having to go cape shopping for now.

"Uh, thanks, Dia," I mumbled quietly.

"Aw, you finally appreciate my superpowers!" Dia chuckled and started pairing clothes into outfits. "So, you're leaving me in a week?"

"Yep. A car is picking me up next Sunday afternoon to take me to a private airstrip. Then it's a plane ride to wherever the Games are being held. I've been assigned a guide or something, who I'll meet when I get there. The e-mail was pretty vague on the details; just lots of 'you shall not' stuff." I finished dressing and stepped out of the fitting room. "Thanks for taking care of Whimsy while I'm gone."

"Anything for my bestie," Dia smiled over her shoulder. "It'll be interesting to do something besides teach."

Nerves and doubts started creeping in again. "Maybe I shouldn't go."

"Lia, you can't back out now!" Dia turned and grabbed my hands. "So what if you don't win the money. This is an adventure. Go snorkeling. Meet some hot guys and have sweaty forget-your-name sex. Spend the day laying on the beach." She hugged me. "Whatever you do, forget about everything happening here and have fun. You need this. What's the worst that could happen?"

6

The sight of the black Lexus pulling into my driveway Sunday afternoon halted my nervous pacing. It was a struggle to fight down the urge to hide in my room and pretend I didn't hear the knock at the door. Time had been my enemy as I watched the minutes tick by all night, unable to fall asleep. Every time I had drifted off my eyes would pop right back open seconds later as a new worry sprang to mind. Counting sheep hadn't worked. They had all turned suicidal and jumped off a cliff. Meditation started out ok until my mind kept conjuring up scenarios on how this could all go wrong. Like being sold into the sex trade to a sweaty old guy who called me Mama. My breath had started billowing in and out so quickly I sounded more like I was practicing Lamaze. I almost coughed up a lung from choking.

My hand hesitated on the doorknob. Was it too late to change my name and leave the country?

No, I was going to do it. This was to save my gallery and to fulfill the promise I had made last night to Dia. To give this thing a chance. Knowing her, she was probably hiding in the neighbor's bushes to make sure I got in that car.

Here we go. Taking a deep breath, I opened the door.

Standing on my front step was a slender young woman in a black pantsuit. Her white-blonde hair was styled in a choppy pixie cut tipped in navy blue to frame her oval face. Her eyes were a smoky blue-gray that seemed to swirl with mysteries as she gave me a quick head-to-toe glance. Her mouth stretched into a mischievous smile as she held her hand out.

"Hi, I'm Molly West. Chauffeur and your personal guide for the Games. Love the outfit."

She gripped my hand in a surprisingly firm handshake as nerves swirled in my stomach. "Oh uh, hi. Thanks. Nice to meet you, Ms. West. I'm Jillian Davies. Um, I thought I wasn't going to meet my guide until I got to the island?"

She shook her head. "Call me Molly. Nope, that would be your Kyrion. You'll meet him there."

"Kyrion?"

"Think of him like a manager, only way cuter." She laughed.

She glanced at my suitcase, her brows pulling together. "That the only bag you're taking? For a four-week trip?"

"Yes, this is it. I figured why pack the house when I'll probably be forced to eat bugs and make my own clothes out of palm leaves or something."

Molly found that hysterical. Her laugh was infectious and the tension eased from my shoulders. "Palm leaves . . . that's great. I like you already. We're gonna get along just fine. Come on, let's get a move on. Can't keep Captain Quickdraw waiting."

Molly walked me to the rear door of the car and ushered me inside. I could hear her talking on the phone as she placed my luggage in the trunk. My clammy hands pressed into the supple leather seat, readying myself to jump from the car depending on what happened next. Hopefully my guide wasn't about to turn into an evil henchman, because I wasn't dressed for ass-kicking.

Blame it on Dia. Somehow she had talked me into "making a statement" my first time meeting a bunch of strangers. Not really sure what statement she was going for, but even I could admit that I looked good. My hair was pulled back and styled into big loose curls. Lush red lips and smoky eyes had me doing a double-take every time I caught my reflection. The girls were showcased in an off-the-shoulder white top and the asphyxiation-inducing bra. Coupled with a burgundy tulle skirt, my waist had never looked smaller. The matching lace-up flats made my legs appear miles long. If it was Dia's intention to make me look like a pin-up girl, she'd hit a bull's-eye.

Molly slid behind the wheel and backed out of the drive-way. Glancing out the window at my condo as we drove away, I was struck by the fact that my life was at a precipice. I would come home with the money to save Whimsy or I would come back to close the doors. Either way, a new chapter of my life was starting. It was all up to me now.

"So, Jillian Davies, tell me about yourself," Molly prompted, glancing at me in the rearview mirror.

"Please call me Lia."

We chatted all the way to the airport. Molly was enter-taining company. By the time we pulled up to a security booth outside a tall iron gate, most of my nerves had disap-peared. Molly talked briefly with the security guard, then pulled through the gate. We drove beside the high stone wall and stopped in front of one of several airplane hangars. Molly grabbed my suitcase, and I followed her over to a small white airplane. There was a small black symbol on the tail of the plane that I couldn't quite make out, but no other identifying marks.

A tall man dressed all in black descended the airplane steps as we approached. He removed his sunglasses as he came to a stop in front of me and tucked them into the collar of his button-up shirt. His smile was friendly and welcoming as he nodded to me but slipped from his face as he greeted my guide. "Ms. West."

"Captain, this is Ms. Davies," Molly stated, suddenly sounding much more formal. "This is Captain Jack Matthews. He will be your pilot for this trip."

"A pleasure to meet you, Ms. Davies," the captain said, bringing my hand to his lips. He smiled up at me as his soft lips brushed my knuckles, and two sexy dimples appeared on his scrubby cheeks. When he straightened, he held onto my hand as his hazel eyes took me in from head to toe. Was this guy for real? This was the most blatant eyeing-up I'd ever seen.

When his eyes reconnected with my entertained ones, the dimples came back out to play. Even someone with my limited experience could tell that this one was an unrepentant flirt. I pressed my lips together to keep from laughing when I remembered Molly's nickname for him—Captain Quickdraw. If that was a reference to his flirting, he was certainly armed and quick on the draw. Finally dropping my hand, he said, "We have clear skies all the way and have been cleared for takeoff as soon as you're settled. Let me help you to your seat."

"Thank—"

"Ms. Davies doesn't need help to her seat. I doubt she's going to get lost making her way up the steps to the only entrance," Molly snapped at him with a glare. Then she turned to me. "Pick any of the four seats and get comfortable. I'll go put your luggage away." She spun on her heel and stomped her way up the steps of the plane.

Captain Matthews jerked as if she had elbowed him in the stomach. His thunderous gaze followed her retreating form. A little too closely. There was definitely some ogling going on. When he finally dragged his eyes back to me, I gave him a knowing look. He ducked his head and ran his fingers through his shoulder-length light brown hair. "Uh, right. I better go check . . . stuff. See ya around." Then he fled toward the hangar.

I must have dozed off at some point because the next thing I knew Molly was shaking my shoulder saying we were about to land. The sleepless night and days of being on edge had caught up with me. My eyes felt gritty, and my brain was in a fog. Yawning, I moved my chair upright and stretched. My fingers brushed my hip by habit, forgetting that my phone was back in my condo. Part of our agreement had been no electronic devices. It felt like my lifeline to the real world had been taken away.

Molly sat in the seat across from me, deep in concentration. A square walnut table had been folded out from the cabin wall, and she was focused on the screen of a sleek black laptop. Apparently, the no electronic devices rules only applied to contestants. At some point, she had changed clothes. The tailored suit had been replaced by a V-neck navy T-shirt that hung loosely on her thin frame. She wore a pair of ripped jeans with a large black skull-and-crossbones on the shin. Her hair was spiked up in the back, and a diamond stud pierced her nose.

She must have felt me staring because her head jerked up in my direction. She smiled at me warmly, seeming to have forgotten whatever issues she had with the flirty captain that had made her so abrupt earlier. Curiosity about the history between those two tempted me to ask questions. The only problem with asking personal questions was that people expected to be able to ask their own in return. Generally, the first question people asked was about your family. That was a topic I would rather avoid.

"Glad you're awake, Sleeping Beauty. Look out your window," Molly directed. Then she immediately turned her attention back to her computer and started hammering away at the keyboard.

Below us stretched a large, roughly triangular island. It was outlined in the aqua blue of the shallows that transitioned into the deep blue ocean as far as the eye could see. Large folds of mountain ridges covered in dense forests came into view as we started our descent. As we got closer, I could occasionally make out sandy beaches at the mountain bases. We turned to follow the shoreline, and the dramatic peaks gave way to lush green rolling valleys stretching toward the interior of the island. The plane banked again, and another side of the island revealed rocky beaches pounded by crystalline blue waves.

The place was breathtaking. These people had to have some serious money to own an island like this. My eyes strained to take in every detail. I could almost feel the sand between my toes already. The only things I didn't see were signs of people. There wasn't anyone sunbathing, swimming, or snorkeling. In fact, there wasn't even a sign of buildings, roads, or even a runway.

Abruptly Molly stood and reached across me to slide the

window shade down with a snap. "That's your peek. Beautiful, isn't it?"

I narrowed my eyes at her. "Yes, it is. Was the sneak-peek part of the Games? Was I supposed to memorize what I saw?"

"The Games started the minute I picked you up. The real fun begins with the competitions, though." She gave me that mischievous smile I was coming to associate with her. "The Paldimori Games happen every year without fail. Six contestants are chosen. Then six competitions are selected and hosted by one of the Kyrion."

"The winner of all six competitions gets the grand prize?"

"Nope," Molly said, giving the "p" a hard sound to make it pop. "The majority winner. Whoever wins the most competitions out of the six. Though every winner of a training session or single competition also gets a prize. The big prize money is only given out after all six competitions are played."

"Who owns the island? Is Paldimori a company or something? And, uh, where's the runway?"

"Can't give away all the secrets this early in the Games, Lia," Molly teased. "What fun would that be?"

I groaned. "Fine. Keep your secrets . . . for now."

"This is going to be fun." Molly rubbed her hands together in anticipation. "Better fasten your seatbelt. The captain likes his landings a little bumpy."

No sooner had she finished her sentence than the plane plummeted sharply downward. I gasped as the sudden descent threw me back into my seat. My clumsy fingers fumbled for the seatbelt. Molly casually took her time stowing her things away. Then she clicked her seatbelt and leaned her head back against the headrest with a sigh as if this were just another day at the office. My fingers gripped the arms of the seat until they went numb as the nosedive continued.

Please god, don't let us end up in a fiery heap on the shores of that beautiful island.

Just when I thought the bagel I'd had for lunch was going to make a reappearance, the tires touched down. The plane shuddered and shook as it tried to slow its momentum. My heart was pounding so hard I thought I might have a heart attack. Beside me, Molly yawned and shifted farther down into her seat as if she was settling in for a nap. My teeth were gritted to keep them from rattling together like castanets as we finally came to a jarring halt.

"See? Fun, right?" Molly asked as she gathered her things and moved toward the cockpit.

"Yeah, super fun." Slowly I pried my fingers from the chair. *Where had Captain Matthews learned to fly—video games?*

The sight that greeted me as I exited the plane looked like a vast underground bunker. The air smelled of jet fumes and the faint mustiness of a cave. My skin prickled in the cold air. Rough-hewn rock walls arched over our heads several stories high with large rectangles of bright lights spaced every couple of feet. A long runway stretched out in the distance outlined in red glowing lines and leading to two-walled airplane "hangars" on either side. Each of the six hangers had a symbol matching those on the invitation card.

"Did we just land inside a cave?"

"Something like that." Molly gave me a secretive smile. "C'mon. This is the boring part. Wait 'till you see your room."

Molly took off toward a set of polished metal double

doors along the back wall. The echo of our shoes and my rolling luggage on the concrete followed us as we walked. She scanned her hand on a keypad beside the doors and they opened with a whoosh. Motion sensor lights winked on overhead as we made our way down a long white hall until we finally came to an elevator. Molly took a key from her jeans pocket and inserted it next to the Up button. The doors opened immediately, and she waved me forward. The oval elevator was large enough to fit a car inside. The walls were paneled in mahogany, and the ceiling looked like an evening sky complete with moving clouds.

"The sky outside is projected onto the ceilings. But you can change the setting in your rooms to whatever you want," Molly explained after pushing a button on the panel. All of the floors seemed to be represented by what looked like Greek numerals, and there were a ton of them.

"This button will take you to your floor." Molly pointed at one. Then she showed me several other buttons for common areas that I might want to visit. The elevator ascended quickly and came to a smooth stop. The doors opened to reveal beige and gold-swirled marble tiles gleaming in the artificial evening sunset. The red symbol of an arrow with wings took up most of the floor front and center of the elevator doors. Beyond that, a crescent-shaped sunken living room faced a wall of windows. The walls were curved and appeared to be made from smooth polygonal stones. There were other areas, but my attention was completely captured by the view dead ahead.

Dropping my luggage by the elevator, I walked toward the wall of windows. My peripheral vision picked up details such as the couches built into the ledge of the sunken living room that were padded with gold-colored cushions, the round bronze fire pit in the center of the area, and the mosaics on the floor. Still, the wall of glass in front of me beckoned. Beyond the floor-to-ceiling windows lay a breathtaking view of the island.

"This is the tallest mountain on the island, called Titan. Yep, we're inside the mountain." Molly stepped up to peer over my shoulder. "Welcome to Sotirìa."

7

Left to my own devices for a while, I spent time exploring the floor that was to be mine during my stay. My inner artist was in heaven with all of the artwork and architecture. Everywhere I looked there was something to be examined. Molly had explained that each contestant had their own floor, each roughly three thousand square feet. One of the six Kyrion owned each level, and it was decorated according to their tastes. And their tastes appeared to be lavish. Guess if you could afford to build a skyscraper complete with an airplane runway inside a mountain, luxury accommodation for your guests wasn't a big deal. My family had been well-off by average standards, but this was a whole other level of extravagance.

Molly disappeared into one of the four bedrooms after giving me a quick rundown on our agenda for the rest of the night. Dinner was to be served in the main contestant dining hall where the guides would give us ground rules. Following dinner, everyone would go to what Molly called the "big-ass room in the sky" to meet the Kyrion. Whatever that meant. She was stubbornly tight-lipped with the information.

At a quarter 'til eight, Molly emerged from her room, and I turned in my seat on the lip of the fire pit to greet her. My greeting never made it out of my mouth. Molly had looked like a chauffeur when we first met. Then she had seemed like the quintessential college student on the airplane. Now an ethereal goddess was walking toward me.

Just who is Molly West?

She wore a floor-length satin dress in a smoky gray. The dress might have been called plain except for the display of one creamy shoulder and the low neckline that showed the top curves of her small breasts. Pinned to the opposite shoulder was a midnight black himation-style cloak trimmed in a red pattern of the flying arrow symbol that kept showing up. The cloak fell over her left arm like a long sleeve then dipped down to drape across her waist and circle around her opposite hip. Her hair had been sleeked down around her face, and the rest pulled back by a double headband of rubies. She was wearing makeup for the first time since I had met her. There were little red jewels at the corner of her dramatic cat eyes, and her lips were painted blood red. A silver torque necklace circled her slender throat and came to rest on her collarbones in an arrowhead shape inlaid with a single large ruby. A matching band circled her right bicep.

"Wow! Did I miss the memo about formal wear?"

Molly snorted. "Nah, the Kyrion just love their traditions. These formal shindigs are the only time I'll ever be caught in a dress. Damn mummy wrap!" She tugged uselessly at the low neckline then adjusted the arrow brooch holding the cloak on her shoulder.

I laughed, appreciating that there was another woman

in the world that hated dresses as much as I did. "You look amazing, but I know the feeling. I can't wait to get out of this skirt and into my pj's."

"Thanks! Yuck, though," Molly said with a shudder. "Let's get this over with before I throw the damn thing in the fire."

The back of the cloak was revealed as she turned toward the elevator. A large flying arrow symbol in red blazed like fire from about knee height.

What's with all the symbols? It was a question Molly had yet to answer.

She explained on our way down that the main dining hall divided the contestant floors: three on lower levels below the hall and three on higher levels above it. My floor was the first of the higher-level contestants' floors, situated directly above the dining hall. Molly also informed me that the Kyrion usually ate on their own floors or in the more formal dining hall in their section of the building located toward the top of the tower above the contestants' levels.

We stepped off the elevator into a spacious hall with a tiled ceiling of lighted arches connecting colonnades on either side of the room. Against the far wall, stone steps led to a semicircular platform with a chandelier overhead. A long wooden table—inlaid with mosaic and big enough to seat an entire team of broad-shouldered football players with room to spare—sat in the center of the hall. Wooden chairs—their high backs carved with the same symbols as on the guides' clothing—were placed far apart, six per side. The center of the table was crammed with enough food to feed a small country. Carafes of coffee and chilled bottles of wine sat before every place setting. At either end of the table, there were small barrels of what I soon found out were bourbon and more wine.

A man and woman stood off to the side of the table in an intense conversation. Molly and I came up next to them just as the woman sternly told the man to take care of something. Then she turned her back on him in clear dismissal. The woman had on a dress exactly like Molly's, except her symbol was a green tree in full bloom. Emerald jewels twinkled at the corner of her eyes and in her headband and necklace. She looked to be in her fifties from the lines that appeared around her kind brown eyes as she smiled warmly at Molly. She opened her arms invitingly.

"Hello, Molly, dear. It's good to see you."

Molly immediately stepped in to give her a hug. "Good to see you too, Den Mother. How you doing?"

The woman patted her cheek in clear affection. "Oh, you know me. Never a dull moment with this rowdy bunch. Now, why don't you introduce me to your friend before she thinks no one around here has any manners."

"Wouldn't want to give her false hope." Molly grinned at me. "This is Jillian Davies, my Potential. Jillian, meet Grace Paxton—Den Mother."

"More like a bloody drill sergeant," mumbled the lanky man behind Grace as I stepped forward to shake her hand. Grace pulled me into a hug instead. Her auburn bob struck through with gray tickled my cheek as I bent down slightly to accommodate her short frame. She smelled like cherry pie. Molly's title for her made sense: everything about this woman said motherly.

"Welcome, dear. You can call me Grace. Never mind either one of these scamps. Molly is sweet but an incurable mischief-maker. And the disrespectful one behind me is Brant Isley, our resident grouch."

The Grouch stood in a wide stance with his arms crossed,

scowling at us. He had on a variation of what the women were wearing: gray dress pants, a gray dress shirt, and a black vest. Similar to the women's cloaks, his vest was trimmed in symbols—in his case, white crescent moons. A matching torque necklace in a thicker, more masculine design hung around his neck. The moon dangling in the opening of his shirt contained a large opal. His dishwater-blond hair was longer on top and combed to one side. His glacial blue eyes bored into me as Grace released me, and I stepped back. With a look of disgust, he turned and headed toward the table.

"Is it me or has he gotten worse? Must be IMS," Molly snapped.

"IMS?" I asked.

"Yep, the male version of PMS." Molly replied. "Irritable Male Syndrome. Although that seems to be Brant's constant state."

"Dear, try not to poke at him unless you want him to lock you in a closet again." Grace smiled at Molly like she and the Grouch were a couple of rambunctious kids.

Molly huffed. "Please, I had that lock picked in two seconds. It was the catapult that I didn't expect."

Grace clicked her tongue. "Full of poison ivy, wasn't it? I don't think I have ever seen someone so miserable. Covered head to toe in that rash and not able to do a thing but scratch. That boy is lucky he left the island before I got hold of him."

I looked at them in horror. A catapult of poison ivy? What the hell have I gotten myself into? *Note to self: Keep your distance from Brant the Grouch.*

"These kids are a handful, I tell you," Grace chuckled. "Oh, before I forget, Cadence will be here tomorrow, Molly. She would like to spend some time with you."

"Sounds good. But why is she coming to the Games?" Molly had narrowed her eyes.

"Dear, I keep telling you. I'm getting old. I've been coming to the Games since I was a young girl. It's time for the next generation to take over." Grace smiled a little sadly. "This will be my last Games."

"Right." Molly snorted. "You say that every year. Then you decide you're too young to retire. You'll be here ordering people around until you're ninety."

"This is it for me, dear. Cadence has been in training for years. She's ready, and so am I. Oh, look, here come the others," Grace said, quickly changing the subject. Molly looked like she wasn't going to let it drop, but Grace didn't give her a chance as she waved for the other guides and contestants to join us.

A woman and two men dressed in the same uniforms as Molly, Grace and Brant brought the total to six guides. The last guide stood out from the rest. He had skipped the shirt and wore only the vest, showing off muscles covered in tattoos from his neck down. The other man was a dark-skinned giant who towered over everyone and marched forward with military precision. The woman was slightly shorter than me with black hair streaked with a smoky purple color that was pulled back in braids that hung to the middle of her back. They were all in peak physical condition and gorgeous to boot.

The contestants were easy to spot in their regular clothes. There was a tall Asian woman in a pants suit and severe bun whose face was carefully blank. A blonde woman, talking animatedly, had on a V-neck halter dress that barely covered her obviously enhanced breasts. She jiggled dangerously as she gestured around the room. More than one set of male eyes were fixated on her chest as if they were waiting for the opportunity to lunge in and assist should she have a wardrobe malfunction.

The remaining three men I mentally labeled the Cowboy, the Geek, and the Lothario. Scanning the group again, I noted how beautiful they all were. The application hadn't listed physical requirements, but I was feeling like the ugly duckling.

My eyes connected with a pair of baby blues staring right at me. A blush heated my cheeks at getting caught sizing everyone up. The Cowboy curled up one corner of his lips in a commiserating smile. He had a well-trimmed beard and ginger hair cropped closely to his head. His blue T-shirt hugged his muscular chest, and well-worn jeans outlined strong thighs. He tipped his white cowboy hat in my direction. My blush deepened as I nodded back to him. He started to walk toward me, but the giant dark-skinned guide asked us all to take a seat.

The seating arrangement restricted any chance for normal conversation due to the distance between the chairs. Unfortunately, the blonde sat next to me and immediately started yelling down the table to talk to me. Her name was Nikki Starr, and she was an actress. It was hard to keep myself from asking what kind of actress, considering how much of her was on display. She was here to get the funding to produce her own movie. Mumbling a few polite replies, I mostly focused on my food.

Twenty minutes of nonstop chatter later and my head was aching. Somehow, Nikki had managed to eat two heaping plates of food in the midst of all that talking. I would kill for her metabolism. Maybe running your mouth that much burned up the calories.

Something was happening with the guides on the other side of the table, but Busty Bigmouth—as I now called her

—was ruining my chances of hearing anything. The giant guide stood at the end of the table with a goblet in hand, leading what appeared to be some sort of toast. The other guides lifted their black goblets in the air and shouted something in unison before sipping their drinks. My stomach was becoming uncomfortably full in my attempts to avoid a conversation with Busty. Eventually, she had to run out of things to talk about, right?

No, I don't want to know about your cousin's childbirth. That's it, bring on the bourbon.

Two shots later and not even Busty could harsh my mellow. Seeing that her audience had drunk herself into a state of blissful oblivion, she set her sights on the person on her other side. The Geek. Oh no, not flirty Busty on top of the chattering. Poor kid, she would eat him alive.

A sigh escaped me as I snuggled back into my chair, feeling deliciously relaxed. From my half-closed lids, I studied the occupants at the table. We were an odd group. Not only in appearance but in personality. What brought this particular group of people together at this point in time? Life was funny. It could lead you down some interesting roads. Here I was in the middle of an island that had never been on any map that I had ever seen. Surrounded by these beautiful people that I didn't know. Participating in a game that I knew next to nothing about. As strange as it was, at that moment it felt like this was exactly where I was supposed to be. Why had I been so worried about coming here?

Dia would really like it here. But she was keeping an eye on my gallery. The mess waiting for me back home stole some of my comfy buzz. Molly's worried look sobered me even more. Drunk wasn't the first impression I was going for. I poured a glass of water and sipped it to clear my head.

The giant was standing once again at the end of the table. Busty quickly stopped talking when his dark gaze pinned her down. Huh, that was a neat trick. Maybe he would teach me.

"Good evening. My name is Devon Harris. I am the Kafàli—or Leader—of the guides." His deep rumbling voice filled the room. "Your guides are here to provide you with what information they can to navigate you through the Games. Heed their advice. They will never be allowed to physically interfere in the Games unless permission is given by the Kyrion. That has never happened." He looked at each of the contestants, his black eyes hard and assessing. "It is almost time for us to ascend to the throne room."

He nodded to the guides, and they moved to stand behind their contestant's chair. "Each guide wears a symbol. No doubt you have seen these symbols elsewhere throughout the day. These symbols represent the six Houses that host these Games. The Kyrion are the rulers of these Houses. All who bear their mark are considered to be under their protection as a representative of that House." His piercing gaze told us all that that this was a special privilege that we weren't worthy of. "You—the contestants—are called Potentials. This means you are the uninitiated champions who have been selected for the Houses. You will be presented to the Kyrion as such for their acknowledgment. They may offer you assistance during the Games, but it is not guaranteed. There are three restrictions placed upon the Kyrion during the Games. Those you will learn in time."

Devon nodded again to the guides. "Your Kyrion have gifted you each with a symbol as the Potential for their House. You must always wear this item while on this island."

Molly's hand appeared in front of my face. Resting on her palm was a torque necklace. The band on this one was much thinner than any the guides wore and had a symbol—almost as large as her palm—of an arrow with intricate silver wings spread wide. Molly bent down and whispered next to my ear. "Put it on and never take it off. It will keep you safe." My gaze searched hers for a moment, waiting for the joke. Safe from what? How could a necklace keep you safe? She must have seen the questions coming because she shook her head. "I can't tell you. Just trust me," she whispered.

Trust. That was in short supply these days. Molly's expression shone with genuine hope, and her eyes were filled with a silent plea. My hand hesitated above hers. There had been an instant connection with Molly since the first moment of our meeting as if we had known each other forever. I had felt more confident about my decision to be here because she was by my side. It seemed she had already wormed her way in without me even noticing.

Picking up the torque, I placed it around my neck. A sudden wave of dizziness rushed over me. My hand smacked the table, causing a clatter as I braced myself. Deep down inside me, a fissure formed, and something slipped from the crack. It moved along my skin, leaving goose bumps in its wake as it coated me from head to toe. Everyone was staring as I fought to gain some equilibrium. Damn it, I was the center of attention again.

Molly loomed over me, brow furrowed and hands poised, ready to grab me if I fell over. Luckily the sensation passed. My shaky smile must not have been too convincing because her hand gripped my shoulder tightly. When nothing else happened the attention quickly shifted back to the Kafàli.

Devon leaned over the table, eyeing each contestant. His intense gaze lingered on me longer than the others, as if he was searching for something. Whatever reaction I'd had to putting on the necklace seemed to have passed. The silence stretched on. Moments later he straightened up as if satisfied with the outcome.

"The symbol is your calling card. It will assist you if you let it. Once you have taken your oath, your guide will provide more information. We will make our way to the throne room now. Stand on your symbol in silence until you are acknowledged." He looked harshly at Busty as he said that last part, and I fought to suppress a smile. "When you are called upon, address yourselves to the Kyrion as Potential and your full name. Then repeat the words they ask you to say." Devon nodded again to the guides. "It's time to meet the Kyrion."

8

The elevator ride to the top of the tower was made in silence. The others looked to be feeling as nervous as I was. Even Busty kept her mouth shut. The guides stood stoically by us with their heads bowed and hands folded before them, as if preparing themselves for something monumental. I started worrying about cults again.

Don't go there. You decided to trust Molly. Besides, it's a bit late to be getting cold feet.

Finally, the elevator came to rest. We stepped out into a small round stone room with dim sconces flickering along the wall. The guides walked us toward an opening to a long hallway and began to line us up in some order that made sense only to them. When they were satisfied with our placement, they paired up with us, and we all began to walk down the hallway.

I kept wanting to catch a glimpse of the other contestants' faces as we walked. Did they feel as creeped out as I was? Unfortunately, being at the back of the line didn't offer me the opportunity to gauge their reactions to this silent pilgrimage. Not that the dim light from the sconces would have let me see much anyway.

We walked for what seemed an hour before the hall curved to the left and a wide stone staircase appeared. The line halted and the first pair ascended the stairs. I fingered the material of my skirt as we waited. Pair by pair, the guides and contestants went up the steps until Molly and I were the only ones left. Molly silently clutched my clammy hand. I was tempted to cling to her but instead gave a squeeze in return before we too headed up the stairs.

The steps curved further around to the left in a gradual incline. Soon a large square opening at the top of lit our way. It took a moment for my eyes to adjust to the brightness after having been in the dim hall. When they did, they were immediately drawn to the place where the rough stone of the hallway gave way to smooth marble. There was something different about the wall there.

My pace picked up as a full three-dimensional relief sculpture in the elegant and sensuous grace of the Greek Hellenistic period came into view. The scene depicted a giant man giving people gifts that looked like the symbols the guides wore. Then the man was being attacked by twelve men and woman with various weapons. The next scene showed a star-like symbol split in two and all of the people fighting. My toe caught the step in my haste, and I would have face-planted if Molly hadn't caught my arm. I glanced at her in thanks, and she arched her eyebrow at me as if to say "pay attention." I nodded.

With difficulty, I managed to keep my focus on getting to the top of the staircase. When we stepped out onto a beige polished marble floor, my mouth dropped open in awe.

No way!

My breath caught in my throat as I gazed upon a familiar

scene. I had been dreaming of this platform of thrones since I was ten. *This can't be real.* The bizarre sense of déjà vu made the hairs stand up on my arms and the torches along the walls suddenly flared higher. Molly gripped my arm, and they immediately died down.

The room was a vast open circle, easily twice the size of the contestant floors. Sculptures and friezes ringed the entire room. One sculpture showed a group of young feminine-looking men fighting around a crumbling throne. A frieze showed a three-headed dog ripping apart a nude woman and her child. A rotunda ceiling, at least two stories above our heads, surrounded a central opening through which moonlight poured. Across from where we stood, several steps led up to a large platform. In the middle of the platform against a solid white wall stood a giant statue. The Greek style of the statue most likely made him a god of some kind, but I couldn't remember one from my art classes that looked like that.

Long hair floated in a vortex around his face, obscuring all but the eyes, which peered back at me as solid white orbs. It could have been the moonlight reflecting on the black marble, but it looked like stars were glowing all over his muscular nude body. He was poised with his arms bent and held out to his sides, palms up, as if gesturing to the sets of three sculptures on either side of him. All six were much bigger than the others in the room and the only others bearing any color. They depicted what appeared to be gods and goddesses each holding the familiar symbols of the Houses. In front of each sculpture was a large black throne. Upon each, a person sat at attention, faces hidden behind hooded robes in colors matching the symbols.

Molly nudged me forward. When we were about two-thirds of the way across the room we stepped into a circle on the floor that looked like a picture of outer space. White stars twinkled against the black background toward the edges of the circle, and a riot of colors that looked like a nebula took up the center. The colors were so vibrant that the nebula appeared to undulate beneath our feet.

Six black rays spread out from the circle and ended at the base of the steps directly in front of each throne. It looked very similar to the image that had appeared on my laptop when I submitted my application. Each contestant stood on the colored symbol at the end of the ray in front of one of the thrones. I started to head toward the only open spot to the far right, but Molly stopped me with her hand on my arm. Following her lead, I bowed my head and waited.

"So nice of you to join us. Perhaps you would like to go ahead and forfeit the Games to stare at the decorations a bit more?" A deep male voice filled the room and seemed to boom from every direction at once. "Well?" the voice barked when I didn't answer.

Hairs stood up on my arms. A shiver raced down my spine. That voice was potent. My mouth felt dry as the Sahara. With a struggle, I managed to unglue my tongue to croak out, "No . . . sir?" What exactly did you call someone who sat on a throne in a hooded robe—besides creepy? I doubted they would appreciate my gallows humor.

"You do not sound very sure." The voice now seemed to be coming from the figure in the black robe to the immediate left of the black marble statue. "Are you dimwitted as well as disrespectful?" it mocked.

A feminine laugh issued from under the white hood at the far left.

Shock at his rudeness finally knocked me out of my daze. *Oh, so the Manson family has a sense of humor.* Good for them, but I'd had just about enough of people's nasty remarks. Straightening my spine, I raised my head to stare at whoever was under that black hood.

"I simply admire good workmanship when I see it. You appear to have an impressive collection of Late Classical Greek sculpture that, if I didn't know better, could have been carved by Praxiteles himself. But then what would a dimwitted girl like me know about that?"

Molly drew in a sharp breath as silence filled the room. What the hell was that? It was as if my mouth was possessed. Nothing to do now but own it. I propped my hands on my hips and glared at each hooded figure as if I wasn't shaking inside. Way to make a lasting first impression. Did they give out a prize for the quickest time a contestant was ejected from the Games?

"I think my Potential is feeling a bit overwhelmed. A good night's sleep will probably help her put things into *perspective.* So, can we move this along?" The amused male voice came from the throne on the far right.

Thanks for the save, red hood. Even if you did imply that I learn my place.

When no one responded immediately, he added in a teasing voice, "I meant—may we proceed with the ceremony, my brother?"

A smirk tugged up one corner of my lips before I could control it. Uh oh, someone was poking fun at their ceremony. Guess I wasn't the only rule breaker.

"Take your place, Potential," the rude male in black clipped out.

Molly and I walked along the last unoccupied black ray until we stood on the symbol of the flying arrow. Molly stepped in front of me in a similar position to the other guides. By some unspoken signal, the guides all began to speak as one.

"I come to you, a servant of your House, to offer the pledge of this Potential. May they be fleet of foot, wise in judgment, brave of heart, and loyal of character. The die is cast!"

There was a rustling sound, but I couldn't see what was happening from my position. "Ruler of the House of Night, I gift you a champion."

"What is your name, *boy*?" The white robed female demanded.

"Chris—I mean, Potential Christopher Erickson," one of the male contestants—the Geek—replied.

"And do you, Potential Erickson, consider yourself a worthy champion for my House?"

"I—yes, I think so," Chris said hesitantly.

"Humph. We shall see," the voice proclaimed, clearly less than impressed with her gift. "I accept what fate intends, Potential Erickson of the House of Night. You may call me Nyx, and I will answer."

A moment of silence enveloped the hall. Then all of a sudden Molly kneeled to the floor and addressed the figure on the throne before us. "Ruler of the House of Arrows, I gift you a champion."

"What's your name, little lioness?" the amused male voice from earlier asked.

"Potential Jillian Davies," I stated, trying to catch a peek at who might be under that red hood.

"Ah, a lovely name for a lovely lady. Do you consider yourself a worthy champion for my House, Jillian?"

"I'll certainly give it my best shot."

A chuckle escaped from beneath the hood. Then long masculine fingers gripped the edges and pulled it back to reveal a gorgeous smiling face. One that had graced the cover of billboards and magazines. I couldn't believe I was staring up into the face of one of the most famous male models in the industry, or so the latest issue of *People* magazine claimed. His blond hair fell in loose waves to his shoulders to frame his lightly tanned face. His midnight blue eyes sparkled with humor, and his full lips were pulled into a sensual smile.

"Oh, I have no doubt, my little lioness." He winked at me. "I accept what fate intends and look forward to the ride, Potential Davies of the House of Arrows. You may call me Eros, and I will answer."

One by one the guides alternated sides "gifting" their contestants and the Kyrion accepting them. My fixation on the gorgeous man upon the throne before me prevented me from catching the others' names. He was practically a celebrity. And his name was definitely not "Eros." What was he doing hiding under a robe on this remote island? Was this some kind of role-playing group? He sat slumped back in his throne, knees spread wide, that same look of amusement still plastered on his face as if all of this was a show put on for his entertainment.

Dragging my attention away from the eye candy, I saw that five of the people on the thrones had revealed themselves. There were three men and two women, all of them beautiful beyond belief. Yet there was something about these people that had my guard up and senses tingling.

I shifted my stance trying to find a comfortable position. My movement caught Eros's attention, and he quirked a brow at me. My gaze must have looked askance because his eyes dipped to the floor then back to mine. Was he trying to tell me something?

I glanced down. Oh, that.

During the time I had been contemplating the Kyrion I had unknowingly edged back until my feet barely touched the symbol on the floor. Goosebumps were standing up along my arms. Rubbing them, I stepped back onto the symbol, nodding at Eros in thanks. My gaze got lost momentarily on all that beautiful maleness. The devil actually winked at me. Heat bloomed in my cheeks and traveled down my chest at my inability to control my wandering eyes. His chest shook with silent laughter, and I ducked my head.

Damn traitorous hormones! This is what happens when you haven't had an orgasm in too long to admit. With all the eye candy on display today, I was close to jumping on the nearest man like a crack addict needing a fix. Maybe Dia was right. Maybe throwing caution to the wind and enjoying all this island had to offer wasn't a bad idea.

My attention was drawn back to the stage when the douche bag from earlier said, "—you may call me Chaos, and I will answer."

The last Kyrion in the black hood revealed himself and a gasp escaped me. A hard, tugging sensation in the pit of my stomach had me fighting not to launch myself at him. My whole body was strung tight as a wire. My hardened nipples rubbed against my bra, radiating a pleasured pain. My ovaries must have melted into a puddle and leaked out into my underwear. That's the only thing that could explain what was going on below. Oh wait, that was my vagina being resuscitated. It had gone from drought to monsoon at the speed of light.

Dark brows were pulled into an intense line above dark eyes as he gazed upon the contestants. When his gaze moved over me, stinging pinpricks erupted across my back. I bit my lip to keep from crying out. Then, abruptly, it was over.

Absently rubbing my lower back, I soaked in his appearance. His lips were thinned into an annoyed line. An angry twitch pulsed along the ridge of a square jaw covered in a five o'clock shadow. Caramel-colored hair stood up in messy spikes as if he had been running his fingers through it all day. He was tall. Even seated I could tell he was easily over six and a half feet. His skin gleamed like bronze in the moonlight.

"You have each signed a contract that you will reveal nothing of what you might learn from the Games. Should you breach that contract or betray us in any way, the consequences will be dire," Chaos threatened. His commanding presence captured the room as we all hung on his every word. "You may know some of us by different names beyond this island. But here, you will call us only by the House name we have given you. I am the leader of all Houses, and I bid you welcome to the Paldimori Games."

My god, the man had ignited a thousand different reactions in me from his voice and a passing glance alone. Every part of me seemed to be at war trying to decide if I should get closer or run away. When Chaos's gaze collided with mine it was like a punch to the stomach. My breath left me so sharply that I went a little light-headed. Somehow, I managed to say my pledge, although I couldn't tell you what I'd promised to do.

My head was reeling when his gaze finally released me. It had felt like my skin was on fire as his eyes had captured mine. It wasn't the kind of lustful fire that had filled me earlier though. This had been cold, so harsh that it burned. What I had seen in those eyes before he blanked his expression had been pure hatred.

A hatred that seemed to be entirely directed at me.

9

"How are you here?" a deep voice echoed from the dark.

"Who's there?" I asked, turning in every direction.

"How are you able to dream-walk?" the voice countered, sounding closer.

Light began to fill the space, but still I couldn't see anyone. I was annoyed now. "This is my dream," I said sarcastically, "so I want you to be my fairy godfather who grants wishes. I wish for a million dollars and smaller hips."

"Again, with the smart mouth. Perhaps I should give you something to keep it busy."

The light expanded to show an enormous room with six black thrones upon a platform—my dream.

Who was the man, though? He seemed familiar, but surely I'd remember meeting a man that handsome? Deep brown eyes, radiating enough heat to warm me from head to toe, stared down at me as I stood at the base of the steps. A cool breeze caressed my skin, making me shiver. Ah, no wonder it felt chilly. The moonlight outlined every curve of my naked body.

My hands tried to cover as much of the important stuff as possible. That was a pointless endeavor considering how much of *me there was up top. The man barked, "I did not give you permission to cover up what is mine. And your body is definitely mine, is it not, Potential?"*

My brows drew down in confusion. Potential what? And why the hell was I naked?

"Come here, Potential," he said, pointing his finger to the place directly in front of his throne. I was torn between wanting to go to him and wanting to run away. He sat motionless, waiting for my compliance. Before realizing what I was doing, my feet carried me up the steps close to him.

"Closer." He beckoned.

Cautiously, I stepped forward, prepared at any moment to flee. My naked thighs almost brushed his knees before he seemed satisfied with my distance. "Kneel, Potential."

Why did he keep calling me that? Who was this man ordering me around and making my body react to his every order like a marionette? In thrall to the sheer perfection of the smooth skin revealed by the open black robe, my eyes traced every inch of him. The sculpted muscles of his bare chest gleamed in the moonlight. I licked my lips, wanting a taste.

"I said kneel, Potential. I will not ask again." His deep voice sent shivers down my spine. There was no conscious decision, only my knees pressing into the cold hard floor.

Was the rest of him just as naked beneath that robe? Curiosity proved too strong, and my hands landed on his knees. My fingers inched along the silky-smooth material, the corded muscles beneath flexing with my every movement. My fingers tingled as the heat of him seeped through the fabric. My hands clenched upon the fabric with the need to tear the robe away.

My head was jerked back by a rough fist gripping the hair at the base of my neck. A startled breath escaped me as I looked into black pools of hatred. "You really are dimwitted if you thought I would fall for this trick, Potential Davies."

"Fuck!" I shouted, jolting awake. The artificial sunlight illuminating the ceiling pierced my tired eyes. Throwing an arm over my face to block out the light, I realized who I had been dreaming about—Chaos. Groaning, I rolled onto my stomach and buried my face in the pillow. Why did it have to be him?

"Well, that's certainly the way I like to wake up," an amused male voice said.

Shrieking, I jumped from the bed, and quickly scanned the room to find the source of the voice. The massive round bed I had been sleeping in was the centerpiece of the room and was surrounded by a wide ring of dancing nymph statues. Several comfortable-looking couches were clustered around a marble fireplace along the wall next to the entrance. The back wall was made up of more windows that looked out upon the island. There were two open arches along another wall that led to closets filled with everything a girl would need to feel at home. The last doorway led to a bathroom that they might have to pry me out of when this was all over. But no one else was in the room.

"I thought men were the only ones who woke up thinking of sex," the voice continued. "But then, my little lioness, I doubt you are like most women. Most women don't go toe-to-toe with our leader. I have to agree with Molly, you do have balls as big as boulders for pulling that stunt last night with Chaos." A rumbling laugh filled the room from every direction. "I wish I could have seen his face! That image would have been a great source of entertainment for decades. Damn annoying robes." A heavy sigh followed. "Ah well, I can still imagine it. I respect your lady balls and applaud anyone who gives my brother a hard time. *But* I'm going to have to ask you to not piss the man off if you want any chance of winning the Games."

Balling my hands into fists at my sides, I glared around the room. "Where the hell are you?" My mood plummeted straight into pissed off. First the dream about douche canoe, now this. Great first day this was turning out to be.

Stomping across the room to the closet openings, my breasts bounced loosely beneath the black T-shirt that skimmed my hips. My hair fell over my face, and I pushed it back with impatience as I leaned into the closet opening. No one there either. A chilly breeze swept through the room, brushing against my bare legs and pushing up the hem of my T-shirt.

"Can I just say that those boy shorts make your ass look amazing?" the voice drawled.

Spinning on my heel, I stomped back over to the bed to grab a sheet. Playing tug of war with the breeze, I fought to wrap the sheet around myself. It hadn't seemed so drafty in here before. Maybe the flue was open in the fireplace.

"I'm not sure which view I like better, the front or the back. Maybe you could stomp around the room a few more times to help me decide?" the amused voice requested. "I find myself strangely fascinated by the dragon character that seems to be peeking out from between your thighs. Normally I'm more of a 'why bother with underwear' kind of guy since they never stay on long anyway."

Eros lay propped up on his side, posed upon the white ocean of a bed as if this was another photo shoot. His red shirt was partially unbuttoned and showed off his toned chest. Faded jeans hugged his long legs. His bare feet should have been ugly—because, you know, they're feet—but even they were sexy. A wave of heat traveled down my body in embarrassment. Ugh, my life sucked! *He* was now privy to my secret passion for Snatch Dragon underwear. Mr. Male Model of the Year. How had he gotten there without my noticing? Breaking and entering was going on my list of grievances.

His eyes traveled from my bedhead down to my feet and back up. "If you're cold, I could warm you up."

His meaning was lost on me for a moment. The sheet! In my shock at finding Mr. Sexypants on my bed, my grip had loosened, and the effect of the cold room was obvious. Scowling at him, I pulled the sheet up to anchor it under my armpits. He chuckled.

Ass.

"What the hell?" I snarled at him. "Where I come from you don't crawl into a woman's bed uninvited unless you're ready to lose a highly valued appendage. And I don't need you to warm me up. Didn't your mother teach you that it's creepy to spy on women? This is my bedroom, not the stage of some strip club."

"That's a shame. You'd make a killing on the stage." He grinned unrepentantly. "Besides, who needs an invitation when most women are falling onto their backs as soon as they see me, eager to do all number of naughty things to my 'highly valued appendage' as you call it. I don't suppose if I were to ask you to join me in this bed, that you would accept?"

A growl escaped me. If I had something to throw that wouldn't cost my life savings to replace, he would be limping. He smiled smugly as if he knew exactly what I was thinking.

"Out!" I pointed to the open doorway. "This room is off-limits, and you can tell the rest of your buddies that too."

"I thought we shared a moment last night." Eros's plump lips turned into an exaggerated pout. Slowly, he crawled across the bed toward me like a tiger stalking its prey. I backed away as he got to his feet. His eyes caught mine as a calculating look crossed his face. "Oh wait, that was before you caught a glance at Chaos, and he made you so wet there was almost a puddle on the floor."

I sputtered in outrage, but Eros continued on.

"I don't think you even blinked once he revealed that mug of his." He laughed. "Don't look so embarrassed; he has that effect on a lot of women. I wouldn't waste my time, though. He has some kind of hate-on for you. I'm not sure why. The stubborn ass won't tell me."

Now would be a good time for the floor to swallow me up. "I don't want anything to do with him," I shot back. "The man is clearly an asshole of epic proportions, and he hates me for no reason! I'd never even met him before last night."

Eros chuckled as he stepped closer. "That's Chaos for you. So, does that mean you'll slide back into bed and let me help you forget his name?"

"Out," I repeated, pointing toward the door.

He brushed past me and a wave of lust hit me hard. Frustration at my unruly hormones had me picking up a pillow to launch at his retreating back. *Oh, that's real mature, Lia.*

He stopped at the doorway and looked back at me. His amused smile was back in place as he looked from me to the pillow that had missed him by several feet. "Well, I had to try. Again, my little lioness, you prove you are not like most women. I'm glad."

Wait, had that been some kind of test? Did I pass?

At least he hadn't sent me packing yet. Shaking my head at the whole encounter, I made my way to the bathroom. Men were weird. This island and its crazy inhabitants were going to have to remain a mystery for now. It was time to get ready and see what my first day as a contestant had in store for me.

A half hour later I emerged from my bedroom feeling refreshed. The smell of coffee lured me to the kitchen, my stomach grumbling the whole way. Sleeping in was unusual for me, but it was probably due to all the hours of tossing and turning before I'd finally drifted off to sleep. Where recurring dreams haunted me with visions of Chaos luring me to him with seduction in his voice only to turn me away in disgust as soon as I gave in. Eros's warning to keep my distance was a moot point: my subconscious was already telling me to stay away.

The fridge in the kitchen was stocked to the hilt, but I stuck to my usual bagel. I was finishing up when the elevator chimed an arrival, and I made my way down the hall. Molly stepped from the elevator wearing black spandex and a troubled expression.

"Good morning, Molly." She didn't acknowledge me. "Um, Molly? Is everything ok?"

She still didn't answer. I placed my hand on her shoulder, and she jumped, staring at me wide-eyed as if she hadn't realized I was there. "Sorry, didn't mean to scare you. Is everything all right?"

"Huh? . . . Oh yeah, I'm fine. Lost in thought." She smiled at me in reassurance, although she wasn't fooling anyone: something still had her rattled. "Is Eros around?"

An affronted voice echoed from the living room behind us. "I think I might be insulted. I've never been overlooked before, so I'm not quite sure. I can see that you are going to be a bad influence, lioness."

We turned to find Eros leaning against the wall of windows. He gave me a petulant stare. My smile took on Cheshire cat proportions. Hmm, if I could nullify his short-circuiting ability on women's brains, I could hire myself out and make a fortune. His lips quirked up in a grin before he shifted his attention to Molly, a look of concern crossing his face. "What's troubling you, imp?"

"You didn't stick around for the rest of the drawings. All six primary competitions were drawn. That's never happened before. One or two a year, sure. But never all six in one year. Could it mean . . .?" The fingers of her left hand tapped out a nervous rhythm along her thigh.

I didn't see Eros move, but suddenly he was right in front of us. He took Molly's left hand in his and rubbed his thumb across her knuckles soothingly. "Don't go getting yourself all worked up over an old wives' tale. The Chosen aren't real. If they were, they would have shown up a long time ago, right? Since they're supposed to be so all-powerful."

Molly nodded mutely. Eros smiled at her and kissed her hand. "The primary competitions being selected means we have our work cut out for us. Back then they barely had knowledge of first aid, so, of course, they were dangerous. We have the gems. They'll protect everyone. Now, Gaia is up first. What do you think we should start this one on? She doesn't look like she's ever braved the elements in her life."

Eros winked at me when Molly turned her attention my way. Some of the color returned to her pale face as she considered his question. "I'm guessing you're not much of an outdoor person?"

"We're talking backyard cookout type of 'outdoor,' right?" I asked, looking back and forth between the two of them.

They exchanged a look and then started laughing. *Guess not.*

Eros rubbed his hands together. "I believe we should find some spandex to cover that lovely ass. It's time to go to training, my little lioness."

10

Humid air caressed more exposed skin than I was comfortable with when the elevator doors opened on the lowest level of Titan Tower. I tugged at the tight black tank top and leggings, wishing there was more material. It had taken Molly threatening to burn my jeans to get me to put on the spandex. I could feel Eros's eyes glued to my butt again as I stepped out onto the rough rock floor of the training level. He grunted as my elbow accidentally jabbed him in the stomach.

The heavy scents of the ocean and a thick forest filled my nose. The vast cavern was lit up like it was broad daylight, but the light seemed to come from everywhere and nowhere. As hard as I looked there were no electrical sources to be found. This area made the throne room look like a closet. Several yards in front of us the rock floor gave way to a grassy field and beyond that lay a dense forest.

It was like we had stepped into an alternate reality. "How …?"

"A freshwater stream flows through the cavern and enough sunlight filters in to allow the growth," Eros offered.

"We helped Mother Nature out a bit with temperature control, and she showed us her appreciation."

"Taking credit for my work, Cupid?" a soft female voice said behind us.

We turned to find a green-robed Kyrion smiling indulgently at Eros. Her sandy blonde hair was piled loosely on top of her head, and daisies peeked out amongst the curls. Loose ringlets framed her face and cascaded across her shoulders. Her flawless peach-toned skin glowed in the bright light of the cavern. The open front of the robe revealed a plain white chiffon dress that fell down to brush the tops of her bare feet.

It hadn't escaped my notice that Eros was also bare-footed. Did the Kyrion have a foot fetish or just an aversion to shoes?

Like the rest of the Kyrion, the woman didn't look a day over twenty-five. Hadn't Molly said something about this group of Kyrion leading the Games for the last fifteen years? Either they were kid geniuses, or they had found the fountain of youth. I made a mental note to ask Molly if there was any "special" water I could drink.

"Gaia, please. Don't call me that horrible name." Eros chided. "Especially in front of my incorrigible little lioness."

Gaia's smile disappeared as she turned to face me. "Yes, I would say she needs no encouragement, given her outburst during the ceremony." Her pale green eyes radiated disapproval. "You might want to remember, Potential Davies, that no matter the results of the Game, you are only here by the grace of the Kyrion."

Her gaze flickered briefly to Eros before she addressed me once more, her tone filled with derision. "Some may find you entertaining. Rest assured that Chaos does not tolerate fools, and neither do I. I hope for Eros's sake that you have some other skills we have yet to see."

Are all of the Kyrion condescending asshats?

A sarcastic response was queued up but slipped from my tongue as a yellow butterfly flew between us. It lighted momentarily on my nose before circling me. I rubbed at the ticklish spot, amazed it had gotten so close. It fluttered in a circle over our heads before landing on Gaia's outstretched finger.

She cocked her head as if she was listening to something before she pinned me with her gaze. "Hmmm, that remains to be seen." She nodded to Eros and turned to glide across the field as if she walked on air. Not even a blade of grass stirred as she disappeared into the forest.

Creepy-assed snob queen.

There was something strange about all of the Kyrion. They tugged at something inside me that I didn't like. Last night at the ceremony it had been an intense reaction. Today it was subtle but still there. It was as if a live current radiated from them and seeped under my skin. It put me on edge. My instincts shouting that they were a threat to me in some way. Especially Chaos.

In fact, my back still tingled from whatever had happened when our eyes met last night. Irritated by that, I asked, "What is with the Kyrion's whole lord and lady of the manor act? Well, except for you. You seem ok mingling with us peasants."

"My little lioness, let's just say that here we *are* the lords and ladies of this land. You should treat us with that level of respect. There are ancient traditions that have to be observed during the Games." Eros grimaced. "The clothes. The language. The annoying pomp and circumstance."

He sobered, all traces of the jokester disappearing as his

gaze bore into mine. "I may push the limits of acceptability, but I never forget that we are honoring our ancestors. As the ruler of my House, I can't be seen to entirely shirk the traditions, even if I find them a bit ridiculous myself. Does that help you to hold that sharp little tongue of yours so that we may avoid pissing off anyone else? The Kyrion may be barred from doing you direct harm, but they can make your time here very difficult."

"I'll try. I'm not usually like this. It's just that there's something about you guys . . ."

Eros wasn't paying attention. He was staring intently at something by my side. Following his gaze, I jerked like I had been caught doing something wrong. Then forced my arms to my sides. The whole time we had been talking I had been scratching furiously at my back where my skin felt hot and itchy.

"Is there something bothering you, Lia?" Eros asked cautiously.

"My skin feels a bit itchy. It's probably an allergy to spandex," I replied sarcastically.

He stared at me for a long moment. "Hmm." Then a lecherous grin spread across his face. "How about I—"

"Don't finish that sentence if you want to be able to walk straight."

He shouted with laughter. "Sheath your claws, lioness. It's time to get sweaty."

Eros led the way to an area around the side of the elevators that looked like your typical gym set-up. If you happened to be someone like Batman who worked out in a cave. The other contestants already occupied various weight machines while their guides either looked on in boredom or encouragement. Eros wove his way through the torture devices, Molly and I following behind.

Dread was filling me already. I should probably warn them about gym equipment's aversion to me.

The thought flew out of my head when my eyes locked on Chaos. He stood over the Asian contestant, Maya Li, as she struggled on the bench press. Her arms trembled as she inched the bar higher. Sweat soaked the chest of her gray T-shirt and dripped from her face. She finally managed to lift the weight and breathed out a sigh of relief. When she attempted to rack the bar Chaos snapped, "Again."

What a dick.

As if he had heard that thought, Chaos turned toward me. Those deep, dark eyes raked me from head to toe. For a second, I could swear that same look of hunger from my dreams filled his gaze. Then a sneer swept his face as his eyes locked with mine. "Potential Davies, tardiness seems to be one of what I am sure is a long list of your faults. If you care so little for training, the offer to forfeit is still on the table."

The banked fire from last night flared to life, and I felt my mouth twist. The urge to push this man rode me hard. There was something building inside that wanted to come out. My mind clicked off, and I was operating on pure instinct. "Oh, I didn't realize I was running late." Pulling my ponytail over my shoulder, I draped the end across my breasts and twisted a strand of hair around my finger. "It isn't every day you wake up to find a gorgeous hunk of man meat in your bed. You can imagine how that would make a girl lose track of time."

Man meat? Really? Where the hell had flirtatious Lia come from?

Chaos looked nonplussed for a second before that tic started in his jaw. Then the ground seemed to vibrate beneath my feet in time with that tic. Uh oh, a mute Chaos was probably bad news.

Damn it, Lia, what were you thinking? Oh yeah, you weren't. Idiot. Time to say goodbye.

I moved to pass him, but he grabbed my arm. A spark ignited from the calloused grip of his hand on my bicep and lit a fiery trail along my nerve endings to shoot straight through my heart.

Holy heart attack!

I stumbled against him. Everywhere we touched seemed to burn.

His fingers flexed on my arm as if he couldn't make up his mind whether to push me away or pull me closer. His gaze searched mine. There was a faint blue ring around his brown eyes that seemed to be growing by the minute. Whatever he saw in my eyes had his brows drawing down into a frown. That tic along his jaw started in double time. I licked my lips, wondering what it would be like to taste that tanned skin. His grip tightened, and he pulled me closer as if he wanted me to find out.

Eros nudged me aside, breaking our contact. Caught off guard, I stumbled back into Molly. She wrapped her hand around my shoulder to steady me, then pulled away with a hiss of pain gripping her hand. It was an angry red as if she had touched something hot.

"Brother," Eros commanded quietly, pulling Chaos's attention from me. "I assure you Potential Davies has been resting. I felt she needed extra sleep this morning to perhaps improve her disposition. That was wishful thinking on my part, but she did look exhausted when I attempted to wake her earlier."

I couldn't see what was happening over Eros's shoulder since he had a few inches on me. However, everyone could feel the tension mounting between the two men. This was my fault. My stupid mouth was getting not only me in trouble but Eros as well. Just like old times. What happened to the level-headed businesswoman I'd prided myself on becoming? She needed to find the on switch for her brain to stop this before it got ugly.

I tried to step from behind Eros, but he put his hand out to block me. Gripping his arm, I leaned to his side to see what was happening. Chaos looked at my hand on Eros's arm, and I could see him connecting the dots. Yep, Eros was the "man meat" most likely to have been in my bed. Chaos took a menacing step forward, closing what little gap there had been between the men. He glowered down at Eros. "The Potential's bedroom is off-limits unless invited by her personally. I will not tolerate the rules being broken, even by you, brother."

The silence was suddenly deafening. The clanging of machines and murmur of voices had ceased. Everyone was watching us. Great, I was once again the center of attention. This time I had no one to blame but myself. *Stop poking the lion, Lia. Eventually, he's going to eat you.*

Chaos looked around the room. The guides bowed to him in acknowledgment. The contestants shifted uneasily. Finally, he pinned Eros with his hard gaze. "Rule number three is that no contestant may be bedded by trickery or coercion, is it not? The rules are in place for the protection of all. You will not break them again."

Eros bowed deeply even though he still gripped my forearm like he thought I was going to do something crazy —or crazier. I glanced at Chaos, expecting him to be basking in the glow of this show of subservience. Instead, that harsh gaze was focused on me. "I will attend the training this afternoon to see for myself if this Potential has

any redeeming qualities that might make up for the disrup-
tion she has already caused. Perhaps you should try a
muzzle on your pet, Eros."

Eros tightened his grip on my arm again. The extra
encouragement to stay quiet wasn't needed; I was done
messing with the king of the jungle. Chaos held my gaze
one more moment as if waiting for my smart reply. When
nothing came, he simply nodded.

Then he turned back to his Potential who had taken
advantage of the distraction to rest. "Again, Potential Li."

Eros dragged me away to the back of the gym where the
stone floor was covered in exercise mats. He finally released
me and turned to Molly who had been trailing us. Crap, had
I managed to annoy the only Kyrion who didn't think I was a
moron?

"Teach her the warm-ups and put her on the track. He
doesn't usually attend the training, but he isn't going to let
this go. Push her. Hard." Eros turned to me. Uh oh, he was
furious. "Congratulations. You've managed to do in less than
one day what no one has ever done in our entire lives.
Chaos prides himself on his control, and you just made him
lose it. In front of a lot of people. You must have a death
wish."

Eros pinched the bridge of his nose and took a deep
breath. When he looked back at me, I could tell he was still
angry but struggling to control it. "Look, something is
different about you. We've all felt it. Nothing has gone right
since you got here. I'm not saying that's all on you, but
maybe you should keep your distance from the Kyrion.
Especially Chaos. I need to look into something Molly said
earlier. It's ridiculous, but I don't believe in coincidence. I'll
be back for the race."

Shamed at my actions and hurt by his words, I whispered, "I'm sorry."

He hesitated as if he wanted to say something but shook his head and walked away.

Molly eyed me in astonishment. "That's a first. You're two for two on driving men crazy. Balls of steel." She shook her head. "Let's go. You're going to hate my guts in about two seconds. For the record, I won't take it personally."

11

A bead of sweat quivered on the tip of my nose before dropping to the mat beneath me. Loose strands of hair had escaped my ponytail and stuck to my sweaty forehead and neck. My breath wheezed in and out like I was an asthmatic at a smokers' rally. Rivulets of sweat ran down my chest and back, making my snug workout clothes feel like a soggy second skin. Molly had called it a dynamic warm-up. If this was only the warm-up, death by exercise was a real possibility.

The heat of Chaos's gaze had swept my body frequently as Molly put me through my paces. As a result, my concentration was crap, and my mood was surly. It hadn't helped that my old clumsiness came back with a vengeance. I'd warned Molly about my propensity for gym-related accidents, but she had shrugged it off as my trying to get out of training. Until she witnessed the train wreck herself.

Molly was the first victim when I accidentally kicked her shin. Then, tripping over my own feet, I'd caused an entire rack of hand weights to fall over. Pretty sure someone's foot was really sore. Mortification had me ducking out behind an exercise machine, so I'd only heard the cussing. Then I got too close to the edge of the mat while doing jumping jacks and smacked Devon right in the face. That behemoth guide hadn't even flinched. He'd stared stonily at me as I apologized, my whole body flushed with embarrassment.

Chaos had snorted and mumbled something too low for me to hear. Probably for the best. My reply was a one-finger salute. Unfortunately, he missed it since he was already walking away toward the forest, snapping at his contestant to keep up.

Molly hadn't let my clumsiness interfere with her drill sergeant routine, though. She'd pushed me harder. Who knew she was such an evil torturer in disguise? I'd cussed like a sailor on every rep. She'd ignored me and added another. She seemed to sense my less than full commitment. She pushed me and pushed me until my whole body was trembling."

"You . . . uhn . . . evil workout dictator," I grunted as I strained through another set.

It was a running joke between Dia and me that I was allergic to all forms of exercise. It wasn't far from the truth. I had tried almost every type of workout you could imagine. It wasn't just that my willpower ran out of—well, power—but things always went wrong. Just when my muscles started burning, and my heart was pounding as I hit my peak, disaster would strike, usually in the form of some bizarre equipment malfunction. Luckily, there had only been minor injuries, but I didn't want to push my luck.

"Get that leg up higher, Lia. C'mon, pick up the pace!" Molly shouted as she tapped the knee of my extended leg to get me to keep it straight.

"Motherfucker!" I glared hard at her perky butt, hoping that at any minute laser beams would shoot from my eyes to set it on fire. "If you had balls . . . uhn . . . I would lift . . . uhn . . . my leg higher . . . uhh . . . just to kick you in them."

"Pretend I'm Chaos then. Get that leg up!" Molly said while she circled me.

A startled screech sounded from nearby followed by a loud crash. Someone shouted, "Look out!"

A heavy weight hit my side and sent me skidding across the mat. My hands burned from the friction, but more importantly, I was being pressed uncomfortably down into the mat.

"Little lioness, you seem to always find trouble. Although I'm quite enjoying the outcome this time," Eros whispered next to my ear as his hips pressed against my butt.

My head thunked onto the mat. "Do you always have to tackle women to get them under you? Get off me, idiot."

"Oh no, my sweaty little lioness," his voice rumbled in my ear. "Usually, it's the women tackling me."

"Oh, my goodness. Oh, my goodness. Are you guys ok?" a breathless woman asked from somewhere above us.

Eros got up and helped me to my feet. The few remaining people in the gym area had gathered around the mat. Damn it, how do I keep ending up in these situations? Busty—er, Nikki—hugged me like we were long-lost friends as she rambled on about how Eros was such a hero for saving me. Finally, she let me go only to launch into a one-woman reenactment of what had happened. Apparently, the weights on her machine had suddenly fallen off when she pulled the bar down. One of the bigger ones had started rolling right toward me. Sure enough, a weight disk the size of a watermelon was now lying on the mat where I had been moments before.

That would have left a mark.

Eros had saved me even after the crap I had pulled earlier. Impulsively, I hugged him in thanks. He squeezed me back. Then he stiffened in my arms and gently pushed me away. My cheeks heated. What did I expect? I'd practically thrown the guy under the bus earlier. He had every right to be mad at me. The apology died on the tip of my tongue as I caught sight of who was standing there. Shit, all of my good luck must have been used up in a previous life.

Chaos stood not three feet from the mat, his arms crossed. His dark accusing gaze swept over me like a wildfire, bringing such heat that my fingernails dug into my palms to keep from crying out. There was a pressure in my brain that pushed and pushed until my head was throbbing. Then suddenly it was gone.

Chaos's gaze raked over me before it snapped to Eros. "Brother, I thought you would be in the library researching this idea of yours."

"The library is extensive, and much time would be wasted in the search," Eros replied carefully. "I decided to have others pursue the information so I could focus on my Potential."

"I see." That tic started up in Chaos's jaw again. "Is your Potential injured?"

"No, there was—"

"If she is not injured, then why is she not on the track? Is this some new form of training that I have not heard of?" Chaos asked with a sneer.

I hoped he was referring to the hug and hadn't seen Eros lying on top of me. Now *that* would be awkward. I stepped forward, drawing his attention. Punching the bastard in the face would have been rewarding. Fortunately for him, my hand still hurt from smacking Devon.

You are a rational business woman able to handle even the most demanding customer; keep it together.

Something flared inside me and what came out of my mouth wasn't what I intended. "For the record, he saved me from being injured," I retorted. "*I* hugged *Eros*. He's clearly too much of a *gentleman* to admit that. Something you obviously know nothing about."

Chaos narrowed his eyes at me but didn't respond. Instead, his gaze lowered slowly to linger on my heaving breasts. Uh oh, there went my nipples, standing right out there for the world to see in this damn spandex. His arms dropped to his sides, and his breathing became more labored as he noticed my reaction. My anger was melting away to be replaced by another type of heat as I felt his gaze like a caress.

I jumped at the phantom brush of hands cupping my breasts. Circles were drawn lazily around each breast, spiraling closer and closer to the tips. Molten pleasure flooded my body as those hands explored me, learning my shape. My thighs clamped together as the heat seared my stomach and continued south.

The invisible hands left my body, and I almost shouted aloud in disappointment, wanting to hold on to the pleasure as long as possible.

A hand landed heavily on my shoulder, and I squeaked in surprise. Whatever trance I had been in immediately disappeared. I blinked rapidly, surprised to find how close I was to Chaos. His arm brushed against my aroused nipple, and I bit my lip to hold back the whimper. My knees threatened to buckle beneath me as whatever too-hot-to-be-real mojo he was pumping out continued to devastate my control.

My whole body was blushing at the curious looks of the

people gathered around us. *Oh god, one second longer and this might have turned into an X-rated show. Damn that man for turning my brain to mush.* My body was so on edge that the slightest movement would probably set me off. I needed to find a way out of this awkward situation that didn't involve me falling into a writhing pile of female hormones at this asshole's feet.

The hand on my shoulder tightened, and Eros stepped up beside me as if he sensed my dilemma. "Brother, Potential Davies has had a near miss with some equipment failure. I'm sure she would like a moment in private to recover herself. Molly will accompany her to the track."

Molly stepped up to my other side and took my arm. "Time to hit the track, people. Move it." She glared at everyone until they took the hint and started walking toward the forest. "I'll show you to the restroom, Lia."

I shared one final long look with Chaos. His expression was carefully blank. Nodding at Molly, I let her lead me away. I could feel the men's eyes following us, but I refused to turn around. Molly didn't say anything until we were far enough away to not be overheard. "Are you ok?"

Not really.

"Yeah, I'm ok. I . . . you know what, I have no clue what just happened."

Molly looked like she wanted to say something but instead shook her head. "Let's focus on getting you through the training."

Thankfully, she left me alone to freshen up. Splashing cold water on my face, I silently gave myself a pep talk about resisting things that were bad for me. Like cupcakes and infuriating men. I leaned my head against the mirror. The cool glass felt good against my heated skin. The sensation of those hands seemed to linger, not letting me come back down from my aroused state. I pressed my hands against my breasts and hissed. *Oh god, that felt so good. How had one look from him gotten me more worked up than sex with any of my boyfriends?*

My fingers traced the same path as those invisible hands. When I pulled at my peaks, I almost came. I don't think I had ever been that aroused in my entire life. I hesitated only a moment before traveling my hands down my stomach. Just as my fingers touched the waistband of my pants, Molly banged on the door.

"Lia, we gotta go."

I stood straight and stared at myself in the mirror. The eyes looking back at me were wide and dilated with arousal. My face was flushed. My nipples pushed out against my shirt. Panted breaths pushed past my parted lips. I looked exactly how I felt. On the edge of an orgasm. What was happening to me? Buttoned-down Lia from Port Lawson would never have acted in that way. She didn't engage in pissing contests or public displays of lust.

Taking several deep breaths, I splashed more cold water on my overly heated skin.

You are a calm and rational adult. You will avoid any more confrontations and do what you came here for. Win the prize. Go home. Save your gallery.

The pep talk helped to calm me down enough to exit the bathroom. Molly noticed my closed expression, and we silently agreed not to talk about what had happened.

As we walked, I asked Molly about the training. There were four days of training before each competition. Then there was the Game day itself. That was followed by a day of celebrating the winner and then a day of rest. The final day of the Games was the ceremony where the grand champion would be announced.

We passed by the now empty gym and trudged across the field to enter the shade of the forest, weaving our way around tall trees and several large boulders. The air became more humid as we moved deeper into the woods. Aside from the sound our feet made as we tromped across the dirt, the forest was eerily quiet. The few times I had ventured into the woods back home, I had been amazed by all of the sounds. Here, it seemed like even the trees held their breath in anticipation of something.

"Are there animals here?"

"Few," Molly answered as she forged ahead. How she picked out a path through all the green vegetation was beyond me.

The forest had become denser as we walked until, suddenly, we stepped out onto a smooth dirt path that stretched as far as I could see in either direction. Light blazed down, and I shielded my eyes at the abrupt change. The trees seemed to close in on the wide path from both sides like an impenetrable wall. I turned to look but couldn't see the gap in the trees that we had stepped through. The other contestants were already lined up at a starting line marked by flagpoles at either side with the black sun symbol. Molly walked me over to an open spot.

"Day one race is two miles. A mile is added to each new training session for a competition. Don't give me that look, I didn't make the rules." Molly huffed. "Look, I don't expect you to be first. I just want your ass to cross that finish line, and so should you."

She cocked her head to the right where I studiously ignored Chaos's presence. "The guides can pace you in the woods and offer encouragement. The Kyrion wait at the finish line. Slow and steady will get you through."

Two miles. It was a miracle I had made it through the

"warm-up." *All right, like she said, get across the finish line. This is only training; we aren't running a marathon.* Stepping up to the line, I performed the stretches Molly had showed me earlier.

Off to the right, the Kyrion disappeared into the woods. Molly waved before she jogged over to join the guides on the other side of the path. Then she gave me a thumbs-up before she too disappeared behind the trees.

All the contestants alone at last.

Looking down the line, I nodded to a few people. Nikki and I looked like bedraggled messes. The Cowboy was doing stretches, his toned muscles flexing with every move. Maya looked as if she was mentally planning her attack on the track. Chris was nervously biting his thumbnail. The Lothario—a handsome black man, whose name I'd finally learned was Mikhail Lorenzo—was on the line already in position to take off. He was clearly built for speed with that lean body and long legs. My bet was on him for first to cross the finish line.

A bird's shrill call broke the silence, and we were off.

The rest of us had barely made it off the starting line, and Mikhail was a yard ahead of everyone. *Called it!* I started off at a walk, focusing on putting one foot in front of the other and hoping that the others would tire themselves out quickly. When a voice spoke up from beside me, I almost tripped over my own feet.

"Sorry. Didn't mean to scare you, ma'am." I glanced over to find the Cowboy keeping pace with me. "Looks like we both had the same idea. No way this lot can run full out for two miles."

He smiled at me and held out his hand. "I'm Kade Downing."

It was awkward shaking hands while walking. "Lia Davies."

"Lia, pleased to meet you," Kade said in his charming southern drawl. "So, this has been some kinda adventure, huh? The fancy rooms and ceremonies. I'm not real sure what to make of it all yet."

"Uh-huh, me too," I answered, trying to conserve my air.

"I noticed you at dinner last night. Wanted to introduce myself but didn't have a chance. Glad I caught up to you." He paused for a moment. "You looked beautiful, if you don't mind my saying so."

"Oh, uh, thank you," I muttered, feeling self-conscious considering how I looked right now.

"Would you like to take a walk after dinner tonight?" he asked.

"I . . . uh . . . ok. I mean, yes. Thank you." *Smooth, Lia.*

Kade smiled at me as if he found my bumbled responses endearing. He started to say something else, but we were interrupted by a loud whistle.

"This isn't a mix and mingle. Close your traps and get your asses in gear!" Molly shouted from around a tree up ahead.

Grace poked her head around the tree next to her and winked at us. "Molly, dear, don't be rude. They're getting acquainted. Don't they make a lovely couple?"

"Uh, sorry about this," Kade whispered. "Grace is my guide. She's almost as bad as my own mother. She tried to set me up with Nikki, the, uh, energetic one."

I looked at him with wide eyes as he gave an exaggerated shudder. We both laughed at his dodging *that* bullet.

Molly groaned and smacked her hand against her forehead. "God save us from your matchmaking, Gracie. They have a competition to train for. How're they ever gonna win that grand prize if they keep yapping?"

"Well, what's a big bunch o' money good for if you don't have someone to share it with? You just wait 'till I find a man that can handle you, dear. Then it's—what do the kids say these days?—on like Donkey Dong."

"Kong. On like Donkey *Kong*. Geez." Molly rolled her eyes. "I don't need— Damn it, you're distracting me. You," she said, pointing at Kade, "keep it in your pants until after training."

Kade and I looked at each other trying to suppress our laughter. I lost my battle and laughed so hard tears streamed down my face. Those two were hilarious. Kade chuckled and shook his head.

Molly barked out, "Scram, Captain Hard-On."

Kade shrugged in a what-can-you-do gesture. Then he sped up, leaving me with my bossy guide.

"Molly, dear, that was very rude." Grace shook her head.

Molly gestured sharply at me, ignoring Grace's comment. "Are you in heat or something? I swear I've never seen so many damn men tripped up over a woman. Grace, I'm gonna need a club."

Molly and Grace argued over the best way to keep the men away from me as I passed by. Molly mentioned nutcrackers, and I picked up the pace.

Good luck finding a man that can handle her.

Then it was only me and the path. A gentle breeze swept through the cave cooling my damp skin. Molly popped up occasionally to shout encouragement. I tried not to think about the fact that everyone else was probably already at the finish line and fed up with waiting for me. The thought of Chaos's condescending voice asking if I wanted to forfeit spurred me to pick up the pace. Not that I would ever admit it, but Molly's warm-up had helped. My muscles were limber and primed. *Look at me go.*

Of course, that was when disaster struck.

I stumbled, falling forward onto my hands and knees. *Ouch, damn it!* Rising to my knees, I inspected the damage. Rocks had gouged my left palm, and blood trickled down my wrist. Tenderly I brushed away the debris. Well, that was going to be painful for a while. Suddenly, there was a vibration under my knees.

What was that?

There it was again.

My good hand pressed to the ground, testing it. The dirt began to shift with the vibration.

Earthquake! Get up! Get up! Get up! The ground rolled and jerked beneath me. *Where do you go when there's an earthquake in a cave?*

Two steps. That's as far as I got before the ground pitched upward and I was flying. My side hit the ground with a sickening thump, knocking the air from my lungs. Pain radiated along my entire left side. I instinctively curled into a ball. The ground split apart a foot in front of my face, and small cracks raced in my direction. Horror filled me. Clawing at the ground, I tried to drag myself away. One inch. Two inches. *C'mon, move!* My hands grabbed for purchase, but the ground crumbled in my grasp. A scream ripped its way from my throat as the ground broke apart beneath me.

Then I fell.

Dirt and rocks pebbled my body. My thigh rammed into something, and I screamed again at the searing pain. My free fall stopped abruptly as I collided with something. Reaching out tentatively in the pitch dark, I tried to feel for my surroundings. The surface beneath me was hard but smooth to the touch. When I applied pressure, it gave against my fingertips. Then a grunt issued from the dark and something grabbed me. My struggles were in vain as the thing cinched its grip around me.

"Cease, woman," a rough male voice demanded, "I will leave you in this hole if you do not calm yourself."

Was this hell? That certainly sounded like the devil.

Wind whipped by us at a furious pace as we shot upward. Wow, they had managed to form a rescue effort fast. Considering who my "hero" was, I was surprised he hadn't left me in the hole.

He shifted me in his arms and pain shot through me. *Arrr, please don't do that again.* My whole body hurt. My leg was the worst, though. Tightening my arm around his strong shoulders, I closed my eyes and leaned my head against his chest. The steady beat of his heart beneath my cheek helped give me something to focus on other than the pain.

Light surrounded us. Voices sounded nearby as we slowed to a halt. I opened my eyes to see that we were at the edge of the woods where a large grandstand overlooked the finish line. Everyone rushed over to us as my rescuer strode forward.

Grace fussed over my injuries and wanted to send someone for a medic. I waved her off, wanting pain meds and a bath to get this mountain of dirt off me. Then maybe a week of sleep. Before it turned into an argument, my rescuer took the decision out of my hands. Ignoring everyone, he headed for the opposite tree line with me still in his arms. His long strides ate up the ground. I glanced up at him for the first time. His face was streaked with dirt, and his shirt was ripped.

It took several tries to clear my throat enough to talk. "Th-Thank you," I managed to rasp out.

Chaos glanced down at me, that angry tic back in his jaw. He nodded, then turned his gaze ahead as we exited the forest. He shifted me higher in his arms, and I winced as pain shot up from my thigh. His gaze traveled to my leg, and his mouth tightened. "Do not think my carrying you qualifies as crossing the finish line. You *will* cross it next time unaided, Potential Davies."

Infuriating jerk wad!

I wanted to rail at him, but his image seemed to be getting fuzzy around the edges. What were we talking about? Oh, look at that tic in his jaw. I had the strong urge to bite it. *What would a little nibble hurt?* Rough stubble brushed my lips as I placed butterfly kisses across his skin before my teeth nipped at him. "You need to learn to relax, Your Holy Hotness. All work and no play makes for a very grumpy boy." I laughed hysterically. The light dimmed around the edges, and the last thing I saw was the look of shock on Chaos's face.

12

I drifted slowly toward consciousness, my body feeling like it was cocooned in an oven. Still in that stage between asleep and awake, I pushed against my wrappings with a disgusted grunt. *Too hot. Need out.* When that produced no results, I attempted to kick my way out. Nothing. Grumbling nonsense, I tried again.

Arrr, damn blanket. Let me go!

Fine, now I was awake. *Asshole blanket.*

Huffing out a breath of frustration, I opened my eyes. The ceiling wavered in the dim light. That was strange. Since when did my bedroom have a stone ceiling?

Movement caught my eye as my foggy brain struggled to puzzle it out. Turning toward the source of the light, I saw a crude fireplace that was no more than a square cutout in the stone wall across from me. The flames leaped higher backlighting some type of mark cut into the wall several inches above the main opening. I frowned at it for a moment sensing that I should know that symbol.

The Games. The earthquake! It all came back to me. That terrifying fall. Chaos rescuing me. My leg injury. Was that why I couldn't move? Panic ratcheted my heart rate up. Please tell me they hadn't amputated my leg. My struggles with the blanket became more frantic. Damn it, it shouldn't be so hard to free yourself from an oversized piece of cloth. Why wasn't it loosening?

A shadow loomed over me and large hands grasped my shoulders. I screeched in surprise, then bucked and twisted until I managed to free an arm to swing at my assailant. A hiss issued from somewhere above me as my fist connected with what felt like warm granite. Working my other arm free, I plowed my fist straight into what I hoped was their face.

A grunt ensued. Direct hit! A pair of calloused hands captured my wrists and roughly pinned them to the bed above my head.

"You son of a bitch! Let me go. I'll—" Before I listed the many unpleasant things I would do to their anatomy, firm lips smashed down on mine. Stubble abraded my cheeks as I bucked my hips trying to dislodge him. His heavy frame lowered onto me, rendering me immobile once more. I went rigid, gathering my strength for the next fight.

Those firm lips slowly softened upon mine. Then they parted to place a tentative kiss against my firmly clamped lips. My refusal to respond earned me a sharp nip on my bottom lip that got a response from parts a bit lower than my mouth.

"Open," a familiar rough voice said from above me.

I relaxed on a stuttered exhale. My instincts registered that I wasn't in any real physical danger, but my brain was still sounding an alarm. Like man rompers, this was wrong in so many ways. I had been warned to keep my distance but it didn't seem that Chaos had gotten the same message.

His grip shifted to anchor my hands with one of his own.

His other hand slid under my head. Then he gripped the hair at the base of my neck and tugged my head back. I gasped at the quick shot of pain to my scalp. Suddenly my mouth was under a full-scale siege before I could batten down the hatches. Chaos teased and tested me as he alternated the depth, pressure, and angle of his kiss. Keeping me off balance, never able to anticipate his next move. His tongue pressed against mine, coaxing it to come out to play. Teeth tugged sharply at my bottom lip and arousal zinged through me.

My resistance evaporated like a lone raindrop in the Sahara. I tugged against his hands, and he reluctantly released them. Pulling him to me, I traced the artistry of his smoothly muscled shoulders. My tongue darted out to taste him, and he groaned. Effortlessly, I was plucked from the covers and rolled until I was sitting astride his firm thighs. Chaos raised himself into a sitting position beneath me and grasped my hips to pull me firmly against his arousal. The thin material of my workout pants left little to the imagination as his cock nudged against my core.

Moaning against his lips, I raked my short nails down his naked back and delighted in the shuddering of his body beneath me. His lips pulled away from mine, leaving them swollen and wanting more. Kisses trailed down my throat as his hands tunneled beneath my clothes to find my nipples. His calloused fingers plucked and massaged my breasts until I was squirming in ecstasy. His lips claimed mine once more, stretching my mouth wide for his invasion like he was attempting to crawl inside me. He jerked his hips up to rub the ridge of his cock between my legs as his fingers plucked at me. My eyes rolled back into my head as I shattered in his arms, calling out his name.

My forehead dropped onto his shoulder as aftershocks

continued to rock me. I was a limp noodle of satiated bliss and I hadn't even gotten naked. Slowly my brain came back online enough to notice that something had changed. Chaos was rigid beneath me and not in the sexy kind of way. His hands no longer held me to him. He had put as much distance between our bodies as he could with me clinging to him. Reluctantly, I sat back. His face was concealed by shadows, but his words were all too clear.

"I am glad to see you have stopped acting like a hysterical female, Potential," Chaos mocked coldly. "After that performance, I would say that you are feeling much recovered from your little accident. Time to find your own room."

My heart still raced from what we had done, and he was already back to being a prick. I jerked off his lap so fast I almost fell over. Finding my footing, I tugged my shirt back down and folded my arms tightly across my chest. Hurt radiated through me. Why did I feel injured by the careless words of an arrogant bastard?

I don't! He's hurt my pride, that's all.

Widening my stance, I lifted my head high. *Arrogant orgasm-stealing fucktard!*

Smiling through bared teeth, I contemplated kicking him in the balls. Hopefully, they were blue and causing him lots of discomfort right now. What kind of man gets a woman off, then dismisses her? Instead of giving me a moment to bask in the glory of finding my O again, he treated me like a paid performer. No way was I going to let his arrogant head swell bigger by realizing he'd rocked my world back into orbit.

"You know, I do feel much better," I said. Stretching my arms over my head, I bowed my back like this was merely another type of warm-up. My lids lowered to watch his reaction as I pushed out my chest. *Ah. Not so unaffected after all, are you?* His eyes shot straight to my breasts and locked on. His hands gripped the edge of the bed as his gaze turned hungry.

Turning abruptly on my heel, I made my way toward the door. "Your medical skills may be amazing," I said over my shoulder, "but your bedside manner sucks. You might want to get some pointers from Eros." Then I slammed the door closed before he could reply.

Vindicated satisfaction filled me when something shattered inside the room behind me. My smile slipped away when I remembered how mad Eros had been. If he found out about this, he was going to kill me. I had practically painted honey on his back and set the angry bear on his trail. Though how did he expect me to keep my distance when he allowed me to get carted off to the bear's cave?

Now how the hell did I get out of here? Having to ask the savage beast for directions would totally ruin my exit. I had only taken a few steps when a shadow detached itself from the alcove of a doorway. Startled, I clutched a hand to my heart. Devon, stepped into the dim light.

"Whew. You people really need to come with a warning system. Errrt! Danger Lia Davies! Danger!"

My attempt at humor was lost on him. He grunted and walked past. I silently followed along behind him. The man intimidated people with a look, but as the leader of the guides, he likely knew a lot. "So, uh, this is an interesting place. I mean, a tower inside a mountain—that's pretty amazing. I've noticed a lot of Greek influence in the architecture and artwork. Is that where you guys are from?"

Devon picked up the pace instead of answering as if he couldn't wait to get rid of me. It was too bad for him that my curiosity was piqued; I could be persistent when I wanted something. "This area of the tower seems to be a bit older than the other parts I've seen. When was it built?"

"You talk too much," he rumbled. Whether it was the post-orgasmic bliss or having met my quota of stoic men for the day, I snorted in amusement. Cupping a hand over my mouth, I tried to smother my laughter with a cough. He sighed as if he was a martyr for having to put up with me. Then, to my shock, he actually responded. "This is the oldest section, built around 1208 BCE. The Chaos at that time left Greece during the Dark Ages. He brought his people here."

Finally, someone had answered a question! But what did he mean "the Chaos at that time?" I had a dozen questions, but they were quickly forgotten when we stepped through an open archway.

A large rectangular courtyard stretched out before us. A stone pathway led deeper into the courtyard, beckoning me to follow it. The path meandered through patches of grass where large trees grew, their limbs heavy with fruit or nuts. The wind suddenly swirled around me and raced through the trees, causing them to sway. A tinkling sound overhead filled the air. Hanging amongst the branches were dozens of chimes. I reached out to set one spinning.

Darkened archways lined every wall of the courtyard on ground level. Potted flowers in a variety of colors hung down from a second-floor balcony above the colonnaded walkway. Did all of the Kyrion live here? No. Molly had said something about them having their own floor. If this was Chaos's floor, then were those rooms for his family?

What if he's married? Maybe he has a dozen kids stashed around here. My stomach dropped at that thought. No more kissing or anything else. Chaos was off-limits.

I continued along the path, brushing my fingers against

the various herbs scattered along the walkway. Plucking a sprig of rosemary, I rubbed it between my fingers, the savory smell mixing with the sweet scent of the flowers.

The walkway led to an open area with an oblong pool in the center. Rock seat-walls about waist height were spaced around the pool area, the top of which contained beds of small black rocks. A giant black statue similar to the one from the throne room kneeled beside the water, and I felt myself strangely drawn to it.

As I walked between two of the seat-walls fire *whooshed* to life as though a chain reaction had been ignited. The heat from the flames was intense as they shot up at least eight feet into the air. It was scenes like this that always ended badly for the female in horror films. My life could stay firmly in the drama category—no horror needed. Shielding my face, I rushed toward the statue putting distance between myself and the flames as they slowly shrank to a more normal size.

The starbursts within the black marble of the statue twinkled in the light of the fire, drawing me nearer. White eyes peeked out at me from swirls of flowing hair that obscured his face, their depths conveying a deep sadness. Streams of water fell from the statue's eyes like tears into his cupped hands and slid with a soft burble into the pool below. Even in his kneeling form, the figure towered several feet above my head. Tentatively, I placed my hand on his huge corded forearm, his form so well defined I could see the tension in every muscle. I leaned forward to splash my face and let the fresh water wash away the dirt, immediately feeling less itchy.

The smooth marble seemed to flex beneath my grip, and I found myself reluctant to remove my hand. It was almost as if the statue were coming alive beneath my touch. As if we were kindred spirits connected by a deep well of anguish, I wanted to comfort him.

Hesitantly, I reached up to place my hand over the location of his heart. Surely, that couldn't be a heartbeat, could it? My only desire at the moment was to help him. Tendrils of fire licked at the base of my spine and spread along my back. My skin ached from the heat that seemed to be building higher. If I could just reach . . .

A startled exclamation broke my concentration. Whirling around, I found Devon standing close behind me. He looked at the statue then at me, his eyes wide in shock. Something smooth and cold pressed against the aching skin of my back in a quick caress. I sighed as the burning feeling receded. Glancing over my shoulder, there was nobody there but the statue. *Strange.*

I turned back to Devon, but he had already schooled his face into its usual blank expression. "Come along, Potential Davies. The Kyrion have arranged entertainment for tonight's dinner. You don't want to be late. *Again.*"

"But . . ." For some reason, all I wanted was for him to go away and leave me alone with the statue. Devon's massive hand wrapped around my bicep before I could form an excuse that didn't sound completely crazy. He all but dragged me to the elevator at the far end of the courtyard. When we got in, my gaze immediately sought out the statue. Just before the doors slid closed, I swear those white eyes looked right at me.

13

Day two of training. Hopefully, we were done with the earthquakes. Despite the dried blood that had coated my thigh, nothing more than a large scratch and some bruises had been found. That didn't mean it was an experience that I would ever forget or wanted to repeat. Much like dinner last night.

Molly had escorted me to dinner in one of the upper levels where a large amphitheater took up the whole floor. The Kyrion had sat on black thrones in front of the stage, while servants dressed in black flitted around them offering food and drink. Deep rows of stone steps were piled with pillows in the House colors. Short wooden tables sat several feet apart along each row, laden with food for the guides and contestants.

Nikki, who had been lying across a mountain of pillows while a young man fed her grapes, squealed when she saw me. Then I was suffocated by her strong strawberry scent and the chokehold on my neck as she hugged me. She regaled Molly and me with a play-by-play of Chaos's heroics as we settled onto a section of pillows. She hadn't been very subtle in her attempts to find out what had happened after we'd left together. My guess was this new "friendship" of ours was about her need to be the star of the show. Next time maybe *she* could be the one falling into the hole. My head was pounding by the time she bounced away to return to her fan club.

Kade and Grace had also stopped by to check on me. My eyes had been drooping by the time the show started. A group of actors in gray robes filed onto the stage, their heads covered in big wooden helmet-like masks with exaggerated expressions. They told the story of the descendants of the gods and how they were betrayed. The traditional Greek tragedy would have been fascinating if I could have managed to stay awake. But it was a pointless battle.

I don't know how much time had passed when something woke me. The room was darker and nearly empty. My eyes were drifting closed again when movement caught my attention. A lone actor still in costume stood several feet away. The laughing mask looked sinister in the low lighting. However, it was the snake swaying hypnotically by my feet that caused my heart to miss a beat as my body went rigid in fear.

The black neck had flared as its tongue flicked out, its beady black eyes watching me intently. Its mouth opened to reveal horrifying fangs.

From out of nowhere, a massive golden-brown dog grabbed the snake in its jaws as it struck at me. The dog had shaken the snake violently before tossing it into the air. The snake flew over three rows of seats to land by the edge of the stage where it lay barely moving. A wet nose nudged my arm. The explosion of breath that left my lungs as the tension released was like a signal that started an enthusiastic game of lick-the-lady.

When Chaos found us, I had been laughing hysterically as I playfully fought off doggy kisses. He'd restrained the dog, whose name was Axol, while I recapped what had happened. Chaos had rewarded Axol—who happened to be his dog—with lots of petting and praise. My heart had melted a little. Who didn't appreciate a man that was kind to animals?

Chaos had said something to Axol, and the dog obediently lay down. Then Chaos knelt beside me as he checked me over for bites. His calloused fingers moved over my skin causing me to hold my breath for an entirely different reason. Axol watched us, ears pricked, probably hoping this was a fun new game. When Chaos pulled me to my feet, I swayed into him, and he held me until I found my balance. Instead of savoring his strong arms, I focused on where the creepy actor had been. The spot was now empty. Had they been trying to warn me about the snake? If so, why hadn't they said something or gotten help?

Needless to say, my sleep last night hadn't been restful.

My already grouchy mood this morning was now rapidly devolving to homicidal as Molly tortured me again.

"Use that anger, Lia. Power through," Molly commanded.

"You sadistic bitch!" I bit out savagely. "I'll show you anger . . . when I plant my foot . . . in your ass!"

"Yep, you're gonna stomp a mud hole in my ass. Got it," she said dismissively. "Last set. Now focus!"

"Ahhh! You . . . you insane . . . sadistic . . . motherfucking-cocksucker!"

Molly ignored my ranting. Days ago, I would have been mortified over my outburst. The calm and reasonable Lia had begun to unravel under the siege back home. Now here on the island the last threads that held rational business woman Lia together were being cut. There was no quiet or routine to help me find sturdy ground. Everything about this place seemed to tug at what was buried beneath the surface, dredging up instincts from that dark time in my life when I learned that you were either a victim or the aggressor. I had been both.

Dead eyes stared accusingly at me. Blood coated my hands. *No! Don't think about it.*

My highway was broken and so was I. All these years I had feared the emotions that had sent me down a path of darkness and destruction. But I had given up so much more than emotions when I buried that time in my life. I'd also buried hard-won lessons and instincts developed on the streets that had kept me alive. And some of those were coming to my aid now.

I finished the set of cable rows and shakily worked my way over to a bench to sit down.

"You did well." Molly sat down beside me and handed me a towel. "How're you feeling?"

Burying my head in the towel to soak up my sweat, I labored to get my breathing under control. "I hate you," I mumbled into the towel.

"Ah, doing ok then. You'll thank me later."

The sounds of gym equipment being put to work filled the air as we sat in silence. Molly had pried me out of bed at some ungodly hour to hit the gym before everyone else. She had started me off at a much slower pace, probably out of consideration for any injuries from the accident. She had been just as surprised as me to find that my injuries were so minor. I should have kept that to myself. The kiddie gloves came off, and she worked me over until my legs shook like Jell-O.

Stretching my sore muscles, I took note of who was

trickling in for their own workouts. Kade nodded hello as he did leg presses several machines down from me. Grace sat in a chair by his side, knitting. I waved to them both. She had stopped by last night to bring me chicken noodle soup and fuss over me for an hour like the den mother Molly had claimed her to be. I'd forced myself to choke down the soup, even though I loathe the stuff. Blame it on my mother who believed in its healing abilities so much that she made me live on it for weeks when I was ten.

Under the guise of continuing my stretches, I turned to watch Devon working with Maya on some kind of ab machine. My gaze roamed on to where Nikki sat on a machine that worked her thighs open and closed. Her guide was the girl with purple-black hair dressed like an emo. She stood over the blonde chatterbox with her arms crossed, glaring threateningly at the two men across from them. Brant the Grouch leaned insolently against the rock wall at the back of the gym area, openly eyeing the blonde like a pirate who had spotted a treasure he was going to plunder. His Potential, Chris, seemed to at least be attempting to keep his eyes to himself as he powered a rowing machine. He looked to be losing the battle, though, as his gaze flickered repeatedly in her direction. His cheeks heated a bright red when he saw me watching him. I shrugged in a what-can-you-do gesture. Nikki was beautiful, and he was a guy. He ducked his head and focused intently on the floor. The poor kid was going to strain something.

The remaining duo of the scary-looking tattooed guide and Mikhail the Lothario were the only ones missing.

"He isn't here," Molly said. "Chaos, I mean."

Busted. Was I that obvious? Why was I even looking for him? The man was a moody bastard. "Good! He's a damn infuriating man and for some reason seems to have it out for me."

"True. I've never seen Chaos act this way. He *seems* to hate you." She looked at me thoughtfully. "But I wonder if it really is *hate* he's feeling." She hesitated a moment as if she wasn't sure she should say anything further. Then she said in a rush, "You were really in his room? *And* you touched the statue? No one else has been on that floor, other than Devon, in forever."

I gave a reluctant nod. I didn't want to talk about Chaos or the statue. Even though Chaos was an asshat of the highest order, everyone was entitled to their privacy. As for the statue . . . There had been a connection made when I touched it like there was something alive under that hard exterior. It roused a possessive and protective side of me. Thankfully Molly seemed to understand my reluctance to talk and didn't push me on it.

"Since we're done here, I want you to meet Ninny and Saam." Molly smiled at me, her eyes bright with excitement.

"I would love to meet them," I said. "Uh, who are they?"

She laughed and stood up. "My horses. Well, they belong to the House of Arrows, but I raised them. C'mon."

Molly headed off with an enthusiastic bounce in her step. It was entertaining to see the transformation from drill sergeant to excited kid. It had me wondering again what her story was. Smiling, I started after her, but bumped into someone. "Oh, I'm sorry—"

"I won't let you win, you know. I expected the big-mouthed one to use sex as a tool. I see now that I assessed you incorrectly." Maya stood with her hands on her hips, a stern expression on her face. "You are no match for me physically, but I did not account for manipulation. I have made adjustments in my strategy. I will win that money. Stay away from my Kyrion."

Maya bumped me again as she walked past to rejoin the ever-expressionless Devon. She hadn't said more than a few words since we arrived, and the first thing she does is threaten me. Was that what everyone thought? That I was having sex with Chaos to win the Game? It never crossed my mind. Besides, that man was nobody's fool. If she thought he could be manipulated, she was underestimating him. And me. I was here to win, and that's what I planned to do.

I caught up with Molly as she entered the far end of the woods. The lush canopy blocked out the light as soon as we stepped into the tree line. The temperature dropped a few degrees, and I shivered in my damp workout gear. We maneuvered through the tightly packed forest that smelled of moist earth and green things, Molly leading the way as we pushed aside damp foliage and carefully chose a path over rocky ground.

We had walked for several minutes when we came to a particularly rough area. I watched as Molly picked her way across large rocks down a narrow, sloped passage. She jumped to solid ground at the bottom and waved at me to cross. Bracing my hand against the rough trunk of a massive tree, I climbed up on the first rock and followed her.

Oh, shit!

About half way down my foot slipped on one of the smaller rocks, causing a cascade of pebbles to tumble down. I jumped to the next rock seconds before the one I'd been standing on shifted and tumbled down the passage. The rumbling sounded extremely loud in the quiet forest. My hands shook as adrenaline from the close call surged through me. I made it the rest of the way down without further incident, but Molly was no longer in sight.

"Molly?" I walked left then right, hoping to catch sight of her. "Molly, where are you?"

The forest had been eerily quiet on our walk, but now there was a rustling in the distance. Suddenly a branch snapped close by, making me jump.

"Haha, you scared the city girl. Good one, Molly," I called nervously. "Come on out now."

I expected to see Molly step from behind one of the tall trees with that signature grin in place. Instead, there was a groan, followed by a slithering sound like something being dragged across the forest floor. Every beat of my heart pounded out an alert signal whispering of danger as I stood in rigid silence. There was something out there.

A spindly root shot from the ground and coiled around my wrist. My scream was part surprise mixed with fright. Pain shot through my knees as the root tugged me to the ground. My wrist burned as I twisted in its grasp trying to free myself. Damp, hairy shoots slithered along my skin, bringing back thoughts of my snake encounter.

I shuddered. *What the hell is happening?*

"Let go, you stupid hairy thing!" I grunted. More roots broke through the ground and slithered toward me. With my free hand, I pried at the root around my wrist. Nothing was working. Grabbing the root, I pulled it toward me, using the leverage to get back to my feet. Then kicked at another root as it attempted to grab my foot. The root around my wrist was trying to use my twisting about to wrap around me.

"Oh no, you don't. I've seen *Anaconda*." Ducking under the root, I got both hands wrapped around it and tugged. The root pulled back, cutting my hands as I was yanked to my knees once more. Blood from my cuts smeared against the root and a zap like static electricity sparked between my hands.

The roots dropped to the ground, now still. Frantically, I looked around for the next threat. And let loose another scream as a hand gripped my shoulder. My fist swung out, and Molly barely leaped back in time to avoid a broken nose.

"Whoa, Lia, it's me. Are you ok?" Molly held her palms out. Then gaped at me in disbelief as she took in my bleeding wrist and hands. "Oh, gods. What happened to you now?"

The adrenaline rush fled, and I wilted to the ground like a popped balloon. I buried my head in my hands mumbling about killer forests and bad dreams. There may have been some pleading to bring back the sexy-time dreams of Chaos. Anything was better than poisonous snakes and possessed roots. At least, in those dreams all I had to deal with was a condescending asshat.

A throat cleared above me, and someone laughed. *Uhh, please tell me that I didn't say that out loud.* My gaze traveled up firm legs braced wide only a foot in front of me, then further up to the stony face of Chaos. He unclenched the fists at his sides to offer me his hand and pulled me to my feet. My shaky knees buckled, and he shifted his hands to cup my elbows to keep me from falling.

"Should have let the ground swallow me," I mumbled to myself.

Molly laughed. Finally, my legs felt solid enough to hold me, and I moved away from Chaos. Those firm hands tightened briefly before he dropped them. His eyebrows slammed down in a fierce scowl as I wrapped my arms around my waist. We weren't friends. We didn't even like each other. He had no reason to be all scowly faced. Besides, I was still mad at him for the way he had treated me in his bedroom. He looked on the verge of saying something that would probably start an argument, so I walked away. My steps faltered for a moment as I noticed not only Eros but also Gaia had joined us.

"The ground did not try to swallow you," Chaos called out. "This island has a very rare form of plant that acts much like a Venus Fly Trap. I am sure that is what you stumbled upon, Potential Davies."

I turned back to him, sarcasm dripping from my voice. "Rare man-eating plant, huh? What's it called? I'd like to look it up when I get back home. You know, for posterity."

He crossed his arms and stared at me disdainfully. "It has a long scientific name which I am sure you would never recall. Do not go wandering around the woods by yourself and you will have nothing else to fear." He stalked toward me, invading my personal space again. "Now tell me what happened. In detail."

I was forced to recount the incident several times while cleaning my cuts with a damp cloth that Molly seemed to have pulled out of thin air. Nope, I didn't want to know; my quota on crazy was filled. Chaos pushed for more details. Damn infuriating man, I'd told him a million times. Finally, I snapped at him that if he wanted more then maybe he should talk to the damn man-eating plant. My cuts were aching. My knees were raw. Somewhere it was five o'clock, and they were serving margaritas. That's where I wanted to be right now.

Everyone had gone quiet at my comment about talking to the plant. Chaos and Gaia seemed to be having some kind of non-verbal communication. She regally nodded to Chaos and then left. Good riddance! The woman had scowled at me the whole time while implying this had all been a bid to get attention. She needed a hobby, preferably far away from me.

Molly handed me a water bottle. Greedily, I gulped down the cool water. The others were arguing over what to do with me as if I wasn't here. Chaos suggested that Molly take me back to my room and tie me up for everyone's safety.

That's it!

I marched over to Chaos and dumped the rest of the water over his head. He blinked at me for a stunned moment before wiping a hand down his face. Molly and Eros's mouths dropped open looking at me like I was a crazy person. I felt like it, actually. Chaos stepped forward until the toes of his shoes nudged mine, those dark eyes burning with anger. "Very mature, Potential Davies."

"So is threatening to tie me down, and talking about me like I'm not here. I decide what's best for me. Got it?" My palms ached to smack that infuriating superiority from his face.

"I am responsible for everyone on this island. If I deem it necessary to tie you to my bed, then that is exactly what will happen." He leaned forward until only inches separated us.

My tongue darted out to lick my lips as I leaned in as well, something besides anger starting to fill me. His eyes traced the movement, their depths burning with an intensity that shot adrenaline back into my system. "No one said anything about *your* bed. The only way you could get me there *is* by tying me down."

His eyes flared as he leaned closer. "There were no ropes last night. Yet I seem to recall you clinging to me as you—"

"Uh, sorry to interrupt." Molly tugged at my arm. "But if it's all right, I thought I could take Lia—I mean, Potential Davies—to the meadow. I can take care of her hands. She can relax there before the race just as well as she could in her room. If you're still joining the race, that is?"

Chaos and I stared at each other a moment, neither of us moving. His eyes dropped to my lips once more. Then he turned and walked away. "Do what you will."

Molly whistled. "Holy hotness, Batman. I thought you two were going to get it on right here."

"Molly." Eros's voice was reproachful.

She shrugged. "What? The I-want-to-rip-your-clothes-off force is strong with those two, Luke."

Eros sighed and turned to me. "You are well enough to race?"

"Yeah, I'm feeling better. I'll be fine." I smiled at him in reassurance, feeling surprisingly amped up. Huh, I guess fighting with Chaos was good for something.

"I'll see you in a couple of hours then." Eros smiled evilly. "Ever raced a chariot before?"

"What?" Alarm shot through me. "Aren't we racing on foot again?"

"Nope. Chariot racing takes lots of practice, and that's the first competition," Molly said, heading into the forest again. "C'mon, you need to get to know the horses."

14

The horse meadow was a beautiful, peaceful spot. Lush green grass dotted with purple flowers covered the expansive area and a small stream ran through the center of it. Horses of various colors and sizes nipped lazily at the grass. Foals romped and played by the stream. I could understand now why Molly said this was her favorite place.

She introduced me to a gray-and-white Appaloosa that she called Ninny due to her goofy puppy-dog behavior. The other she introduced as Saam, aka Stubborn as a Mule. He was a reddish-brown color and tended to stomp his hoof like an obstinate child when he didn't get his way. Molly cooed to them and rubbed them down until they were putty in her hands. Here was yet another side to her.

"C'mon, let's get those hands cleaned up."

We walked to the creek where she pulled supplies from a hollowed-out stump that bore the House symbol. I washed my hands in the cold, clear water, laughing as Saam tried to steal the medical supplies every time Molly turned her back.

"Stop that, you little thief. Behave, or there won't be any apples for you."

Saam stood frozen as if he couldn't believe Molly was serious. Then Ninny nipped him on the rear, starting a game of chase. Molly patted the spot beside her on the bank inviting me to join her. What I really wanted was to strip down and roll around in the creek like one of the foals. Ah well, maybe later. I dropped down onto the soft grass with a sigh. If we could stay in this spot forever, I would be content. No worries or obligations. No one trying to destroy my life.

"Let me see 'em." Molly nodded at my hands.

"They aren't that bad. The blood must have made it look worse than it was," I replied, turning my hands up for her inspection.

"Hmm, I guess." She frowned but shrugged it off and applied ointment to the shallow cuts, taking away the remaining sting.

"The horses seem very attached to you. Do you spend a lot of time here?" I asked.

Molly pulled two apples from the bag and handed them to me. "Not as much these days. When I was little, I would sneak out here every night. I thought the horses were going to fly like in my books. Mom would find me sleeping with the foals. Freaked her out the first time, but she gave up trying to stop me. I was a real handful."

A nudge against my back had me turning around to find myself eye to eye with Ninny. "Uh, hello there," I said, leaning away to put some distance between us.

"She won't hurt you. She just wants the apple. Here, let me show you how to give it to her." When it was Saam's turn, it became clear that he was a picky eater. Molly laughed her head off when he nipped me on the ass when I stretched out to pick up the apple I kept dropping. It took me three times to present it to him the way he wanted. His name was well deserved.

The horses wandered off again, and we stretched out in the sweet-scented grass. Curiosity got the better of me. "Molly, what is this place, really? At first, I thought you guys were like one of those role-playing groups. You know, the ones that dress up like elves and stuff. But this place is old, like ancient Greek old. You aren't running around pretending to play a part. Who are you people?"

The only sounds were the burbling of the creek and the occasional snorting of a horse as I waited to see if she would answer. A yellow butterfly fluttered in circles over our heads before landing on the back of the hand Molly lifted. She stared at it intently for a moment before she turned to me. I knew she had decided to tell me from the relieved smile she sent my way.

"It's rare for us to share anything about ourselves. We're very private. Eros was right, though. There's something different about you. We all know it." She nodded to the butterfly as if to acknowledge that it too thought so. "We call ourselves Paldimori. You won't find us in any of your history books, but our people have been around for a *very* long time. All but a few—like me—are direct descendants of the original six families."

"Wait, so if you aren't from the original family line where do you come from?"

Molly shifted uncomfortably, and the butterfly flitted over to land on my bent knee. "There were other families at one time. I was adopted into the House of Arrows. It's not forbidden, but it's frowned upon. The Houses are all about keeping the lines pure. I guess Eros saw something in me. Or maybe it was because he was adopted. Who knows?"

Whoa, that got my attention. "Eros is adopted? He and Chaos aren't really brothers?"

"No. Chaos's parents adopted Eros and his sister when

they were little. Eros *is* a direct descendant, though, for his House. In a lot of ways that made it easier for him. As for me, an outsider becoming a guide is unheard of." She stared fiercely at her balled fists. "But that's all I'd ever wanted to be since the first time I snuck in to see the Games. Even with Eros's support, it's been a long hard road to get here. Don't get me wrong, I'm thankful for everything he's done for me, but I've earned my spot. No one can say any different."

We were both silent a moment. Molly tucked her hands under her head and focused back on the sky. When she spoke, her voice was soft, reverent. "It's beautiful here, isn't it? This was once the home for all Paldimori. Then someone made the decision to spread the Houses out and give them territories," She snorted. "Stupid decision if you ask me. Who wouldn't want to live here? Now we only come here for the Games. The rest of the time we stay in our territories. The House of Arrow's base in Mexico is beautiful, but not like this. And before you try to find a way to ask that isn't obvious—but really is—Chaos's base is in the U.S."

"Thanks, I think. I'm not sure what all that means but you don't have to worry. I'll keep your secrets."

"I know. I trust you." Molly said sleepily.

We dozed for a time until the other guides came to retrieve their horses. The meadow I woke up to was not the same one I had fallen asleep in. Where there had once been an impenetrable wall of trees surrounding the meadow, there was now a large pathway to one side leading out toward the track. When Molly saw my puzzled look, she mumbled something about the gate being released. I shook my head, adding one more strange thing about this island to my list.

All around the meadow, guides singled out two horses each. They didn't do it using dogs or ropes. They walked right up to a horse and made some kind of quick hand gesture near the horse's flank. Then they mounted one of the pair of horses bareback and took off through the opening, the other horse following along behind. It was a truly spectacular sight.

Molly insisted that I ride Ninny so that we could get better acquainted since she was the easier to win over of the two. She showed me how to place a bridle on her. Then came the fun part. Getting on the horse.

For the record, big girls can't jump. We also don't possess a lot of upper body strength to pull our weight up onto the back of a horse. I fell off. Repeatedly. We were all frustrated and sweaty by the time I finally got on. Ninny was irritated enough to try to shake me right back off, but there was no way I was going through that again. Clinging to her neck like a burr, I proved I was the more stubborn. Luckily, she was easily sidetracked. All it took was Saam walking by giving her a look like he would never be caught dead in such a situation.

Molly had called out pointers as we exited the meadow. Then the crazy woman left me. She raced away on Saam, shouting over her shoulder that I would figure it out and she'd see me at the starting line. What exactly was I going to figure out? How to fall off again? Pretty sure I had that down. Ninny and I stood there in shared disbelief—if I interpreted her snorting correctly. Then she took advantage of my inexperience to turn her happy horsey self back toward the meadow.

"Oh no, you don't. I'd love to stay and relax in the meadow too. But we have training to do." I pulled on the reins to get her to turn back around. She ignored me while she sniffed at every blade of grass and flower around. Gah, this horse had the attention span of a toddler in a toy store.

Ok, time to take control. Animals respected that, right? Wrong. Ninny did not respect my authority.

"You should have been named Stubborn Ass. Will you just cooperate, you crazy animal?" I shouted in frustration. "Do you want Saam to show you up? He's probably strutting his stuff at the starting line right now. I bet he's telling all the other horsey ladies that you can't even get your rider to the line."

Ninny stopped sniffing, lifted her head, and flicked her ears back. She snorted then shook her head. Her mane flopped around, hitting me in the face. She did it again. When she did it yet again, I grabbed hold and she took off. Apparently, she liked playing at being a fool, because the horse was incredibly smart, and by the time we reached the starting line we had formed a partnership.

She taught me how to ride, and I guaranteed her we were going to beat the hooves off all the other horsey girls. We pounded down the dirt path toward the finish line, making a late grand entrance. I stayed braced low over her neck as we galloped up to the starting line at breakneck speed and slid to a dusty stop inches from Eros. He grinned up at me in approval and helped me down.

What a rush! For the first time since I started training, confidence filled me. We were going to kick some ass.

That feeling stayed with me right up to the point when I was standing in the chariot. *Deep breaths. It's only a little chariot racing, what can go wrong?* Gripping the leather reins tightly in my sweaty palms, I slid my feet into the boots that were welded to the platform similar to skis. Molly hooked locking carabiners attached to wide leather straps through metal rings on the top edge of the chariot. Then ducked around me to hook the other end of the straps through loops that circled the waist of my tight leather tunic. A black motorcycle helmet with the flying arrow symbol fitted snugly onto my head.

The chariot was a wooden barrel that had been painted red and placed on a single axle connected to spoked wheels. The platform was a bit of a tight fit when Molly strapped herself in behind me. Her voice crackled over the speaker in my helmet. "Doing ok?"

My breathing was fast and shallow, like an asthmatic Darth Vader as I responded, "Uhhrr . . . Not . . ."

"You got this. Stay in your lane." Molly pointed to the black lines on the dirt path that formed six lanes. The lanes continued around a bend a couple hundred yards down the path. "First sets are the straightaway. Go to the green line then back. Full track will come later."

Ninny and Saam whinnied and tossed their heads, filling the air with the sound of jangling harnesses as if to say, "Let's go." A man carrying a green flag walked onto the track. He faced the grandstands and bowed. Flipping up my visor, I scanned the covered box area at the top of the grandstands to see the Kyrion seated upon thrones. Flags for each House waved in the breeze along the roof of the structure. Servant women in simple black chiffon dresses poured wine and set out dishes of food at small tables beside each throne.

Chaos rose from his seat at the center, and the servants scattered, quickly disappearing from sight. He strode to the balcony edge and braced his hands on the railing as he leaned forward to address us. His voice echoed through the area in that weird way that made it seem as if it were coming from all directions. "The chariot race is a game of great excitement, but also of great danger. A steady hand and trust in your team are essential. We do not wish harm to befall any of you during this training or during the competitions." I felt the heavy weight of his gaze land on me briefly before he continued. "Gaia will be your host for the contest two days from now. May your teams be fleet of foot, and your judgment wise and swift."

When Chaos resumed his seat, the flagman rose from his bow and faced us. He had an Irish accent and was dressed in a black toga-style garment. His gray hair fell to his shoulders, but his eyes were a sharp green as he took the measure of each charioteer.

"Ah'right, then. There're two parts to this trainin' day. You get an hour to test yer teams out there on the track first, and then ye race 'em. Time'll start when I drop me flag."

I dropped my visor, then held my breath as he raised the flag over his head and brought it down swiftly before running to the sidelines. We lurched forward with a suddenness that made me thankful for the straps that kept me from falling. Gripping the loops of the reins tightly, I used them to hold me up. Molly barked orders rapid-fire.

"Don't hold the horses back."

"Balance against the chariot wall."

"Don't pull to one side."

Oops—that one came a little too late. Mikhail the Lothario flipped me off when I veered into his lane.

I got us safely back on course, and we whipped down the path, kicking up dust in every direction. I focused on the ground churning under the horses' hooves and my stomach dropped out. We were so close to those hooves. Molly yelled at me to not look down—again instructions that came too late. The green line appeared much too quickly. My already sore muscles strained as I followed Molly's directions on how to get the horses into a U-turn to go back down the straightaway. I learned that chariots don't corner like a car.

So did Mikhail when I clipped his gold chariot before finally straightening us out.

An hour later my whole body was shaky and I was slick with sweat. We halted the chariots at the starting line and were given a break before the race. Molly helped me unhook and dropped an arm around my shoulders to support me as I stepped down from the platform. Ugh, sea legs. My body was still bouncing and swaying. My thighs protested every step, which made it all the more difficult to keep my balance.

God, it felt good to peel off the stuffy helmet and take big lungfuls of fresh air. The breeze cooled my overheated skin as I used the warm-up poses Molly had taught me to stretch my tired muscles. A robust young man in another black toga-like outfit escorted Molly and me to a circle of plush benches set in the shade of the tree line. We had barely settled onto a bench before he took up a huge black palm frond to fan us. Another male servant handed us each a platter of fruits, cheeses, and nuts. Another brought us goblets of water that I gulped down, not caring about the excess that trickled down the sides of my face. I shoveled down food until my stomach no longer growled as if it was ready to eat someone. Nibbling contentedly on a succulent strawberry, I glanced around the circle.

At every bench, a contestant was being fussed over by barefooted servants of the opposite sex. Chris almost choked on a grape when a young blonde servant flashed her ample cleavage as she bent forward to refill his cup. Finished with my strawberry, I relaxed back against the bench.

Immediately one of the male servants approached and bowed to me. "Potential, permit me to give you a massage?" he asked in a lightly accented voice.

The boy couldn't have been any older than his early twenties. He glanced up at me when I didn't answer right away. His tanned skin glistened like sun-kissed bronze, setting off the perfection of his pearly smile. Jet black hair tumbled in messy curls around his face, and sharp hazel eyes full of life twinkled back at me.

"Uh, no thanks. I'm good," I mumbled.

He frowned and darted a glance at Molly. "Potential, if I do not please you perhaps you would pick another?" He looked at me like I had kicked his puppy.

Crap, I didn't want to hurt his feelings. "What? No . . . I—"

"Grayson, this one is stubborn. Let me," Molly told him and turned to me. "They are the prizes," she said bluntly. She saw the look on my face and rushed on. "Hold the phone, warrior princess. Don't go storming the grandstands. They volunteer."

I glanced at Grayson who nodded his head in agreement. "It is my honor, Potential. I demonstrated much skill to win the privilege of first approach." When I looked puzzled, he stepped closer. "Let me ease your sore muscles, and I will tell you. Yes?"

"Um, ok," I reluctantly agreed. He gifted me with a boyish smile that lit up his whole face. Then he dropped to his knees and reached for me. I pressed myself against the back of the bench. "Whoa, what're you doing?"

"I'm sorry, Potential." He looked up at me with solemn eyes and my heart melted. "I did not mean to startle you. I am not permitted to do more until the victor of the race has been declared, but I would massage your hands. Perhaps your arms and shoulders. This is agreeable?"

"Oh, yeah, sorry," I said, embarrassed that I had been so jumpy. He gifted me with another of his smiles. The little brat had just conned me. God help the woman that he set his sights on; she would be a goner before she knew what hit her.

Grayson waved over one of the other men who handed him a bottle of almond oil. For the next half hour, I sighed and groaned in bliss as he massaged any exposed skin he could reach with those magic hands. He talked to me as if I was a skittish horse, soothing me when his hands delved beneath the collar of my shirt to ease the knots from my shoulders. All the while he did exactly as he had promised by explaining things to me.

He belonged to the House of Shadows, which was based in Spain. He was the youngest of five and the only son. He claimed that his older sisters were the reason why he was wise beyond his twenty years, then he shot me another of those smiles. I couldn't help but laugh. What a charmer; he was definitely going to break some hearts.

When I asked him about being a prize for the Games, he explained that every year each House opened its doors to allow members aged eighteen to twenty-one to present themselves as volunteers to be awarded to the contestants in the Games. Among their people, it was a great privilege to serve the Potentials. After all, the Potentials were champions representing the Houses. There was nothing sexual involved unless both parties were willing. He seemed genuinely happy to be here.

Grayson had earned the right to approach me first out of the four men assigned to me, because of the ranking he received when all the volunteers demonstrated their skills to the Kyrion. He puffed out his chest with pride as he told me he was ranked first out of all the volunteers and would, therefore, have more freedom at the Games than the others. He gestured at his solid black attire, saying that the Games were the only time in their lives that members did not wear their House symbols and were given a chance to be ranked across all Houses. The ranking helped both the Kyrion and the young volunteers since it acted like a placement test for determining what each young person's role would be within their House.

I was so fascinated by his stories that I lost track of time. Molly interrupted to tell us that it was time for the race to begin. Before I could stand, Grayson leaned down to brush a kiss against the back of my hand. He grinned up at me. "We are friends now, yes?" I nodded. "I will find you after the race," he said as his hand brushed against my cheek before he walked away.

Molly rolled her eyes. "C'mon, before your harem kidnaps you."

15

The grass tickled my bare feet as I tiptoed through the trees, avoiding the pathways. The wind swirled around my bare legs, causing me to shiver in my sleep shirt. I scanned the area, diligently searching every shadow. The coast was clear.

My bare feet raced across the path not making a sound. The fires were already lit and swayed merrily in welcome as I passed into the center of the Chaos's courtyard. Skirting the edge of the pool, I made my way directly to the statue and pressed my palm over his heart. Hello, remember me?

A moment of silence ticked by before a whispered voice responded, "Lyannìa . . ."

From the depths of the statue a presence surged forward to invade my body. Fire sparked to life across my back. My mouth fell open in a silent scream as the breath was seared from my lungs. Every cell of my body felt as if it were being stretched and remolded. Stop! Please, make it stop. My back bowed in agony. My lips stretched wide around screams that there was no air to sustain. Bright starlight twinkled from the statue, growing brighter with each passing moment until it exploded out around me.

I was hurtled across the courtyard, my raw back crashing into the ground. Pain arched my body up into the heavy weight that was trying to hold me down. My eyes were blinded to all but the starlight. Distantly, I felt a rough grip around my wrists pulling me into a sitting position. Hands cupped my face, and Chaos's incredulous voice floated to me as if from a great distance. "Your eyes! They are the white of a god's. How . . . What have you done, Jillian Davies?"

But I was lost to the will of the starlight as it carried me into the vast field of darkest space. There we became as one. And though the light burned me still, I felt no pain. It taught me the wonder of creation as together we formed a world with a single thought. I tapped my finger upon the world of my creation, and it shattered to dust.

Creation and destruction. Change. Yes, these were worthy endeavors.

"Jillian, focus on me. Follow my voice. You need to remember who you are. Remember your friends, Claudia and Molly. They need you to return to them." Fingers swept through my hair and caressed my cheeks. "The horse Ninny. You remember her? You enjoyed riding her. Come back, and you can ride her any time you wish."

Was this also creation? This tiny voice that called to me? A speck of light, brighter than the thousands surrounding it, beckoned me near.

Destroy?

No, this creation did not need destruction. But change. Change without destruction was transformation. Yes, this creation needed to transform. I reached for that small speck.

"Jillian . . . Lia, do you remember Ja—Eros? My little brother cares for you. He would miss you if you did not return." My hand paused over the speck. The voice sounded different. There was change. This creation could change but not transform? This was

. . . emotion. The creation did not want the brother to care. Why would the creation have this . . . jealousy?

"No! Do not stop. Keep moving toward my voice. I . . . I, too, want you to come back, Lia." His fingers tightened around my neck. "I do not want this attraction, but I will no longer deny it. My people need me. Now more than ever they need a strong leader. Not someone who is so distracted. You shatter my concentration and occupy my thoughts when I need to be focused on my duties. You fight me over even the smallest of things. Yet I like that you do not bow to my every whim. Come back. Come fight with me again, beautiful Lia."

My hand wrapped around the creation and a tumble of emotions filled me. They spread like a ravenous cancer—joy, frustration, arousal, resentment. My grip tightened around the creation. How dare it force these emotions upon me! I do not transform. It must be destroyed!

"Come back to me, Lia," whispered across my lips. Warmth spread through me as his lips breathed new emotion into me. My hand bent on destroying the creation stilled as other sensations came to me. Cold air against my skin. The grass beneath my bare legs. Chaos's hard body cradling me.

I released the spark of creation view of Chaos and focused on the flesh-and-blood man. My lips clung to his as the kiss deepened. My hands delved into his silky hair, tugging him closer. He grasped me tight then swept the sides of my breasts before sliding around to my back. His palms flattened against my spine to pull me closer and molten lava poured down my back. The tide of pain crashed over me until I threw back my head and screamed.

My hoarse throat cut off mid-scream as I bolted upright in bed. Breath sawing from my lungs, I untangled myself from the blanket and stumbled to the bathroom. Leaning over the bathroom sink, I splashed water onto my face. My pale, wide-eyed reflection stared back at me in the mirror.

I caught sight of something stuck in my hair. Plucking a leaf from the tangle of curls, I twirled it between my fingers. How—? My grimy feet brushed across the cold floor, scattering dirt over the tiles. A large grass stain smeared the hip of my sleep shirt. Terrified of what I might find, I turned my back to the mirror and slowly lifted my shirt.

Oh, god. Oh, my god.

My whole back was an angry red and dotted with blisters that seemed to form a kind of star shape.

Don't panic. Don't panic. There has to be a good reason for this.

A knock sounded at the bedroom door, forcing me to get my hyperventilation under control. Molly called out, sounding worried. Rushing to the door, I silently turned the lock. It took me a couple of tries to get my voice to rise above a strained whisper. How long had I been screaming?

"I'm all right, Molly. Just a bad dream." I rested my forehead against the door.

"Wow, that must have been some dream. You want to talk about it?"

"I just want to go back to bed. Thanks, though."

She left a couple of minutes later, and I breathed a sigh of relief. What would I have told her? Oh, it was one of those dreams where you get possessed by a statue with a god complex. You know, the ones where it's so real that you wake up with dirt on your feet and leaves in your hair as if you were really there. Yeah, she would probably laugh her ass off—or have me committed.

I was way too wired to sleep, so I took a quick shower and got dressed. I paced the room trying to puzzle through the craziness of everything that had happened since I came to this island. Molly had told me a bit about the Paldimori, but what were they really about? Why did they need to stay hidden? I could understand not wanting to be inundated by scientists and historians clamoring to make a name for themselves, but weren't they risking that each time they brought outside people here for the Games? It was incredible that no one had sold the story of their time here and turned it into a movie. The Games seemed almost vitally important to them as a people. Was there something they gained from the Games that made it worth the risk?

Ugh, this was getting me nowhere.

There was someone who would have the answers. Sure, it was an excuse, but I would take it. There was an almost frantic need to find him that had been clawing at me since I woke up. That dream was still bothering me. As crazy as it sounded, if even a portion of it had been real—and I'd brought back evidence that something had happened—he had been there. The common denominator in all my crazy dreams lately had been him. I needed answers, and he was going to give them to me.

Silently, I crept from my bedroom to the elevator. Then stood there looking at the long line of buttons. His rooms were higher up, but which floor was it? Choosing a floor at random, I impatiently waited for the elevator to ascend. As soon as the doors opened, I knew it was the wrong floor. But it also felt as if this was exactly where I needed to be. Chaos could wait.

The smell was the first thing I noticed. A comforting scent that reminded me of my father's study, that combination of metallic mustiness with hints of vanilla. In awe, I turned in a circle to take in the books that covered three stories from floor to ceiling. A giant tree stood in the center. Its gnarled branches spread throughout the room in every direction. The elevator I had stepped from was set inside the wide trunk. Dark green vines dropped from the branches and dangled down to the moss-covered ground. Hanging from the vines were dozens of what looked like giant purple bean pods.

The ground felt spongy. I kicked my shoes off and wiggled my toes in the cool moss. A sense of childlike joy overrode all the concerns and the tension I had been carrying since the dream slid away. A pod hanging a few inches above the ground caught my eye. It was maybe a foot taller than me, the surface a shiny, dark pinkish-purple. A darker seam ran down the front. I poked it with my finger and jumped back, half expecting an alien to pop out and start sucking on my brains.

When nothing happened, I moved closer to trace my finger along the waxy surface of the seam. The pod opened like a zipper, making me squeak in surprise. Nestled in the hollow curve of the pod were three large flat white seeds. This was looking eerily like a bad sci-fi movie where the curious idiot was poking at alien pods instead of running for her life. I took a step back and something pushed me from behind. I landed against the seeds with a muffled screech as they molded to my body like memory foam. I twisted about, fully intending to leap out when the seeds adjusted to cup my body perfectly. The pod tilted back until I was reclining. Then there was a rustling sound as the pod started to move.

"Whoa!" I shouted, bracing my palms against the walls of the pod.

From the opening of the seam, I watched in amazement as the tree branches carried the vine along. The pod stayed surprisingly stable as the tree moved me around the room. This couldn't be real. *Ouch, damn it! Ok, the pinch test says otherwise.* Welcome to the island where Mother Nature took the right-to-work law to a whole new level. Your ficus wants to be a bank teller? Sure, why not!

Panic was threatening to overwhelm me. That, or hysteria. Any minute now I would be rocking in the corner, thumb in mouth, or running around screaming. What the hell kind of place was this?

Up and up the tree took me until it stopped before one of the highest bookshelves. Another vine slithered across the row of books and plucked one from the shelf. It came toward me, and I cringed. No more slithery things! Snakes and roots and vines, oh my!

The vine held what appeared to be an ancient book. The cover was a weathered brown with a few flecks of other colors here and there. The binding looked as if it had been replaced at some point, but so long ago that it barely held the thick, yellowed pages together. A familiar symbol was centered on the cover and surrounded by eighteen smaller symbols.

The vine carefully opened the book to a page filled with faded writing. Curiosity overcame panic for the moment, and I leaned forward to try to make out the words. The seeds immediately shifted to place me in a comfortable seated position from which to read the text. *That's handy. My clients would love something like this.* If I had any left, that is.

Scanning the page, I began to read aloud the sections that were legible.

"… and God did seek companion opposite of his order, born of purest light and unquenchable darkness . . . Uh, something about the creator who was also the destroyer and balancing the two." I skimmed along the page. It mentioned something about the companion becoming obsessed with creation. There were a lot of terrible and hideous beasts created before the companion got the bright idea to take a piece from himself. He finally made a son. Then the son created three brothers and two sisters. Together they ruled the Earth as the Primordial Gods. "The son was named after his father . . . Chaos."

The vine closed the book and placed it back on the shelf.

My mind was whirling with everything that had just happened, but the one thought that kept popping into my head chilled me to the bone. Were the Kyrion the Primordial Gods? From the beginning there had been something different about this place and these people. This couldn't be written off as a mental breakdown from stress or an overactive imagination. The tree had wanted me to see that book. That wasn't freakin' normal!

If I believed what was in that book, then there was a lot more going on here than rich people with too much time on their hands. Had my dream earlier been *real*? Had I somehow been mind-melded with the companion from the book? The whole creator and destroyer thing certainly fit. Was that what—or who—I was feeling within the statue?

It was almost as if there were two entities within the statue. One that had scraped out everything that was me and replaced it with the cold detachment from my dream. The other was something very sad and lonely. It sounded stupid, but I got the impression that the portion that called to me was searching for something and didn't mean me harm. It needed me.

If any of that had been real, Chaos had saved me from a fate I'm sure I didn't want to know about. Had he known what was happening because he had read this book, or was he really the son of a god?

The tree handed me back down to the ground, and I stepped out before the pod resealed itself. I was reaching for the seam again to see if the tree would show me something else when an annoyed voice startled me.

"Interesting that you were able to find this floor on your

own." Chaos's condescending tone grated on my nerves. "It is not a place that is open to merely anyone. It is almost as if someone wants you to discover all of our secrets. What did the Tree of Knowledge show you, Potential Davies?"

I turned to face him. Oh no, that was so not fair. Muscular pecs and a washboard stomach had my hands twitching for something to draw with. Those smoothly toned muscles needed to be captured in charcoal, or maybe clay. The low band of his sweatpants revealed the V-line of his hips, and my tongue darted out to moisten my suddenly dry lips. My fingers itched to trace every line of those muscles—purely for artistic research, of course. Maybe my tongue too. Sweat beaded his skin as if he had come straight from a workout. My mind was conjuring up all kinds of things we could do to get sweaty, and they didn't involve gym equipment.

"My eyes are up here, Potential," Chaos's rough voice growled, making me shiver.

I could feel the blush blooming on my skin as I dragged my eyes up to meet his. There was so much heat there my skin tingled. We stared at each other, and somehow the distance between us shrank until only inches separated us. He brushed a strand of loose hair over my shoulder.

"What did you learn?" he demanded.

"I . . . It wasn't anything important," I lied.

His eyes narrowed. "I find that doubtful. The tree showed you something. What did it think you needed to know?" His hand settled against the side of my neck, his thumb stroking my jumping pulse.

"That's ridiculous. A tree doesn't think," I scoffed, trying hard to ignore the effect he was having on me. "Uh, that's an interesting way to browse the library though. You could make a fortune on that technology."

"That is the path you are choosing? Denial?" His fingers tightened on my neck. "Yes, I suppose you would. My father once told me that humans will rationalize anything. They blame great feats on an adrenaline rush or luck. It seems the bastard was right about something."

Humans? Dear baby Jesus in the manger. "A-Are you saying that you're not human?"

"Now that would be 'ridiculous', as you say," he said with a mocking smile. "We are merely a society that chooses to maintain our privacy. Is that not what you have learned?"

"Maybe there's more to your people than that. The things that've happened here—"

"Accidents or pranks," he countered. "What else could they be?"

Pranks my ass. Damn stubborn man! We were getting nowhere. "Right. Well, it's time I got back to bed. Don't want to be late for training again. Goodnight."

His hand tightened around my neck, preventing me from leaving. He studied me as if I were a fascinating puzzle that needed to be solved. His other hand came to rest on my hip, then slowly slid along the hem of my shirt before burrowing under to rest against the skin of my lower back. His fingers lightly caressed the still-tender skin. "Has anything else happened that you would like to tell me about?"

Your mouth looks yummy. If your chest keeps rubbing against me like that, I might spontaneously combust. Probably not what he was referring to, but still true. Breathlessly, I said, "Nope. Nothing new going on here."

"Hmm. Maybe there is more to you too." He moved into me, pressing our bodies tightly together.

My breath escaped in a gasp at the evidence of his

arousal. He stole the rest of my breath when his lips sipped softly from mine.

"Wh-What are you doing?"

"Testing a theory," he mumbled.

Then his tongue darted out to lick my bottom lip before he captured me in a slow deep kiss. Brain cells melted. Lightning shot through my body. This was a bad idea, but for the life of me, I couldn't remember why. Nothing else mattered except easing the ache he had created.

One hand drew arcs along my back, while his other sank into my loose hair, tugging my head back. His lips traveled straight down my neck to the curves of my breasts visible above my tank top. His tongue dipped into my cleavage at the same time that he pressed a knee up into my core. A low moan issued from my lips and I gripped his shoulders to keep my legs from collapsing. He palmed my breast, pushing it up for his seeking lips to find more of me. With the other hand he cupped my butt, forcing me to grind on his knee. Then suddenly it was gone.

A whimper escaped me. *Nooo, bring it back!*

There was a tug on my jeans as they were pushed down to mid-thigh. A shiver wracked me as the cool breeze caressed the wet cloth of my panties. Then long fingers tugged aside the wet fabric, exposing me fully. His mouth captured mine again as one finger traced me down below. His finger tapped against my clit, and I almost came on the spot. I gripped his spiky hair to pull him deeper into our kiss and my hips arched against the finger that was rubbing me just right. My world was preparing to go nuclear when he pulled back with a curse.

He gripped my shoulders roughly, putting distance between our bodies. "This is what I meant. You are a distraction. I am supposed to be dealing with the fallout from another attack, yet here I am with you." His eyes blazed with a mixture of longing and disgust as he took in my half-naked state. "Every time you are near, I want to pin you to the floor and fuck you senseless. I will not let you turn me into my father. My control is essential. This will not happen again. Do you understand?"

My brain was still trying to clear the fog of lust. He shook me when I didn't answer. "Y-Yes. But—"

"No. There is nothing between us. There will never be anything between us." It sounded as if he was trying to convince us both. "I must go, but first you will tell me what you learned here."

Anger flashed through me and wind swept through the room, sending the pods swinging in the trees. "I'm not one of your subjects to kiss your ass. If I learned anything here, it was meant for me, and doesn't concern you. Let me go."

"So be it." A cold mask settled over his face. Then he turned and walked away, leaving me aching in more ways than one.

16

The fourth day of training, Molly and I were once again strapped into the chariot. The lanes had been erased from the dirt track this time. Gripping the reins with a bit more familiarity, I leaned into the chariot and waited for the signal. As soon as the flag dropped, we were off. After those first fumbles, I had taken to chariot racing like a natural. Molly kept asking if I'd had training somewhere. It felt right. Working with the horses. The thrill as we whipped down the track. The exhilaration of outmaneuvering the other drivers.

I was neck and neck with Kade in his green chariot down the straightaway. Taking the lead, I skidded around the first turn. One of the wheels left the ground, and I used my body to counterbalance, just as Molly had taught me. Clouds of dust kicked up all around us, and the noise would have been deafening if not for our helmets.

Mikhail pulled along beside me as we entered another straightaway. His gold chariot suddenly lurched toward me, attempting to cut me off. We were so close I could reach out and touch him. Our wheels bumped. Mikhail tried to correct too hard. The horses reared, and the pole that ran between them snapped. They were too close. We were going to crash.

"Yah! Yah!" I yelled at my team even though they couldn't hear me.

Mikhail's chariot veered over to where we had been a second ago. I glanced over my shoulder to see if he was ok. The broken pole dragging on the ground between the horses caught on something, and the chariot flipped up into the air, tipping wildly as it bore down on us. There was no time to alter course. We were going to be crushed.

Snapping the reins furiously, I did what I could to put distance between us. The gold chariot crashed down, clipping the back end of our platform. Molly was thrown forward into me, and we slammed against the front wall of the chariot. Pain blossomed along my ribs. Molly cussed virulently over the open speaker as she tried to shift her weight from me. Something was wrong. The chariot platform seemed to have more give and sway than before.

Chris in his white chariot pulled alongside me as the second curve came into view. He gave us a wide berth until we came to the turn and then suddenly crossed behind me to take the inside track. Leaning against the turn, I kept as close to his chariot as I dared.

C'mon guys, let's win this.

Abruptly the platform beneath my feet cracked down the middle. Molly pitched into me again, and this time the chariot collapsed. Molly's scream blared through my earpiece as we were thrown forward, hitting the ground with a jarring thud. My world turned into a topsy-turvy nightmare of pain and fear. There was no up or down, only the vacuum of silence created by the tornado of agony as it tossed me about.

Molly's weight was banging against my back. *Thank god, she's still with me.* Every ounce of strength I possessed was put into keeping my grip on the reins. My arms felt as if they were being pulled from their sockets, but I couldn't let go. If we got disconnected from the horses, there was a real chance we could end up being trampled beneath the hooves of another team. I had to hang on.

A small section of the front panel was being dragged along by the cords latched to my tunic, straining my arms further. My fingers were going numb, but I locked my hands as tightly around the reins as I could. Molly shifted her weight against my back. I swallowed down the scream that tried to claw its way from my throat at the fresh shot of pain. My voice sounded ragged as I begged over our headsets, "Don't. Move."

"Sorry," Molly gritted out. "Trying to cut the straps. Can you hang on?"

"Wait. Turn," I gasped.

The horses took the turn, and we went into another tumble. My visor was coated with dirt, preventing me from seeing anything. That didn't matter because the image of the horse's deadly hooves thundering only feet in front of our faces was embedded in my brain.

Molly slammed heavily into my back. She gripped me tightly to keep us from rolling again until we were back on the straightaway.

"Now," she shouted.

She shifted again. Her position was putting too much weight on my right side. I could feel my grip starting to slip. She fumbled a hand under my hip to reach the straps connected to the piece of the chariot we dragged with us. Then she leaned to the other side and repeated the process, an extremely risky move. One bump and that knife could cut into either one of us instead of the straps. When the last strap released, it lessened the sensation of being pulled in opposite directions. We might make it through this.

My grip abruptly gave out. Pain slammed into me. My eyes squeezed shut as I waited for the first hoof to land. The world turned eerily silent once more. Then we were moving again, but this felt different. My stomach dropped, and my head got fuzzy from the speed. Someone rolled me onto my back and removed the helmet. The tickle of soft grass pressed against my cheek. Bright light pushed against my closed eyelids. Was I dead? My eyes squinted open to find the anxious face of Chaos leaning over me.

"Damn it, I must be in hell," I mumbled.

Strong hands cupped my face. Firm lips stole my breath. This hot and cold thing with him was going to give me whiplash. Chaos lifted his head to stare down at me. Unfortunately, my big inhale to rant at him made my chest feel full of broken glass. Crying out, I tried to curl up into a ball, but that made it worse. My arms flopped uselessly. My skin was raw and burned everywhere the sun touched.

Molly knelt by my side as Chaos shouted orders above me. Her long-sleeved tunic was ripped in several places. Her hands were bloodstained and two of the fingers on her right hand were clearly broken. Whimpering, I could only take shallow breaths as I lay as still as possible trying to ease the pain.

"Hang on, Lia. The doctor will be here soon." Molly pushed my damp hair out of my face. Even that small movement made me wince, and she withdrew her hand. "You were so brave. You saved us both. I've never seen anything like that, and I've been around the Games since I was a kid."

I tried to talk, but the pain had leached my voice from me. Molly gave me a sip of water from the palm of her hand.

Where she got it from would have to be a question for another day. Waves of pain wracked me as she continued to talk. Soon the doctor came and with him fresh pain as he prodded my battered body. The diagnosis was cracked ribs, both shoulders dislocated, and sprained wrists. That was on top of all the cuts, scrapes, and bruises.

Bless that doctor; he prescribed some really potent painkillers that went to work almost immediately. Lots of bed rest was in my future. Chaos ordered a bedroom set up right there in the woods instead of making me suffer the journey all the way back to my own room. People scrambled in every direction to do his bidding. Mr. Bossybutt was handy to have around sometimes. *I wonder if he does dishes?* If you could get rid of the asshole and keep the sexy, women everywhere would be lining up to get one.

Grace came over and shook her head at the battered pair of us. She sent Molly to be looked over by the doctor and I could hear her complaining the whole way. Grace pulled my hair from its half dangling ponytail and brushed her fingers through it while humming softly. The sound coupled with the soothing motion was relaxing.

I must have dozed because the next thing I knew I was gasping in pain again. Chaos barked at my handlers to be careful as they lifted me onto a stretcher, hoisted it from the ground, and carted me into the woods behind the grandstands. It was a bizarre parade as people followed my stretcher to a clearing in the woods where a tent had been set up.

Chaos was still issuing orders as we entered the tent. "Leave them alone," I weakly commanded but he ignored me. All I needed was a bath and a bed, not a freakin' five-star resort set up in the woods. Stubborn man was determined to get his way. A couple of men transferred me to a large bed. Then Molly and Grace were there, making me as comfortable as possible. Frustration and anger warred in me. Stuck in my immobile body, I stared up at the canvas ceiling. This was a disaster.

"I need to be in the race tomorrow," I said a little desperately. "Tell them I need to be in the race."

Molly sat on one side of the bed while Grace dipped cloths into a basin on the other. Grace leaned over me to touch the cool cloth against my sweaty skin, wiping away layers of dirt. She turned to rinse the cloth out, and movement at the foot of the bed caught my attention.

Chaos stared at me with an indecipherable expression on his face. "You are unfit to participate in the Games, Potential Davies. One day or one month will not change the fact that you are too injured to compete any longer. Eros will forfeit your place."

If I had been able to move, I would have thrown something at him. My voice came out as more of a whispered shout as I said, "No! Damn you, I've worked my butt off training for this. I won't forfeit."

Chaos's gaze sharpened as he rounded my bed to stand over me. "Why? You mock our traditions. You show disdain for the Kyrion. Why would you choose to stay here?"

The miserable state of my life wasn't up for public consumption. I didn't need anyone's pity. Especially from the man who had it all. He'd treated me like I was worthless since I'd arrived. How much more pathetic would he think I was if he knew why I was here. "None of your business."

He briefly looked disappointed before blanking his expression. "There is no shame in forfeiting the Game due to injury. You were brave today. You fought hard to save Molly and yourself from much greater harm. Any Kyrion would be proud to have you as their champion. Rest for now, and we will discuss what may be done later."

When Grace turned back, he shifted his gaze to her. They peered at each other for several moments, as if they were conducting a conversation that only the two of them could hear. He glanced back at me once more and then disappeared out the flap of the tent. Grace studied me carefully as she loomed over me once more. Her hand flexed, wringing drops of water onto the bed from the cloth clutched in her grip. She didn't seem to notice.

"You're the one. The prophecy is true," Grace said in a stark voice.

Molly slapped her hand on the bed, making me jump and hiss in pain. "Oops sorry," she said sheepishly. Then she looked at Grace. "Damn, I should have known. The odd things that kept happening around her. Chaos's reaction. The statue. The healing. I just—wow. It's happening."

"What the what? No more riddle me this." I demanded, my words slurring together as the painkillers took over. "What about the statue? I'm one what? What's happening?"

Grace looked down at me with a blinding smile that didn't quite reach her eyes. "That's entirely up to you, dear. You are Chosen. Will you save us or destroy us?"

17

I bolted upright in bed panting. These dreams were going to drive me crazy. I had been on an island this time. There were some similarities to Sotirìa, but this one was unlike anything this world has ever seen. I had been playing with the butterflies in the garden and hanging strands of jasmine flowers while waiting for my husband to join me. Someone had called my name. Someone I recognized. I turned to greet him with a smile when pain lanced through my back. Terror spiked through me as I grabbed my heavily pregnant belly before pitching forward. I woke up right before I hit the ground.

Rolling over, I buried my head in the pillow and let out an exasperated yell. Maybe I really was losing my mind.

"I often feel a good yell helps to calm the soul," a husky voice said.

I lifted up onto my elbows feeling only minor aches from my injuries. The medicine they had here was amazing. Grayson walked closer to the bed, his boyish grin in place. "I am glad you are alive, Potential. I feared I had gained and lost a friend all in one day. You must not scare me so."

"Yeah, well it wasn't my idea of fun either," I grumbled. "Uh, do you think you could get Molly or Grace? I'd like to get up." I looked about the tent, expecting one of them to poke their head in. They definitely had some explaining to do after that conversation last night. Right now, though, there were some other pressing needs to take care of.

"Permit me." Grayson scooped me up from the bed before I could protest.

"Whoa, slowly," I admonished while gripping my spinning head. "Put me down, Boy Wonder."

"I apologize, Potential Davies, if my excitement at your speedy recovery caused you harm." His sad puppy-dog expression made me feel like I should be the one to apologize as he helped me stand. The sneaky little manipulator knew I couldn't stay irritated with him when he gave me that face. I rumpled his hair, and he grinned. Then he wrapped his arm around my waist for support as I tested out my legs.

"Huh, I do feel pretty good for being dragged around behind the horses yesterday." I took a tentative step and then another until my legs felt solid beneath me. My chest expanded with the first full pain-free breath in what felt like forever. My shoulders and wrists were a bit achy but there was no major pain to be found anywhere. The doctor was a miracle worker. "Was I out long?"

"Several hours as best I can tell." Grayson kept pace with me as I stretched.

Now that I could move about on my own, the restroom was my next stop. Grayson wanted to carry me to the restroom at the grandstands, but I refused. That ended up being a poor decision on my part. By the time we made it there, I was shaky and covered in sweat. Grayson was practically dragging me as my feet stumbled over the ground the last few yards. At the door to the restrooms, I gathered my flagging strength and insisted that I go in alone. He hadn't been happy about it but let me have my privacy.

When I exited, Molly was waiting at the edge of the woods. "How're you feeling?"

"Surprisingly good. You guys could make a fortune on those painkillers," I said as she hugged me.

"Painkillers?" She raised an eyebrow. "Oh, right."

"Was anyone else hurt in the accident?"

"No, everyone is fine. I'm all bandaged up." She held up her splinted fingers. "Kade won. He, ah, claimed his prize. If it makes you feel any better, she was the one who, uh, initiated things."

"Great, I'm happy for him. There wasn't anything between Kade and me." That brief moment on the track when he had flirted with me seemed so long ago. And my interests seemed to be focused elsewhere on the broody and obstinate leader of the House of Chaos. "It makes sense that he would win. He was doing well in training and I heard him mention that he owns a ranch. He was certainly more comfortable with the horses than most of us."

"Weird though that their sister would choose to be the prize. She's never participated in the Games before. Eros wasn't happy about it." Molly looked off into the distance with a puzzled expression, then shook her head. "Who knows. They tell us guides only what we need to do our jobs, which isn't much."

"Who was the prize?" I asked. "Eros's sister?"

Before Molly could answer, Grayson tugged my hand. "I would give you a massage now, Potential. Please come."

He pulled me along toward the wide trail leading back to the tent. I glanced back at Molly, but she seemed to be grinning at something in the grandstands. "Bye. I'll see you in a little bit," I called.

Her gaze shifted to me, and she looked as if she was having trouble holding back a laugh. "Oh, I'm not expecting to see you until tomorrow. Scratch that, maybe a few days from now. That look totally said someone was going to mark their territory soon. Almost makes me jealous."

"What?" I tried to pull free so I could talk to Molly, but Grayson swept me up in his arms mumbling about taking care of me.

"Don't worry," Molly called out. "I'm sure you'll find out soon enough. Have fun."

I decided I would track Molly down and find out what she was babbling about later. Right now, I was tired and still in my dirty chariot clothes. It was pointless to fight Grayson when he was only looking out for me. He carried me past the tent onto another path but refused to tell me where we were going. *Why is getting answers around here like trying to break into freakin' Fort Knox?*

Several minutes later we came to another small clearing. A ring of six trees formed a large rotunda in the center of the area. Their twisted trunks rose into the sky before they arched together to form a roof of interlocking branches. Pink and white blooms hung down from the limbs, creating a ceiling of fragrant flowers. A lush green carpet surrounded a large oval stone bath in the center of the structure.

Grayson let me down and we stood for a moment at the edge of the clearing admiring the view.

"Beautiful, yes?"

"It's amazing," I sighed, wishing again for my drawing supplies.

"Come." He pulled me forward.

We entered the rotunda and I breathed in deeply letting

the warm, fragrant air fill my lungs. Steam rose from the water, and I almost groaned in anticipation. Grayson led me to the side of the bath where a black robe and several bottles sat.

"Let me help you undress," Grayson said as he reached for the leather ties that laced down the front of my tunic. "We can bathe, and then I will give you the massage."

"Uhm, I think you've got the wrong idea. See—" His nimble fingers worked the laces on my tunic loose, and I smacked at his hands.

"Grayson, I believe the Potential prefers to bathe in private," Chaos's deep voice grated from behind us. "Perhaps you could assist Molly with the horses." His tone implied this was not a suggestion.

Grayson's jaw set in stubborn refusal, then relaxed as he smiled softly at me and ran the tip of his finger along my cheek. "I will see you soon, Potential Davies."

"Grayson," Chaos snapped.

Grayson gave me his boyish smile, then turned and walked away. Molly was right; something was weird here. Back home guys had paid attention to me, sure, but nothing like this level of sensual pursuit. First had been Eros. I had mostly written that off as him being a flirt, but maybe there was more to it. Hadn't Chaos said he had broken a rule by being in my bedroom? Eros was a rule bender, but to blatantly break one of the rules he was held to didn't sound like him.

Next was Kade. Now Grayson. None of this seemed to have started until after the pledges were made in the tower room. Kade hadn't approached me until the next day, even though we'd shared a moment at dinner before our pledges. I had met Grayson days later. Chaos had hated me on sight. But then after the pledges, he couldn't keep his hands off me. Did someone douse me in pheromones during the pledges?

Lost in thought, I'd forgotten that I wasn't alone until a rough finger nudged my chin up. A brief flash of jealousy flared in the dark eyes assessing me. "Potential Davies, you are a danger," Chaos said solemnly. I sputtered in protest, but his hand shifted to grip my throat. "To yourself. To my people... To me."

His fingers tightened on my throat until I thought he was surely going to strangle me. Then his lips crashed down on mine, and he pulled me tight against him. He cupped my butt, pulling me into his arousal. A moan buzzed my lips at the feel of him against me. Then his tongue delved into my mouth. His hand tried to tunnel beneath my shirt, but the tunic was too tight. He growled in frustration and ripped his mouth from mine.

He impatiently yanked at the laces of my tunic. Moments later it lifted over my head. Kisses landed on the top curve of each breast as his hands deftly worked at my back to release the clasp of my bra. The world was tilting this way and that like I was once again being pulled behind that chariot. My body was caught up in a whirling vortex, but it was a different kind of agony that flared through my veins and pooled low in my belly. Chaos pulled my bra from me and tossed it to the ground. He cupped me gently, my breasts overflowing his hands as he leaned down to lick each nipple.

My pants and underwear were shoved down my legs as kisses trailed along my stomach. Chaos growled again when they became tangled around my tennis shoes, and I hurriedly kicked them off. He looked up at me as he kneeled on the ground to remove the last of my clothing. The fire that had smoldered for days was now raging out of control in his eyes. He must have seen the same in mine because he shot swiftly to his feet, yanking his clothes off.

A naked Chaos was a work of art. Every line of him was defined perfection. I watched as his muscles flexed beneath my touch, feeling like silk poured over granite. I traced the V-lines at his pelvis and his cock jumped in response.

The hard length of him curved up toward his belly button. I licked my lips as I imagined the taste of the drop of moisture seeping from the slit. He groaned but held still for my perusal. My eyes followed the path of that drop as it trickled down the shaft to the cleanly shaven sacs below. We both watched as my finger traced the path back along the throbbing veins and thickly engorged head.

Chaos groaned again, then lunged as if his lauded control had finally snapped. He claimed my lips once more. My arms went around his neck, and he gripped my butt to hoist me into his arms. His cock pushed against my core, and he hissed in a breath as my wetness coated him. The swollen head of his penis bumped against my clit, making me shudder with every step as he walked us around the bath and down the steps into the water.

His lips continued their assault as the warm water lapped at my thighs when we neared the center. Then he abruptly pulled away. My breath sawed heavily through kiss-swollen lips as we stared at each other.

"This is a mistake," Chaos muttered.

Oh no, you're not doing this to me again. I pushed against his chest and kicked my legs, trying to dislodge his hold. "You son of a bitch. Let me go."

He swatted my ass. "Be still, Lia." I was too shocked to do anything but gape at him. "You could have died today." There was a haunted look in his eyes. Did he really care so much? His grip tightened, and he lifted me higher against him. "I cannot let you go. I have tried to stay away, but something about you draws me." A tortured look crossed his face before his jaw tightened in grim determination. "You are mine. If only for tonight."

Then he plunged me down upon his hard shaft. My head tipped back, my eyes closed as a pleasured squeal escaped. His wide girth stretched me to capacity as he pulled out and plunged back in, forcing me to take more of him.

"So tight. Take it all," he said through gritted teeth.

My thighs trembled as we fought to move together. I slammed my hips down, forcing a gasp from both of us as I took him all the way to the hilt. Chaos dropped to his knees in the warm water, his rough hands keeping us joined. "Ride me, Lia." Then his thumb found my clit and my hips jerked against him. "Ride. Show me how you take your pleasure."

The water lapped against the sides of the bath as I began to move on him. His hands traveled up my spine as he laid me back in the water. My hair floated around me, and my breasts were pushed up toward the sky in offering. Chaos wasted no time taking what was offered, drawing first one nipple and then the other into the hot cavern of his mouth. He suckled and nipped as I worked myself upon him. Lightning bolts zapped through my body every time I sank down. Moans and whimpers escaped my lips as pleasure wracked me.

One hand delved between us to thrum my clit, and I screamed out his name as fireworks burst behind my eyelids. My walls tightened and contracted upon him as my orgasm powered on and on. When I opened my eyes, Chaos was smiling at me. "You are beautiful. I want to see you cum on my cock over and over again."

He pulled from me and led me over to the ledge of the

bath. He spun me quickly and pushed against my back until I leaned over the ledge. "Spread your legs."

I braced my arms on the ledge and widened my stance. His firm tongue speared into me then lapped at me. I was too sensitive and tried to pull away. His strong hand landed on my ass with a smack that made me jump. "Stay still."

Bastard.

His tongue played over me as I bit my lip to try to keep from squirming. Then he rose up behind me and coated himself in my wetness before he dived back inside. He felt impossibly larger in this position. "Deeper, Lia. Take me deeper."

I wiggled my hips, trying to work myself over him. He pulled out and slammed back in, gaining more ground. Panted moans spilled from me as I struggled to take all of him. He ground his cock into me as his fingers worked me. He withdrew and slammed back into me, finally seating himself all the way inside. "Mine. So wet and tight. I'm going to take you now. Are you ready?"

"Y-Yes," I stammered.

He wasted no time in setting a hard and fast rhythm that tore gasps of pleasure from my lips. He dropped kisses along my shoulders and back as he continued to pound into me. His hands roamed everywhere as if he was committing every part of me to memory.

He pulled from me and twirled me around. Then kissed me fiercely as he picked me up again and laid me back on the wide ledge. His eyes were pitch black as he stared down at me, hunger blazing in their depths. He nudged against my opening. "Look. See me as I take you."

Rising up on my elbows, I watched as he took me. That thick shaft sank deeper and deeper. "Look how I fill you up.

I like that I have to force my way in. It is like a victory when I am finally all the way inside you."

It was my turn to groan. His words excited me almost as much as what he was doing. We both watched as he slid out slowly and then back in. It was erotic the way my glistening pink walls clung to him as he pulled out, then stretched wide for his entrance. "Is that the way it feels, Lia? Do I win something from you when you take me to your depths?"

I had been drawn to him from the first moment my eyes landed on him in the throne room. His touch was something I now craved. Even in my dreams he was there, pulling at this deep well of desire and wild abandonment that I never knew existed. He wasn't the only one who both craved and despised this attraction between us. We had given in. God help me, but I wasn't sorry.

That raging river of emotions I had paved over and left for dead was ready to erupt. I didn't know if either of us was ready for that. He had given me honesty, though. I could give him this in return. After all, it was only for tonight.

"Yes." I hissed.

Deep down inside the pavement was starting to crack. Instinctively, I knew that he could be the one to break my lonely highway wide open. No one else had ever been a threat because I had never *wanted* to give anything of myself. This was a man who could handle anything. My past. My present. My future. It was the temptation to give him all of me that had me wanting to take back some control. "Just as I win something from you."

He gazed at me intently, seeming to understand that I'd given all I was willing to. He nodded. "Then we will both be conquerors tonight." His hips slammed against mine, and I collapsed onto my back as he held true to his words.

The tension mounted in my body as he drove me higher

toward climax with each brutal thrust of his hips. I exploded again in ecstasy, calling out his name. Then he jerked against me, and I felt the warm rush of his release inside me. A tingling spread throughout my body, and I felt him tense above me. He collapsed forward onto his hands, leaning over me with a look of awe.

I smiled languidly up at him, feeling more relaxed than I had in years. He continued to stare at me, a kaleidoscope of emotions shifting across his face too quickly for me to name them all. "You cannot be . . . how did . . ." He drew a deep breath and seemed to gather himself. "You surprise me at every turn, Jillian Davies."

"Uhm yeah, it's been—you know—a while." I blushed hotly. "I, uh, didn't expect that either."

He chuckled. "That, too."

"Chaos—" I gasped, as he began to move inside me again. Heat filled me to an almost burning pitch, concentrated along my back.

"Bennett." He kissed my lips. "My real name is Bennett Young."

18

We bathed together, teasing each other as we lathered our bodies in the warm water of the tub under the rotunda. Afterward, we returned to the tent by the light of a lantern, bringing along the scented oil. Bennett used that oil on my body in the dim light of the tent to tease me to a state of feverish longing. Those magic hands wrung promises and threats from me that I would never admit to in the light of day. Only when I was on the brink of combusting with need did he sink back inside me. Then he whispered those promises back to me and made sure I fulfilled every one.

He drove me hard toward my peak then denied me as he withdrew. He used that sharp tongue of his to bring me to orgasm again and again. My voice grew hoarse from begging and pleading before he declared me ready for him. My body was so sensitive that even the slight breeze was too much. Delirious with exhaustion and overwhelmed by endless pleasure, I swore I couldn't take any more.

He proved me wrong. Pulling my hips up until I was resting only on my shoulders, he made me watch as he took me. The things he said as he claimed me with every inch of himself brought my desire roaring back to life. He had me on the razor edge of release as he took his time exploring my depths. The first jets of his seed spilling into me and the single thrum of my clit had my climax exploding through me, before we collapsed in a sweaty heap of tangled limbs.

We reached for each other again in the middle of the night. It was fast and intense, our competitive streaks coming out to play as we tried to see who could make the other climax first. The rotten bastard won, of course. I'd never been so happy to lose in my life. We made a quick trip to the grandstands to clean up, then crawled back into bed and talked about meaningless things—mostly Axol.

As the first rays of the sun slipped over the horizon to light the tent in a reddish glow, my lips trailed down that amazing body. Tasting and touching until my mouth wrapped around that delicious cock. The jerking of his hips and the sounds wrenched from his lips were my rewards as I paid him back for every moment of torture he had put me through. His rough demands sent delicious shivers through my body. Finally giving in, he called out my name as his warmth spurted on my tongue. Wrapped in his arms, I sank finally into a contented sleep.

The thrust of his cock into my depths woke me. Oh god! Crying out in pleasured pain, my body sore but willing, I met that dark gaze. There was such a look of intensity on his face that it was almost frightening as he drove himself as deep as possible like he was trying to mark me from the inside. This was it. This would be our last time together. Ignoring the stupid ache in my chest at the thought, I rose up to take his lips tenderly. He pushed back hard and deep, trying to drive me back into a lust-filled frenzy. *Not this time.* Each time he tried it, I pulled away. Only to start all over. Grunting in frustration, he finally let me take control.

I didn't want another feverish skirmish to see who would claim victory over the other. This last time I wanted something deeper. Something that meant more than merely scratching an itch. Pushing him into a kneeling position, I straddled his thighs and slowly sank down onto him. His hands gripped my thighs to hold me in place. My arms wound around his neck as we watched at each other. His lips parted on a hissed breath when I rolled my hips. A blue circle around the outer edge of his eyes seemed to be pulsing in time with the hard beat of his heart. It was mesmerizing, drawing me in like a moth to a flame. Our hearts were beating as one as the pleasure climbed higher with every slow glide upon him. Nothing existed of the world beyond us and this perfect moment.

There were gentle caresses and whispered words of praise. Through it all, our eyes never left each other. When we climaxed together, it was as if there was a feedback loop between us that kept the waves of pleasure pouring over us. His pleasure was mine and mine his. It felt as if a part of me now resided in him, forging a link between us. Neither of us spoke as we settled back upon the bed.

He stroked my back as I lay draped across his chest. We lay like that in silence for some time, lost in our own thoughts. Until Bennett asked quietly, "Why did you come here, Lia?"

I hesitated, wondering what we were doing. This felt like more than the one night of no-strings-attached sex that we had agreed to. Lying here in his arms, I couldn't deny that tonight had only whetted my appetite for more of this man. And not only the sex. There was a funny and caring side to Bennett that had slipped through during our time together. It made me want to get to know the real Bennett.

And that was the danger of answering his question. Did

I open the door to share more of myself or slam it closed? The smart thing to do was to give him an answer that he would expect: one motivated by money. But I found myself strangely wanting to say more. To tell him that I was starting to believe I was here for something more profound. I stood on the broken pavement of my lonely highway questioning if I had the courage to resurrect what I had buried here— myself. But at the last moment, I backed away. "Coming here was a gamble to try to save my art gallery."

What I couldn't bring myself to say was that I was almost sure I was here to save myself. My lonely highway was crumbling and there was no gallery here to help smooth the jagged pieces back into place. No routine of solitude as business owner Lia where I knew all the moves to make. Pieces of the old me were seeping through with each day that I spent here. They were melding with pieces of the new me, and I wasn't sure who I would be in the end. For the first time in years, though, I wasn't going through the motions. I was living.

I was living every gloriously, fear-inducing moment, and it hadn't destroyed me. Instead it was reshaping me.

Bennett was a big part of my waking up. He stirred up something inside me that wouldn't let me hide from life. He forced me to take notice and participate. He made me feel. And for the first time in years I wasn't locking those feelings away in the prison I had built to protect myself. It was terrifying but there was a part of me curious to see what life could be like without the shackles I had kept myself contained in.

Bennett had gone rigid beneath me. His voice was bitter when he asked, "Is this because of the rumors?"

Sickening dread filled me, and I scrambled to sit up. "H-How did you know about that?"

Bennett pulled himself up against the headboard, his face carefully blank. "How do you think we keep word of this place and our people from spreading? Only those who are meant to will see the invitation to the Games. We are even more cautious about those we allow in. We knew everything about you from the moment your application was accepted."

"Blackmail? Is that how you're planning to keep me and the others quiet about this place?"

"You would not say anything about us. You consider Molly a friend. Possibly Eros as well." Sarcasm dripped from his voice, "Oh yes, and let us not forget the charming Grayson."

"That's not an answer. I can't believe this," I said incredulously. "You people are supposed to be unsullied by the outside world or something. Instead, you're like mobsters."

"Hardly. We are people like any other. Maybe I should be the one to worry. Were the rumors true?"

How had we gone from those moments of tenderness to this? That he could ask me that after the night we shared made me nauseous. Humiliation and anger gnawed at my chest as I pulled the sheets around me like a shield. Tears welled up, and I ducked my head to hide how much he had gotten to me with that question.

"What do you think?" I said, as a tear slipped down my cheek and I roughly brushed it away. "We spent the night together in this bed. You tell me if I lived up to those rumors."

"That was careless of me," Bennett said gently. "I am sorry, Lia. Please forgive me."

He reached out to me, but I jerked away. "Go to hell!" My fists clenched the sheets as my tear-filled gaze met his. "Nothing about those rumors was true. Nothing! It doesn't matter though, right? Guilty until proven innocent. It's my word against whoever's out to ruin me. Congrats to them, they're doing a damn good job."

This night had gone from amazing to shit quickly, and I needed to leave before I had more to regret. "I knew this was a mistake. I almost opened up to you. How stupid. To think for a minute I could trust anyone—especially you." Bennett grabbed my arm as I tried to slip from the bed. Tears fell unchecked as I fought his grip. I landed a punch to his shoulder. He grunted and then roughly captured my wrists.

Bennett's heavy weight rolled into me, taking me down onto the bed beneath him. I struggled harder, but he pinned my hands beside my head and waited until I tired myself out. He stared guiltily down at me as another tear slipped from the corner of my eye. His voice was husky with remorse when he said, "I did not mean to hurt you, Lia. Please forgive me."

"Fine. I jutted my chin up, daring him to keep me pinned even a moment longer. "Let me go."

"That is something I cannot do." His fingers tightened where they were twined with mine. There was a tugging sensation along my spine and the room spun for a moment feeling as if he was pulling my energy from me. Then he loosened his grip and gave me a small smile. "I can help you, though. You *can* trust me, Lia. Please. Will you tell me what you were going to say before I messed this up?"

"You—" I started to protest.

"Please."

Taking a deep breath, I nodded. He slowly backed away as if waiting to see if I would run. Then lay down beside me and propped himself up on his elbow. His lips grazed mine as he whispered, "Thank you."

My anger melted away. Those lips should be outlawed. "Kissing me when I'm angry at you is cheating."

"Is there a rule somewhere that I did not know of?" He pretended to be serious but was fighting back a grin.

"Yes, my rule. I just made it up," I bantered back. This man could make me run the gamut of emotions in sixty seconds flat. There was too much to feel, and I was inexperienced at processing it all. So, I winged it. "You are in violation of rule one of Lia's Law."

"So sorry, officer. Is there a penalty? Perhaps there is some way that I could make it up to you." His gaze traveled down to where the sheet barely concealed my breasts.

"Are you attempting to bribe an officer of the law, sir?" I asked sternly.

"Only if it is working. Would hours of servicing you—I mean community service—take care of the issue?" The corner of his mouth curled up.

I licked my suddenly dry lips. *Oh boy.* "Umm yes, I believe that would do it."

"Indeed. I look forward to putting in my time." His dark gaze had heat pooling in my belly once more. "For now, I believe you were going to tell me something of yourself. I want to know you. Tell me."

"Bossy. You probably have a file on me already." The fact that he knew so much about my life already still annoyed me.

"The minimum details. You are a single child. You were raised on Mercer Island in Washington. Your father was a prosperous shipbuilder. Your mother stayed at home but was very involved in your activities. Throughout high school and into college you were active in gaining artist support for causes. You founded a couple of non-profits, I believe."

"Yes, one for child abuse education and the other was

focused on supporting women." More reminders of what I had walked away from. I had been such a crusader in those days. Convinced I would change the world. Instead, it was me that had changed.

"Then your parents died, and you disappeared, only to resurface almost a year later in Port Lawson." He studied me closely, obviously curious. "There you set up shop and have been a good taxpaying citizen for the last three years. Leading a very quiet life until recently."

"See, you do have all the details."

"None of that tells me about you as a person. Your hopes and fears. What drives you. Where you went that year you disappeared."

His voice was gentle, but I immediately turned ice cold as memories tried to pry their way up through the cracks. *No!* Push them down. Pave them over. No one needed to know about the things that I'd seen living on the streets. The things that I'd done to survive them. "There's nothing interesting to tell. How 'bout we talk about you? Growing up with Eros as a stepbrother must have been interesting."

His rough fingers traced my mouth. "Your lips say it is not important, but your eyes say differently. One day you will tell me. When you are ready. What about your parents? What were they like?"

"They were . . . beautiful. Inside and out." My heart ached remembering the way they were. "My mom was kind and smart. She had my dad wrapped around her finger, but she never asked for much. She was good at everything. Except baking. She was horrible at baking. But she kept trying. Bake sales for art camps were the worst. My dad and I would have to buy back everything she donated. It was a win–win for me though. I got the money for camp and didn't have to console my mom when she sent everyone to the hospital with food poisoning."

Bennett chuckled, and the tension eased a little. "My dad came off all gruff, but he was a big teddy bear. He lived to make my mom smile. They were so in love. And so comfortable with each other. Half the time I swore they could read each other's minds. They were always holding hands or had their arms around each other. They were inseparable. One would have never been able to live without the other."

My thoughts inevitably turned to the day of the boating accident. Losing both of my parents at the same time was horrible, but it was true what I had said. If one of them had lived, it likely would have only been for a short time longer. The will to live on without the person who was their other half would have been gone.

"Tell me," Bennett softly coaxed as he twined his fingers with mine.

19

Bennett was asking me to tell him about the worst day of my life. To dredge up memories that I had never discussed with anyone. For some reason, it felt right that he would be the first.

"I had just gotten my art degree and was ready to take the world by storm. My artwork would be hanging in the galleries alongside the most famous artists in the world. I was so naive. But my parents believed in me, and that was all that mattered."

My fingers toyed with the bedsheet as I lost myself in the memories. "The plan was to spend a few weeks at home before I decided what my next steps were. Usually, Dia joined me, but she was sick. So, it was the three of us, like old times."

Selfishly, I had been glad to have my parents all to myself for a little while. "It was good to be home. We spent a couple of days catching up and dreaming big dreams about my future. My dad wanted to celebrate my graduation by taking me out on our boat that weekend. I was so excited to get back out on the water.

"It had been a perfect spring day. Not a rain cloud in sight and warmer than usual. We had joked around as we packed for our day out on the lake. Mom and Dad had shared secretive glances the whole time." A smile tugged at my lips. "I pretended not to notice, letting them think that they were so sneaky when they surprised me with whatever it was they had planned. My dad had always been big on surprising us, but he was horrible about actually keeping it a secret. It was just that he got so excited, he gave himself away. My mom was normally much harder to read.

"We got an early start so we could make a full day of it. We stopped at all my favorite spots along Lake Washington. Laughing over stories about Dia and this older guy she had started dating. Talking about Dad's plans for a new ship. We had sandwiches in the Japanese Gardens at the Arboretum in Washington Park. It's amazing there in the spring when the flowers are in bloom. We shopped. Drank wine and gorged on chocolate. It was the best day."

Memories pushed against the pavement of my highway. The echo of my mother's scream. Those dead eyes accusing me. I took a deep breath and forged on.

"Later in the afternoon, Mom started feeling anxious. She said we needed to get home. We didn't question her. It probably seems strange to you, but she had a sort of sixth sense when something was wrong."

"Did she do this often?" Bennett seemed very focused on my answer.

"It was usually big things. Like a bad wreck that was going to happen on the road I'd take to school." I shifted onto my side to face him. "Stuff like that didn't happen a lot on our little island. But she was always right when she got one of her feelings."

Bennett pushed a lock of hair behind my ear. "Do you find it odd that she could do that?"

"No. Maybe if I hadn't grown up seeing her *know* when something was going to happen, it might've been different."

"Then you believe that there are things beyond the normal human abilities?"

"I guess. I mean, I didn't really see Mom as different. But what she could do was real. She can't have been the only one."

He looked pleased. "Thank you." He smiled down at me. "I promise not to interrupt again."

I nodded. Tension built in the pit of my stomach as I thought about what had happened next.

"Mom had paced the bow of the ship as we headed home at full speed. She was frantically scanning the shore and the water, even the sky. I asked over and over again what was wrong, but she never answered." I had never seen her so scared. "She hugged me tight and told me she loved me. Then my dad was there, holding us both so tight I could barely breathe. He kissed my mom like he knew it would be the last time. Then hugged us both again. They ordered me to get below deck and stay in my cabin until they came to get me. I hadn't taken more than a few steps when the wind roared over our boat, almost sweeping us all over the side.

"The storm came out of nowhere a few miles from home. One minute we had been enjoying a sunny afternoon and the next it was as dark as night. The wind and waves tossed the boat about like it was a toy. I've been on that lake since I was a little girl, but I'd never seen anything like that."

I shuddered as the dread that had weighed so heavily in the air that day came rushing back. I'd never feared the water before then.

"Below deck, the wind was barely a howl, but it was still frightening to hear. I sat on my bed only to tumble off moments later as another wave hit. Angry at being sent to my cabin as if I were a child, and more than a little scared, I went back up on deck. Waves sloshed over the boat. My feet slipped. Cold rain pounded down, soaking me. Thunder boomed so loud it rattled my bones. Lightning flashed, striking the water within feet of our boat. My dad struggled with the sails, and I rushed to help him.

"Dad and I fought to bring the sails down. Somehow one of the rigging lines got wrapped around him." Tears slipped from the corners of my eyes. "I t-t-tried to grab him, but he pushed me away. He was d-dragged overboard."

Not once since giving my statement to the police had I spoken about it. That paved highway of buried emotions deep down inside split wide open, and everything came crashing over me. Tears poured unchecked down my cheeks as I struggled to breathe. There was a burning in my chest that felt like my heart was being ripped out all over again. The need to run from the pain swamped me, and I surged up needing to put distance between us.

Bennett pulled me into his arms. "Let it out, Lia. You need to let this pain go."

"You don't understand! You weren't there. You didn't see the look on my mom's face. I couldn't save him. I just stood there staring at where he had gone over. You didn't hear her scream like I had stabbed her straight through the heart. I can still hear it in my dreams. And that look. The way she looked at me. Th-then she—" Sobs wrenched from my throat as my heart shattered. It felt as if an explosion burst from me. The acrid smell of something burning filled my lungs before Bennett wrapped himself tighter around me.

He rubbed his hands along my back and kissed the tears from my cheeks. "What did your mother do, *asteràki*?"

"S-S-She hugged me to her. Then there was a b-bright light. It must have been the lightning. Somehow, we were beside the rail and . . . and she p-pushed me overboard! I caused them to d-drown. They died hating me—" I sobbed until I cried myself out of tears and a heavy numbness filled me.

"Do not doubt that your parents loved you deeply, *asteràki*. They protected you with their very lives. Your father knew you would be dragged overboard with him if he let you touch him. Your mother's . . . heart was broken at his loss. Likely she knew the ship would go down. She threw you overboard to save you. Deep down you know this is true. This burden you carry is not yours." His calm voice slid over the jagged edges of my emotions like a cooling balm. "Your parents would not want this for you, *asteràki*. You must let it go."

Some part of me knew he was right. "But I don't know *how*. I've been running from my past for a long time. Hell, I ran all the way to the other side of the world and headlong into trouble. I did the only thing I could to keep myself alive: I buried the pain."

Everything about my life had suffocated me after the accident. All I felt was rage and pain. Making our lawyer the power of attorney for everything, I'd walked away and never looked back. The few thousand from my bank account and a full tank of gas only got me so far. Pawning the car got me a little farther. After that, it was a vicious cycle of hard lessons, fear, and hunger. I'd been one of the lucky ones, though. I had gotten out.

There had been several times on the streets when things could have gone a different way. Looking back now I wondered if I hadn't had a guardian angel watching over me. The turning point for me was the day I had been staring down at the needle gripped in my hand. The thin mattress beneath me smelled of old sweat and urine. Garbage piled around me from what I had scrounged as my "treasures."

That flophouse in Shanghai was an active one. The sounds of sex and fights were my constant background noise. After almost a year of living that way, my lines had become blurred. My moral compass was worn down by the need to survive. It was harder each time to say no to the drugs, the sex, the violence. And sometimes I hadn't. My dirty hand trembled as I pressed that needle to my skin. There was no coming back from that decision. Was that what my parents would have wanted? Was it what I wanted?

I'd thrown the needle away and left. Every last penny I'd saved from odd jobs went into getting me back to Washington. It took a while, but when I set foot back in my home state, I knew it was for good. There was no going back to the streets. Not if I wanted to live.

Surprisingly enough, I did. That meant I had to mold myself into someone who could make it in the nine-to-five suburban world. I tracked down the only friend I'd ever had. After she was done chewing my ass out for disappearing on her, she'd helped me build a new life. Dia had never pried into what happened to me. She had simply been there for me, and I owed her so much.

"Pouring everything I had into my gallery helped. It became my sole focus. My life. It was the first thing that was truly mine. Built with my own blood, sweat, and tears." It was also my shield, I could see that now. I had buried myself in the persona of the perfect business woman. Being a gallery owner was predictable and gave me an identity that I had lost somewhere on the streets. "Now someone is trying to take that away from me by spreading vicious lies. I've been shunned by half the town, not to mention the art community, and my bank has called my business loan due."

"I am sorry for your loss, Lia. I understand your pain. It never completely goes away but letting yourself remember the good helps to dull it." Bennett's stubbled jaw clenched, and a haunted look entered his eyes for a moment. "I lost my mother when I was nine. I may as well have lost my father too. He was never the same after she passed. I would not wish the pain of losing a loved one upon anyone. Many would have crumbled under the weight of grief after facing such a tragedy as yours. You ran. Yet you came back. You built a life that your parents would have been proud of. That took courage." His voice hardened. "As for your current predicament, people might have been misled into believing something false. It is your courage in fighting for yourself and your business that will weigh in your favor."

I pulled away to sit with my back to him on the edge of the bed, cringing at the thought of him realizing what a coward I was. I didn't deserve his praise.

"I haven't, though," I confessed. "Fought, I mean. I hid out to avoid people whenever I could. I never even tried to defend myself. Now I've taken a month off, leaving Dia in charge to deal with it all." I swallowed thickly realizing what I had done. "I ran again, didn't I? I should have stayed. I should have gone to the police or someone to help me find out who was targeting me."

The silence stretched on uncomfortably for several long moments as I awaited his judgment. A rough finger trailed along my back, tracing some invisible pattern in the darkness.

"The money from the Games would perhaps solve your loan problem. There is still a battle to be fought." He gripped my chin turning my face toward his. "Vindictive people do not usually give up until they feel they have found justice. You came here to arm yourself. You have taken up the sword. The question now is, what will you do with it?"

20

A gasp dragged me from my much-needed sleep after Bennett had left the tent. I quickly tucked the blanket around my naked body and rolled to see who it was. Grayson and Molly stood a couple of feet from my bed. Grayson's face was a mask of utter shock. Molly, however, smiled at me like I was the failing student who had scored the highest grade in the class.

"What?" I asked, hoping there hadn't been any accidental flashing.

"You bonded," Grayson whispered.

"Well, if that's what you guys call it around here, sure I 'bonded' last night. Can I avoid the walk of shame this morning or is there a crowd waiting?" I asked sarcastically, pushing my messy hair out of my face.

"No, you misunderstand, my lady. You are—"

"Later, Grayson. She has a competition to get ready for."

"But she doesn't—"

"No, but that's for him to explain. The Games can't be stopped. That's the way *they* set them up. Once the contestants are pledged, all six competitions must be played out within the year." Molly stared at Grayson meaningfully. He looked reluctant but didn't say anything else.

"Right. Naked here. Can you two go discuss things somewhere else so I can get dressed?" I asked pointedly.

"Wait," Molly said. "Grayson, walk back out and tell me when you notice the difference."

Grayson walked out of the tent and then back in. Then repeated the process. He stopped several feet away from the bed on his return trip. Then said, "Here."

"Uh, why is he 'my ladying' me and walking in and out of the tent?" These people were so weird sometimes.

Grayson immediately dropped to one knee like the servants did for the Kyrion and bowed his head. "I am my lady's man. If you do not wish others to know of your status, I will assist you."

Was getting laid a status? "Yep, I'm good with the assisting. Assist away if it keeps me from having to flash my butt to everyone."

Molly snickered. "No worries. I brought fresh training gear."

"I am good with distractions, my lady. Leave this to me." A sly smile stretched across his face that made me fear for whoever he was plotting against. Then Grayson rose from his knees and marched out of the tent with a determined stride.

"I'll probably have to post bail. Seems you've got yourself a loyal servant. Still, don't know what all the fuss is about. You can't run or lift worth a damn." Molly playfully stuck her tongue out. "But you do drive a pretty mean chariot."

We laughed together at that. I caught sight of something strange on the ceiling. There, right over the bed, was a large hole with blackened edges. "Uh, why is there a hole burned in the tent?"

Molly laughed hysterically. "Guess things got a little *heated* last night. Looks like someone lost control. Good for you."

Blushing, I quickly changed the subject. We chatted about the competition as I got dressed. I was brushing my hair back into its customary ponytail when I noticed that Molly had gone quiet. She fidgeted with the seam on her blue yoga pants as if she was debating something. "C'mon, spit it out. What?"

Molly bit her lip. "Don't freak out, ok? I want to show you something."

"Molly, that is a surefire way to get someone to freak out. Never start with that. But ok, no freaking out. Got it. So tell me. Has my time here turned me into one of your alien race, and I'm going to turn green?" She continued to stare at me nervously, my attempt at a joke falling flat.

"We're not aliens. The teenagers do love their crop circles, though. Keeps the media guessing. But that's not what I wanted to talk about." She flashed me a grin before she sobered and said, "You *are* one of us."

"You mean like right now I'm part of the House of Arrows?"

"No. I don't know how, but I think you were one of us from the start. A Paldimori. Eros is looking into it. That's why he isn't here right now. He got a call back from one of his contacts," she said in a rush.

"I should let Chaos tell you this. I really should." Molly pinched the bridge of her nose then blew out a frustrated breath. "But the ass is playing the me-man, me-know-what-best-for-you card. You need to know. So here we are. There is a symbol that appears on each of us to show which House we belong to. We're born with it. It's . . . Well, let me show you."

She pulled up the bottom of her shirt and showed me a tattoo above her belly button. It looked like dark blue waves that peaked into three sharp points. "I'm originally from the House of Water. You won't see this symbol around here. But that's a history lesson we don't have time for."

She tapped the tattoo on her stomach. "The placement of the symbol on our bodies has meaning. Think of a circle drawn around your torso. The lowest point close to the navel, like mine, would mean the weakest. The highest point, around your collarbone, means the greatest strength. Usually, that would signify a guide or House leader. Although House leaders' symbols are often larger than the average. That's how they're identified to start training early for leadership. And then there are those rare ones . . ." She walked over and took me by my shoulders.

"Ok, you are seriously freaking me out right now," I said, getting more nervous by the second. "I know I promised not to, but can we stop with the cryptic speak before my head explodes?"

"I'm trying to show you," Molly said. Giving my shoulders a squeeze, she looked at me as if to say "be brave," and backed me over to a floor-length mirror that stood near the foot of the bed.

"Lift your shirt," she demanded. I looked at her as if she had lost her mind. "Please, Lia. I'm your friend. You've trusted me this far. Can you please trust me a little further?"

Swallowing hard, I pulled the spandex shirt over my head and glanced down at my chest and stomach in dread, but let out a sigh of relief when I saw nothing but pale skin. No tattoos for me. I looked back up at Molly, ready to tease her about getting me all worked up, but she wasn't looking at me. Instead, she was focused on the mirror behind me, an expression of awe on her face.

Reluctantly, I looked over my shoulder. The vague image of something on my back had me twisting around to get a better look. *What the hell?* Molly tapped me on the shoulder and gave me a hand mirror so I could see my full back. Reflected in the mirror was an odd, star-like shape. There was a ragged hole in the center with bursts of various colors spreading out from that ring to the base of six black arched points.

The tattoo covered my back from between my shoulder blades to the base of my spine. It was faint but still beautiful. This was a work of art that I would have loved to discuss with the artist. If it had been any other kind of artwork that didn't involve my skin. "How . . . Bennett, that bastard. He tattooed me, didn't he? I'm going to grind his balls into sausage!"

"Whoa! Whoa! He didn't do this—well, he did—but not the way you think. And yuck, way to ruin sausage for me." Molly wrinkled her nose. "He didn't tattoo you. I'm pretty sure you were already marked. You had to be. If you were born one of us, you would have had a symbol. Yours was hidden. I don't know why or how. But when Chaos's uhm . . . stuff was . . . you know . . ." Molly mimed jacking off complete with squirting sound effects.

I laughed. "He jacked off on me, and his cum took up tattoo art?"

She looked to the ceiling, mumbling something about the gods giving her a vacation soon. "When a man from our Houses makes his 'deposit' *inside* the right woman, it forms a temporary bond. That bond usually shows up as a faint mark over the heart of the person they bond with, if they aren't Paldimori." She tapped her finger over her heart. "If they *are* Paldimori the stronger symbol is overlaid on top of the existing House symbol and replaces it when they complete the bonding. If they complete the bonding vow, the weaker partner is initiated into their bond-mate's House."

"You're saying that my having sex with Bennett caused this tattoo?"

"Not a tattoo. It's called the Desmòs—or Soul Bond. I think that's what this is, anyway. The reason Grayson knew right away what had happened was because he was being warned off." Molly flopped down on the bed and crossed her legs. "See, once the person has been marked with a bond symbol there's a sort of—well, it's like a repellent, I guess—that sends signals to the opposite sex to tell them you're taken. I think what was happening before, with all the men following you around like you had a leash on their dicks, was because you already were a Paldimori and one with strong talents. Strong powers are sought out to breed strong bloodlines. It's only happened a few times, but fighting over the chance to be taken for a test drive to bond with a powerful partner can get fierce." Molly looked at my mark thoughtfully. "It's very similar to Chaos's mark, but the colors are different. I'm not sure what it means, except that you are very powerful."

I looked into the hand mirror again. I hadn't noticed anything on his back last night. Of course, the light had been dim and there were far more interesting parts of his body to focus on. There were way too many questions and not enough time for answers. "He has this tattoo on his back?"

"Birthmark. Not tattoo. Yes, very similar. He is unique

even for us. He's the strongest Chaos we've ever had, since the original anyway."

"But what does it mean—"

Screams sounded in the distance, interrupting us. Molly and I looked at each other. "Grayson," we said together and then burst out laughing.

21

Whatever Grayson had done to clear a path worked well, and we made it back to my room without seeing a single person. After taking a quick shower, I threw on workout clothes. Molly had some explaining to do. Unfortunately, she rushed me out the door to do more training before I could ask my questions.

We went to the horse meadow. Molly had secured a chariot for us, and we practiced in the field. It was different than driving on the track. The new challenge soon had me forgetting all about my mysterious body art.

We hurried back to my room afterward to get dressed for the competition. When I exited the shower for the second time that day, Molly stood by my bed holding out scraps of an outfit that immediately had me balking. Leather. Leather and chunky chicks was not a good combo. I told her that repeatedly. She asked nicely, I'll give her that. She needed to understand that it wasn't going to happen.

"Do I need to have Chaos come help you dress?" Molly threatened, tapping her foot.

"Like I'm scared of him." I crossed my arms defiantly.

"He better keep his distance if he doesn't want to feel my foot on his balls."

"Great!" She smiled brightly. "Let me call him up here."

"Er, that's ok. He's probably doing important stuff for the Games. Like flower arrangements. You can never have too many of those."

"Oh, I'm sure he'll make time to come help his mate. You guys could work out your differences. Show him your ball stomping skills." She was struggling not to laugh. "I'm sure he'll be impressed."

"He would be. But maybe later. I've got a competition to win. And I'm *not* his mate." I glared at her. "Aren't you supposed to be telling me not to get distracted?"

"You're right. You lust monkeys can't be in the same room together." She held the clothes out to me. "Time to strap on *your* balls and put on your leather."

"Gah, that's a horrible image. You're damn annoying, do you know that?" Grimacing, I grabbed them and stomped toward the bathroom. "Fine. If I break something trying to contort my way into this, you only have yourself to blame."

Lots of grunting and cursing later, my leather-clad-self followed the sound of voices to the kitchen. Grayson stood at the counter eating an apple. His black hair was a bit more mussed than normal, but he didn't look the worse for wear for his escapades. On our way downstairs he regaled us with how he incited a bunch of bats to attack the other contestants in the gym. His descriptions of the scene of the crime had us laughing all the way down to the training area.

Molly turned right from the elevator and led us past the forest. We continued walking for several minutes until we turned into a corridor I had never seen before. We followed the dark passage until we came to a wide opening in the cave. The early afternoon sunlight shone brightly beyond the opening, and a warm breeze caressed my cheeks.

We were going outside! Finally. It felt like we had been locked away in that cave for years. I breathed in deeply, filling my lungs with the fresh air.

Lined up inside the opening to the cave, the chariots stood in a magnificent spectacle. The crude training chariots had been replaced by deadly but elaborate works of art that brought the House symbols to life. I waved at Kade and Grace as we passed by. They were checking over a chariot that looked like a short tree. The front portion was made from a massive hollowed-out tree trunk covered in inch-long thorns. Spiny branches twisted back on each side to form the sidewalls. Green leaves lined the top edge of the chariot all the way around and down to the platform in the back. Thick giant green leaves padded the inside, offering some protection from all those sharp spikes.

We moved down the line. Mikhail was leaning insolently against his gold chariot letting two female servants polish his tall boots. "Stay out of my way out there today, little girl." He sneered at me. "Wouldn't want there to be any more accidents."

Arrogant prick. As if the accident had been my fault. He was the one trying to cut me off. Well, that wasn't going to happen today. He was going to lose. "We certainly don't. I'll make sure I'm way out front so you won't have to worry about hitting me again."

"Bitch! You almost hit me a dozen times during training. Don't tell me you haven't had it out for me. Best just watch your back." He pointed his finger at my chest threateningly. "We all know you've done whored yourself out for that money. I'm here to tell you, ain't nobody winning that but me."

"We'll see about that." I turned on my heel, ready to get away from him.

Balls of flame suddenly erupted from his chariot. Backing away sharply, I bumped into Molly and sent us both sprawling. Mikhail was laughing his damn head off. I expected to see the chariot burning to the ground, but instead, it looked as if the flames were part of the design. Hammered gold formed the eye area of a face from above the brow line to mid-nose. The patina of the gold created shadows that gave the face an almost skeletal look. Within the open eye sockets were roiling balls of flame that hissed and leaped. An intently furrowed brow passed judgment over every person that walked by.

"You mind getting off me?" Molly grunted.

Oops. "Sorry."

"You've got to learn some control," Molly said, dusting herself off a bit more vigorously than was warranted. "That could have been bad."

"What? *I* didn't cause that. Did you see his chariot? The punk did that on purpose." I sent Mikhail a look that I hoped showed how much my fists wanted to make his acquaintance.

"The flames aren't supposed to shoot out like that." Molly rubbed her butt and sighed. "*You* made them do that. I felt you."

That couldn't be right. Could it? People couldn't make fire do what they wanted. Nah, Molly was just hangry or something.

There was no mistaking the next chariot as belonging to anyone but the House of Arrows. The exterior extended out like the bow of a ship into a black arrowhead point that matched the sharp blades protruding from the wheel hubs. Large arched wings in red swept back on either side of the point and wrapped around to create the body of the chariot. The horses wore red leather bridles lined with sharp black arrowhead tips that stood up at an angle atop their heads and chest plates with the House symbol. It looked like I was going into battle rather than competing in a race full of amateurs.

Even my outfit felt more suited to combat. Tight black leather pants were tucked into knee-high black boots with red flying arrow buckles. My shirt was a long-sleeved red leather tunic. That wasn't the worst part though. No, I couldn't be "Dominatrix Girl" without my trusty corset. Dia would be laughing her ass off if she could see me now. All I needed was the cape.

The corset was black with wide red seams and red laces down the back. The front was covered in a lightweight black metal plate that started below my breasts and came down to a single arrowhead point right at the top of my thighs. The sides were longer and covered my hips. The back was cut high enough to display my ass—designed with input from Eros no doubt. The bust part cupped me perfectly and was covered in red metal pieces that looked like feathers.

"You realize I look like a reject from one of those comic conventions, right?"

"Warrior princess looks good on you," Molly teased. "Lucky for you there aren't any nerds in sight. I have enough trouble keeping your harem away."

While Molly pointed out the differences in handling this heavier chariot, Grayson acted as a human force field. He sent anyone packing who attempted to get too close to me, even the other servants bringing my meal. He was telling everyone that would listen that he was now my personal servant. Between watching Grayson and feeding the horses, the time slipped by quickly.

We were signaled to mount our chariots. Molly wished me luck then left to take her place. The guides would be positioned throughout the forest to monitor the competition. Grayson helped me with my helmet. He would be waiting here for my return. I slipped my booted feet into the leather straps of the platform and gripped the reins ready to get this party started.

"All right, guys, time to kick some ass," I said through my headset.

"You got this," Molly encouraged. "Don't hold the horses back. They know what they're doing. So do you. Good luck."

We started forward, keeping the chariots in the line formation. With my visor up, I was momentarily blinded as we passed through the opening into the sunlight. Ah, real live sunlight. How I had missed it. Everything seemed more vivid. I wasn't sure if that was due to having been cave-bound or because it was absolutely beautiful here. The sky was a vibrant blue. The meadow where we halted was a sea of rich green dotted with millions of flowers. My nose tingled with a dizzying mix of lavender, rose, hyacinth and many others I couldn't name.

Stretching out beyond the meadow was a lush valley nestled amidst several mountain ranges. This would have been a spectacular view by itself. However, it was the scene that surrounded the Kyrion that awed me.

In the center of the meadow stood six tall trees that fanned out in spectacular displays of fruit-laden branches. Sitting nestled in their centers, amidst boughs that formed perfect thrones, sat the Kyrion. The men all wore black leather pants that showed off their toned legs to perfection. Eros nodded to me. Then plucked a peach from his tree and took a bite. He sprawled in his seat running a finger along the open collar of his red shirt as he seductively licked away the juice that coated his lips. A blush heated my cheeks. That man was sinful seduction wrapped in angelic beauty and splashed with mischief. God help the female population.

My eyes roamed against their will to the man in all-black surrounded by limbs of blood-red apples. Even from fifty yards away I could feel the heat radiating from him as he stared back at me. I narrowed my eyes, visualizing throwing those apples at him and knocking his ass from that tree. If he thought the tattoo on my back meant I was his mate or whatever, he had another think coming. Confusion crossed his face, and he leaned forward as if to say something.

I turned away to survey the rest of the scene. Thanks to Molly, I could now put a name to all of these beautiful faces on display. Erebus slouched insolently in a gray shirt amidst the arms of a tree bearing dark green avocados. Nyx posed seductively in a lemon tree with her assets barely concealed by a white strapless dress with an indecently short skirt. Tartarus, in a golden shirt unbuttoned to his navel, sat in rigid intensity within the arms of a tree filled with dark purple figs.

All of the Kyrion looked otherworldly sitting on their tree thrones, but Gaia was clearly the belle of the ball. She sat in the center in a massive tree that eclipsed the others by half, surrounded by branches of golden pears. Her hair fell in a cascade of curls down her bare shoulders. Her green eyes sharply measured each contestant as she lazily petted a red fox curled in her lap.

Her dress reflected every season. Springtime vines dotted with flower buds cupped her generous breasts. The vines circled around her stomach, offering large glimpses of pale skin as the buds opened into a summertime rainbow of colors. They circled her hips and a skirt of vibrant green leaves joined the array of flowers. As it reached her feet, the vines grew into tree limbs and continued to spiral toward the ground.

Birds of all kinds sat amongst the green-tipped branches, singing songs that should have sounded discordant but were oddly melodic. The green leaves transitioned into a fall medley of red, orange, and yellow. The last section of limbs, some twenty feet below where Gaia sat, showcased winter's splendor with ice-covered red berries framing a tunnel that ran through the base of the tree.

The birds abruptly stopped their song as Gaia raised her hand, and a few moments of silence filled the air. "The House of Seasons welcomes you to the first competition of the Paldimori Games. Remember rule number two. No Kyrion may aid you once the race has begun unless a unanimous decision is reached. The first to make it back through the tunnel wins. May you be as cunning as a fox and as fast as the falcon. The Forest of Epochès awaits you."

I flipped down the visor of my helmet and gripped the reins as Gaia finished her speech. Suddenly, the birds screeched then took flight, signaling the start of the race. I cracked the reins, feeling a jolt of adrenaline spike through my system as the horses took off.

We thundered across the meadow toward the tunnel of Gaia's tree. We would be forced to go through single file, which could help or hurt depending on my position in line. I reached the tunnel first. The darkness of the tunnel disorienting after the full sun of the field.

Then we were out the other side in the blink of an eye and racing toward the edge of the green forest. Once amongst the trees, I scouted for the wide dirt path just as Molly had instructed. The path was marked by a procession of tall green trees on either side, some with tightly closed buds lining their branches. Smaller saplings between the trunks of those giants struggled to make their way to the sun. Further down, the path disappeared around a sharp turn. Glancing over my shoulder, I spied Kade gaining ground. The path was wide enough for two chariots to run side-by-side, but it would be close. Snapping the reins, I urged the horses faster.

We flew down the path and entered the turn. One wheel of my chariot left the ground, and I fought to keep it level. We came to a straight section as Kade pulled ahead of me. He hadn't prepared for the change in terrain, though. Every thirty yards or so, a tree root was exposed on one side of the path or the other. Kade hit the first one head on and was knocked down onto his butt. He held on to the reins trying to keep his balance, which caused the horses to slow down considerably.

Taking advantage, I dodged around him and cut over in time to avoid the next root. Back and forth I maneuvered, missing most of the roots until the ground leveled back out. Chancing a peek over my shoulder, I was thankful to see I had gained quite a bit of ground.

Omph! Tree limbs smacked against my helmet and sent a riot of orange flowers floating all around us. *Shit! Pay attention to the road, Lia.*

We skidded around a right turn that dropped sharply downhill into a large meadow of thick grass and yellow flowers. I silently thanked Molly for this morning's training and let the horses choose their way through the knee-high grass while I scanned the tree line at the opposite end, looking for the path. Unlike the thick green forest I had left behind, the one ahead was awash in the colors of fall. The path lay beneath a set of trees that leaned heavily against each other to form an X.

I made it to the halfway point and glanced back to check on the competition. Kade had used the beaten down trail we had made to catch up with me. Now he dogged my heels while letting my horses do all the work. *Damn freeloader!*

Mikhail had taken a different route and was skirting the edge of the forest. *Damn. Damn. Damn.* He was going to beat me to the other side if I didn't do something. Redirecting the horses to cut across to the tree line several yards in front of his chariot, I hoped we would come out ahead. Mikhail picked up speed when he realized what I was doing. I urged my horses on even faster.

Minutes later, I pulled alongside him. Then Kade pulled up to my other side. We closed in on the path quickly, none of us giving way. With the trees angled over the path the way they were, two abreast would take some work. There was no way all three of us could pass through together. I yelled encouragement to Ninny and Saam, probably deafening Molly through our headset.

Mikhail edged into me, bumping my wheels. The spiked hammer protruding from the hub of his wheels slipped between my wheel spokes. *Crack!* Splinters of wood flew up. My own arrowhead hubs sliced back. With our wheels interlocked and Kade on my other side, there was nowhere to go. Seeing his opportunity, Kade pulled ahead and passed under the leaning trees first. Finally able to put some space between Mikhail and me, I urged the horses on again. If only we could gain a little ground to cut him off.

Mikhail rammed into me hard enough to throw me into the sidewall. Steadying myself, I gritted my teeth at the sound of the damage being done as our wheels locked together again. This was going to be a tight fit. The horses passed beneath the crossed trees, and I ducked down to keep from being knocked off. The side of my chariot scraped the tree, sending pieces of rough bark flying. Mikhail wasn't so lucky. His chariot rammed into the tree on the right with a horrible scraping noise. He had leaned over instead of ducking to avoid the trees and his shoulder took a direct hit. He leaned heavily against the front of his chariot and switched the reins to his one good arm.

The trees gave an ominous groan as we cleared the opening. Mikhail panicked. One-handed, he haphazardly whipped his horses into a frenzy. Idiot! With our wheels still locked together, his horses were dragging my chariot along with them. The popping of breaking roots sounded like gunshots only feet behind us. I spared a quick look back to see the trees starting to fall in our direction. They were going to topple right onto us.

We needed to free our wheels. Up ahead a break in the trees on my side of the path caught my attention. I steered the horses sharply toward it and, with a horrible crunching noise, the wheels disentangled. My chariot flew off the road and was suddenly airborne. The fall leaves on the ground had concealed a dip in the terrain. Behind me, the trees smashed to the ground.

I braced myself as the chariot slammed back to solid ground and went skidding. My poor abused wheel broke away from the hub. My side banged into the chariot wall once more and I grunted in pain. Pulling with all my might, I worked to bring the horses to a stop as the bare axle of the chariot dug up mud and leaves along the way.

Dropping my head onto the tilted lip of the chariot, I let out a relieved sigh. So much for kicking ass. Broken down was not how I saw this going. "Molly, are you there?"

"Hey, how's it going?"

"Well, it could be better." I sighed in frustration. "My wheel is shredded, thanks to Mikhail. I'm broken down."

"Shit! Ok, I'm allowed to help with this at least. I'm in Winter. Where are you?"

"My guess is Fall. Just look for the downed trees. You can't miss me," I replied with more than a hint of sarcasm.

"*What?* Never mind. On my way."

22

I took off my helmet, placing it inside the chariot as I stepped down to the ground. Ninny and Saam were a little skittish. I talked to them as I rubbed them down, checking them over for injuries. Thankfully, they were fine. My muscles, however, were tense and sore. I worked through some of the warm-up stretches, then walked back toward the path. The forest was eerily quiet and still, except for the falling leaves.

Maya, in a chariot of black flames with red tips, picked her way through the forest to get around the downed trees. She looked right at me as she passed within feet of me, but never once slowed down. She maneuvered back onto the path and then raced away.

One of the horses neighed, drawing me back to my chariot. I walked over to them, talking soothingly. The next thing I knew I slammed face first into the ground. Dazed for a moment from my forehead smacking the ground, I lay there, until the horses' whickering got me back onto my feet. I scrubbed at my dirty face with equally dirty hands, achieving little except for smearing mud around.

"Shhh. I'm coming," I told Ninny and Saam.

In the distance I could hear the sound of the other char-iots making their way around the downed trees. Strike one for me. Please let the rest of the competitions go much better than this one.

I'd only taken a couple of steps when I was flying through the air again, only to slam down to the ground several feet from where I'd been. "Owww! Son of a bitch," I hissed as pain radiated from my butt and back.

The air had felt like it thickened into a massive fist before punching me into last week. Something bizarre was going on here. Why was it that strange seemed to be attracted to me these days? I took a deep breath and inched my way onto my feet, hissing in pain with every movement. Massaging my butt, I turned in circles, listening. The empty forest surrounded me: nothing but tall trees and colorful leaves. A cool breeze filtered through the trees bringing a swirl of falling leaves. Their rustling sounds the only thing to be heard. Sweat dripped down my face, and my damp hair clung to my neck.

Something moved in the air around me. Then the air started to thicken. I spun around and raced toward the path, hoping to catch one of the other chariots. Fear shot through my veins at the thought of what—or who—could be stalking me. My feet pounded over the ground, reaching the dip I had flown over earlier. My eyes widened in terror, but my scream stayed trapped in my throat as my body was wrapped up in a boa constrictor's embrace.

The air squeezed me in its grip. There was a tugging sensation at my neck, then the grip tightened even further. My chest was burning for air, and tingling pinpricks started in my limbs. I could hear my bones creaking as they were compressed to the point of breaking.

God, please don't let me die, I pleaded. *Please don't let me be squeezed to death.*

I closed my eyes. White dots floated behind my eyes as my body began to shut down. The feeling in my limbs was gone. The creaking of my bones turned to splintering as they gave way under the pressure. Then I heard the most beautiful sound in the world.

"Lia?" Molly called. "Lia, where are you?"

Released, I fell limply to the ground. I gulped air, gasping. My dry lips tried to form words, but nothing came out. Every swallow brought agony to my bruised throat as I worked to croak out, "Molly. Here."

The sound of an ATV drew closer. My forehead dropped to the damp ground, my whole body shaking. My ribs ached with every breath. I felt pretty sure something had cracked. Cautiously, I tested my body, starting with my toes and working my way up. Miraculously, nothing seemed to be broken. Just bruised to hell.

Molly pulled up beside me and rushed over to my side. Her knees hit the ground beside my head, and her hand smoothed over my back. "My gods, Lia. What happened? Are you ok? The path is a mess back there."

My whole body shuddered before I locked it down and slowly pushed to my feet. I held up my hand warning Molly away. When my eyes met hers, she took an involuntary step backward. Anger and pain warred for supremacy as I advanced on her, backing her up several more steps before she decided to stand her ground. Wind whipped through the trees making the branches above creak and groan.

"I don't know what the hell is going on around here, and I don't care." Anger had won, and it suffused every inch of my body. A limb crashed to the ground behind her. "I'm done with this. Do you hear me? Done! I want to know what you people are and why someone is trying to kill me."

"Ok, Lia. Ok." Molly held her hands up in front of her as I stopped mere inches from her face. She looked worriedly at the branches above us. "Let's just calm down. Tell me what happened."

"*What happened?*" I stepped back and spread my arms wide to encompass our surroundings. "This damn island is what happened. The ground and the roots already tried to eat me. I was dragged around by horses. Now the damn air tried to squeeze me like I was a fucking tube of toothpaste."

"Are you saying that something attacked you?" She looked skeptical. "Did you see anything?"

"No, Molly. I didn't see a damn thing because there was nothing there!" I shouted and another branch fell. "The damn air felt like it was thickening or something. Then it lifted me up, so my tiptoes were barely touching the ground and started squeezing the life out of me. I'm telling you it was the air. The stuff that does a body good. Required to breath. Fucking air!"

"Ok, I believe you. Breath, Lia. Calm." Molly mimed taking in deep breaths, and I followed her lead. The wind died down and she looked around the forest. "Get on the ATV and go. I'll get the horses."

"I can't. I don't know how to drive that thing." I didn't need to wreck another vehicle today. "Let's fix the chariot. I'll drive it. You can follow me."

She nodded, and we got to work replacing the wheel. Molly looked over the horses once more and stayed with me as I got them back on the path.

Then we were off. My ribs and pounding head complained from the jarring ride, but I was glad to be getting out of there. Of all the things that had happened to me since I had arrived, being almost squeezed to death was the creepiest. Things were weird here. It wasn't my imagination. When we got out of this damn forest, someone would be giving me some answers.

The path became more and more covered in leaves as we went, making the chariot slide about. I drove the horses hard, ready for this to be over. The fall forest gave way to a snow-covered woodland that made me thankful for the drivers who had gone before me to mark the path. Here, pine boughs dipped with the weight of inches of snow. Icicles dangled from branches and tinkled in the breeze.

The path took us first down a steep snow-covered hill that strained every muscle and nerve I had to navigate. Next was an archway of black roses encased in ice that led down into a cave of massive icicles. They protruded up from the floor and down from the ceiling, making a hazardous obstacle course. We made it through and came to another hill. In the distance, I could see the boundary where winter ended, and the green meadow began. The finish line! We were nearly there. We just had to cross the frozen pond that separated us.

"All right, guys, last part. We're almost home free."

Slowly, we eased out onto the frozen water while Molly waited on the hill. Ninny and Saam took it in stride like they walked across ice all the time. Maybe they did. They trotted across the frozen expanse, the wheels of the chariot slipping about. White-knuckled grip on the reins, breathing shallow, I listened to the ice beneath us. The creaking and groaning sounded almost like an eerie song.

Oh, thank god! We made it across. The end was in sight. Pulling off my helmet, I breathed in deeply, taking in the fresh scent of snow. Then I turned and waved to Molly. Her turn to cross the pond.

"Let's do this, guys!" I said as I gathered up the reins.

Excruciating pain exploded in my chest. Something wet dripped onto my hand then down to the ground. Red drops trickled down like rain to stain the white snow below. My lungs struggled for air. What was wrong? What was happening? I looked down at my chest where a black arrow with red fletching protruded from under my breastplate.

That didn't make sense. Surely that couldn't be an arrow stuck in my chest. People only get shot by arrows in the movies. Then the trees swayed in a sudden gust of wind and a great flock of birds flew overhead. My uncooperative body slumped against the chariot wall. Directly overhead, the birds circled around and around in a cyclone of beating wings. Roaring sounded in the distance and the ground trembled. Another earthquake? No. The ground stopped shaking and the sound tapered off into an anguished howl.

"Lia!" Molly screamed in panic somewhere behind me. "Go! Get to the Kyrion."

The path before me began to change as the snow melted away and dry dirt took its place. Weakly, I called to Ninny and Saam. The horses seemed to sense the urgency and flew over the ground as if they had wings. Dizziness assailed me, and I wasn't sure if what I was seeing was real. "How . . .?"

The dips in the path leveled themselves flat only feet ahead of the horse's hooves. My grip on the reins and the wall of the chariot were all that kept me upright as my legs gave out. Darkness crept in and beckoned me to come rest. A jolt of pain dragged me back from the darkness. Cold. It was so cold. My heart was beating rapidly like the fluttering of all those wings.

A gray-brown owl landed on the lip of the chariot in front of me, looking me over with its big dark eyes. "There's an arrow in my chest, Owl. Who-who shoots someone with an arrow?" My weak laughter turned to wet coughing. The owl merely cocked its head.

My wheezing breath sounded abnormally loud, filling my ears to drown out all else. The darkness was visiting me more frequently with every moment. The owl still watched me from its perch on my chariot. Was any of this real? Pain ripped through my chest and I came back from the dark once more. The owl had its beak wrapped around the arrow. "D-don't ..."

It let go and looked at me as if to say, "Don't make me do it again." Oh god, as crazy as this was, it was all too real.

We thundered through the tunnel directly toward the crowd of people gathered at the finish line. We needed to stop, but my body was no longer obeying my commands. Bennett appeared beside me in the chariot. Wrapping his arm around my waist, he took control of the reins and brought us to a skidding, grass-flinging halt feet from the crowd. Then he was laying me down on the grass.

He brushed my hair back from my face. "Lia, stay with me. The doctor is right here." He looked pale and worried. He gripped my hand, then leaned down to lightly kiss my lips. When he pulled back, blood coated his lips like a garish red lipstick. Fear spiked through me. I tried to talk, but nothing came out.

Then the doctor was by my side and moved Bennett out of the way. Coldness seeped through my pores and leached into my veins. My eyes drifted to the late afternoon sunset that painted the sky in beautiful shades of orange, pink, and purple. A tear trickled from the corner of my eye as I took in the beauty.

I wish Dia was here. There was so much I wanted to tell her. My breaths came farther apart as the coldness encased my bones and organs in ice. I barely felt the doctor as he worked over me.

Molly and Grace knelt on my other side, sobbing. It was like watching a movie with the sound turned off. Everything was silent. Bennett leaned over me again, shouting something. I stared at his gorgeous face and smiled at the crazy mess of his hair that looked as if he had been trying to pull it out. I wanted to run my fingers through it, but I could no longer feel my limbs. Then I sank down into the cold depths and the darkness welcomed me home.

23

I drifted up out of my body, my astral presence floating over Bennett's shoulder. My pale body lay still on the ground, dirt-and-blood-streaked face set in a serene expression. *That's me lying there. Which means . . . I'm dead.* If I could feel anything I'd be hyperventilating right about now. The thoughts were there, but it was getting harder to reach the emotions tied to them.

This was the suckiest "vacation" ever. After all of my near misses only to end up dying at the first competition. My afterlife better be filled with me being treated like a princess, including all the chocolate a girl could eat, or I might hurt someone.

Bennett pulled me up, shaking my unresponsive body as he raged at me to open my eyes. Eros, his shoulders slumped, tried to get Bennett to let me go. "Brother, she is gone."

"No!" He jerked away from Eros's hand on his shoulder and held my body to his chest.

The arrow bumped into him, and rage suffused his face. His hand waved jerkily above the arrow, and it pushed through my chest flying several feet to embed itself in the ground. Bennett rocked me against him for a moment, whispering words too soft for me to hear. Then he lay a gentle kiss on my lips before pressing my eyes closed. He kissed each lid then smoothed the hair back from my face.

Did he really care so much?

Bennett lay me back on the ground. He dropped his head, breathing erratically as his fists opened and closed on his knees. A shudder racked his body. Gradually that vaunted control of his slipped over him like a long-lost friend as he regained his composure and rose to his feet. He held out his hand and the bloody arrow flew into his grasp as though yanked by a string. He held the arrow out, blood coating his palm as he looked over the crowd.

"Who?" he asked softly. Silence. "*Who has done this?*" he bellowed.

Bennett had mind-ninjaed that arrow to come to him. *Wasn't someone a special snowflake?* The shock should have been pouring over me, but even that was absent. Anger would have been there somewhere too. The damn man had punched a hole through the other side of me with that arrow. My body had enough holes in it already, thank you very much. I kicked his shin for good measure, and my foot passed right through him. I couldn't even be a vengeful ghost.

It figures some answers would finally come when it was too late. My suspicions were confirmed. There was something extraordinary about the Paldimori. Everything that had happened on this island I had rationalized or blown off. No more. Bennett was the son of a god or maybe a wizard. Whichever, he wasn't human.

The other contestants were showing the level of shock and anxiety I should be feeling. They stared intently at

Bennett from where they had separated themselves far away from the Paldimori. Chris had finally gotten his chance to play hero and hid Nikki behind him. She clung to him, squishing up against him so tightly his face was a comical slideshow of pleasure and horror. Maya stood defiantly at the front, narrowed eyes assessing everyone. Likely she was recalculating her strategy. Kade stood wide-legged, arms down at his sides prepared for whatever may come. His sad eyes occasionally flickered to my still form. Mikhail, his arm in a sling, scowled as if he were two-vvseconds away from kicking everyone's ass.

The guides and servants looked uneasily at each other. Still, no one came forward. Molly leaned over my body and pointed at my throat. "Look, h-her necklace is gone." Tears tracked down her face. "I-In the woods. Someone used air manipulation. Tried to crush her. It must've happened then. Someone took her protection so they could kill her."

Had that happened when I'd felt the tugging sensation at my neck? Probably. Jewelry had been the last thing on my mind while fighting to breathe. After that, all I'd wanted was to get out of there.

Who the hell would want to kill me? I was a fucking nice person.

"We have traitors amongst us." Bennett gripped the black arrow so tightly his knuckles turned white. "The accidents that befell Potential Davies were created by someone with the intent to do harm. Those attacks against our honored guest have brought shame on our Houses. But this . . . To kill a contestant . . ."

Bennett's voice was filled with vehement rage as his hands fisted around the arrow. "Someone has violated our number one rule: it is a Kyrion's sworn duty to protect all contestants who enter the Games and no intentional harm may be visited upon them. This is an act of treason; to attack a Potential is to attack your Kyrion." His dark gaze scanned the crowd. "These Games were created to help our people. To find those descendants who were lost to the human world. To strengthen our people once more. Whoever you are, you have betrayed our people in a manner we have not seen since we were forced to this sanctuary. Confess now, and your punishment will be swift. I vow that no consequences will befall your House beyond those who are responsible. Confess, so you may yet restore some honor to your House!"

Bennett stared stonily at the gathered crowd as if he could bend them to his will with only a look. The other Kyrion moved into position at his back to form a united front. Molly's sobs filled the silence. Grace sat on her knees, stunned, staring at my body. Her shell-shocked voice drifted through the air.

"She can't be dead. She's going to wake up. She has to. It was just to scare her. That's all. She was only supposed to leave."

Stunned gasps rang out as everyone turned toward her. "Grace? No. What are you saying? You . . . You wouldn't . . ." Molly stared at her in disbelief. She reached out to Grace, but Eros pulled her to her feet. She struggled, but he wrapped his arms around her.

"I'm so sorry, Molly. You can do nothing," Eros said as he pinned her to his chest. Molly kicked at him, trying to break from his hold. He murmured to her until she finally stopped fighting and stood rigid in his embrace, never taking her eyes off the older woman still kneeling on the ground.

Bennett held the arrow tip against Grace's throat. "Rise."

Grace stood clumsily and reluctantly met his gaze. Bennett jerked his head to the side, indicating she should move around my body. He glanced down briefly at my life-less form, a look of anguish crossing his face before he hardened his expression.

"I will hear your confession." When the silence stretched out, he roared, "*Speak!*"

Tears trickled down Grace's stricken face as she looked into the mask of fury before her. "It was only to scare her. Something kept going wrong. The power swelled out of control." She looked puzzled for a moment before she continued on. "I refused to do any more. They weren't happy with me, but they wouldn't do this."

So, they did have some kind of magic powers. I knew I wasn't crazy. Man-eating plants, my ass.

What I had experienced and Molly's talk about the symbol position indicating strength made sense now. Each House had their own powers, and their mark was a physical representation of the strength of that power. Grace was from the House of Seasons, whose leader was Gaia. People had once believed that Gaia was a goddess who held power over the Earth. It made a kind of crazy sense that Grace's powers had to do with the Earth. It would explain the earthquake and roots. Maybe air was another one of her tricks.

Grace continued to babble about surges of power and Houses rising. I had no idea what she was rambling on about, but she was clearly having a breakdown. Her whole body was trembling. Her fingers were wrapped in her hair as she rocked back and forth.

I was still struggling with the fact that Grace had been the one trying to kill me. It seemed surreal that this motherly figure who thought of everyone as her children could really be a cold-blooded killer.

Bennett sliced his hand through the air to cut off her ramblings. "There were others?" He pushed the arrowhead against the delicate skin of her throat. A trickle of blood traced a path down her pale neck. "Who?"

Eros left Molly to step between them and placed his hand on Bennett's arm. "Grace. Thank you for doing the right thing. You said 'they.' Air manipulation is not a power in your family. Who else was involved? Was my sister part of this?"

Grace shook her head as tears continued to pour down her cheeks. "Sh-she wouldn't."

Bennett pressed harder, cutting into her skin. Grace gasped in pain, then sobbed reluctantly, "It was—"

Her eyes rounded in surprise. Gurgling sounds issued from her gaping mouth as she clawed at her throat. Eros grabbed for her, but she was hoisted into the air before he could reach her. She flailed back and forth, clawing at her throat until bloody scratches appeared as she hung several feet above everyone's heads. People screamed, scrambling in all directions. Uselessly, I jumped to grab her foot to pull her back down. What good was being a ghost if I couldn't *do* anything?

Bennett threw the arrow aside and brought his hands up toward her. He closed his fists, made a pulling apart motion, and she plummeted downward. Bennett's power caught her and lowered her gently to the ground.

Air manipulation was clearly a power of *his*. Could someone from the House of Chaos be responsible for the attack?

"Quickly, place this band around your arm. It will null your powers but will also protect you from power intended to do you harm." Gaia stepped forward with a silver band of leaves. Grace's fingertips were an inch away from the band when she jerked backward, crying out in alarm. Then a sickening crack sounded as her head was violently wrenched to the side.

Molly screamed. Grace's body tumbled to the ground. Screaming and shouting filled the air, but I couldn't drag my eyes away from the body that lay mere feet from my own. I knelt beside her in shock.

Molly threw herself across Grace's body, wailing in agony. A great roar ripped through the air pulling me from my stupor. Bennett stood alone, his head thrown back as that terrifying roar issued from his open mouth. The ground shook, trees swayed, and anyone near him was thrown to the ground.

I should have feared the powers Bennett was channeling, but instead I ached to hold him. Even without being able to touch my emotions at that moment, that lone figure wrapped in the eye of his own storm of rage and anguish called to me. I had been there before.

The wind whipped around him in a frenzy. Dark clouds filled the sky directly above him. Tremors were still shaking the ground. He had lost all control. Now I understood why it was so important to him. I took a step toward him, wanting to offer comfort even if he couldn't feel me, but an urgent tugging sensation flared along my spine and stopped me in my tracks. It felt like a rope connected to a point between my shoulder blades, and someone was pulling on it.

Glancing around, I saw that most people had fled to the safety of the cave, the Kyrion and Molly, the only ones remaining.

That tugging sensation pulled at me again. Maybe I was still tied to my body. Catching sight of Devon and the tattooed guide carrying my body on a stretcher heading for the cave, I was torn. I sought out Bennett again. The energy around him seemed to be growing more violent. Trees were being uprooted. Lightning was scorching the ground around him. Fire writhed along the grass like snakes. Overhead, a funnel cloud was forming. The other Kyrion were cautiously approaching him, Eros in the lead.

Please help him. The rope pulled violently, almost wrenching me from my feet. I glanced at Bennett one last time. *Goodbye. I wish there had been more for us. Thank you for what you gave me in the short time we were together.* Then I let myself be pulled away.

The tugging sensation came more insistently, but it wasn't leading me into the cave after my body. I glanced up in the direction I was being pulled. It must be time to move on.

Some instinct told me what to do. Bending my knees, I pushed off the ground. To my surprise, I shot up in the air several yards and then continued to rise. The mountain was a beautiful sight against the backdrop of the sun setting over the ocean, but my attention was drawn back to the ground. Eros had braved the elements to pull Bennett into a hug. The aching in my chest eased slightly knowing that Eros would be there for him.

I had thought I was no longer capable of letting anyone get close to me, but I had been wrong. Dia had always been there, but now there were others I would've called my friends. Molly, Grayson, Eros. Even Bennett. If only I'd let them in, there could have been so much more to my life. Now, when it was too late, I wondered what exactly I had been so scared of that running away from people was easier than letting them in. I would give up heaven in a second to get another chance to truly live.

As if someone had heard me, the rope tugged harder, pulling me ever upward. The top of the mountain came into view. Heading into the twilight sky, I sensed I was no longer alone. The familiar scents of ocean and cedar reached me as the form of my dad appeared.

Dad? He smiled at me as he had a million times before and wrapped me in his strong arms.

"My little star, I've missed you. He hasn't given us much time with you, and there are things you need to know." I burrowed into his chest as he stroked my hair. "Most important you need to know we never blamed you for what happened. We knew what it meant the moment you were born, but we tried so hard to protect you. We left you unprepared for our world. We failed you, Jillian. Please forgive us."

A slender body pressed against my back and familiar fingers smoothed over my hair. "Your father is right, sweetheart. We were afraid of the prophecy. What you will be tasked with. There are so many enemies out there that still hunt us. We only wanted to protect you, but it's happening anyway."

Dad released me, and I turned to face my mom. She was as beautiful as ever, but lines of doubt that I had never seen before marred her face. "I'm so sorry, Jillian. I know you must hate me for what I did to you." She gripped my hands when I would have protested. "No, let me finish. I felt your father die and I was overcome with grief. All I could think about was that I wouldn't let them take you as well. There was so much to tell you and no time. You've walked into our world completely blind, and that is too dangerous. There are things you will have to face that we should have prepared you for. Your Bennett will do what we failed to, if you let him."

Tears slipped down my cheeks as my emotions broke through the ice. "I could never hate either of you." I hugged them to me. "You were the best parents a girl could have. I thought you hated me. I couldn't save you. I didn't—"

A sob tore from my mom's throat, and she wrapped me tightly in her embrace. Dad joined us, wrapping us both in his arms. "No, baby. Never. We could never hate you. We were so blessed to have had you. We love you, Jilli-bean."

"I love you both so much."

Dad whispered against my hair. "Be brave, my little star. You are far more special and stronger than you realize. We love you so very much, and we know you will do your best to make things right. We must go, but know we are always with you. Always."

They started to fade away and I grasped them tighter. "I love you too," I cried out. "I can't wait to see you again."

Suspended there in the evening sky, I wondered what happened now. No sooner had I finished that thought than I plummeted straight down. A vast black hole beneath me looked like the mouth of a giant beast. Surely, I didn't deserve to go to hell! Screaming, I fought hard to climb my way back up toward the sky. Then darkness swallowed me. Too afraid of what I would see, I clenched my eyes closed as I was pulled further down.

Finally, I came to a stop. Listening for sounds that would confirm I was in the depths of the devil's playground, I heard only the tinkling of water. My nose scrunched in confusion as the sweet smell of flowers drifted through the air. Surely hell didn't smell that good? Then again, maybe that was what hell was all about: teasing you with a peek of heaven that was beyond your reach.

My eyes cracked open, and I caught a glimpse of trees. This seemed familiar. I was in the courtyard on Bennett's floor. The sound of sliding stone came from behind me, and

I spun around quickly. The statue that I was so drawn to was no longer beside the pool. In its place stood a man.

Everything about him was massive. Considering that he was completely naked, I mean every golden inch of him. He was easily seven feet tall, and his midnight black hair fell in waves all the way down to the floor. His body had been chiseled by a master craftsman showcasing powerful muscles from head to toe. His face was exotic yet rugged, framed by a strong jawline. His eyes pulsed with starbursts of color, a supernova exploding over and over again.

Those mesmerizing eyes captured mine, and I couldn't look away. He took a tentative step as if testing his legs like a newborn foal. One hesitant step after another he closed the distance between us until he finally stood barely a foot from me. He lifted his hand to caress a lock of my hair, and his fingers brushed against my cheek.

"*Lyannìa, astèri mou.*"

He continued to murmur to me in a language I couldn't understand as he trailed his finger along my jaw. I was lost in the beautiful cadence of his voice and the kaleidoscope of his eyes. He pressed his lips against my forehead. Then tilted up my chin as his lips neared mine. I shook my head, breaking the trance.

"Whoa, buddy." I pushed him away, and he let me. Then I jerked my hand back, my fingers tingling as if there was a live current under those rock-hard pecs. "I don't know who you are, freaky-eyed naked guy, but you need to keep your lips to yourself."

He gave me a puzzled look then stepped uncomfortably close and gripped my face in both hands. His eyes pulsed dizzyingly as he stared into mine. Pressure built in my head. It felt as if someone was flipping through the Rolodex of my memories. "You . . . you are not my beloved." His voice was bitter. His hands tightened on my face briefly before he let me go and stepped back. "Yet you are her blood."

I blinked rapidly. What the hell was that? *Note to self: Don't look the naked dude in the eyes.*

"Ok, big guy, whatever you say. You need to respect the personal space, though. Got it?" I gestured to the distance between us, and then tapped my finger against my temple. "That means whatever freaky mind meld you pulled, too. Uh, and can you put Mr. Winky away before someone gets clubbed with that thing?"

"Mr . . . Winky?" he said with a husky accent.

He tilted his head to the side as if trying to piece together what I meant. Hopefully, he'd figure it out soon, sex-ed not being my forte. He glanced down at himself and seemed to make the connection. Then he laughed in a booming voice that made me jump. "This is—how do you say—comedy?"

"Comedy? Oh, you mean a joke. Yeah, haha. For real though, can you put that away?"

He smiled, and, all of a sudden, a purple himation was draped about his body. The man could set a new trend for sheet-wearing he looked that good. *Ignore the eye candy, Lia.*

"Thanks," I mumbled. "So, I take it you're not from around here. The freaky eyes kinda give it away. Who are you?"

"I am Chaos."

Yeah, he was channeling Groot like a pro. "Uh-huh, guess that makes two of you then. Is there a numbering system I need to know about? Should I call you Number Two?" I smirked, but he stared back at me, clearly not sharing my sense of humor. Oh well, I was an acquired taste.

"I am Chaos," he repeated. "You would prefer my human name?"

"That would probably make things less confusing."

"I was once called Titan Theophanes. The Chaos you refer to is—how do you say—my seed?"

"Geez, do you guys have no imagination or is it an ego thing to name everything after yourself? You know what, never mind. I can guess. I don't know about 'seed,' but maybe you meant like a relative?" He nodded. "Clearly you don't mean your son. You guys look about the same age. What kind of relation are we talking about?"

"My age is incalculable. Your Bennett is but a babe. He is many times the son of my son. He is mightier than many before. This is good. Necessary. What comes will not be easy."

He stared off over my shoulder for a moment as if he could see the future that clearly, the sharp angles of his face set in grim determination. Then he looked down at me, and his expression softened. "That is why you are here. You woke me from my slumber."

"What do you mean? This is the first time I've ever met you."

"You touched my other form." He struggled to find the right words. "My ... phallus?"

I glanced down before I could stop myself. "I have *not* touched your penis! If anything, it was touching me." I glared at him. "Personal space, know it and respect it."

He seemed taken aback for a moment before he roared in laughter. "I did not mean Mr. Winky, as you call it. When I was stone. You touched me then."

"Wait, you were the statue?" I glanced at the spot where it had been. Guess they weren't redecorating. "How could you be a statue?"

"Yes, statue. It is one of many forms. My father is the God of Chaos. I am made of him. I created my brothers and sisters, also blessed by him. The six Houses are . . . relations."

"They're your descendants. That's why they have powers." He nodded. "Wow, so you were never born? You didn't have to suffer through teenage acne. You just poofed into existence." My god—or gods—this was insane. I was talking to a magical being who was possibly the first to set foot on Earth.

"We were formed as adults, yes." He looked at me intently. "I cannot tell you all you need to know. Our time grows short. You must go back, or all is lost. I see the path that must be taken. You are needed, but there are others."

He held out his hand, and a dark orb appeared. The starry nebula within the orb swirled and pulsed like his eyes. Then it floated up above our heads. Six black rays descended from the orb and formed into the House symbols I recognized. Then other lines formed and connected to other symbols beneath those. They all glowed brightly for a moment before some of the second set of symbols faded until they were barely visible. The six main House symbols faded only slightly. All except the one for the House of Chaos, which shone almost as brightly as before.

"The House strengths are as they appear. The six Houses of the Order of Chaos have grown weak—impure. The enemy has been invited in. They rise once more. You must find the others for the Order to regain power. The Game must continue. Gather your soldiers, little warrior."

"What . . . How—" I gasped as my chest felt as if it had been ripped open. "What's happening?"

"You must go back. Remember what you have seen." He gestured to the group of symbols. "Enemies hide amongst allies. Allies amongst enemies. Two Houses had healing power such as yours. There you might find answers."

There were so many more questions. Pain ripped through my chest again, taking away my breath. Cold seeped into my body and made me shiver. It felt as if I had been submerged too long in an icy lake and my body was bursting to take a desperate breath. Titan's hand caressing my cheek drew my attention back to him. That rolling bed of emotions within the statue—within him—reached out to me as he stared sadly at my face. "You look so much like her. Take care, blood of my beloved. Perhaps one day we shall meet again. I must return to my slumber. It is not yet my time. Find the twin Houses of the Olympian Omàda."

Titan held his hand out toward me, and something pushed against my chest.

I tumbled down ... down ... down.

24

I opened my eyes with a gasp. Where was I? What had happened? Fighting to sit up, my lungs thirstily gulped for air. My eyes burned against the light, and my head throbbed painfully. My throat felt raw as if I had been screaming for hours. And my chest—my chest felt so sore.

"Easy, my lady. Easy. Please, you must not injure yourself again," Grayson said as he gripped my shoulders to ease me back down onto the hard surface.

"Wh . . . Wha . . ."

Grayson lifted my head and placed a straw to my lips. My raw throat objected to each swallow, but the cool liquid felt good as it went to work quenching my thirst.

"Slowly, my lady," he cautioned and pulled the cup away when I finished.

My eyes closed against the pain as I struggled to take a full breath. Systematically, I flexed my muscles to work the blood back into my stiff extremities as I tried to remember what had happened.

I had crossed the frozen pond and the finish line was in sight. Then agony unlike anything I had ever experienced exploded through my chest. The chariot wall had caught me as the strength left my body. Blood had flowed from around the arrow imbedded in my chest with an ominous slowness like the world had been shifted into slow motion. It had dripped onto the snow, soaking into each ice crystal to create a vivid Rorschach painting. Frantically, I patted my chest, still expecting to find an arrow lodged in my lung.

Grayson grabbed my hands. "You are still healing. By the gods, I thought we had lost you, my lady!" His hazel eyes glistened wetly as he squeezed my hands against his chest. "Never worry me so again."

"Don't worry." I squeezed his hands in return, my voice a raspy whisper. "No more chariots or arrows for me. Thank you for taking care of me."

"It was my honor, my lady. But I fear our friendship may cause my hair to gray. Perhaps I will appear sophisticated enough to capture the ladies' hearts." His smile was strained as he tried to lighten the mood.

"The ladies would love you even if you were bald, Grayson."

"Never jest about the hair, my lady." An exaggerated look of horror crossed his face. "Women prefer men with hair they can run their fingers through. I would never disappoint them."

Fresh waves of pain ripped through my chest when I chuckled. "Ouch! Ok, no laughing."

Grayson placed a kiss upon the back of each hand. "Please rest. I will be but a moment."

When he disappeared, I traced the hole where the arrow had pierced my clothes and probed the tender skin beneath. I whispered a prayer of thanks that I was still alive. A shiver shook me bringing me back to the present. Light rippled across the low rock ceiling above me, and the sound of running water filled the air. Goosebumps peppered my skin as the cold rock floor I was laying on stole what little warmth I had. My clothes felt welded to my skin with grime and dried blood. All I wanted was to strip every piece of clothing from my body and soak in a hot bath until warmth replaced the cold ache. As weak as I felt, that wasn't going to happen anytime soon.

Grayson knelt beside me again, assessing me with a concerned look.

"Where are we?" I asked.

"The hot springs. It is part of the training floor, but inaccessible to the Potentials. This place is sacred to our people. We will not be disturbed. We thought you dead, my lady." Grayson looked as if he still wasn't sure if I was a figment of his imagination. "Ordinarily, women are selected to care for our dead. They bring the loved one here to be cleansed and anointed for proper burial. Molly would have seen to you, but she grieves so for her mother. I was granted permission to perform the honor in her stead."

Holy schnikes, I had died! Fear and anxiety rolled in my belly. "Wait, are you saying Molly's adoptive mother died?"

"Sadly, yes. Grace adopted Molly when she was found as a young child." Grayson hesitated a moment. "I am sorry, my lady. I have sad news that I am sure will burden your heart, but I feel you should know." He wrapped his long fingers around my hand and stared into my eyes sadly as he explained what had happened after I died.

Poor Molly. I knew the pain of losing a parent all too well. "Molly shouldn't be alone right now. Please take me to her," I said.

"I do not think it wise, my lady," Grayson replied. "There is much unknown about those who wished you harm. Kyrion Eros is with her." He pulled a large vase near and withdrew a wet cloth. "For now, let me help you refresh."

Too bone weary to be stubborn, I didn't argue. "Grayson, I don't understand. Why would anyone want to kill me?"

Grayson wiped the warm cloth across my forehead slowing removing the dirt and grim. He worked his way down my cheeks and to my neck, his brow furrowed in thought. I sighed and closed my eyes in bliss.

Then his soft voice broke the silence. "The Games are more than contests to my people. The Potentials are necessary." He worked the cloth over my arms. "Do you remember the invitation for the Games?" At my hummed response, he continued. "What is seen when holding the card is different for every person. Most will see nothing. Others—special people like you—see the invitation."

That explained the changing messages on the card. What made them—me—so special? "Potentials are important to us," Grayson explained. "They are protected, always. To harm a Potential is to harm our families. The rules that govern the Kyrion have never before been broken. Now that they have, I fear what the consequences will be for my people."

He dipped the cloth back into the vase with a trouble expression. "We have enemies that would see us wiped from the earth. There are rumors that you are one of the Chosen we have been searching for and that our enemies know this. That Grace was working with them. I only know that you are special. I felt it the moment we met." His fierce expression pinned me. "I have bound myself to your service, and I would die to protect you."

They had the wrong girl if they were looking for a savior. I couldn't even save myself. "Grayson, I'm not—"

He balled the cloth tightly in his fist. "Do you understand who we are as a people, my lady?"

There was something that tugged at the back of my mind, something important. I focused on that thought for a moment, but every time I tried to bring it into focus, it slipped farther away. Giving up, I fumbled my way through a response. "As crazy as this sounds, I think . . . there is some kind of power that your people possess. It's insane, but the things I've seen . . ." I shifted, feeling self-conscious about the crazy pouring from my mouth, but I couldn't deny what I had experienced here. "Each House seems to have their own power. Like the House of Seasons has power over earthy stuff."

"You are not crazy, my lady." Grayson gifted me with his boyish smile. "Yes, it is true that we all have a degree of power. But who we are is not only what we can do. You have met Kyrion, guides, and servants from all of our Houses. What do you see when you look at us?"

Words rolled off my tongue before my brain engaged, "Tradition. Inequality. Arrogance." I blushed when I realized what I had said. "Uh, sorry, that was rude. I was never good at pop quizzes."

He laughed. "You may always be truthful with me, my lady. Yes, those things exist. Your time here has been short, and we are good at hiding what we do not admit even to ourselves. I will tell you something of our history so that you may understand."

He dipped the cloth in the vase once more and picked up my hand. "A very long time ago our people were once called Chaonians. We were a proud and powerful people who thought ourselves invincible. Superior. Over time civilizations rose and fell. Sometimes the Chaonians played a guiding hand, sometimes they simply watched from afar.

They did not fear for themselves, for who would ever dare oppose them?

"When I was a young boy my abuela would tell me stories of our ancestors." A fond smile spread across his lips. "Her favorite tale was what she called the Dawning. She said it was an end for our people and a beginning. A beginning that I would one day play a part in defining. She would recite this old proverb when she spoke of it: 'Faces we can see, hearts we cannot know.' She would say, love and hate are two sides of the same coin and somewhere between the two lies treachery."

When I looked at him strangely, he laughed. "It was not a fairy tale kind of story, my lady. It began with a great celebration that is held by my people during the winter solstice each year. For those days of celebration, all Houses are welcome, and everyone is treated as equal." Grayson dipped the cloth angrily into the vase. "It was during one of those times that our ancestors were betrayed. Many died that day. Whole families were lost. Our leader saved those he could by hiding them away here on this island. Now our people call ourselves Paldimori. It is a name for what we have become—descendants of power who have hidden so long that we have become the shadows.

"You are an artist?" Grayson asked abruptly, looking up from his task.

"I like to think so. Although I haven't created much myself since I opened my gallery," I admitted.

"What type of art do you create?"

"I do charcoals, but my real love is glass work. I've always wanted to create glass that shows the depth and breadth of life. I'm drawn to realism." The window in my gallery was symbolic of the paths in life, but it was a realistic representation of the divergence of my own life. "I've always thought that there is beauty enough in the real world without having to create the abstract."

"The Paldimori are like your abstract art. We have been remolded until we barely resemble our heritage. That is who we have become, shadows who live in shadow. Fear is our cloak, and we wear it well. Yet there is promise buried beneath the surface, my lady." Grayson gave me an imploring look. "It is there, waiting to be shaped by the right hands. We could be a powerful people once more."

His boyish face was so full of hope. My heart hurt that I would be the one to extinguish that light. This person they were looking for wasn't me. Inside, I was still that scared young girl who had tried to outrun her problems. It had taken actually dying to finally understand that you can't outrun yourself.

Looking back now, I could admit that I had panicked. The threat of losing the gallery—of losing something else I loved—had dredged up the pain of losing my parents and weakened the pavement of my lonely highway. That pain and loss, which had never been dealt with, combined with everything going on in Port Lawson had sent me spiraling. I'd run again, in a way. Winning these Games wasn't going to stop the rumors or give me back my reputation. It wouldn't stop the person who started the rumors or heal the gaping wounds I'd tried to pave over. Nothing and no one could do that but me.

My journey of healing had begun the night I opened up to Bennett. There was still a long way to go, but I had shined a light on that darkness revealed by the cracks in my highway. Now the landscape was changing. Where once there had barren wasteland, grass now dotted the landscape. My mother's screams and the roaring of the water that the highway had concealed had quieted. The pain and grief were still there, but they weren't a debilitating force driving me to self-destruction. I doubted I would ever stop missing my parents, but now there was something else. Hope and the realization that my path in life didn't have to be lonely.

I realized now that I'd never stopped running. From my past, from relationships, and from myself. It was time to let things go. To stop locking myself away from life and those who were important to me. Especially Dia, who deserved so much better. She had let me set boundaries on our friendship these last few years, but she deserved a friend who was as vested as she was.

I knew now what I had to do when the Games were over. It was time to face my past. It was time to live instead of keeping myself locked away like a ghost in an empty estate where I was too afraid to open the door. Whatever waited for me when I got home, I would handle, because life gave you hope. Only death was final.

"I'm sorry, Grayson. I'm not sure who you think I could be, but you've got the wrong person," I said regretfully. "I'm no crusader. I have a life and a terrific friend waiting for me back home. I have a lot to make up for. I've been a coward. But I've got a second chance at life. I plan to make the most of it."

My heart ached to see the hope in those bright hazel eyes die out. "We are a resilient people, my lady. Do not worry for us." A tear slipped down my cheek as he pasted on a fake smile. "Whatever life has in store for you, I wish you much luck and happiness. I am grateful to have been able to serve you while you have been here. Now, I will go and secure your clothing. I am sure you would like to change."

He dropped the cloth back in the vase then stood abruptly, putting distance between us as if he couldn't stand to be near me one second longer. His forced smile made me want to be what he needed if only to not disappoint him. "Do you need assistance into the water?" he asked.

"Grayson, I—" I started awkwardly, but I wouldn't make him false promises. Sighing, I gingerly pulled myself into a sitting position. "I think I've got it. Thank you for everything." Looking up at him through teary eyes I asked, "Is this goodbye?"

His expression softened. "My people do not believe in saying goodbye, my lady. We say, 'Until we meet again may the gods guide you and look favorably upon your House.'"

Shakily, I got to my feet to give him a hug, but my stiff legs couldn't get the hang of walking again so quickly. I started falling, and overcompensated plowing right into Grayson. He hadn't expected to be tackled by a wild woman and lost his balance.

Tangled together, we hit the water and sank. My muscles seemed to be turning liquid with the warmth of the water, making me a useless weight that was pinning Grayson to the bottom of the well-lit pool. He grinned in amusement at our predicament. I nodded sharply toward the surface and he placed my arms around his neck to help me to my feet. I thunked my forehead onto his chest, breathing heavily in the chill air. Grayson pulled my limp body closer, securing me to him as I mumbled against his chest.

"What was that, my lady?"

The water level was right around my collarbone. Right now, it was looking pretty inviting. Maybe I could sink back underwater and stay there. Forever. Or at least until I was sure I wouldn't die of humiliation. "I'm so sorry! I'm a walking hazard. You should probably escape now before I manage to drown you."

Grayson laughed. "My lady, there is no need to apologize. I do believe you gave me exactly what I needed. A dip in the water to wash away my bad manners." He brushed my hair back over my shoulders. "I am sorry for the way I acted. You have been through much. I had no right to ask you to give up your life for people who have shown you little kindness and much pain." I looked up into those kind eyes. That wasn't true, I had found a few friends among the Paldimori. "Here, let me help you to the ledge so you may sit."

Grayson scooped me up and carried me across the pool to sit on a sunken ledge that brought the water line down to my navel. I was relieved to see those beautiful eyes shining once more. "We are already wet," he said with a grin. "Would you like me to help you bathe, my lady?"

My skin tingled in awareness that we were no longer alone. "That will not be necessary, Grayson," Bennett's said softly, sending my pulse spiking. "I will assist Potential Davies with whatever she may require."

So much for being my dedicated servant—Grayson fled without a backward glance.

25

Bennett stood before me, bare chest gleaming with droplets of water. I refused to let my eyes follow those droplets to see what the crystal clear water would reveal as they headed south. He plowed across the cave pool with purposeful intent and came to a stop, mere feet in front of me. Dark eyes scanned me from head to toe, leaving a trail of heat in their wake. His face was a blank mask, but an almost tangible river of emotions churned in the air around him. There was so much tangled together that I couldn't decipher one emotion from another. His hand lifted as if he would touch me. But his fingers curled into a fist, and he let his hand fall back to his side.

Caution was required here until I could figure out which side of this complicated man was standing in front of me right now: the lover who had held me while I cried or the condescending asshat who expected everyone to bow to him. "So, I'm Potential Davies again?" I said. It hurt to hear him call me that after everything we had shared.

His jaw hardened, and his eyes narrowed. A blast of

emotion almost knocked me over. It was almost like I was tuned into his radio frequency. Right now, it was blaring.

"You do realize Grayson is several years younger than me, right? You have nothing to be jealous about."

Bennett crossed his arms over his chest, staring at me intently. "*Then why was he going to bathe you?*"

His reply was sharp and clear although he never opened his mouth. I notched my chin into the air and glared back my own response. "*Because he's a friend. Some people actually have friends. The kind that will help you out when you're too weak to even bathe yourself. I'm sure you wouldn't know anything about that.*"

Bennett's eyes widened in surprise a moment, and then his scowl deepened. "*You are mine. No one else may touch you in such a fashion. Tell me.*"

"*Stubborn, pig-headed man.*" Mockingly, I crossed my arms. Outrage was refueling my energy. Bennett's lips twitched as if he had heard my thought. "*I'm not property. You can't go around saying I'm yours. I decide who I let touch me and how.*"

"*You* are *mine.*" His rumbling voice floated through my mind.

"Did . . . did you just speak in my head?" Call me slow. Blame all those wet muscles on display. What woman's brain wouldn't be fried?

Bennett stilled, his expression carefully blank. That roiling ball of emotions swirling around him suddenly cut out of existence. "Yes."

"*Cryptic much?*" I would have missed his reaction if I hadn't been looking for it. His jaw flexed, and those sexy pecs twitched. "You heard that too, didn't you? What have you done to me? How is this possible?"

"There is a connection between us." That tic started in

his jaw. "It is special amongst my people. An honor. When two people are able to share themselves through such a connection."

Holy alien cooties! He'd infected me with their unique brand of crazy. "Unplug us or whatever. I didn't agree to any kind of 'connection' with you. I told you I'm not a damn piece of property! You are invading my privacy."

He gripped my thighs, pushing them apart to make room for himself. I couldn't stop him even if I wanted to, with my stupid body still not working right. I tipped my head back, pissed off that he had outmaneuvered me. His fingers trailed along my cheek, leaving my skin tingling in their wake. Damn sexy bastard!

The temptation to lean into that touch was almost overwhelming. His fingers tangled in the hair at the base of my neck, and he gently pulled my head back. His other hand traveled up my thigh and around my waist to rest on my lower back. Then he brought my hips up against his. I balanced precariously on the muscular arm against my back as I flailed about searching to find purchase. The smug bastard left me with no choice but to cling to him. Gripping his shoulders, I wrapped my legs around his waist.

A menacing smile crossed his face as he bared his teeth and said, "There is no unplugging. And I will invade you in any way I see fit. Possession is nine-tenths of the law, so they say. Should I wish it, you would be locked away in this tower for eternity."

"Like hell!" I thrashed against him. "I am *not* your possession."

He tightened his grip on me, pulling me more firmly into him. Then leaned over me until he was inches from my face and growled, "I have watched you die this day. Do not think to fight me on something we both know to be true."

Bennett's mouth slammed down on mine. His lips stole any further protests and replaced my fury with a different kind of heat. It sank beneath my skin at every point we touched and settled low in my belly. My fingers tangled in his damp hair, giving the locks a tug. He grunted against my lips.

Suddenly, wind whistled all around us and had my mouth not been occupied in other ways I probably would have screamed. Then my back hit a wall. Bennett released my mouth momentarily to gaze down at me. The air around him pulsed with an intense need that made my skin buzz. "Stay with me this night."

Could I? *Yes.*

Should I? *Most definitely not.*

This man wrecked my composure and brought things out of me I never knew I could feel. So why did I find my lips forming the word "yes"?

He lowered me until my feet touched the floor, and then turned me to face the wall. His hands traveled down the tight leather encasing my hips and around to my rear to give it a squeeze. His nimble fingers made quick work of my corset ties, and it fell with a damp clatter to the floor. The rest of my clothes were peeled from me slowly as he kissed every inch of exposed skin.

My forehead rested against the wall, my hands balling into fists as I shifted my stance, trying to ease the ache that had settled at my core. Bennett pressed against me, his hard, naked body covering mine from head to toe. His fingers twined with mine as he pulled our hands up above my head and pressed them to the wall, silently telling me what he wanted.

He nudged my feet apart and curled his hands around to my front to tug at both of my nipples, eliciting a moan from me. His hands dropped down to my hips where he traced along my groin before plunging two fingers into me without warning. *Yes!* A gasp of pleasure escaped my parted lips as lightning shot through my body. His fingers slipped from me, and I whimpered in protest. His cock pushed between my thighs to rub me. My wetness coated him and a rumbling sound like a purring lion came from behind me.

"Brace yourself, *asteràki*. I need to be inside you now," Bennett said gruffly as he placed a kiss between my shoulder blades.

My fists clenched against the wall as I felt him nudge against my opening. He felt impossibly large as the head of his cock pushed into me. I squirmed against his relentless invasion, and a loud crack split the air as his hand landed on my ass cheek. The stinging sensation only added to my excitement. "Take me, Lia. Let me feel the tight warmth of your embrace."

Need clawed inside me so intensely I was sure I would combust. An eternity seemed to pass as he slowly worked himself inside me. My fist pounded at the wall as I bit my lip. The urge to push back and take him all the way had me fighting against the pressure of his hold on my hips. His hand landed once more. *Smack!* Oh god, yes! That was almost enough to push me over. "Do you feel me, Lia?" He pressed a kiss between my shoulder blades when I felt him bottom out. "Do you feel how your body takes me perfectly? This is who we are. Pieces of a puzzle that fit together perfectly."

He pulled out slowly, hitting every pleasure point as if he had a roadmap. Then he moved back into me just as slowly. His torturous pace had me keening with need. My nipples felt impossibly tight. My core was on fire. If he would just move! His hands traveled around to cup my breasts, and I hissed as his fingers grasped my hard peaks.

"Tell me," he said. "What do you feel when I do this?" When I didn't answer right away, he slammed into me. "What about this?"

The breath exploded from my lungs, and I dropped my head against the wall, panting. Need pulsed through every nerve ending. My palm slammed against the wall as he held motionless inside me. My hips twitched, trying to move on him. So close. Just a little more. He pressed me flat against the wall. "Ahhh. *Move*. You bastard." A wail of frustration left me. "I'm going to kill you if you don't move!"

He only chuckled and nipped my earlobe, spiking my need even higher. I tightened around him where we were joined. Bennett's quickly drawn breath brought a smile of smug satisfaction. He withdrew and rubbed against my butt. "Should I leave you like this, Lia? Wet and wanting while I spill my seed on your beautiful bottom?"

"No, damn you!" I cried out. "I-I feel heat and fullness. I feel like lightning bolts are zinging through my veins straight to my core every time you move. Like my heart could explode at any moment, and I wouldn't care as long as you keep touching me. Is that what you wanted, you bastard? Is that enough?"

"For now." He pressed the head of his penis against my back opening. My cheeks clenched involuntarily at his double meaning. He eased us away from the wall and pulled me flush against his chest. He tugged my hair until I rested my head against his shoulder and turned my face up to him. Dark eyes rimmed in light blue stared back at me, seeming to pulse in time with the heavy thud of his heart against my back.

Another pair of eyes that were an explosion of supernovas flashed through my mind. Then Bennett kissed my lips tenderly, and the image was lost. My moan whispered against his lips as he slammed back into me once more. The frantic pace rocketed me into an orgasm as I pried my lips from his to cry out his name. Slumping against him, my shaky legs could no longer hold my weight. He slipped from me and hoisted me up into his arms. I got a brief glimpse of his bedroom as he carried me across the room.

No wonder he was always popping up unexpectedly. He could teleport. These Paldimori and their powers were scarily amazing. I would definitely have to put a bell on him.

Bennett lay me gently down on his bed and settled between my thighs. He took my hand and wrapped it around his shaft. He let me explore him for a moment before he grunted and wrapped his hand around mine to still my movements. "Do you accept me, Jillian Nova Davies?" He searched my eyes as he used our joined hands to place himself at my opening. I tried to pull him into me, but he held still. "You must say the words as you take me, Lia. Say 'I accept you, Bennett Theo Young.'"

I growled at him. Literally growled. My grip tightened as we worked together to slide him into me one inch at a time. "Yes! I accept you. You demanding . . . oh . . . orgasm-with-holding-ass, Bennett Theo Young."

He laughed triumphantly as he finally slid all the way inside me. The blue around his eyes pulsed brighter as he slowly leaned down to take my lips. Finally, he started to move. The pleasure built slowly, but soon we were both covered in sweat. The tingling started in my toes and moved up my body as I neared the precipice. My hips rocked up impatiently to meet him, making him groan.

Bennett rolled us until I straddled him. Wasting no time, I set a faster pace, racing headlong to my pleasure. Damn this man, I couldn't get enough of him. Our eyes locked and I stared in fascination as the blue rings started to bleed inward toward his pupils. The air around us felt charged with electricity. Every time I impaled myself upon him a spark seemed to ignite within me that had me hovering on the razor's edge of release. He brought one hand up between my breasts and pressed the other between my shoulder blades. A kaleidoscope burst behind my eyes as I tripped over the edge into bliss. Bennett's warmth spilled inside me as he grunted his own release.

My eyes drifted slowly open to find in his a full explosion of the cosmos as he whispered, "Body of my body. Soul of my soul. We are one."

26

The afternoon sun shone brightly through the plane window as I looked out at the fluffy white clouds below. I sipped from my water bottle, ignoring the meal on the tray in front of me. My thumb rubbed absently at the ring on my finger as my thoughts drifted back once again to the morning.

Waking to the heat of Bennett's body pressed along my spine had been a glorious feeling. My left leg draped over his thigh, his calloused fingers caressing my skin. Shifting back against him had been all the encouragement he'd needed to sink inside me. We had made slow, silent love, letting our hands and lips map each other's bodies. We'd found our release together as we watched the first rays of sunlight pour across the sky from the wall of windows in his bedroom. He had silently held me in his arms until our breathing slowed and the sweat on our bodies started to cool.

I was sinking toward sleep when his gruff voice stated, "You are leaving."

"What?" Wide-awake now, and with a sinking sensation

settling in my stomach, I pulled myself into a sitting position against the headboard. "What are you talking about?"

"You cannot stay on the island." He got out of the bed to pull on his pants. His carefully blank expression when he turned back to me cut me to the core. "You must leave now before everyone wakes. The fewer people that know you are still alive, the better."

That was the condescending voice of Chaos, the arrogant leader of the Paldimori that I had met that first night. My heart squeezed painfully. Why was he doing this? If he wanted to get rid of me, why ask me to stay the night? His expression said clearly that our time together had been a cheap thrill that had now grown tiresome. Grabbing the sheet, I wrapped it around my naked body as I shot out of the bed we had made love in only minutes before.

My throat burned with unshed tears, feeling too tight to form words. My shoulders were rigid as I walked over to the wall of windows. *Don't you dare cry! He isn't worth it.*

He had been so attentive and understanding the night I told him about my parents. Each time we made love he had claimed me as his own and wrenched that same confession from me. He had believed in me and brought me back to the world of the living. He had made me lo—No, it wasn't that! I didn't love him—this was just sex. Amazing sex.

"I thought you said I was a warrior that needed to use my sword?"

Rustling sounded behind me as he pulled on the rest of his clothes. "I was wrong. You are an artist. What would you know of wielding swords?" His tone dripped with contempt. "I will make the arrangements for your departure. Grayson and the others must be seen mourning your loss, to avoid suspicion."

I pulled the sheet tighter around myself like armor to

deflect his callous dismissal. My shovel was poised to bury this and start a new section of my lonely highway. No, not anymore. Mentally I pitched the shovel aside. I wasn't going to locking myself away again because of a man. Besides I was here to win the prize and there were five more chances. I turned to face him. "No."

His gaze swept over me and for a moment I thought I saw relief written there. Then his expression hardened as he stalked toward me, his hair a wild mess. My fingers twitched as I remembered running them through that soft hair. That was over. Lust wasn't going to control me.

"You have no choice, Potential Davies." Bennett growled. "I am the law here."

"I came here for a reason," I said as I crossed my arms and planted my feet. "And I'm not leaving until I complete the Games."

He stepped right up against me, making my traitorous body tremble in reaction to his nearness. I checked my instinct to step back and stood my ground. His dark eyes blazed down at me in fury that I would dare defy him. "You *will* be on that plane if I have to carry you there myself."

"You're done with me, fine. Message received. I didn't come here for you. I came here for me." I pushed past him. "Now get out of my way. I need to get to training."

He grabbed my arm and before I knew what was happening, we had been swept away. The times before when he had teleported me, I had been too distracted to pay attention. This time I experienced it all. It was like riding a rocket into outer space without a suit. The wind whipped by at a dizzying speed. The breath was sucked from my lungs. My body felt like it was ready to break apart into a million pieces.

We came to a halt seconds later, and I stumbled into

him. My stomach churned as I struggled to regain my balance. He held me to him as he whispered against my hair in that lilting language of his. Forcing down the bile trying to choke me, I pushed away from him. Gripping my spinning head, it took me a moment to realize we were in my bedroom on my floor of the tower. Eros watched us with a smug smile as he leaned against one of the nymph statues near the bed.

His gaze filled with appreciation as he took in my disheveled state. Then his brows pulled down in puzzlement, his eyes darting back and forth between us. He squinted at me. Then abruptly straightened from his position. "Holy shit-bagel sandwich. What were you thinking, brother? Or maybe I should ask what you were thinking *with*."

I would have laughed at Eros using a Molly-ism if all my energy hadn't been focused on not throwing up. Ignoring them both, I went to the bathroom. Taking small sips of cold water from the sink to settle my stomach, I silently hoped Bennett would leave. After a quick shower, I pulled on my workout gear. He thought I wasn't a warrior. Well, time to prove him wrong.

Bennett was alone when I walked out. We stared at each other across the room, each of us determined to get our way. None of his emotions or thoughts were filtering through to me. Mine were locked down tight as well. He wouldn't get any free ammo from me. Bennett approached me and took my hand in his. I wanted to pull away, but I was done letting him see how strongly he affected me. He gazed into my eyes, his own doing the pulsing thing again as he slipped something onto my finger. That lilting language poured from his lips again as his hands cupped mine. Then he walked away.

That had been too easy. Something was wrong. I glanced down at the weight on my finger. And rubbed over the smooth surface of the black ring. Beneath the clear top layer, a blue-black mountainous terrain glimmered. I don't know how long I had been standing there before Eros came to get me. Eros refused to tell me about the ring but warned me not to take it off. Assuming it was another piece of protective jewelry, I let it go. This time I would make damn sure to keep it on.

We headed off to training. Or so I thought.

That assumption was rectified as soon as we stepped off the elevator into the hallway I had first walked down after we landed. That sneaky ass jerkwad had let me believe I had won, only to have Eros do his dirty work. My fist pounded the Up button, but nothing happened. *Shit!* It required a key to open the doors at this level.

Eros leaned against the wall and crossed his arms looking amused as I cussed and kicked the elevator door until I ran out of steam. Using my nonexistent flirting skills didn't help either. Apparently whatever pheromones I had been giving off when I first arrived had worn off. Eros laughed his ass off. After which he had the nerve to ask how I had ever managed to get a date. The kick to his shin provided some short-lived satisfaction.

With no other alternative, I reluctantly walked to the airplane. Turning to Eros, I held my hand out to him. "You're just as bad as he is," Eros snorted. "Stubborn and determined to get your way. Luckily, you both have me. No, no, don't thank me. The entertainment of seeing you two trying to figure it out has been reward enough. Thank you for keeping me from dying of boredom."

"Glad I could entertain you." I grimaced. "You do know if I don't win the money from the Games that I'm going to lose my business? Likely my home too, since I won't be able to pay my bills. I need to go back, Eros."

"Bad call on his part. Always check your sources," Eros said not at all surprised about my situation. "Anyway, I think you might find that things are not quite as you left them in Port Lawson." Then he pulled me in for a hug and whispered near my ear. "This is not the end, Lia. Take care of yourself. Until we meet again, may the gods guide you and look favorably upon you."

What did that mean? I shrugged it off. "Thank you. I really am going to miss you even if you are a perv." We laughed. "Please take care of Molly. She needs someone now, and I can't be there for her. If you ever get the chance, can you tell her that I'm still alive? You know her; she's going to want to hunt someone down for all of this. I don't want her to put herself in danger. And if either of you are ever in the neighborhood, I hope you'll stop by."

He nodded. I turned to head toward the plane when I felt a smack on my butt. "Ouch! What the hell?"

Eros winked at me. Perv! I jabbed my elbow back, catching him in the stomach.

"Omph! Sorry, sorry. Couldn't resist. You know how I feel about your ass. You're wearing yoga pants again, that's practically an invitation." Then he suddenly stumbled forward, rubbing his hand along the back of his head. "Ow, damn it! As I said, just alike."

I boarded the plane and we were airborne within minutes. Captain Jack's kamikaze takeoff not even fazing me as I stared out the window at the island until it disappeared from view. My brain was whirling with too many thoughts as the hours ticked by. There was something I was missing.

"Ms. Davies, I wanted to let you know we will be landing

in twenty minutes." The captain's voice pulled me from my thoughts.

The flight attendant came to pick up my untouched tray a few moments later. I stowed the foldout table and fastened my seatbelt. Almost home. Part of me was looking forward to going back. Another part of me was seething in frustration and anger that Bennett had taken the choice away from me. He was so sure that he knew best for everyone. Well, he could keep being Mr. Bossybutt to his people. He no longer had any say in my life. For some reason, that thought brought a heaviness to my chest that had tears welling up again. There was a hollowness inside me that was growing the farther away from the island we got.

I rubbed my eyes and lay my head back against the seat. The questions circled round and round in my head with no answers in sight.

No longer able to stand my own what-if game, I grabbed the first bottle my fingers encountered from the mini fridge beside my chair. Taking a large gulp, the fire burned all the way down my throat and into the pit of my empty stomach. I raised the bottle in cheers as I mumbled, "Here's to fate, you evil bitch. I'm done towing the line. As Molly would say 'Mama is rockin' some shit kickers and your ass will be wearin' tread marks.'"

By the time the plane touched down, I was feeling much more relaxed. I plucked a few more bottles from the fridge and hurriedly stuffed them into my bra. It wasn't like they couldn't afford to restock. Waving my middle finger around the plane, I hoped Bennett could see me.

So long, sexy asshole.

I got a little dizzy when I stood up but congratulated myself on only stumbling once as I exited the plane. Captain Jack smiled knowingly at me as I carefully picked my way down the steps. Oops, twice. That last step came out of nowhere. I saluted the captain, nearly taking out my eye. He took my hand—probably to save me from injuring myself—and pulled it to his lips. I giggled. Then slapped my other hand over my mouth in surprise. Those little bottles may have been a bit stronger than I thought. He smiled at me but sobered quickly when he looked back down at my hand still clasped in his. "Is this a bond ring? I've never seen one, but I've heard of them."

I blew a raspberry. "Bond, shpond. It's for pro-proteshion. Shmexy basthard put it on me 'n' walked away. C'you believe that?"

He laughed again. "Not even a full week with my people, and they drive you to drink. Was it Molly? That woman needs to be locked up for the safety of others."

The shocked look on his face when I patted his cheek was priceless, and I giggled again. "You l-i-i-ke her. You want to do na-a-a-ughty things to her," I sang.

He winced as I topped that off with a little booty dance. When I almost toppled us both to the pavement, he wrapped his arm around my waist. "Damn it," he said as he wrapped his arm around me and heaved a heavy sigh as I continued to try to dance. "Looks like I'll be driving you home. Uh, can you stay here for a minute while I tell my crew? Right here, ok? Don't move."

"Aye aye, capthain," I said as he backed away slowly, ready to catch me if needed.

The runway was mostly abandoned, except for a taxi near the hanger. I waved happily at the man behind the wheel. He waved hesitantly back before checking his watch. A ray of late afternoon sun peeked through the gray clouds. I reached up, laughing as I tried to grab the beams of light.

The weak rays grew brighter, and within moments I was standing in a circle of bright sunlight.

"Shit, did you do that?" Captain Jack grabbed my arm tightly and pulled me quickly toward the hanger. His co-pilot rushed over to take care of the annoyed cab driver. The captain mumbled to himself as I struggled to keep up with his long strides, "What am I saying? Of course, she didn't do that. No one but a Kyrion could control the sun like that."

In the hanger, he pulled open the back door of a black Lexus and helped me in.

"Oh goody, minibar!"

"It's going to be a long night," Captain Jack groaned as he closed the door.

27

Pain shot through my skull as my eyes opened on a whimper. Quickly I closed them and pressed my hands to my pounding temples. The slight movement caused my stomach to roll, and I gritted my teeth against the urge to gag. My dry mouth tasted like something had died in there. My back ached from the hard surface I was lying on and something heavy was squishing my breasts.

Several careful swallows later, my stomach felt a little more stable. I patted at my chest and my hand connected with something furry. Uh, was that a head? I remembered that Captain Jack had driven me home. After that, things were pretty blurry.

Please tell me I did not sleep with Captain Jack.

The person snuggled deeper into my cleavage then mumbled, "Mr. Skittles, don't eat that."

Oh, thank god. I knew that voice. But how did Dia get here? And why were we sleeping together on the floor? Thinking hurt my brain so I gave up trying and rubbed at my tired eyes. A huge yawn caught me by surprise, and I took the opportunity to stretch my sore body.

Dia grumbled and tried to fluff up her "pillow." Grunting, I said, "Wakey, wakey, Sleeping Beauty. This is about to turn into a water bed if you don't let me up."

"Lia?" she mumbled sleepily. "Tell the head to stop moving, my bed hurts."

Dia was not a morning person. She was all dazed and confused until she finally woke up all the way. Unfortunately, my bladder couldn't wait. Shifting her aside, I carefully sat up and the room began to spin. When the tilt awhirl stopped, I pried open my eyes only to have them assaulted by the sunlight coming through my living room windows. It pierced my retinas like knives, and I covered my eyes with my hands. *Kill me now.*

When the pain eased, I squinted at the bathroom door all the way on the other side of the room. What I wouldn't give for Bennett's teleportation powers right now. Everything protested as I rolled to my hands and knees, my stomach sloshing uncomfortably. *Oh god, please don't puke. Please don't puke. Please don't pee my pants.* Crawling seemed the safer bet. I made my way across the floor and leaned my perspiring forehead against the closed door. More deep breathing to prepare for my next move, then I reached for the doorknob to hoist myself up. So far so good, although it would help if my legs stopped trembling.

My death grip on the door was the only thing keeping me upright. I turned the knob, my added weight against the door swung it open quickly and sent me careening into the sink. I muttered about the stupid door as I took care of business. I washed up and splashed water on my face, feeling a bit sturdier.

Where the hell was the singing coming from?

The shower cut off, and the curtain opened. A naked Captain Jack stood in my shower, his shocked look likely mirroring my own. I screeched and spun around. Then hissed in pain as my head threatened to explode. Starbursts lit up behind my closed lids as my head pounded in protest, and I braced myself against the sink.

"What you doin' in my shower?" I demanded, gripping the edge of the sink like a lifeline.

"Don't leave a man hanging in the wind here," he said in amusement. "Hand me a towel."

I handed him the towel off the counter, making sure to keep my eyes closed. There was a hot naked man in my shower, and all I wanted to do was cover him up. This was a sad day, and I blamed Bennett for ruining all other men for me. The captain chuckled as I awkwardly slipped from the bathroom, my face heated in embarrassment.

Dia was sitting in the middle of the living room floor with a confused look on her face. "Have you seen my bed? It went for a walk and didn't come back."

"Mmm," I replied, absently patting her on the head as I walked past toward the kitchen. I stood in the front of the open fridge as I took some aspirin with a glass of water. C'mon headache–be gone. Setting the empty glass inside, I stood there dumbly staring at the contents of my fridge as if it held the answers to life's questions. The taste in my mouth was grossing me out and my toothbrush was all the way upstairs. No way I would make it up there. I skimmed the mostly empty shelves and plucked up a jar. This would have to do. I gargled a sip of pickle juice, then put the jar back in the fridge. That was mildly better.

Several minutes must have passed while I stood there in a daze. Goose bumps pebbled painfully across my skin bringing me back to the present. For the first time I noticed what I was wearing. A snug white T-shirt molded to my bra-less chest practically making the material see through. The hem landed mid-thigh showing off my pale legs. There was a dark liquid stain near my belly button. What the hell had happened last night?

The bathroom door opened and Dia squealed, making me jump. "Best. Dream. Ever," she gushed. "Are you gonna strip now? Pooh, I think my bed took my purse. Or maybe it was Mr. Skittles. Do you take IOUs?"

Captain Jack stood in the doorway with my peach towel wrapped around his lean waist and miles of damp muscle on display. He looked amusedly at Dia still sitting on the floor and flexed his biceps for her. She squealed again in delight, bouncing in place. She was wearing only his pilot jacket, and we were dangerously close to seeing if there was anything under it. I coaxed her to stop bouncing and asked where everyone's clothes were.

"You guys are wearing most of mine." Captain Jack calmly lounged against the door of the bathroom as if this happened to him all the time.

The doorbell rang. "Eeek, more strippers!" Dia shouted. "Get the door, Lia,"

A strident male voice sounded through the door, "Ms. Davies, this is the Port Lawson Police Department. We have a warrant to search this property."

A warrant? For what?

Dia curled back up on the floor closing her eyes, mumbling about her cat again. Captain Jack stalked across the room with animal grace, all traces of the easy-going man from moments before were erased.

"Do you know why the police would want to search your property?" he whispered next to me while studying the door.

"The police want to search my property?" I repeated in shock. "They must have the wrong address."

"Listen, I have a bad feeling about this." He gripped my chin and turned my face toward him. "You don't know me very well, but I need you to trust me right now. Let them in. Ask to speak to your lawyer. Call this number. They're going to lock up all of your stuff. Give me your hand." I watched still in a daze as he pulled a pen from thin air and wrote a number on the back of my hand. What was happening here? "I'm going to slip out the back and get in touch with the Kyrion. I'll be close by keeping an eye on things. If you feel like you're in danger, run." He stood up, gave my hand a squeeze, and placed a quick kiss on my cheek. "You girls sure know how to show a guy a good time."

He gave me a wink, then whipped off the towel as he walked away, tossing it over my head. By the time I extracted myself from the towel that smelled of peach body wash and sexy man, he was gone. I jumped as the front door handle rattled. Holding the towel to my chest, I went to unlock the door.

Blinking rapidly against the bright morning sunlight, I came chest to face with an angry policeman. He looked up at me, his scowl deepening as if my height offended him even more. Jaded blue eyes scanned me from head to toe, and a sneer of disgust tightened the thin mouth below his gray mustache. His barrel-chest and the beginnings of a potbelly strained the buttons of his uniform.

Behind him, a female officer peered over his head through the door, sharp green eyes cataloging every detail. Her dishwater-blonde hair was pulled tightly into a bun at the base of her neck, and a flush of excitement tinged her cheeks. A small flip notepad was held at the ready. The blue police uniform and gear dwarfed her lean frame.

"I'm Officer Landish," the man harrumphed and hitched a thumb over his shoulder at the woman. "And the pup behind me is Officer Quinn." A flash of annoyance passed across the woman's face before she could hide it. "Are you Jillian Nova Davies?"

"Yes, that's me," I answered nervously. "What's going on?"

Officer Landish puffed up his chest as he shoved a sheaf of papers at me. "Ms. Davies, we have a warrant to search this residence and your place of business. We need you to step aside."

I took the paper. "Search? For what?"

"Ma'am, are you refusing to allow us entrance?" Officer Landish's hand inched toward a can of mace.

"No, I-I just don't know what this is about," I stammered. Then I made the mistake of glancing behind me when I heard the back door ease open.

Officer Landish drew his gun and shouted, "Police! No one move! Put your hands on your head."

I immediately put my hands up, and the towel that had covered most of my indecent attire floated to the ground. Landish eyed my damp white shirt that left nothing to the imagination with contempt. He spun me around and twisted my arm behind my back, marching me into my living room.

Officer Quinn worked her way around the perimeter of the room, gun drawn. When she reached the open back door, she called it out to Landish. Then she closed it and locked it. She put her gun away before heading over to check on Dia. "She's alive. From the liquor bottles in the kitchen, I would say drunk." She shook Dia's shoulder. "Ma'am, can you hear me?"

"Mmmm . . ." Dia hummed.

Landish pulled out his handcuffs and slapped one around my wrist. "Sir, she's not—" Quinn started.

"Quinn, when I want your opinion, I'll give it to you," Landish barked as he hauled me to the steps and placed the other cuff around the spindle of the railing. "The suspect is secured. Clear the upstairs."

Quinn drew her gun again and eased her way up the stairs, leaving me alone with Officer Asshole. Landish turned to me. "Who is she? Why is she lying on your floor?"

"My friend, Claudia King," I choked out as the nauseating smell of the alcohol fumes leaking from my sweating pores made my stomach churn. I gulped nervously wondering what in the hell we had done last night. "I don't know why she's on the floor, we drank a lot last night. Whatever we did, it was a mistake. I don't usually drink—"

Landish told me to shut up and walked over to Dia to nudge her with his shiny black shoe. "Ma'am, can you hear me?"

"Mmhm, take your clothes off," she mumbled sleepily.

Landish shot a contemptuous glance at me before he crouched down beside her. "Ma'am, are you ok?"

"Mmmm, I'm too tired to do it." She slowly opened one eye. "Hey, what happened to the other guy? Can you tell him to bring my bed back?"

Quinn came back down the stairs. "Clear, sir."

Landish nodded toward Dia. "Call this in for a squad. I think she's on something. I'll start the search upstairs."

"Hey!" I shouted, fed up with being bullied. "What the is this about? You can't go around cuffing people for no reason. I want to talk to my lawyer."

Quinn spoke quickly and quietly into her radio while Landish headed for the stairs. The silence stretched out as Officer Quinn stood at the ready with her back against the far wall, continuously scanning the room. I tried to explain to her that Dia was maybe still a bit drunk and not a morning person. She ignored me. When I asked what I was suspected of, her gaze darted to the forgotten warrant lying in the foyer. Then she went on to list the allegations that were being brought against me.

My mouth gaped in shock. I couldn't begin to make sense of half of what she said, but certain things stood out. Things like human trafficking and embezzlement. *My god, what was happening here?*

Then Officer Asshole came back downstairs carrying a black duffel bag in his gloved hands. A duffel bag that I had never seen before in my life. His sinister smile sent ice down my spine. "Gotcha," he said. Then he opened the bag to show me the contents.

Neat piles of hundred-dollar bills lined the bottom of the bag, but it was the pictures I couldn't look away from. There were tons of pictures of different people. Most of them people that I knew, shown in all kinds of depraved sexual poses. The one that caught my eye, though, was front and center.

Natalie, my former assistant. Her hands were tied to my four-poster bed. Tears leaked from her terrified eyes as she appeared to be screaming around a gag. The painful instruments and toys abusing her body made me gag. My stomach finally lost the battle to keep down its meager contents, and acid burned my throat as I threw up on Landish's shoes.

28

How had my life come to this?

I scanned the gray ceiling of my jail cell again as if it held the answers. Worry for myself and Dia had kept me on edge since they had pushed me into the back of the police car. Dia had been rushed away in an ambulance while I sat there helpless. Then they had carried out my laptop, my phone, my camera, even my trusty vibrator. It had all disappeared into the back of a van while the local newspaperman took pictures. A crowd had gathered to watch the drama. Most wore looks of shocked disbelief, but I occasionally caught a look of superiority as they whispered about how justice was finally served.

"Davies, your lawyer's here." The jail door clanked open.

I stared from my seat on the uncomfortable cot, too numbed by all that had happened to register what the guard was saying.

"Davies, you meeting with the lawyer or not?" he snapped.

The inmate uniform chafed against my skin as the jailor escorted me to an interview room. To my astonishment,

Eros was standing in the middle of the plain white room in a no-nonsense blue suit and matching briefcase. His hair was slicked back, and a pair of gold glasses sat on his nose. He winked as I stared at him in confusion. My heart shriveled a bit in disappointment that he was alone. Why had I thought Bennett would come?

"Ms. Davies, good to see you again." Eros greeted me and shook my hand as if we were strangers. "Although I'm sure, we both wish it was under different circumstances."

"Ero—"

"No need to be so formal," he interrupted, his eyes darting to the mirror on the wall. "You can call me Jaxon."

Right, someone was watching. I wouldn't give away his secret double life, but why would they let a cover model in to see me? "Thank you for coming, Jaxon. Do you know what's happened to Dia?"

"Ms. King is fine. She was taken to the county hospital for examination, which she submitted to quite reluctantly. She sobered up enough to give a statement." He laughed and I smile weakly thinking of the police trying to get a straight answer from her. "After which she checked herself out of the hospital and started a one-woman picket line to free you from jail. Her boyfriend was called in to take her home and keep her there. Do you know that she threatened to 'bedazzle the inside of my underwear' if I didn't get you out of here? Fascinating friend you have there."

The twinkle of amusement and interest in his eyes could only spell trouble. Those two together would be entertaining to watch. After I got these charges taken care of.

"Please have a seat." He motioned to the chair on the opposite side of the metal table. I slumped into the seat and watched with mild amusement as Eros—er, Jaxon—made a production out of sitting down. He slowly unbuttoned his suit jacket, then draped it meticulously over the back of the seat, making several adjustments before he was satisfied with the way it was hanging. Then opened his briefcase on the table and laid out all of the contents in a neat row. I fought back a grin as I imagined the steam pouring from Officer Landish's ears. Jaxon had clearly taken to playing his role with glee.

"I have reviewed your file, Ms. Davies," he said as he finally lowered himself into the metal chair. He retrieved a gold pen and legal pad from his briefcase. "I have to say that the evidence looks quite damning. Photos of individuals allegedly being held against their will at your work or your home. Piles of money in a duffel bag and more found in a box of inventory at your gallery. Testimony from one of the alleged victims, who also picked you out of a lineup. Need I go on?"

"I didn't do any of those things! Please. I know I sound like every bad guy cliché, but none of that is mine." Panic beat in my chest. My hands turned clammy where they gripped the edge of the chair. "I've never seen that duffel bag, and I certainly don't have money to spare. If I had all those piles of money, why wouldn't I have paid my loan off? Th-those disgusting pictures weren't me. I've never done those . . . things in my entire life. Ask my exes. My sex life is boring as hell—why else would they have cheated?"

"Very good questions, Ms. Davies." Jaxon adjusted his glasses and took a few notes. "A couple of the many questions that I also have. It seems the overeager detective skipped a few steps in his investigation. Don't worry, I'll be addressing those lapses on your behalf soon enough."

Oh, he was good at this. But where was my real lawyer?

"In the meantime, let's talk about you. The date stamp on some of those photos goes back a few years. But I would like to go back even further. Let's start with when you were born."

I stared at him in confusion. "What on earth does my birth have to do with these charges?"

"Maybe nothing. Maybe everything," Jaxon said, clicking the pen. "Please begin."

Time passed slowly as I talked him through my life. What this would accomplish, I had no idea but I wasn't in a hurry to go back to my cell. Sometimes I rambled, analyzing my own actions now with the distance of adulthood. We laughed together at the stunts Dia and I had gotten into. When it came to the day of the boating accident, it wasn't as hard as I expected. Having talked about it once already seemed to make it easier. It didn't stop the tears that beaded the table when I laid my head down and sobbed. To my surprise, the guilt had been absent, and all I felt was grief at their loss. Jaxon hadn't done anything visible that would have made prying eyes suspicious, but I felt arms wrapped around me in comfort more than once.

Sometimes Jaxon barked rapid-fire questions, and other times he stared through me as if he was somewhere else. Throughout the whole interview, he had taken copious amounts of notes but had never flipped the page. Once I had stopped talking, curious to see what he was writing. The words he scribbled across the page were written in another language, possibly Greek. The fascinating part though was that as soon as he finished a line, it disappeared from the paper. More Paldimori magic.

We took a short break. The squat guard waddled into the room and slammed down our requested glasses of water. I stretched my legs, keeping my distance from the scowling man who huffed at me on his way back out. Then it was back to my life story. There was only one part I left out. If Eros was concerned that I'd skipped over the year when I had run away, he didn't show it. My words dried up when I came to the part about going to Sotirìa and I glanced at the mirror, but Jaxon motioned for me to keep going. His expression grew grim when I talked about everything that had happened to me there. He smirked at the blush heating my body as I glazed over my time with Bennett. He didn't push me on that, thankfully, but asked a lot of questions about my reactions to him.

Exhaustion weighed me down as I finally finished. This is what I should have done with Dia all those years ago. As soon as I got out of here, I was going to talk to her. *Really* talk to her. Taking a sip of the tepid water, I watched Jaxon continue to write for several more minutes before he laid his pen down and folded his arms on the table.

The lights suddenly flickered, and then it was as if we were in a vacuum. All of the muted background noises—the air coming through the vents and the murmur of voices beyond the door—were gone. "I've placed us in something like a bubble so that we can speak freely," Jaxon said. "I've been doing that off and on for the last few hours, in case you were wondering. Prying ears will only have the information I allowed them to hear. Thank you for telling me everything. Now it's my turn to share with you. Do you know what I found when I had my people dig into your background?"

I shook my head, bracing myself for what he might say.

"You, my little lioness, are Paldimori," he said very matter-of-fact.

I shook my head. "Molly thought that too. But it can't be. I would have known if I was one of your people. I mean, I would have had a birthmark, right?"

"I have verified the information several times. There is no mistake." Jaxon watched me closely. "Your father was born Hector Acesius in the City of Aegletes in Sicily. His parents were high-ranking members of the House of Light. He was being groomed to take over his grandfather's position as Kafàli, but he disappeared days before the ceremony to appoint him to his position.""

"What? That can't be. You're wrong." A strangled breath escaped. "My dad was a shipbuilder from Seattle. He was an only child. His parents passed away when he was twenty. He worked at a local shipyard where the owner saw his skill and took him under his wing. He eventually went out on his own and built a successful business" I recited the story my parents had told me many times. "He met my mom when she was on spring break from college. They fell head over heels and were married within a week."

Jaxon examined me as if I were a fascinating new species to be picked apart so he could understand how I worked. "Your father *was* an only child. And yes, he worked for Jack Lawson—whom I believe you know—and several people claim they became good friends. From what I can tell, he must have met your mother during the Madonna della Luce celebration at Cefalù Harbor. Then he went underground for several years before re-emerging as Henry Davies of Washington accompanied by a wife and their six-month-old daughter."

Could it be true? My parents had told me the story of how they met dozens of times. However, thinking about it now, they had never talked about the details. The story had always been about how they had locked eyes and knew right away they had found someone special. They had talked about their love and happiness in finding each other. There had never been any pictures of their families or stories about them. The only pictures I had ever seen in our house were of our family after I was born.

"Lia, your father was a descendant of Apollo. As are you. That is why you survived the arrow. You healed yourself."

That can't be right, could it? My parents would have told me if they had powers—if I had powers. Some part of me said this was all true, but after everything that had happened, I couldn't take one more betrayal. Violently, I pushed away from the table and rounded on him in fury. "No, take it back, you're wrong."

Jaxon stood slowly from his chair. His midnight blue eyes assessed me for a moment before he let his gaze drop. My guard dropped, hoping that he was going to claim it was all a joke. But he continued to stare down at some spot. If he was staring at my breasts . . . All the air escaped from my lungs as I saw what held his attention. There, hanging in the air between us, was his gold pen, the pointy end only an inch from his heart.

"I can only guess your powers were locked away for your safety. As you grew, so would they. They may have occasionally slipped through the block during times when you were upset or exerting a lot of energy. Like working out—or sex." He smirked at this before continuing. "I suspect Grace's power was mingling with your own to amp up the attacks on you. Certainly, you can now call them without conscious thought." He nodded toward the pen. "You are very powerful, but you need training. And as interesting as it has been to be held at pen point, I do not wish to be stabbed." He took a hesitant step back and the pen followed him threateningly "Please focus on moving the pen back to the table."

How was I supposed to control it when I had no idea how I had even made it do what it was doing? I gulped. "Uh, stop that, pen? Bad pen?"

"That isn't going to help." Jaxon gritted his teeth. "Your will controls it, Lia. You have to make it return to the table."

"Hey, I'm new to this magic crap. Give me a break," I snapped. *Ok, deep breath. You can do this. Focus! Be the pen or something.* "Pen, go to the table."

Instead, it stood upright and tipped back and forth like it was shaking its head no. "Why you little . . .! Get back on that table right now before I pull out your ink cartridge."

The pen flew over to the table and dropped with a metallic clang. Then a snick sounded as the pen clicked itself and the ballpoint disappeared. I smiled triumphantly at Jaxon, but his expression had the smile slipping from my lips.

"I need to dig deeper into your background," he whispered in awe. "Only the originals had creation powers. You are imbuing a bit of yourself into whatever you give life to. My gods, try not to use your powers or we'll be overrun by sassy office supplies."

Holy shit, was he saying I had brought a pen to life?

I wasn't sure whether I should feel freaked out or fascinated. But I had more pressing things to worry about. "So, it's true?" My heart ached with the knowledge that my parents had lied to me. "I really am one of you. How could my parents have kept that from me? You know what, it doesn't matter right now. We have to figure out who's framing me and how we get these charges dropped. Any ideas?"

"A few. I don't think getting you out on bail will be much of a problem. It's keeping you out of here and safe that are my top priorities. In the meantime, try to remain calm and keep those powers in check." He paused, his expression troubled as his gaze swept over me. "Is there anything you need at the moment?"

"I can't recommend the accommodations, but no one has tried to make me their bitch." I gave him a half-hearted smile, but what I wanted to do was beg him to take me with him. "I'm fine for now."

He carefully dropped the pen into his briefcase and gave me a wink. "The real crime here is that jumpsuit. How am I supposed to ogle your ass in that thing?"

29

True to his word, Jaxon had me out of jail the next morning. How he did it I wasn't questioning. He greeted me at the door of the jail, amused by my bewilderment that he was actually able to get me out. Then ushered me to a car where he handed me off to Captain Jack who was ordered to stick to me like glue. When we arrived at my condo it was to find nearly every single inch covered in fingerprint dust and my things trashed. Thankfully, the captain had sent someone to the store to pick up bedding, clothes, and toiletries for both of us.

I spent an hour scrubbing myself down before I exited my guest bathroom. Unfortunately, I couldn't scrub the last two days from my mind as well. My gut clenched as I walked down the hall to my bedroom, torturing myself, but I needed to face the scene of the crime. I should have taken the captain up on his offer to find a hotel, but I was determined not to let anyone force me from my home. Not the smartest decision. My skin crawled being here. The heavy weight of wrongness now tainted everything about the home I had loved.

I paused in the doorway to my bedroom, taking in the sight of my stripped-down bed. The picture of Natalie being abused right here popped into my head. Disgust and regret slithered through me. Had she been trying to get my attention all this time? To let me know that she was being abused by someone who knew me and had access to my home?

Turning away, I walked down the hall to the guest room. To my surprise, the room had been cleaned and the bed pushed against the far wall. A comfy-looking air mattress covered in purple bedding took up the middle of the room. A breakfast tray sat beside it with a wrapped sandwich and chips. On the other side of the mattress sat a beautiful wooden trunk with carvings of various scenes. The lid was raised, revealing new clothes in my exact brands and sizes. My fingers ran over the delicate scene on the front of the trunk that depicted a beautiful floral garden. I would have to ask the captain where it came from.

I slipped on the comfy pj's and sat down to devour my meal, then stretched out on the air mattress with a sigh, barely able to keep my eyes open. I drifted into that in-between state of awake and asleep. Bennett's voice whispering to me to rest was all I remembered before dropping off to sleep.

Rough fingers trailed along my outer thigh, making me arch toward that touch. "I have missed you, *asteràki*." Tender kisses traced my spine. "The glimpses I have had through Jaxon are not enough. The touch through our bond is not enough."

Those fingers grazed my stomach and traveled up to cup my breast. I whimpered but held still, afraid this dream would end too soon. "*Asteràki*, you are temptation itself. I vow that when the Games are over, I will tie you to my bed and devote days to pleasuring your body." Teeth scraped against my neck and made me shiver. "I will hear you scream my name as I make you cum upon my tongue and fingers. When you become so sensitive that even breathing is torture, only then will I slide into your tight depths and ride you to oblivion. This I promise you, but tonight I am here for another purpose."

I groaned and tried to pull his hands back to the parts of my body that ached for him. He chuckled as he pressed a kiss to my shoulder. "We will have many years to explore each other, but, even then, I doubt it will be enough. Come, *asteràki*. We have work to do."

The bedroom faded away, and we were standing on top of a mountain peak under the night sky. The wind whipped through my thin pj's, and I wrapped my arms around myself. Hundreds of feet below us a walled city circled the mountaintop like a crown. Spaced along the wall were turrets that spiked into the sky, their tops lit with glowing balls of fire. In the center of the fire rotated the black star-like symbol for the House of Chaos. Like the one on Bennett's back. A luminescent street circled up the mountain, terminating at a giant archway that led directly into the mountain peak upon which we stood.

"This is the seat of the House of Chaos," Bennett said as he wrapped his arms around me and pressed himself against my back. "One day soon I will bring you here for real to meet our people. First, you must learn to control your powers. Now we begin."

Then we were in the middle of a desert under the bright sun. Bennett let me go. I stumbled forward, the sand shifting beneath my bare feet. Blech—my stomach did not agree with this form of travel. Drawing in deep breaths to settle it down, I paced along the sand.

"Whoa, whoa, whoa. I did not sign up for a dream about

zipping around the world and having to take lessons from you. I should be dreaming about sexy guys bringing me margaritas and giving me foot massages."

He scowled at me. "Who are these other men?"

"Nope, no sidetracking. This is my dream. Shoo! Be gone, nightmare." I closed my eyes and wiggled my nose. Then peeked one eye open. Damn, that had worked for Tabitha.

He gritted his teeth. "Lia—"

"Why isn't this working? Maybe I need to go more traditional. Abracadabra." I swished my hands about. "Why are you still here?"

"Dream-walking is not like a normal dream. Although our physical bodies are still asleep, our consciousness is projected anywhere we choose. We started out in your dream, but I brought you into mine," Bennett explained. "Just as you brought me into your dream of the throne room that first time. In time, you will be able to master this to create the dreamscape and pull in whoever you like."

Right, because I was a magical Paldimori like him. "Can you at least warn me next time before the poofing?" I glared at him.

"My apologies, *asteràki*. This form of travel is natural to me. I will tell you next time before the 'poofing', as you say."

I nodded when I saw his contrite expression. "What does that mean? As-asky, something?"

"I will make you a deal. If you agree to dream-walk with me nightly and allow me to guide you in learning to control your powers, I will tell you."

"I don't know how it works," I confessed. "It just kinda happened before."

He stepped forward, and I stepped back. "Lia, you must

trust me. Promise me, and I will show you what you need to know."

I snorted. "Trust you? Really. I seem to recall being booted off your fancy island like I was a filthy commoner who wasn't fit to be in your presence."

"That wasn't—"

Anger built in me. "Oh, but I was good enough to be in your bed, right? Maybe that's your thing. Lure in a group of people with the promise of a bunch of money and dazzle them with your whole King of the Paldimori thing. I bet the women fall at your feet."

"There have been women, but—"

Bastard! Bennett flinched as if he had heard that.

"Then there's the bond thing" Hurt mixed with the anger, and I lashed out. "Do you have any idea what it was like to wake up alone with a big-ass tattoo on your back that wasn't there before? I didn't even get roses or chocolate. Not even a fucking note! Molly was the one who had to explain the Paldimori version of the birds and bees to me."

"Lia, please—" He stepped forward to try to grab my hands.

The air around us simmered with building heat as I held my palms out to stop him. He halted, a look of frustration crossing his face. "I poured my heart out to you that night. You were the first I ever told about my parents. I shared not just my body with you but who I am. You held me and cherished me like I was precious." My voice broke on those words and I swallowed thickly. "The next morning you belittled me and had your brother escort me off the island. Why would I trust you?"

A single tear trickled down my cheek and my heart cracked in two. A fiery blast shot out from me in all directions and everything went dark.

30

A week had passed without incident. I opened the gallery again. The occasional tourist stopped in, but mostly I was left to tend an empty store. A few good things had happened though. The first was that I spent an entire evening with Dia and told her everything. Well, almost everything. I'd made a promise to tell her about that year on the streets and I would. In time. We had laughed and cried over pints of our favorite ice cream. A little more of the guilt and darkness was chipped away.

The second thing was the phone call I received from Brice. He sounded uncharacteristically nervous as he apologized for the way he had treated me over the years. Apparently, his bank had been purchased by a large corporation that had paid off several loans as part of a publicity stunt. My loan had been one of the ones selected. I had sat there in stunned silence as he vented about the changes that the new company was making. Then he offered to open the line of credit that I had tried to get months before. I had laughed hysterically, both in relief and at his predicament. Then told him to go fuck himself and hung up.

Ms. Myrtle and Mr. Lawson had stopped in to check on me as well. They were dating. Mr. Lawson had told me his children now lived in fear that he would marry and leave their inheritance to Ms. Myrtle. From the gleam in his eye, I had no doubt he was considering it.

My life was almost back to normal. If you ignored the fact that I now had a permanent shadow in the form of Captain Jack. That I had burned two alarm clocks with no more than my fingers. Had a town full of people who still hated me. Oh, and a powerful Paldimori invading my dreams at night. Maybe it wasn't exactly normal, but at least no one was trying to kill me.

Bennett and I had come to an agreement—about training at least. When I blew him up in my dream, I hadn't expected to ever see him again, but the next night there we were, right back in the desert again. He hadn't taken any chances that I would blast him again. The rotten man had trussed me up like a turkey.

"Hello, Lia," he greeted me as I glared up at him unable to speak or move. "I would prefer to speak to you without the bindings, but you left me no choice. Do not try to escape. Those bindings are made specifically for our people. You will not be able to access your powers while you wear them.

"That was an impressive display of your fire gift last night. Although I would rather it not have been directed at me." He crouched down beside me and pushed my hair back from my face. I attempted to kick out at him, but the ropes tightened around me. "I understand why. I have mistreated you. For that and more, I am sorry.

"You were right in all that you said last night. I had my reasons, but there is no excuse I can offer to change what was done. I will only say that you took me by surprise from the moment I first saw you and continued to surprise me at every turn. I never expected to find my bond-mate." He reached for me but curled his hand back before making contact. "When I first felt our connection form, I was shocked. Then I saw your symbol, and I knew what it meant. I was angry and in denial. I convinced myself that everything was a lie, even the bond." He paused as he looked down at me with a vulnerability I had never seen before in his eyes. "When you . . . died I felt it through the bond. It was a pain I do not ever wish to feel again, Lia. Please let me train you in your powers so you can keep yourself safe."

My resentment faded a bit at his confession. A flash of pain and images filtered through our bond as he relived the moment I died. Feeling what he had felt in that moment, I couldn't hold onto my anger. I nodded, and my bindings disappeared. He helped me to my feet, and my clothes changed to my workout gear.

"Fine. I promise to meet you here to practice my wizarding skills. Now I want a promise from you." My voice was filled with the pain I had been trying to deny. "Promise me that you won't come to my bed or try to seduce me again."

A look of regret filled his dark eyes as he searched my face. "I promise I will do nothing unless you want it. I know that I have hurt you, Lia. I will offer you another promise. I promise I will make this right between us. For now, know that I need you to be safe. Come. Our time is short, and there is much to learn."

He held his hand out to me, and I cautiously took it. He pulled me closer and placed my hand over his heart. My fingers tingled as what felt like a current of electricity seeped into me.

"There is energy all around and within. Feel the energy that flows between us. A bonded pair are like a closed circuit." He said gently as if afraid I would flee at any moment. "We can share not only energy but our powers as well. My line is descended directly from the God of Chaos, and I am very powerful. We do not yet know all of your inherited powers, but you manifested several before our bond. Now that you can also tap into my powers it makes you formidable, but it is also very dangerous for you and those around you should you lose control."

The training was hard work as I learned to tap into my power and control it. Bennett was gifted with all the powers of a Paldimori, but fire was one of the easiest for him. It also seemed to be the easiest for me to call. I was a pro at making things explode. It was *not* making them explode that was the problem. The training was slow going, and I had lots of time on my hands. Which is how I found myself making a decision that I hadn't expected to be facing quite so soon.

I contacted my dad's lawyer friend who had handled the estate after my parents' deaths. We had talked a couple of times and completed all of the necessary paperwork. I was now the owner of a nearly eight-thousand-square-foot home on the coast of Mercer Island.

Tomorrow I would be setting foot in my childhood home for the first time in over four years. My feelings about that were a jumbled mess. Dia wanted to come with me, but I'd asked for time to face everything I had walked away from. She had agreed to meet me there in a couple of days.

I needed the time to myself to not only face the past but the future. The life I had come back to after Sotiria no longer felt right. I had changed and couldn't fit myself back into the mold I had created in Port Lawson. But what did I want from my life now that I had started living it?

31

The late-morning sun reflected brightly off the water lapping at the dock. The trip to Mercer Island had been a quiet one. I had stared out the window the majority of the time, lost in thought. Nightmares about the boating accident jolted me awake the few times I had nodded off. I had ignored the captain's concerned glances.

James, the young man who was part of the staff that routinely maintained the house, greeted us in the drive. He was overjoyed that someone would be living there again, even if it was only for a few weeks. "Ms. Davies, welcome. Here, let me take your bags."

"Thanks, James. Is anyone else around?"

"No. Don't tell Mr. Renner, but sometimes I come out here by myself." He gave me a pleading look hoping I wouldn't tell my lawyer. "My dad has been sick, and my little brothers are a handful. I come here to lie on the dock and listen to the water. I promise I never go into the house."

Poor kid, he couldn't have been older than seventeen. "Your secret is safe with me. And you can come hang out on the dock anytime you want." He had beamed at me and insisted on taking my bags inside. Since I wasn't quite ready to go in, I let him.

I wandered the grounds and eventually ended up on the dock myself, staring down the coastline. The area where our boat had gone down wasn't visible from that spot, but the place where I had washed up on shore was. That small section of beach was where I had woken terrified and disoriented. Weak and trembling, I'd stumbled to one of the houses for help, only to knock and knock until my knuckles bled. Using a flower pot, I had broken the window beside the door and let myself in to call the cops.

A chill chased down my spine, and I shook the memories away.

Captain Jack joined me; his sympathetic gaze was too much to handle, and I looked away. "Do you want me to come in with you?"

I glanced over my shoulder at the house looming in the distance. "No, I need to do this alone."

"Strength isn't about how many times you can stand up again after getting knocked down, you know," he put his hand on my shoulder. "It's also about letting someone help you get back up. If you asked, there would be plenty of people who would not only help you to your feet but would weather the blows with you." He squeezed my shoulder, then turned back toward the house.

Logically, I knew he was right. That didn't mean it was any easier to ask for help. My first step in the right direction would be to call Dia. She would be worried about me and wasn't the type to stand being on radio silence for too much longer. I loved Dia, and I knew she'd be by my side in a heartbeat. But when the captain spoke of someone to weather the blows with me, I hadn't thought of her. No, the shoulder I saw myself leaning on was much too muscular to belong to my best friend.

Heat pulsed along my back as I imagined him reaching for me. The tension eased from my shoulders as I was wrapped in his strong embrace. For a moment, I sank into the comfort. Then I stiffened my spine and cut our connection. I had learned that I could control how far I opened the door to let Bennett in. The heat abandoned me abruptly to be replaced by a cold hollowness that seemed to eat away at my last reserves of energy. Between his nightly visits and the nightmares, I was exhausted.

I glanced across the manicured lawns at the house nestled amongst the tall green trees. There was more to do before I could rest. Then I focused on putting one foot in front of the other. It was only a house. All the memories it contained were already imprinted on my mind. I had already faced the hardest ones that night in Bennett's arms. My life had gotten stuck on the deck of that boat where the storm raged, and the water threatened to swallow me down as it had my parents. It was time to remember the love and laughter we had shared here. It was time to let light cast away the dark.

Gripping the handle of the double doors at the rear of the house, I felt something ripple across my skin. What was that? When nothing else happened, I cautiously stepped inside. It felt as if I was stepping through a layer of Jell-O. *Could there be some kind of shield on the house?* I turned and extended my arm back through the doorway. Again, it felt like pushing through a thick substance, but I couldn't see anything.

"Why do I get the feeling that there's a lot that my parents didn't tell me?" I asked the empty room.

I passed through the lower level and took the stairs up to

the main floor. The slate tile of the central foyer radiated warmth from the bright sunlight filtering through the wall of windows overlooking the lake. I barely noticed the spectacular view as I made my way to my destination.

My dad's office was just as I remembered it. A tall sculpture of the anchor from his first ship took up a prominent place near the door. Miniature models of the ships his company had built over the years lined one wall. A large walnut desk sat in an alcove of windows that I had called his fishbowl.

Easing into his leather chair, I pushed myself up to the desk, the rollers squeaking. A smile tugged at my lips. A ray of sunshine broke through the darkness. How many times had Dad grumbled about that squeaking? The chair had been passed down to him from his grandfather. Had he never had it fixed because it reminded him of the life he left behind? Did any of his family—my family—still live in Sicily?

I settled my head back onto the chair, breathing in the faint scents of ocean and cedar. Those scents used to be stronger and my chest ached at the thought of that part of him fading away.

A flicker of yellow light amidst the ship models caught my attention. That was strange. None of the models had working lights. Then another flicker of yellow appeared in a different spot. A few moments later there was another one and then another. I walked over to the shelves to investigate. The lights seemed to be flickering in a pattern starting from the left and circling around. I counted as the pattern repeated: seven lights in all. My fingers trailed along the shelf until I came to a schooner that was approximately where I had seen the first light. I examined it from top to bottom, but didn't find anything. The pattern started again. Patiently I waited, peering closely at the ship. There! The light wasn't coming from the ship but from the wall behind it.

I quickly moved the ship to the side. A golden, wavy triangle shape tipped on its side protruded from the wall. It was a solid gold piece about the length of my thumb. I rubbed the smooth metal, the surface glowing brighter as it warmed beneath my finger. Dragging one of the visitor chairs away from the desk, I took a closer look and found other pieces. They were all the same size and shape but positioned at different points on the wall.

What were they for? Stepping back to scan the whole wall, I could see that they were arranged in a circle with their longer sides turned to the inside of the circle, suggesting they were spreading out from some kind of center. I drew a line in the air from each point. If I was correct, they all converged at one center point. At one ship.

The design of the ship was much older than any my dad had built. The body of the ship was long and narrow with the bow resembling some type of serpent. It had one large square sail and dozens of oars on each side. I reached for it, intending to look behind it. As soon as my hand touched it, the ship turned to solid gold.

Holy crap!

I tried to yank my hand away, but it was stuck. More by accident than design the ship was pushed toward the wall, but instead of smashing into the wall, the stern started to sink into it. The oars lifted, and the sails fluttered as the ship rowed itself into the wall. I was freaking out as I yanked frantically at my hand. The sound of crashing waves filled the room, and suddenly the seven gold pieces were growing.

They stretched and rippled across the wall, glowing brighter as they converged upon the ship. Like liquid, they poured into the wall where half of the ship had disappeared. A brilliant light lit up the room.

I shielded my face with my free hand, expecting at any moment to feel the blast of a bomb. It wouldn't surprise me if I exploded something else. All of a sudden, my hand came free, and I stumbled backward. My hand was unusually hot to the touch when I cupped it to my chest. I was relieved to see there wasn't any damage.

A giant golden sun was now displayed on the wall. Then everything the sun touched started to dissolve from the center outward. A blinding golden light beamed from the hole that was swallowing up the entire wall of the office. The light wrapped around me, cradling me like a warm cocoon. It felt safe, comforting.

Finally, the light dimmed. Even after everything I had seen and learned since I went to the island, I stared in awe at the sight before me. Walking forward, I dropped to my knees at the edge of the opening and cautiously inched my fingers across the threshold. When nothing happened, I extended my hand even further and skimmed my fingers through the thick grass. A ripple spread out from where the green blades tickled the palm of my hand. I watched, slack-jawed, as the ripple traveled across a field of hyacinths to a tall golden tower that sat near the edge of a cliff. When the ripple reached the top of the tower, a ball of orange-yellow light grew until it filled the circumference of the top of the tower and began to rotate. The light of the tower barely reached the deep valley below where more land stretched out toward the backdrop of the starry expanse of outer space.

"You are full of surprises aren't you," said a sarcastic female voice from behind me. "Congrats, I guess you really are one of us. Not that it matters."

The cocking of a gun froze me to the spot. Slowly, I turned on my knees. "You! How did you get in here?"

"You mean how did I get through the barrier placed on the house?" Natalie grinned menacingly. "Oh, you could say I hitched a ride. Your friend needed a little persuasion to let us in. Unfortunately, my associate's methods are not quite as enjoyable as mine. No real harm done, yet. See for yourself." She gestured toward the desk.

So there really had been a barrier on the house. Dread filled me. If the barrier had repelled her, there was likely an excellent reason. I climbed to my feet. *No!* James was tied and gagged in my dad's chair. His left eye was swollen nearly shut, the other wide with fear. Blood trickled from a cut on his cheek.

"You must be Paldimori too. I never would have guessed. Of course, I had no idea what that meant until a couple of weeks ago," I said, my thoughts racing. *Had Captain Jack let Jaxon know I was here? Was the captain waiting for an opening to jump her?*

A hazy figure clad all in black stood behind the chair. The frame suggested a man, but I couldn't make out any other details due to the white glow that surrounded him. His hands were splayed in front of James's face as a sizzling rope of white light arched threateningly between his palms. Another figure sprawled face down on the floor in front of the desk. Damn, it was Captain Jack.

"Who's your friend?" I asked cautiously, clenching my hands to hide their trembling.

"Oh, I never kiss and tell. Wait a minute. Yes, I do." She

laughed maniacally. "But only when it benefits me. My associates are a little on edge since you pulled your whole undead thing. They're ready to end this. But where's the fun in that?"

The crackling light jumped around in the man's hands as if in agitation at her comment. I was all for dragging this out until I could find a way for us to escape. Catching James's eye, I silently tried to tell him it was going to be all right. We were going to get out of this. "This is my fault," I said to him. "I'm so sorry."

At his subtle nod, I shifted my gaze to the too-still figure on the floor. "What did you do to Captain Matthews?" I couldn't see any injuries, but his tanned skin looked unnaturally pale. "I need to check on him. He doesn't look good."

"I like you right where you are. Don't worry, I'll take good care of Captain Cutie." She smirked nastily. "You know how much I like to play with your boyfriends."

"They're only the hired help," I tried to convince her. "Why don't you let them go? You want me, right? Well, you've caught me. C'mon!" I snarled in frustration. "You're the one holding the gun, what am I gonna do?"

She smiled gleefully. *Keep your cool, damnit. The last thing you want is to let her know how much she's getting to you.* That vicious bitch got off on torture of all kinds. To lose control would be to play right into her hands.

"Poor little Lia. Never able to hang on to her men," she taunted playfully.

I could play her games until I figured a way out of this. "Why are you doing this?"

"*Why?* Because you've ruined everything!" she snapped, her composure briefly slipping. She took a deep breath then walked toward the desk, offering the glowing man the gun.

"Turn off the bug zapper and take this. She's not going to try anything."

Again, his light snapped in agitation, but he did as she said. He moved to the opposite wall from where I stood, keeping everyone in sight. He never made a sound as he raised the gun to point it at me.

"Guns are so old-school. They're crude tools that hold back creativity. You're an artist, you know what I mean." Natalie trailed her fingers along James's arm. His throat worked convulsively, recognizing that the greater threat came from the less obvious of the two.

Her hands wandered along his shoulder, and up his neck; then she viciously ripped the tape from his mouth. James yelped in pain as a cut on his lip reopened. She smiled down at him then crashed her lips onto his. He struggled as she ground her lips harder against him, but then something changed. He was fighting his restraints, but he wasn't trying to get away. He was trying to get closer to her, pushing up into her kiss and moaning. She pulled back with a delighted giggle and licked the blood from her lips.

James watched her with a hungry look. She ran her fingers through his hair and jerked his head back. His mouth dropped open as his breath hissed out. In pleasure or pain or both, I wasn't sure. She moved behind him and stared down into his eyes, then wrapped her fingers around his throat and started to squeeze. Another moan rattled in his chest, and his face turned red. His arms began to twitch, but he never looked away from her.

"Stop it! You'll kill him," I shouted, taking a couple of steps forward. Mr. Glow-Stick took a threatening step forward as well, halting me in my tracks as I stared down the barrel of the gun.

A sound of pleasured pain came from the desk area,

drawing my attention back to Psycho Barbie. She had released James, but the torment wasn't over. She ripped open the buttons of his shirt to rake bloody claw marks across his tanned chest. He stared up at her with a dazed look of unconditional devotion as her hand wandered down his chest to disappear beneath the desk.

"Mmm. There are so many things I could teach you," she purred to him, all the while watching my face.

My stomach lurched in revulsion. She had to be using some kind of power. *Was this how she had seduced all the other men?* I swallowed down the acid threatening to rise up my throat. "Hey! Hey kid, snap out of it! You don't want this. Trust me, everyone has had a ride on that bicycle." A hissed laugh came from Mr. Glow-Stick.

"You think you're so clever," she sneered at me. "But it's no use. He's mine now. Like every other man in your life. You thought you could take what was mine, but instead, I've taken everything from you."

"What are you talking about? I've never taken anything from you. You showed up in my life out of the blue and started smashing it to pieces!"

She made a growling sound then pushed the chair away violently. Holding her hand out, an icy blast of wind sent the chair careening across the floor straight at me. I tried to side-step, but it clipped me in the hip and sent me sprawling. I scrambled to my knees trying to grab the chair. James's panicked eyes met mine as my fingers closed around air. He spun past me to smack into the barrier leading to the cliff top.

James screamed, finally released from his trance. The wind pinned him down no matter how much he struggled. I crawled toward him, keeping my body low to avoid as much of the wind as I could. I managed to get my fingers wrapped around the base of the chair to pull him toward me, but as soon as I made contact, the chair shot through the barrier as if it wasn't there.

A horrified scream was wrenched from my throat. The momentum carried James into the world beyond, tearing a path through the field of flowers. The chair caught on something that caused it to topple and roll several times before coming to rest upside-down. I strained to see any movement, but there was nothing.

"Oopsie. Sometimes I just don't know my own strength," Natalie cooed innocently behind me. "One little doll left to play with. I always did have problems with breaking my toys."

Rage burned through me, incinerating everything but the thought of vengeance. One moment I was kneeling beside the barrier, the next I plowed into her. Teleportation. Finally, a useful power. We hit the ground with a jarring thud, but I barely noticed. My fist connected with her face. I straddled her thighs, my heavier weight keeping her pinned down as she bucked wildly, those sharp claws drawing blood everywhere she could reach. Mr. Glow-Stick backed into the shadows, content to watch as we pummeled each other.

I pulled my fist back to hit her again, and she punched me in the stomach. Air rushed out of me, and I lost my concentration. She quickly rolled, dislodging me. Before I could get my breath back, a kick landed in my ribs, then another. Something broke, and agony swept my torso. I rolled several times until I hit the wall and used it to pull myself up. Her fist came down on my kidney. I screamed. Then kicked backward, satisfaction filled me to hear her pained curse.

"STOP THIS NOW!" boomed a familiar angry voice that filled the room and shook the windows.

I turned my battered back to the wall, panting hard. Bennett stood in the doorway to the office looking seriously pissed as he shifted his gaze between us.

"Someone will tell me why my wife and my sister have beaten each other bloody."

32

"What?" we both shouted at him in shock.

"Of all the bitches in all the world . . ." I muttered.

Natalie recovered quickly from her shock, a flash of glee sparking in her eyes. She wiped at her bloody nose, whimpering as tears filled her eyes. The evil torturer from moments ago was transformed into a scared little girl as she rushed across the room to fling herself into Bennett's arms.

"Oh Benny, I'm so glad you came," she sobbed. "Lia invited me here saying she wanted to settle our differences. Then attacked me as soon as I walked in the door. I was trying to defend myself. It was awful!"

"Lia would not—" Natalie kissed his neck and whispered into his ear. Bennett glanced at me in confusion, then shook his head as if he were dazed. His arms came to wrap around Natalie and rub her back as she continued to cry on his shoulder. His voice sounded different, almost robotic when he said, "Shhh. Do not cry, sweetheart. We will get to the bottom of this."

Something seemed off but I was so angry at them both

that I didn't care. "Give me a break. Are you seriously falling for this little act?" I laughed rather than stalking over to rip her hair out. "I thought you were supposed to be some great and powerful wizard."

Bennett glared at me over her head. "You know I am not a wizard."

He mumbled soothing words to Natalie, cradling her as if she were a fragile gem. Then placed a kiss on top of her head before leading her to a chair in front of the desk. He checked over her injuries as she whimpered looking small and vulnerable.

"Your precious little sister killed someone." I snarled at him. He never paused fawning over her and my heart crumbled to dust. "Fine, you two can catch up on old times somewhere else. Like a jail cell. I'm calling the cops."

"Lia, wait—" Bennett called as he stumbled to his feet.

"Piss off."

I was halted mid-step as the rope that had been part of the anchor sculpture wrapped snugly around my waist. Slowly I was pulled backward to be plopped unexpectedly down into the other guest chair. The rope slithered around me once more, tying me to the seat-back before the whole chair was dragged backward. *Stupid powers.* I cussed at Bennett and struggled against the ropes to no avail. If I weren't afraid of killing us all in an explosion, this rope would be toast.

The chair came to a stop several feet away from Natalie where she clung to Bennett's arm. "Now," he said shakily, as a bead of sweat rolled down his temple, "we will discuss this rationally. I want to know how that portal came to be here later as well. But the more important questions are who died and what is wrong with Captain Matthews?"

His eyes dilated as Natalie kissed his hand and launched into another series of lies. "It was Lia. Poor Jack tried to defend me, but she knocked him out with her powers. The other guy was trying to calm her down and got thrown through the portal."

Bennett frowned at me and took a tentative step in my direction. Something shifted in the shadows. I had been so distracted by Bennett that I had forgotten about my other uninvited guest.

Frustration had me wanting to claw against the ropes that kept me defenseless. "The captain drove me here," I said. "He stayed behind to help James—the hired staff, *the dead kid*—unload the car. You should ask sister dear what happened to him. In fact, why don't you use your wizard skills to *assess* the situation? You might be *surprised* by what you find."

Bennett gave me a puzzled look as I tried to subtly nod toward the man hiding in the shadows. Natalie gasped, "Benny, I don't feel too good." She lurched to her feet, wobbling.

Bennett caught her as she started to fall. "Nat, what is it? Are you ok?"

"I feel dizzy." She grimaced as she laid a hand against her forehead, her body shaking as though terrified. "It feels like someone is using their powers on me. I can feel them in my head."

Someone give the girl an Oscar! With acting skills like those she was in the wrong profession. Bennett glared at me. "Lia, stop. Your powers are too new. You could damage her permanently."

"You're an idiot." I barked, frustrated to the point of screaming. "I wouldn't want to go on a field trip in her head even if I knew how. She's psychotic. Don't you understand that every time she opens her mouth, she's *lying*?"

Bennett stared at me a moment, his sweaty brow wrinkled in confusion. He started to say something, but Natalie put her arms around his neck and pressed her lips to his. *Oh, hell to the no she didn't!* Bennett stiffened against her, his trembling hand reached out for mine. Then, just like James, he was under her spell. He gripped her tightly and took control of the kiss to ravage her mouth.

Natalie moaned as she pressed against him. Bile rose up my throat when he hitched her into his arms and sat on the edge of the desk with her astride his thighs. His eyes were wide open and blank, as she trailed kisses down his neck.

"Gross, he's your brother. Do you have dick-slaying power in your kiss or something?" I shouted in disgust, struggling once again to free myself from the chair.

"Stepbrother actually," Natalie purred as she turned to me with a triumphant look. "You could say my kiss is like ambrosia from the gods." She giggled, tracing a finger over his bottom lip. "Men are so easy, I hardly need to use my powers. Stroke their dick and their ego and they're putty in my hands. They'll do anything I want."

Her hands roamed under Bennett's shirt, and she leaned up to lick his bottom lip. "Mmm. He's delicious, isn't he?" She tugged on Bennett's hair and bit his ear. "Stay right here pet, until I'm ready for you."

Natalie hopped off his lap and turned to glare at me. "I've wanted him since I was four years old, but he only saw me as his little sister. I got as close to him as he would let anyone. Until you." She shoved her finger into my chest. My skin crawled when she leaned her head against mine and stroked my hair. "It was so much fun watching you two at first. He hated you for what you had done to me. His poor baby sister abused at the hands of a monster like you. He was so close to setting you on fire the day of the pledges. I was mad at him for not killing you, but I realized later that would have been too quick."

My heart stopped beating. My lungs no longer pumped air into my body. Please no. Bennett cared for me. He wouldn't have believed I could hurt someone like that, could he?

"He's a man though. His dick was bound to get in the way. He struggled so hard with his attraction to you. I really don't get it." She pushed away with a huff of disgust. "I had to remind him why he should hate you but he couldn't keep it in his pants. I thought he would fuck you and be done, like all the other sluts he's taken to bed. But he became obsessed with you." Her face turned red, and spittle flew from her mouth as she stalked toward me. Then slapped my face. "He was supposed to love *me*!"

Pain exploded across my cheek and in my heart. My bruised cheek would heal but I wasn't so sure about my heart. From the beginning, Bennett had been poisoned by Natalie's lies. He had gotten close to me, closer than anyone had ever been, all to avenge his sister. Why else would you sleep with the person you thought abused your sister?

"Oh ho, big brother hasn't shared as much as I thought." She laughed maniacally as tears slipped down my cheeks. "Honestly, I can't blame you. With a body like his, who needs pillow talk?"

The pain took my breath away and I realized finally what I had been denying. I loved Bennett. I loved a man who only wanted to destroy me.

"You took Douglas from me and I got my revenge. On

both of you." She smiled pleasantly at me. "But taking Bennett from me—for that you have to die."

"What are you talking about? You introduced me to Douglas."

"Do you know how long it took me to turn him into my little puppet." She pressed her face close to mine, madness burning bright in her blue eyes. "I could see his lust for those young girls in his classes, but he thought it was wrong. I was so close to tempting him, then he met you and never looked at me again. I wanted to keep him, but I had to break him— because of you."

"Everyone should have the freedom of choice. Please don't do this."

She patted my cheek. "Cheer up, Lia. Our playtime will be over soon. Honestly, it was getting boring dealing with that whiny bitch Grace anyway. But it was sweet, really, the way she wanted to protect me from you." Natalie clasped her hands over her heart. "Grace may not have had the guts to kill you, but I do. And the best part is once you're dead, Bennett and I will finally be together."

She blew Bennett's still form a kiss. Mr. Glow-Stick stepped out of the shadows all lit up again. He turned toward Bennett, sparks shooting from his fingers, but Natalie's words stopped him in his tracks. "Nah-ah-ah, he's mine."

Lights sparked from his fingertips in agitation, but he shifted toward me, holding his hand out. A beam of light lengthened into the shape of a sword. *You've got to be kidding me. Glad to meet another fan of the light saber, but seriously?* Death by light saber was epically cool in the movies. In real life, it screamed never gotten laid.

"This time there will be no coming back. That was very naughty of you, by the way. My friends weren't happy that you didn't die from that arrow." Natalie stood back and motioned to Mr. Glow-Stick. "My associate is going to carve you into a million pieces and then burn this house to ashes. It's a pity that you won't be around to watch me enjoy every inch of Bennett's body, but I can't have my future husband thinking he's already married to another woman."

"Now you're just adding insult to injury. *Shut up!*"

A blast of wind burst from me hitting Natalie and she went flying backward into Mr. Glow-Stick. My chair pitched over backward, smacking into the floor with a thump. Whether from Bennett's weakened power in his dazed state or dumb luck, I managed to slip free of the ropes. My aching ribs protested as I crawled across the floor to Captain Matthew's side hoping he had a weapon on him. The dumbass duo would untangle themselves any minute. I needed a plan.

My hands slipped into the captain's pockets coming up empty. Wait, there was something in the breast pocket of his jacket. I pulled out the slim rectangular black box and quickly flipped it open. A familiar gold pen was the only thing inside. I hung my head in disappointment. Then the pen clicked itself several times rapid-fire as if excited to see me, before shooting up out of the box to rub against my hand.

This was the pen I had brought to life. This just might work.

I motioned for the pen to hide under my sleeve and stood to face my enemies. Mr. Glow-Stick was approaching with his sword extended. I tried to use my powers but nothing was working. *Why couldn't the force be with me right now?* Natalie watched him advance on me with a disturbing look of lustful anticipation. Mr. Glow-Stick drew back his sword ready to strike me down. My arm shot out in a stop gesture as I yelled, "Now! Click!"

The pen launched itself from my sleeve directly at the man's face. He lurched backward in surprise. The pen dipped and dived, driving him further back. Mr. Glow-Stick swung his sword about trying to chop at the pen and almost took Natalie's head off. Unfortunately, she ducked under his swing and came at me instead.

I only had enough time to chuckle as the glowing man backed against the wall and Click drew a quick outline around him. Then Natalie was in front of me, throwing out a burst of wind that I barely managed to sidestep. Picking up Click's discarded box, I threw it at her head. She batted it away, and I tackled her. We hit the floor with a jarring thud in front of the office door, with me on top. She rammed her fists into my back and wrapped her legs around my waist, using her leverage to roll us over. Her muscular thighs squeezed me tightly, battering my broken ribs. I screamed and punched at her, but she wouldn't let go.

I did the only thing I could think of. I bit her stomach. She yelped and finally released me. Lacing my fingers together, I shoved my arms up then slammed them down. Something snapped beneath my hands. Natalie fell backward with a scream. I followed her down, and my extra weight finally paid off as I pinned her in place. She sobbed beneath me, cupping her broken collarbone.

"If that wasn't my sister under you, the girl fighting would really be doing it for me," Jaxon's amused voice said from the doorway. "Although having your ass on display is now my new favorite way to be greeted at the door." A loud smack followed, and then he growled, "Damn it, woman! Stop sticking those damn things on me."

"Lia, are you all right?"

"Dia?" I squeaked.

Dia crouched beside me, and I stared up at her

wonderful face in disbelief. When she grasped my hand I burst into tears, mumbling incoherently about how glad I was to see her. There may have been some stuff in there about being in love with Bennett and him being possessed by his sister. It was all pouring out like water through a broken dam. I doubted the tears would be stopping anytime soon. She pulled me up off Natalie and into her arms, mumbling encouragingly to me until I finally calmed down.

My crying jag had sapped what little energy had been left after the fight. Jaxon had tied Natalie to a chair as he checked on Bennett and the captain. She was making quite a racket as she continued to wail and accuse me of hurting her. "What happened here?" Jaxon asked, snapping his fingers in front of Bennett's face. "He's under some kind of thrall."

"Ask her." I wiped the tears away and pointed to Natalie. "She kissed him and he turned into a lust zombie."

Jaxon studied Bennett more closely, then turned toward Natalie. "Nat? Nat! Stop crying and tell me what you did to Bennett."

She cut off the hysterics and glared hatefully at Jaxon. He teleported to her side in a flash, his hands wrapped loosely around the base of her throat.

"You've been busy, sister. I saw those photos from Lia's condo." His grip tightened. "I've been tracking you for days and imagine my surprise when I realized where you were. I would have gotten here sooner but I had a little sidekick that refused to stay at home where she belongs." His glanced at Dia and she gave him a little finger wave. He shook his head and turned back to his sister. "I'll ask once more. What did you do to Bennett?"

"Fuck you!" She spat at him. "He wanted it. He wants me. We were meant to be together. I love him. Let me go!"

"You always were obsessed with him." Jaxon shook his head sadly. "I thought it was a harmless crush you would outgrow." He pinned her shoulders back against the chair. "He would never want you. You're a manipulative, self-absorbed, vindictive little brat. Everything he would despise if ever saw the real you."

"You don't know anything about me. How could you?" Natalie sobbed. "You both left me there."

Guilt settled over his face. "Nat, it wasn't like that. We had to get out." His voice gentled as he stroked her hair. "I'm sorry, sis. We shouldn't have left you there alone with father." He pressed a kiss to her forehead. "We won't abandon you again. We'll get you the help you need and be there by your side this time. But you have to let this obsession with Bennett go. Look at what you've done to the man you claim to love."

They both looked at Bennett who was still sitting motionless on the edge of the desk. Her lip trembled and she dropped her head. "I release you."

Click nudged against my hand and slide under my sleeve. Clutching my ribs, I slowly walked toward Bennett. We all watched him anxiously. Jaxon smoothed his hand over Natalie's bowed head. "Thank you. Bennett deserves to be happy, and so do you. But Lia is his bond-mate."

Bennett blinked rapidly as if he was coming out of a long sleep. He turned to me, and a smile spread across his face. Hesitantly, I smiled back. A huge gust of wind hit me and sent me flying backward. I tumbled through the doorway of the office out into the living room where I smashed into a wooden support column. Bones shattered and blood poured down to the floor below. All that escaped was a huff of air as my lungs collapsed. I slid down to the floor, spots dancing before my eyes. There was shouting in the distance. Then the great roar of a lion shook the floor.

Darkness crept around the edges of my vision. Just before it pulled me under, I heard a voice in my head say, "*Blood of my beloved . . . find the twin Houses of the Olympian Omàda.*"

33

"So, you haven't heard from him?"

"Nope," I responded nonchalantly. "Jaxon and Grayson have stopped by a couple of times. Grayson says he's part of my House now, whatever that means. I've offered him my guest bedroom numerous times. He just smiles and tells me not to worry because 'the gods have it in hand.' I'd swear that little punk was related to Yoda," I grumbled. "I can't imagine either of them being very comfortable staying at Vern's Hotel. But maybe Jaxon is hanging around for some *other* reason."

Dia became very interested in the napkin on the table as we had our first dinner at Mussels in forever. Something had happened between her and Jaxon while I was in jail, but she wasn't talking. He seemed to be equal parts fascinated and annoyed by her. Watching them had kept my mind off Bennett and what he had said to me the day he left.

It had taken me three days to wake up after Natalie blasted me into that column at my parent's house. Apparently, my body had simply been through too many traumatic experiences in such a short time frame. Surprisingly, we Paldimori aren't perfect little Energizer Bunnies with unlimited powers. What we do takes up a lot of energy, and I'd needed to recharge. On the morning of the fourth day, I'd sat up gasping for air. This incredibly realistic dream had been playing on repeat in my mind. That I had died and met a man named Titan Theophanes who said, "Blood of my beloved. Find the twin Houses of the Olympian Omàda."

"You have been saying that same phrase for days," Bennett said as he leaned against the bedroom doorframe.

He was dressed casually in well-worn jeans and a tight black T-shirt that made my mouth water. My ogling had been short-lived as Dia rushed in, throwing herself on top of me and squeezing me until I couldn't breathe. She had cried and promised never to use my boobs as pillows again if I would stop scaring years off her life. By the time I had untangled myself and promised to not get dead, Bennett was gone.

Those first few days were rough. My energy level was still low from being nearly depleted on top of the healing. I had refused to let Bennett lend me his strength through our bond. I was relieved that he was ok, but I didn't trust him after what Natalie had told me.

Grayson had been a mother hen fussing and worrying over me the whole time. It was cute but annoying. Like when he refused to let Captain Jack—who was fully recovered—visit me on his way out of town because Grayson thought I needed a nap. He wouldn't make that mistake again. My gift for explosions had finally come in handy.

The captain and I had spent a couple of hours catching up. He'd still refused to tell me what happened the night we got drunk. But he did at least clear up how Click had ended up in his pocket the day Natalie came to crash the party. Apparently, Jaxon was delayed but teleported Click with a note that he might come in handy. And he had. The captain and I spent a lot of time talking about that day and the what ifs. James's death sat heavy on both our hearts.

No one had been able to get past the barrier to retrieve his body, except me. We weren't sure about the environment on the other side of the barrier, so I'd knelt at the edge and stuck my hand through. It was the one time I'd let Bennett take complete control of my powers. He'd brought James's body through while I'd sobbed uncontrollably for the young life that had been snuffed out because of me. I'd asked the family to let me pay for the memorial service and host it on my dock since it was his favorite spot and because he had broken his neck while in my employ. The sight of his sick father and young brothers grieving during the service had almost driven me to hunt Natalie down.

Memories from these past months tortured me and drove me to seek out the water's edge. I may not have set foot in the water since the accident, but the gentle lapping of the waves still managed to soothe me. The pinks and purples of the setting sun was a beautiful sight. My thin Snatch Dragon pj's offered little barrier to the dropping temperature, and I was dotted with goose bumps, but I refused to go inside. Grayson was in there somewhere, probably counting the minutes until he thought it safe to come get me without being yelled at.

The heat reached me first. That warmth along my spine that let me know he was near even when the door between us was closed. My senses became hyperaware of every sound and smell as if my body was searching him out. My heart fluttered when he sat down beside me. For the first time in days I felt whole as if he carried the other piece of me.

From the corner of my eye I watched his strong profile.

He looked tired. We'd both had our share of ordeals lately. I couldn't imagine what he must have gone through when he found out that his little sister had killed people because she wanted him for herself.

The silence stretched out for some time with neither of us knowing quite what to say. Bennett sighed and turned to me. "There is much I need to tell you. Things that I am only just now learning. Others . . . that I should have told you before. Will you please look at me, Lia?"

It had been the "please" more than anything that had me meeting his gaze. He was not a man that was accustomed to asking nicely. His eyes were full of regrets and profound sadness that made my chest ache. He lifted his hand as if to touch me but hesitated. He stared down at his palm as if it was covered in filth that no amount of scrubbing would erase and dropped it back to his side. "I apologize for all that my family has done to you. Natalie is . . . not well. My father has taken custody of her, and she will get the help she needs. Help that we—her family—should have realized she needed long ago."

Bennett explained how she had been sleeping with Officer Landish who, as it turned out, was also the friend that Mr. Lawson had asked to look into the rumors. Landish had fallen head over heels for Natalie and her lies. He had promised her he would see me locked away where I couldn't hurt her anymore. Spurred by her tear-filled pleas to help her, Landish had planted the evidence in my condo that Natalie provided.

Luckily the partner, Officer Quinn, was a damn good police officer. She was suspicious of Landish's passionate conviction of guilt and started digging on her own. Natalie hadn't tried too hard to cover her tracks since she had Landish. She had used the credit card that her father paid for to purchase the camera equipment and sex devices used in the photos. The money was from the college tuition that their father thought he was paying. Turns out Natalie hadn't attended college in several years and was having the money sent directly to an account under her name.

Several of the victims had also come forward to give statements. They had initially been too afraid of Natalie but when she left town and Officer Quinn started questioning them more thoroughly, they had caved. They were running into dead ends on the embezzlement part, but enough evidence had been found for all charges against me to be dropped. Landish had been forced into early retirement. So many people had fallen victim to Natalie's plotting, I wondered if we would ever know the full extent.

Bennett was silent for a moment, his hands balled tightly. "For me, there are no excuses. I wanted you, and I took you. I had no care for what my actions meant for you. I took everything from you that I could. Your freedom and your choice. I am no better than Natalie."

"Bennett, you aren't like her. You wouldn't—"

"Please let me finish," he interrupted softly. "That night in the training glen I knew that there was a connection between us. It was like a siren song pulling me nearer every time I touched you. I should have walked away. I convinced myself that I *could* walk away. I only needed to be inside you and the craving would end."

He looked at me, his eyes full of a weary resignation. "That first time, I felt the bond forming between us. The gods help me, it was like pouring gasoline on a fire! I could feel you inside me like a warm caress, and it only heightened the pleasure. You made me feel out of control. It was a feeling that I loathed and craved all at once. Like any drug addict, I came back for more, each time knowing that I was strengthening the bond between us."

"I felt it too," I confessed.

"You do not understand!" he thundered, his fist hitting the ground and making it shake. "I selfishly married you in the way of my people to take your power. To take control. The bond could have been left incomplete. We would have both been free to carry on our lives as before. But the thought of you with anyone else drove me mad. With the bond, I could have you *and* your power." His words shot out like bullets, tearing through me.

He grasped my arms and pulled me up onto my knees before him. "All that power, and you had no idea what to do with it. I did." His eyes were full of desperation. "Your powers are too great to fall into the hands of our enemies. As much as I hated the idea of the bond, I knew it would help my people. I forced you to accept me—to bond with me. I thought the bond would allow me to control you."

I tried to pull away, but his fingers tightened painfully. "The bond is more than being able to hear each other's thoughts. When it is truly open, there is nothing the pair can hide from each other. With your lack of knowledge, I could take full advantage. That is why I was so reluctant to tell you anything of the bond." He pulled me so close his breath touched my lips. "You made me forget my duties. You became the most important thing in my life. More so than the people I am sworn to protect. I am the leader of my people. I cannot be seen to be weak. Not when our enemies grow stronger every day. Not when my people are suffering."

My breath was locked in my throat. The already aching pieces of my heart shattered. He *had* used me. But it hadn't been in the way I thought. It hadn't been to get vengeance for Natalie's false accusations. He was the bully on the playground taking all the toys so others couldn't have them. He really did think of me as his possession, no better than a tool to be taken out of storage for his purposes.

Every touch, every shared moment that had meant so much to me, had all been an act to pull me into his web. Any hope I still clung to that we could work this out now that the lies were out in the open vanished. No wonder he wanted to train me. He had probably been siphoning power off me all along. Well, no more.

No one was taking anything else from me. Using one of the moves I'd learned on the street, I broke his hold and scrambled to my feet. Anger was overtaking the hurt with each rapid beat of my heart. He got to his feet as well, and for a moment I thought I saw regret and love tangled in his eyes. But I wouldn't be fooled again. He didn't try to block me as my hand lashed out leaving a red print upon his cheek.

"You son of a bitch!" I pushed him and he let me. "You don't own me. Or my powers. People are not pawns in your game to be moved around to soothe your overinflated ego. I make my own decisions, and I didn't choose you."

My fists raised as my anger built. The urge to hit him again was almost overwhelming. The now familiar feeling of my powers was stirring. Let them come. He was so greedy to have them, he was going to get a taste. Fire engulfed my hand and lit the ground around us. Bennett didn't move as the fire crept closer, lapping at his sneakers.

"No, you did not choose this," Bennett whispered. "I did."

The ring on my finger glowed a turquoise color. Then lines of violet joined the blue, then a bright green, and so on, until there was a rainbow of colors shining from the band. My rage faltered. Then died completely when I saw the blackened circle of destruction all around me. What was I doing? I wasn't a killer like Natalie. My whole body shook as I closed my eyes and fought to pull my power back. When I no longer felt the heat, I opened my eyes. Bennett's shoes were melted, the hem of his jeans' legs burned away. I had done it, though. I had finally drawn back the power and didn't explode us into bits.

"Congratulations. You are learning control." Bennett smiled at me with pride. "Lia, I told you all of that because you have the right to know my intentions were not honorable. At least, at first. When you died—"

"Stop. Just stop." Bitter resentment filled my voice. "You've lied to me from the very beginning. You believed every sick lie Natalie fed you, and you wanted to see me suffer. Were you helping her try to kill me too?"

"No. Never. I could never hurt—"

"Was having sex with me her idea or yours?" Disgust dripped from my voice. "Did you want to walk on the kinky side and thought I would show you the ropes?"

"I told you the truth. You drew me from the first moment I saw you. I looked forward to our confrontations even when I was so frustrated with you." The tick started in his jaw. "I watched you interact with the other contestants. With Molly and Jaxon. Nothing I saw matched the person I was expecting. I suspected there was more to the story long before we were together."

He stepped closer, his eyes boring into mine. "Then we had sex. Because I wanted you as much as you wanted me. Not for any other reason. After that first time—when the bond formed—I could no longer afford to suspect. I had to know. You told me that someone had started those rumors. That they were not true. But Natalie had pointed you out as her abuser. Someone was lying, I just did not know who."

His hand wrapped around mine and his thumb rubbed against the ring. "Until we completed the bond-mate ceremony. I saw you—all of you—through our bond. I knew then that you were telling the truth. I wanted—needed—to protect you." His other hand cupped my cheek as he continued, "How could I convince you of that when I had so much to atone for? You would have never believed me. But I did not give you a chance. I ruthlessly pushed you away. In the end, I hurt us both. I am sorry, *asteràki*. For everything."

I edged the door open between us. The strained tension in Bennett's body seemed to ease a bit as if with the restored connection he could breathe again. Bracing myself, I peeked through the crack.

"Ask what you want to know," he said. "The bond will show you."

There were too many questions. Though maybe there was one that would answer them all. *"Why did you bond with me?"*

Images whirled past. A kaleidoscope of scenes and emotions filled me. When it was over, I dropped my head onto his chest, breathing deeply. "I-I saw you," I whispered. "I saw what is happening to your people. Every decision that led you to bond with me."

He stroked my hair. "Yes."

"There is so much about your world I still don't know. But what's happening to your people isn't right. No one should be killed because of who they are." Tears glazed my eyes as I looked up at him. "I understand why you bonded with me but what you did was wrong."

He nodded. "My people were not the only reason. You cannot deny that I wanted you for myself." Bennett brushed his lips across mine. "You saw inside me. You felt my emotions. Do you deny it?"

I pushed him away and he took a single step. His look said that was all the space he was willing to give me. "No, I won't deny it. You wanted me. But that's not enough." The dimmed lights of the ring winked out when I pulled it from my finger. Gently, I placed it on his palm. He gripped my hand and folded his other over mine. "I can send you some of my power when you need it but that's all. We don't trust each other. Hell, we barely even like each other. There is too much wrong between us, and sex only confuses things."

Bennett's voice was hoarse when he finally spoke. "There is more between us than lust. You know it is true. You had to have felt—"

"You should know," I went on, ignoring his plea, "that thing I kept saying about the twin Houses? When I . . . died, I met someone. It's all fuzzy, but there was definitely a man. He said his name was Titan Theophanes. And that I had to find the twin Houses of the Olympian Omàda. That I would find answers there." Shoving my hands awkwardly into my pockets, I focused on the last rays of the sun peeking over the horizon. "I don't know where to start looking, but they're somewhere out there. I need to find them. There is so much that I don't know still. About your world. About my past. Does that mean anything to you?"

"No, neither are familiar to me." Bennett gritted his teeth. "Lia—"

He must have seen my resolution because that tic in his jaw picked up the pace. "Don't," I said. "I've made up my mind. We can work together. But that's it."

The door closed between us once more. This time it hadn't been me that shut it.

"We will try it your way. For now," he reluctantly conceded. "As for the man, Theophanes was my original family name before it was changed. Each leader always carries some part of their original family name. That is where my middle name, Theo, comes from. Jaxon may know more." Bennett smirked knowingly at my skeptical look. "Do not let his lazy-playboy-Neanderthal routine fool you. There is a reason he is our lawyer for all Paldimori and human issues."

"I thought he was playing a role with the whole lawyer thing. This is Er—Jaxon we're talking about here. His dream job is to be a bikini contest judge. Preferably with hands-on judging. Are you telling me he's *really* a lawyer?"

Bennett nodded. "Yes, but he would rather you think him playing a role. If you tell him I said otherwise, I will deny it. He prefers that people underestimate him."

"Unbelievable," I said in awe. "You don't have to worry though. I mean, I won't be seeing you guys again, now that the Game is done, right?"

Bennett ran his fingers through his hair in the first nervous gesture I'd seen from him. "We will return to our home bases until a sixth Potential is found to replace you but the Games must go on until a champion is crowned." He turned the ring over and over on his palm lost in thought. "Even if you wanted to return, you would not be allowed to continue. Your powers give you an unfair advantage. Each competition is designed to push the contestants into revealing any latent powers they might have. Once the sixth is found, we will recall the other Potentials and finish the Games."

"Molly said something about the Games having to be finished within a year."

"Yes." He tugged at his hair, but his hand quickly dropped when he noticed me watching him. "This has never happened in the history of the Games. My people are worried."

It didn't seem like it was only his people that were worried. "Good luck. I hope you find someone." I meant that. They weren't human but they deserved peace just the same. "Uh, before you go there is one more thing I remembered. Titan said that there were enemies amongst the Paldimori." I rubbed my chest where the arrow had pierced me. "He definitely needs to work on his timing, but I get the impression he means there were others besides Grace. Tell our people to be careful, Bennett."

He smiled when I called them "our people." I may not fit into their world, but I was one of them.

"Thank you, Lia. You did not have to tell me this. After everything that has happened that you still find the compassion to think of our people speaks highly of you. You would be an honorable Kyrion." He held the ring out to me, and I hesitantly took it. "Please keep it. You are one of us, whether or not you claim House membership. The ring will help protect you."

I closed my fist around the ring. Then turned and walked away as tears slipped silently down my cheeks. "Goodbye, Bennett."

EPILOGUE

"Click! Damn pen, come back here." My flip-flops made popping sounds as I rushed from my office out onto the gallery floor, dodging around boxes searching for my errant pen.

The decision to close Whimsy had been one of the hardest choices I'd ever made. The town had mostly welcomed me back after everything came to light. The art community wasn't as forgiving. There were those few who accepted me back as if nothing had happened, but it would take a long time to rebuild my reputation. It was a challenge that I could have taken on, but it wasn't the right one for me. Just as Port Lawson no longer the right place for me.

Mr. Lawson had purchased the gallery as a wedding present for Ms. Myrtle. We had worked out a deal that benefited both of us. I got paid to pretend to still be the owner—unfortunately that still included doing all of the paperwork—and he got to surprise one of the biggest gossips in town. I also had full access to the studio to finally create my masterpiece. I had ripped up the pavement where I'd buried the real me and the creativity had come back to me.

I'd poured every emotion into the glass, pushing it to its limits to bend it to my vision. Globes within globes sat upon a pedestal of fire. Flames flared up around the outer globe in places, seeking to touch the center but never reaching it. Shadows danced across the layers, some distinct and others only hinted at. Nestled at the center stood a naked female form, head tilted back as if in joy or anguish. Her outstretched hands seemed to call to the fire. It was the best work I had ever done in my life, but it was for me. *Beckoning Fire* wasn't for sale. Today was my last day managing the gallery and it would be coming with me back to Mercer Island this weekend.

I searched the table that held replicas of nineteenth-century dessert plates, cups, and flatware. Click had spent the last week trying to talk to the silverware, but he wasn't there. Rounding the checkout counter, I looked over the display of handmade wooden pens.

Oh no, this couldn't be happening. Click had managed to hook his clip through that of a pink buckeye-burl pen with gold plating. He appeared to be waltzing "her" through a series of dance moves. *This is what I get for letting him watch TV.* His new favorite show was *Dancing with the Stars.* Now he was putting his moves to the test. I was going to need therapy soon. There were no self-help books on raising an adolescent ink pen with all the accompanying hormonal issues.

"Uh, Click. Can you put the nice pen back where it belongs, please?"

He continued twirling and then went into a low dip. I planted my head in my hands and rubbed at my temples. My afternoon of finalizing paperwork had hit a snag when I realized all of the bank documents I needed to turn in before I left had a new ink logo. Every page contained variations of the new bank manager riding backward on donkeys. I would give Click points for being clever since the man's name was Jack—hence Jack-Ass—but his artwork would not be appreciated. Jack was fastidious and ran the bank like a mini dictator since Brice had been fired. He wasn't as bad as Brice but I wasn't looking forward to dealing with him. Click was going to get a lecture, as soon as I could get his attention.

Clicking noises sounded from the table, followed by rattling. Uh oh, that couldn't be good. Peeking through my fingers, I was left momentarily speechless. It seemed males of any type all shared the same trait. They were all horn dogs. Click had unscrewed the top on the pink pen and was working it off. My hands went to my hips in classic mom-scolding style. "Click! Stop that right now, young man. You don't go for second base on the first date."

A throat cleared behind me. "Ah, that is good to know."

I stood frozen on the spot. *What is he doing here? Oh gods, it had to be today when I'm a mess from packing.* My hair was sticking out like a lion's mane from tugging on it in frustration as I did paperwork. I was wearing faded jeans, and a rumpled yellow T-shirt. My notorious luck strikes again.

Click abandoned his girlfriend to nudge against my chin, as though he sensed my embarrassment. He was like a puppy at times and, at others, a fearless guard dog. I winked at him and patted the pen pouch on my belt. The lecture would have to wait. Click zoomed inside as I plastered on a smile and turned to greet my unexpected visitor. "Hello, Bennett, I'm surprised to see you. You're a long way from Oz."

His hair was longer and even messier than usual. His

skin was a shade darker than normal as if he had spent a lot of time in the sun recently. His gray jeans and maroon T-shirt hung a bit loose on his frame. There were dark circles under his eyes but he was still as heart-stoppingly gorgeous as ever.

"I told you I am not a wizard."

"Yes, I guess you did. How are you?" I asked politely.

"I am good. How are you, Lia?" he replied just, as politely.

Oh, this was awkward. "I'm good. Uhm, Grayson isn't here. I had Click chase him around the block the last time he tried to hover near me while I was doing paperwork, so he's out picking up groceries."

Bennett chuckled. "I am glad you are keeping him on his toes. But it is you I came to see."

"Oh." I glanced down at Click as if he could offer advice. "I could use a break, anyway. Would you like to take a walk?"

He smiled and gestured toward the door. "It would be my pleasure. After you."

The wind blew briskly bringing a bite to the air. I wrapped my arms around myself, as we walked along the street. Without even realizing it, my feet had set me on a direct path for Mussels. But I didn't want to taint my favorite restaurant with memories of him. Switching directions at the crosswalk, I led us across the street to the boat docks. We reached the pier and kept going until it ended. I stood back away from the rail and gazed out where the sun was descending over the water."

"It is beautiful, is it not?" Bennett stepped around me to lean out over the rail and took a deep breath. "I have always enjoyed the ocean. I often wished as a boy that my affinity with water was stronger. My power over it does not come as easily as the fire."

"I never thought to ask. What's my strongest power?"

He turned to face me, leaning against the railing. "It can vary amongst families. I would say that yours is healing, but your powers need to be tested. There were some from the House of Light that could heal others as well as themselves." His gaze swept over me and heat followed in its path. "I heard that Grayson is working with you on your control. I am glad that you are continuing to train. I apologize that I have not contacted you myself. We agreed to work together, but I think we both needed some time. We could begin training again, if you wish?"

"I, uh, could probably use the help. Thanks." My cheeks heated in embarrassment. Hopefully, no one had told him how my lessons had gone so far. My control was even worse now than it had been weeks ago.

The silence stretched out for several minutes as the waves crashed beneath us. Some of the tension started to ease from my shoulders as the relaxing rhythm of the ocean rocked me. My eyes closed, and I breathed in the salty air. A warm hand settled on my bicep then slowly traveled upward, following the line of my shoulder. My muscles jumped beneath his hand. His fingers curled around the back of my neck before slipping up to thread through my loose hair. My eyes fluttered open. Raw hunger burned in his eyes, taking my breath away.

"Axol and I have spent the last few weeks on board my sailboat. Do you know what I discovered?" I shook my head slightly, excitement zinging through my body at the tug on my hair where he still held it. Blue light lit up the outer edges of his eyes. "I discovered that no matter how far I traveled I could still feel you inside me like a warm fire on a cold night. I discovered that the scent of you is branded upon my senses, so much so that I would turn, expecting you to be by my side. The memory of your touch found me in my dreams and brought me to the brink of madness with pleasured pain. I have tried this your way, *asteràki*. Now we are going to try mine."

He stepped into me, pressing our bodies together. *Not fair.* My teeth sank into my bottom lip to suppress the moan that wanted to escape. Being this close to him again after all these weeks was torture. His eyes caught on my lips. "You were brave enough to face your past, and you held your own against my sister." Irritation flashed across his face, then he tugged my hair, using it as leverage to tilt my head back. "Do not hide from me. Not even from something as simple as the fact that our bodies crave each other. I am done with denying us. I thought I could give you time to come to terms with what my sister and I did to you. But I cannot." His lips brushed mine in a gentle kiss. "This is not about control because I have none when it comes to you. None. And before you say something to piss me off, I do not care about your powers. I want *you*."

"What're you saying?" I demanded. "You'll come see me when you have an itch to scratch? The sex was great, but I'm not interested."

"I love you. That is what I am saying. That you are mine, my wife. *Astèri tis zoìs mou.*" He growled as the blue around his eyes grew brighter and brighter. "If I have to tie you down and pleasure you until you are delirious to make you agree to be with me, then that is what I will do."

"Y-You love me?"

"Yes, *asteràki*, I love you." He cupped my face in his hands. "I did not think it possible, but I do not want to be without you. I think I have loved you from the moment you defied me in the tower room. You were not afraid of me even from the beginning. You stood up to the Kyrion—to me—when you could have just as easily bowed to our every wish like so many others. I love your strength and your passion. Even your delicious, smart little mouth."

"I was planning to track you down," I laughed as tears streaked down my face. He had beaten me to the punch. Of course. "I made some decisions about my life while I was convalescing. I don't need Whimsy anymore. I funneled all of my focus into my gallery because it was all I thought I would ever have. Then you came along. I was sleepwalking through life, and you woke me up. It was you who made me see that I'm strong enough to face anything."

"*Astèri tis zoìs mou.*" Bennett crushed me against him and pressed his lips against mine. When he pulled away, I struggled to catch my breath.

"You have shown me that my life does not have to be only duties," he continued. "With you, I see a future that is no longer hollow and cold. I have nearly lost you too many times. To my enemies and to my own foolish pride. I need you with me. I need to know you are safe, always. Lia, will you marry me?"

Whoa! Hadn't seen that coming. He had already married me according to his traditions. That he would do things the human way, thawed my heart even more. Still, there was so much that had happened.

"How about we start with a date?"

His look turned thunderous, and his grip tightened as if he were afraid I would try to run away. Holy hotness, that look right there was going to be featuring in some dreams.

"I'm not saying no," I rushed to assure him. "I'm not trying to run away. I'm done with running, but my life has been turned upside-down again. I'm still discovering who I am. I need to learn about my real family history. About my powers and what this prophecy means." I smoothed my hand along his stubbled jaw. "I want us to have time to get to know each other. To build a solid and lasting relationship. I want to take my time." My lips pressed against that agitated tic along his jaw. "So, what do you say, Mr. Wizard? Want to go on a date with me?"

He growled as I nipped his jaw. "*Asteràki*, you never do things the easy way. Yes, I agree to your dating. The gods help any man who dares look at you." He plucked the necklace from under the collar of my shirt. The black ring dangled from the end. "I want you properly wearing my ring so that they know you are mine."

"Oh, I think you've marked your territory, caveman. I've got the tattoo to prove it." Giggles spilled from my lips when he pulled me to him and swatted my ass, mumbling about sassy females. "What does it mean?" I asked. "The asky thing you call me."

He chuckled. "*Asteràki* means 'little star.' Even before I could admit that I loved you, your light drew me like a moth to a flame. I felt your presence before I ever saw your face. I feel you like the warm caress of the sun on my skin when you are near. I should have known that the blood of Apollo runs through your veins, but you destroy my focus."

"How appropriate, I'm your own personal chaos-maker," I laughed. "At least, life will never be dull. What was the other thing you called me? The ass-moo thingy. You've called me that before, haven't you?"

He laughed out loud and then repeated the phrase several times until I could pronounce it. "Yes, I have called you that before. When you recovered, and we were together after the hot springs. I will tell you what it means when you agree to wear my ring again. Now stop distracting me. I need to hear you say the words. Tell me."

"Fine, I'll tell you," I huffed. "You're bossy." His irritated expression made me smile. "Oh, that wasn't it? I know. You're stubborn. Still not right? It must have been that you have a hot body."

"Lia." He growled and kissed me senseless. "Tell me."

When he let me up for air, I could barely remember what we had been talking about.

"You never give up, do you?" I asked in faked affront, then wrapped my arms around his neck. "I love you too, Bennett. I promise I'll try to keep myself safe. I'm done living with my head in the sand, but I won't live in a bubble either. That means you're going to have to be ok with me being on the front lines. I've taken up the sword, and I will use it if I have to. I'm going to find the twin Houses. I don't know how or where. I don't know what will happen when I do find them, but I need answers."

He groaned and mumbled about the gods saving him from strong-willed females. "My warrior princess, I never give up when there is something I want. You should know this. If you are planning for battle, I will teach you what you need to know. I will be by your side to face whatever may come."

"Are you sure?" I asked nervously. "I'm jobless since I sold the gallery. I have a horny teenage pen living with me along with a twenty-something mother hen. My powers are still a mystery, and my control sucks. There's a portal in my study." I tilted my head back as I needed to see his face as I itemized all my baggage. For once we were going to lay all of the cards on the table. There would be no more secrets between us. "Oh, and let's not forget that I've been given a quest. Then there's a prophecy about me that nobody is sure if it means I'm going to perform a miracle or doom us all. Are you sure you want to sign up for all that?"

The whole world paused as I waited for his answer.

Bennett cupped my face. "If you come with the package, tell me where I must sign. I love you, Lia. That means we are in this together, no matter what."

ALSO BY T.L. CALLAHAN

Paldimori Gods Rising Series

Dawning Chaos

Waking Chaos

Unearthing Gaia

Rising Chaos

Illuminating Nyx

ACKNOWLEDGMENTS

Thanks so much to the mighty Callahan Clan Street Team who provided invaluable feedback and support in making this book happen.

A special thanks to Detective Rick Haney for his advice on police matters and not getting mad when I broke all the rules!

Thank you so much to you, the readers, for giving my book a try. You all are awesome and I look forward to sharing many more adventures together.

ABOUT THE AUTHOR

T.L. Callahan is the author of the fantasy romance adventure series Paldimori Gods Rising. She has always been a book lover; devouring romance, fantasy, and poetry since she was a young girl growing up in Kentucky. Her love for the outdoors inspired hours of wandering the woods pretending to be on adventures discovering magical creatures and being the heroine of her own stories. That hasn't changed much these days. Never knowing what you can find around the next corner keeps her seeking out new adventures from backpacking in the Wind River Range of Wyoming to piloting a sailboat down the Tagus River in Portugal. T.L. lives in Ohio with her husband, son, and a cat that thinks he's a dog.

www.ingramcontent.com/pod-product-compliance
Lightning Source LLC
Chambersburg PA
CBHW062009170626
46813CB00001B/93